PS, I LOVE YOU

PS, I LOVE YOU

Cecelia Ahern

HYPERION NEW YORK

For David

Lyrics to WITH A LITTLE HELP FROM MY FRIENDS, appearing on pages 115–116, Copyright 1967 (Renewed) Sony/ATV Tunes LLC. All rights administered by Sony/ATV Music Publishing, 8 Music Square West, Nashville, TN 37203. All rights reserved. Used by permission.

The Library of Congress has cataloged the original hardcover edition of this book as follows:

Ahern, Cecelia
   PS, I love you / Cecelia Ahern.—1st ed.
      p. cm.
      1. Loss (Psychology)—Fiction. 2. Widows—Fiction. 3. Grief—Fiction. I. Title.

   PS3601.H47P78 2004
   813'.6—dc22

                                                                2003056686

Movie tie-in edition ISBN: 978-1-4013-0916-9

Hyperion books are available for special promotions and premiums. For details contact Michael Rentas, Proprietary Markets, Hyperion, 77 West 66th Street, 12th floor, New York, New York 10023-6298, or call 212-456-0133.

10 9 8 7 6 5 4 3 2 1

Fear drives us to do many things in our lives. For me, the fear of losing a loved one, and all those terrifying thoughts of what it's like to be left behind and feel alone, drove me to conceive and write this story.

PS, I Love You is a story about losing a loved one—and continuing to love that lost one. It's also a positive message of love and hope—how our love for someone will never die because they live on in our hearts, in our memories, and, in Holly and Gerry's case, through Gerry's letters. In this story, the very person that Holly is grieving is the one to help her through the process; Gerry's final gift for her. Through writing his letters and preparing her tasks, he prepares himself for leaving this world and for Holly's years left without him.

This was my first book, written during the night at my dining room table. It was a story meant only for me. I never imagined that the story, not least the sentiments, would reach so many people around the world, nor did I ever imagine that I would receive so many heartfelt letters from people sharing their own precious private moments of similar stories.

And now, as it has been adapted to a film, the story, but I think most importantly, the message, will be shared even more. This book, this story, these characters changed my life. I hope that in some way, they either entertain or help a moment in yours.

We haven't lost everything, if we haven't lost our hope. *PS, I Love You* is a story not just about love and grief but also about hope.

One

HOLLY HELD THE BLUE COTTON sweater to her face and the familiar smell immediately struck her, an overwhelming grief knotting her stomach and pulling at her heart. Pins and needles ran up the back of her neck and a lump in her throat threatened to choke her. Panic took over. Apart from the low hum of the fridge and the occasional moaning of the pipes, the house was quiet. She was alone. Bile rose to her throat and she ran to the bathroom, where she collapsed to her knees before the toilet.

Gerry was gone and he would never be back. That was the reality. She would never again run her fingers through his soft hair, never share a secret joke across the table at a dinner party, never cry to him when she got home from a hard day at work and just needed a hug; she would never share a bed with him again, never be woken up by his fits of sneezes each morning, never laugh with him so much her stomach would ache, never fight with him about whose turn it was to get up and turn the bedroom light off. All that was left was a bundle of memories and an image of his face that became more and more vague each day.

Their plan had been very simple. To stay together for the rest of their lives. A plan that anyone within their circle would agree was accomplishable. They were best friends, lovers and soul mates destined to be together, everyone thought. But as it happened, one day destiny greedily changed its mind.

The end had come all too soon. After complaining of a migraine for a few days, Gerry had agreed to Holly's suggestion that he see his doctor. This was done one Wednesday on a lunch break from work. The doctor thought it was due to stress or tiredness and agreed that at the very worst he might need glasses. Gerry hadn't been happy with that. He had been upset about the idea he might need glasses. He needn't have worried, since as it turned out it wasn't his eyes that were the problem. It was the tumor growing inside his brain.

Holly flushed the toilet, and shivering from the coldness of the tiled floor, she shakily steadied herself to her feet. He had been thirty years old. By no means had he been the healthiest man on the earth, but he'd been healthy enough to . . . well, to live a normal life. When he was very sick he would bravely joke about how he shouldn't have lived life so safely. Should have taken drugs, should have drunk more, should have traveled more, should have jumped out of airplanes while waxing his legs . . . his list went on. Even as he laughed about it Holly could see the regret in his eyes. Regret for the things he never made time to do, the places he never saw, and sorrow for the loss of future experiences. Did he regret the life he'd had with her? Holly never doubted that he loved her, but feared he felt he had wasted precious time.

Growing older became something he wanted desperately to accomplish, rather than merely a dreaded inevitability. How presumptuous they both had been never to consider growing old as an achievement and a challenge. Aging was something they'd both wanted so much to avoid.

Holly drifted from room to room while she sobbed her fat, salty tears. Her eyes were red and sore and there seemed to be no end to this night. None of the rooms in the house provided her with any solace. Just unwelcoming silences as she stared around at the furniture. She longed for the couch to hold out its arms to her, but even it ignored her.

Gerry would not be happy with this, she thought. She took a deep breath, dried her eyes and tried to shake some sense into herself. No, Gerry would not be pleased at all.

Just as she had every other night for the past few weeks, Holly fell into a fitful sleep in the early hours of the morning. Each day she found herself sprawled uncomfortably across some piece of furniture; today it was the couch. Once again it was the phone call from a concerned friend or family member that woke her up. They probably thought that all she did was sleep. Where were their phone calls when she listlessly roamed the house like a zombie searching the rooms for . . . for what? What was she expecting to find?

"Hello," she groggily answered. Her voice was hoarse from all the tears, but she had long since stopped caring about maintaining a brave face for anyone. Her best friend was gone and nobody understood that no amount of makeup, fresh air or shopping was going to fill the hole in her heart.

"Oh sorry, love, did I wake you?" the concerned voice of Holly's mother came across the line. Always the same conversation. Every morning her mother called to see if she had survived the night alone. Always afraid of waking her yet always relieved to hear her breathing; safe with the knowledge her daughter had braved the ghosts of the night.

"No, I was just dozing, it's OK." Always the same answer.

"Your dad and Declan have gone out and I was thinking of you, pet." Why did that soothing, sympathetic voice always send tears to Holly's eyes? She could picture her mother's concerned face, eyebrows furrowed, forehead wrinkled with worry. But it didn't soothe Holly. It made her remember why they were worried and that they shouldn't have to be. Everything should be normal. Gerry should be here beside her, rolling his eyes up to heaven and trying to make her laugh while her mother yapped on. So many times Holly would have to hand the phone over to Gerry, as her fit of giggles would take over. Then he would chat away, ignoring Holly as she jumped around the bed pulling her silliest faces and doing her funniest dances just to get him back. It seldom worked.

She "ummed" and "ahhed" throughout the conversation, listening but not hearing a word.

"It's a lovely day, Holly. It would do you the world of good to go out for a walk. Get some fresh air."

"Um, I suppose." There it was again, fresh air—the alleged answer to all her problems.

"Maybe I'll call around later and we can have a chat."

"No thanks, Mum, I'm OK."

Silence.

"Well, all right then . . . give me a ring if you change your mind. I'm free all day."

"OK."

Another silence.

"Thanks, though."

"Right then . . . take care, love."

"I will." Holly was about to replace the phone when she heard her mother's voice again.

"Oh Holly, I almost forgot. That envelope is still here for you, you know, the one I told you about. It's on the kitchen table. You might want to collect it, it's been here for weeks now and it might be important."

"I doubt it. It's probably just another card."

"No, I don't think it is, love. It's addressed to you and above your name it says . . . oh, hold on while I get it from the table . . ." The phone was put down, the sound of heels on the tiles toward the table, chairs screeched against the floor, footsteps getting louder, phone being picked up . . .

"You still there?"

"Yeah."

"OK, it says at the top 'The List.' I'm not sure what that means, love. It's worth just taking a . . ."

Holly dropped the phone.

Two

"GERRY, TURN OFF THE LIGHT!" Holly giggled as she watched her husband undress before her. He danced around the room performing a striptease, slowly unbuttoning his white cotton shirt with his long slender fingers. He raised his left eyebrow toward Holly and allowed the shirt to slide from his shoulders, caught it in his right hand and swung it around over his head.

Holly giggled again.

"Turn off the light? What, and miss all this?" he grinned cheekily while flexing his muscles. He wasn't a vain man but had much to be vain about, thought Holly. His body was strong and perfectly toned. His long legs were muscular from hours spent working out in the gym. He wasn't a very tall man, but he was tall enough to make Holly feel safe when he stood protectively beside her five-foot-five body. Most of all she loved that when she hugged him her head would rest neatly just below his chin, where she could feel his breath lightly blowing her hair and tickling her head.

Her heart leapt as he lowered his boxers, caught them on the tips of his toes and flung them at Holly, where they landed on her head.

"Well, at least it's darker under here anyway," she laughed. He always managed to make her laugh. When she came home tired and angry after work he was always sympathetic and listened to her complain. They seldom fought, and when they did it was over stupid things that made them laugh afterward, like who had left the porch light on all day or who had forgotten to set the alarm at night.

Gerry finished his striptease and dived into the bed. He snuggled up beside her, tucking his freezing cold feet underneath her legs to warm himself up.

"Aaaagh! Gerry, your feet are like ice cubes!" Holly knew that this position meant he had no intention of budging an inch. "Gerry," Holly's voice warned.

"Holly," he mimicked.

"Didn't you forget something?"

"No, not that I remember," he answered cheekily.

"The light?"

"Ah yes, the light," he said sleepily and pretended to snore loudly.

"Gerry!"

"I had to get out of bed and do it last night as I remember."

"Yeah, but you were just standing right beside the switch a second ago!"

"Yes . . . just a second ago," he repeated sleepily.

Holly sighed. She hated having to get back out of bed when she was nice and snug, step onto the cold wooden floor and then fumble around in the darkness on the way back to the bed. She tutted.

"I can't do it all the time you know, Hol. Someday I might not be here and then what will you do?"

"Get my new husband to do it," Holly huffed, trying her best to kick his cold feet away from hers.

"Ha!"

"Or just remember to do it myself before I get into bed."

Gerry snorted. "Fat chance of that happening, my dear. I'll have to leave a message on the light switch for you before I go just so you'll remember."

"How thoughtful of you, but I would rather you just leave me your money."

"And a note on the central heating," he continued on.

"Ha-ha."

"And on the milk carton."

"You're a very funny man, Gerry."

"Oh, and on the windows so you don't open them and set the alarm off in the mornings."

"Hey, why don't you just leave me a list in your will of things for me to do if you think I'll be so incompetent without you?"

"Not a bad idea," he laughed.

"Fine then, I'll turn off the bloody light." Holly grudgingly got out of bed, grimaced as she stepped onto the ice-cold floor and switched off the light. She held out her arms in the darkness and slowly began to find her way back to the bed.

"Hello?!!! Holly, did you get lost? Is there anybody out there, there, there, there?" Gerry shouted out to the black room.

"Yes, I'm hhhhowwwwwwwcch!" she yelped as she stubbed her toe against the bedpost. "Shit, shit, shit, fuck, bastard, shit, crap!"

Gerry snorted and sniggered underneath the duvet. "Number two on my list: Watch out for bedpost . . ."

"Oh, shut up, Gerry, and stop being so morbid," Holly snapped back at him, cradling her poor foot in her hand.

"Want me to kiss it better?" he asked.

"No, it's OK," Holly replied sadly. "If I could just put them here so I can warm . . ."

"Aaaaah! Jesus Christ, they're freezing!!"

"Hee-hee-hee," she had laughed.

So that was how the joke about the list had come about. It was a silly and simple idea that was soon shared with their closest friends, Sharon and John McCarthy. It was John who had approached Holly in the school corridor when they were just fourteen and muttered the famous words, "Me mate wants to know if you'll go out with him." After days of endless discussion and emergency meetings with her friends, Holly eventually agreed. "Aah, go on, Holly," Sharon had urged, "he's such a ride, and at least he doesn't have spots all over his face like John."

How Holly envied Sharon right now. Sharon and John had married the same year as Holly and Gerry. Holly was the baby of the bunch at twenty-three, the rest were twenty-four. Some said she was too young and lectured her about how, at her age, she should be traveling the world and enjoying herself. Instead, Gerry and Holly traveled the world together. It made far more sense that way because when they weren't, well, *together*, Holly just felt like she was missing a vital organ from her body.

Her wedding day was far from being the best day of her life.

She had dreamed of the fairy-tale wedding like most little girls, with a princess dress and beautiful, sunny weather, in a romantic location surrounded by all who were near and dear to her. She imagined the reception would be the best night of her life, pictured herself dancing with all of her friends, being admired by everyone and feeling special. The reality was quite different.

She woke up in her family home to screams of "I can't find my tie!" (her father) or "My hair looks shite" (her mother), and the best one of all: "I look like a bloody whale! There's no way I'm goin' to this bleedin' weddin' looking like this. I'll be scarlet! Mum, look at the state of me! Holly can find another bridesmaid 'cos I'm not bleedin' goin'. Oi! Jack, give me back that feckin' hair dryer, I'm not finished!!" (That unforgettable statement was made by her younger sister, Ciara, who on a very regular basis threw tantrums and refused to leave the house, claiming she had nothing to wear, regardless of her bursting wardrobe. She was currently living somewhere in Australia with strangers, and the only communication the family had with her was an e-mail every few weeks.) Holly's family spent the rest of the morning trying to convince Ciara how she was the most beautiful woman in the world. All the while Holly silently dressed herself, feeling like shite. Ciara eventually agreed to leave the house when Holly's typically calm dad screamed at the top of his voice to everyone's amazement, "Ciara, this is Holly's bloody day, *not yours!* And you *will* go to the wedding and enjoy yourself, *and* when Holly walks downstairs you *will* tell her how beautiful she looks, and I don't wanna hear a peep out of you *for the rest of the day!*"

So when Holly walked downstairs everyone oohed and aahed while Ciara, appearing like a ten-year-old who had just been spanked, tearily looked at her with a trembling lip and said, "You look beautiful, Holly." All seven of them squashed into the limo, Holly, her parents, her three brothers and Ciara, and sat in terrified silence all the way to the church.

The whole day seemed to be a blur to her now. She had barely had time to speak to Gerry, as they were both being pulled in opposite directions to meet Great-aunt Betty from the back arse of nowhere, whom she hadn't seen since she was born, and Grand-uncle Toby from America, who had never been mentioned before but was suddenly a very important member of the family.

And nobody told her it would be so tiring, either. By the end of the night Holly's cheeks were sore from smiling for photographs and her feet were killing her from running around all day in very silly little shoes not designed for walking. She desperately wanted to join the large table of her friends, who had been howling with laughter all night, obviously enjoying themselves. Well for some, she had thought. But as soon as Holly stepped into the honeymoon suite with Gerry, her worries of the day faded and the point of it all became clear.

Tears once again rolled down Holly's face and she realized she had been daydreaming again. She sat frozen on the couch with the phone still off the hook beside her. The time just seemed to pass her by these days without her knowing what time or even what day it was. She seemed to be living outside of her body, numb to everything but the pain in her heart, in her bones, in her head. She was just so tired . . . Her stomach grumbled and she realized she couldn't remember the last time she had eaten. Had it been yesterday?

She shuffled into the kitchen wearing Gerry's dressing gown and her favorite pink "Disco Diva" slippers, which Gerry had bought her the previous Christmas. She was his Disco Diva, he used to say. Always the first on the dance floor, always the last out of the club. Huh, where was that girl now? She opened the fridge and stared in at the empty shelves. Just vegetables and yogurt long past its sell-by date leaving a horrible stench in the fridge. There was nothing to eat. She smiled weakly as she shook the milk carton. Empty. Third on his list . . .

Christmas two years ago Holly had gone shopping with Sharon for a dress for the annual ball they attended at the Burlington Hotel. Shopping with Sharon was always a dangerous outing, and John and Gerry had joked about how they would once again suffer through Christmas without any presents as a result of the girls' shopping sprees. But they weren't far wrong. Poor neglected husbands, the girls always called them.

That Christmas Holly had spent a disgraceful amount of money in Brown Thomas on the most beautiful white dress she had ever seen. "Shit, Sharon, this will burn a huge hole in my pocket," Holly guiltily said, biting her lip and running her fingers over the soft material.

"Aah, don't worry, Gerry can stitch it up for you," Sharon replied, followed by her infamous cackle. "And stop calling me 'shit Sharon,' by the way. Every time we go shopping you address me as that. If you're not careful I might start taking offense. Buy the damn thing, Holly. It's Christmas after all, the season of giving and all that."

"God, you are so evil, Sharon. I'm never shopping with you again. This is like, half my month's wages. What am I going to do for the rest of the month?"

"Holly, would you rather eat or look fab?" Was it even worth thinking about?

"I'll take it," Holly said excitedly to the sales assistant.

The dress was cut low, which showed off Holly's neat little chest perfectly, and it was split to the thigh, displaying her slim legs. Gerry hadn't been able to take his eyes off her. It wasn't because she looked so beautiful, however. He just couldn't understand how on earth that little slip of material had cost so much. Once at the ball, Ms. Disco Diva overindulged in the alcoholic beverages and succeeded in destroying her dress by spilling red wine down her front. Holly tried but failed to hold back her tears while the men at the table drunkenly informed their partners that number fifty-four on the list prevented you from drinking red wine while wearing an expensive white dress. It was then decided that milk was the preferred beverage, as it wouldn't be visible if spilled on expensive white dresses.

Later, when Gerry knocked his pint over, causing it to dribble off the edge of the table onto Holly's lap, she tearily yet seriously announced to the table (and some of the surrounding tables), "Rule fitty-fife ov the list: *neffer effer* buy a 'spensive white dress." And so it was agreed, and Sharon awoke from her coma from somewhere underneath the table to applaud and offer moral support. A toast was made (after the startled waiter had delivered the tray full of glasses of milk) to Holly and to her profound addition to the list. "I'm sorry 'bout your 'spensive white dress, Holly," John had hiccuped before falling out of the taxi and dragging Sharon alongside him to their house.

Was it possible that Gerry had kept his word and written a list for her before he died? She had spent every minute of every day with him up until his death, and he had never mentioned it, nor had she noticed any signs of him writing one. No, Holly, pull yourself together and don't be stupid. She so desperately wanted him back that she was imagining all kinds of crazy things. He wouldn't have. Would he?

Three

HOLLY WAS WALKING THROUGH AN entire field of pretty tiger lilies; the wind was blowing gently, causing the silky petals to tickle the tips of her fingers as she pushed through the long strands of bright green grass. The ground felt soft and bouncy beneath her bare feet, and her body felt so light she almost seemed to be floating just above the surface of the spongy earth. All around her birds whistled their happy tune as they went about their business. The sun was so bright in the cloudless sky she had to shield her eyes, and with each brush of wind that passed her face, the sweet scent of the tiger lilies filled her nostrils. She felt so . . . happy, so free. A feeling that was alien to her these days.

Suddenly the sky darkened as her Caribbean sun disappeared behind a looming gray cloud. The wind picked up and the air chilled. Around her all the petals of her tiger lilies were racing through the air wildly, blurring her vision. The once spongy ground was replaced with sharp-pebbled stones that cut and scraped her feet with every step. The birds had stopped singing and instead perched on their branches and stared. Something was wrong and she felt afraid. Ahead of her in the distance a gray stone was visible amid the tall grass. She wanted to run back to her pretty flowers, but she needed to find out what was ahead.

As she crept closer she heard *Bang! Bang! Bang!* She quickened her pace and raced over the sharp stones and jagged-edged grass that tore at her arms and legs. She collapsed to her knees in front of the gray slab and let out a scream of pain as she realized what it was. Gerry's grave. *Bang! Bang! Bang!* He was trying to get out! He was calling her name; she could hear him!

Holly jumped from her sleep to a loud banging on the door. "Holly! Holly! I know you're there! Please let me in!" *Bang! Bang! Bang!* Confused and half asleep, Holly made her way to the door to find a frantic-looking Sharon.

"Christ! What were you doing? I've been banging on the door for ages!" Holly looked around outside, still not fully alert. It was bright and slightly chilly, must be morning.

"Well, aren't you going to let me in?"

"Yeah, Sharon, sorry, I was just dozing on the couch."

"God, you look terrible, Hol." Sharon studied her face before giving her a big hug.

"Wow, thanks." Holly rolled her eyes and turned to shut the door. Sharon was never one to beat around the bush, but that's why she loved her so much, for her honesty. That's also why Holly hadn't been around to see Sharon for the past month. She didn't want to hear the truth. She didn't want to hear that she had to get on with her life; she just wanted . . . oh, she didn't know what she wanted. She was happy being miserable. It somehow felt right.

"God, it's so stuffy in here, when's the last time you opened a window?" Sharon marched around the house opening windows and picking up empty cups and plates. She brought them into the kitchen, where she placed them in the dishwasher and then proceeded to tidy up.

"Oh, you don't have to do it, Sharon," Holly protested weakly. "I'll do it . . ."

"When? Next year? I don't want you slumming it while the rest of us pretend not to notice. Why don't you go upstairs and shower and we'll have a cup of tea when you come down."

A shower. When was the last time she had even washed? Sharon was right, she must have looked disgusting with her greasy hair and dark roots and dirty robe. Gerry's robe. But that was something she never intended to wash. She wanted it exactly as Gerry had left it. Unfortunately, his smell was beginning to fade, replaced by the unmistakable stink of her own skin.

"OK, but there's no milk. I haven't got around to . . ." Holly felt embarrassed by her lack of care for the house and for herself. There was no way she was letting Sharon look inside that fridge or Sharon would definitely have her committed.

"Ta-da!" Sharon sang, holding up a bag Holly hadn't noticed her carry in. "Don't worry, I took care of that. By the looks of it, you haven't eaten in weeks."

"Thanks, Sharon." A lump formed in her throat and tears welled in her eyes. Her friend was being so good to her.

"Hold it! There will be no tears today! Just fun and laughter and general happiness, my dear friend. Now shower, quick!"

. . .

Holly felt almost human when she came back downstairs. She was dressed in a blue tracksuit and had allowed her long blond (and brown at the roots) hair to fall down on her shoulders. All the windows downstairs were wide open and the cool breeze rushed through Holly's head. It felt as though it were eliminating all her bad thoughts and fears. She laughed at the possibility of her mother being right after all. Holly snapped out of her trance and gasped as she looked around the house. She couldn't have been any longer than half an hour, but Sharon had tidied and polished, vacuumed and plumped, washed and sprayed air freshener in every room. She followed the noise she could hear to the kitchen, where Sharon was scrubbing the hobs. The counters were gleaming; the silver taps and draining board at the sink area were sparkling.

"Sharon, you absolute angel! I can't believe you did all this! And in such a short space of time!"

"Ha! You were gone for over an hour. I was beginning to think you'd fallen down the plughole. You would and all, the size of you." She looked Holly up and down.

An hour? Once again Holly's daydreaming had taken over her mind.

"OK, so I just bought some vegetables and fruit, there's cheese and yogurts in there, and milk of course. I don't know where you keep the pasta and tinned foods so I just put them over there. Oh, and there's a few microwave dinners in the freezer. That should do you for a while, but by the looks of you it'll last you the year. How much weight have you lost?"

Holly looked down at her body; her tracksuit was sagging at the bum and the waist tie was pulled to its tightest, yet still drooped to her hips. She hadn't noticed the weight loss at all. She was brought back to reality by Sharon's voice again. "There's a few biscuits there to go with your tea. Jammy Dodgers, your favorite."

That did it. This was all too much for Holly. The Jammy Dodgers were the icing on the cake. She felt the tears start to run down her face. "Oh, Sharon," she wailed, "thank you so much. You've been so good to me and I've been such a horrible, horrible bitch of a friend." She sat at the table and grabbed Sharon's hand. "I don't know what I'd do without you." Sharon sat opposite her in silence, allowing her to continue. This is what Holly had been dreading, breaking down in front of people at every possible occasion. But she didn't feel embarrassed. Sharon was just patiently sipping her tea and holding her hand as if it were normal. Eventually the tears stopped falling.

"Thanks."

"I'm your best friend, Hol. If I don't help you, then who will?" Sharon said, squeezing her hand and giving her an encouraging smile.

"Suppose I should be helping myself."

"Pah!" Sharon spat, waving her hand dismissively. "Whenever you're ready. Don't mind all those people who say that you should be back to normal in a month or two. Grieving is all part of helping yourself anyway."

She always said the right things.

"Yeah, well, I've been doing a lot of that anyway. I'm all grieved out."

"You can't be!" said Sharon, mock disgusted. "And only two months after your husband is cold in his grave."

"Oh, stop! There'll be plenty of that from people, won't there?"

"Probably, but screw them. There are worse sins in the world than learning to be happy again."

"Suppose."

"Promise me you'll eat."

"Promise."

"Thanks for coming round, Sharon, I really enjoyed the chat," Holly said, gratefully hugging her friend, who had taken the day off work to be with her. "I feel a lot better already."

"You know it's good to be around people, Hol. Friends and family can help you. Well, actually on second thought, maybe not your family," she joked, "but at least the rest of us can."

"Oh, I know, I realize that now. I just thought I could handle it on my own—but I can't."

"Promise me you'll call around. Or at least get out of the house once in a while?"

"Promise." Holly rolled her eyes. "You're beginning to sound like my mom."

"Oh, we're all just looking out for you. OK, see you soon," Sharon said, kissing her on the cheek. "And *eat!*" she added, poking her in the ribs.

Holly waved to Sharon as she pulled away in her car. It was nearly dark. They had spent the day laughing and joking about old times, then crying, followed by some more laughing, then more crying again. Sharon gave her perspective, too. Holly hadn't even thought about the fact that Sharon and John had lost their best friend, that her parents had lost their son-in-law and Gerry's parents had lost their only son. She had just been so busy thinking about herself. It had been good being around the living again instead of moping around with the ghosts of her past. Tomorrow was a new day and she intended to begin it by collecting that envelope.

Four

H OLLY STARTED HER FRIDAY MORNING well by getting up early. However, although she had gone to bed full of optimism and excited about the prospects that lay ahead of her, she was struck afresh by the harsh reality of how difficult every moment would be. Once again she awoke to a silent house in an empty bed, but there was one small breakthrough. For the first time in over two months, she had woken up without the aid of a telephone call. She adjusted her mind, as she did every morning, to the fact that the dreams of Gerry and her being together that had lived in her mind for the past ten hours were just that—dreams.

She showered and dressed comfortably in her favorite blue jeans, trainers and a baby pink T-shirt. Sharon had been right about her weight, her once tight jeans were just about staying up with the aid of a belt. She made a face at her reflection in the mirror. She looked ugly. She had black circles under her eyes, her lips were chapped and chewed on and her hair was a disaster. First thing to do was to go down to her local hairdresser's and pray they could squeeze her in.

"Jaysus, Holly!" her hairdresser Leo exclaimed. "Would ya look at the state of ya! People make way! Make way! I have a woman here in a critical condition!" He winked at her and proceeded to push people from his path. He pulled out the chair for her and pushed her into it.

"Thanks, Leo. I feel really attractive now," Holly muttered, trying to hide her beetroot-colored face.

"Well don't, 'cos you're in bits. Sandra, mix me up the usual; Colin, get the foil; Tania, get me my little bag of tricks from upstairs, oh and tell Paul not to bother getting his lunch, he's doing my twelve o'clock." Leo ordered everyone around, his hands flailing wildly as though he were about to perform emergency surgery. Perhaps he was.

"Oh sorry, Leo, I didn't mean to mess up your day."

"Of course you did, love, why else would you come rushing in here at lunchtime on a Friday without an appointment. To help world peace?"

Holly guiltily bit her lip.

"Ah, but I wouldn't do it for anyone else but you, love."

"Thanks."

"How have you been?" He rested his skinny little behind on the counter facing Holly. Leo must have been fifty years old, yet his skin was so flawless and his hair, of course, so perfect that he didn't look a day over thirty-five. His honey-colored hair matched his honey-colored skin, and he always dressed perfectly. He was enough to make a woman feel like crap.

"Terrible."

"Yeah, you look it."

"Thanks."

"Ah well, at least by the time you walk out of here you'll have one thing sorted. I do hair, not hearts."

Holly smiled gratefully at his odd little way of showing he understood.

"But Jaysus, Holly, when you were coming in the front door did you see the word 'magician' or 'hairdresser' on the front of the salon? You should have seen the state of the woman who came in here today. Mutton dressed as lamb. Not far off sixty, I'd say. Handed me a magazine with Jennifer Aniston on the cover.

"'I want to look like that,' she says."

Holly laughed at his impression. He had the facial expression and the hand movements all going at the same time.

"'Jaysus,' I says, 'I'm a hairdresser not a plastic surgeon. The only way you'll look like that is if you cut out the picture and staple it to your head.'"

"No! Leo, you didn't tell her that!" Holly's mouth dropped in surprise.

"Of course I did! The woman needed to be told, sure wasn't I helping her? Swanning in here dressed like a teenager. The state of her!"

"But what did she say!" Holly wiped the tears of laughter from her eyes. She hadn't laughed like that for months.

"I flicked the pages of the mag for her and came across a lovely picture of Joan Collins. Told her it was right up her street. She seemed happy enough with that."

"Leo, she was probably too terrified to tell you she hated it!"

"Ah, who cares, I have enough friends."

"Don't know why," Holly laughed.

"Don't move," Leo ordered. Suddenly Leo had become awfully serious, and his lips were pursed together in concentration as he separated Holly's hair to get it ready for coloring. That was enough to send Holly into stitches again.

"Ah, come on, Holly," Leo said with exasperation.

"I can't help it, Leo, you got me started and now I can't stop!" Leo stopped what he was doing and watched her with amusement.

"I always thought you were for the madhouse. No one ever listens to me."

She laughed even harder.

"Oh, I'm sorry, Leo. I don't know what's wrong with me, I just can't stop laughing." Holly's stomach ached from laughing so hard, and she was aware of all the curious glances she was attracting but she just couldn't help it. It was as if all the missed laughs from the past couple of months were tumbling out at once.

Leo stopped working and made his way back round to the mirror, where he propped himself back on the counter and watched her. "You don't need to apologize, Holly, laugh all you like, you know they say laughing is good for the heart."

"Oh, I haven't laughed like this for ages," she giggled.

"Well, you haven't had much to laugh about, I suppose," he smiled sadly. Leo loved Gerry, too. They had teased each other whenever they met, but they both knew it was all in fun and were very fond of each other. Leo snapped himself out of his thoughts, tousled Holly's hair playfully and planted a kiss on the top of her head. "But you'll be all right, Holly Kennedy," he assured her.

"Thanks, Leo," she said, calming herself down, touched by his concern. He went back to work on her hair, putting on his funny little concentrating face. Holly giggled again.

"Oh, you laugh now, Holly, but wait till I accidentally give you a stripy head of color. We'll see who's laughing then."

"How's Jamie?" Holly asked, keen to change the subject before she embarrassed herself again.

"He dumped me," Leo said, pushing aggressively with his foot on the chair's pump, sending Holly higher into the air but causing her to jerk wildly in her chair.

"O-oh Le-eo, I-I-I-m soooo sor-reeee. Yo-ooou twooo we-eerree soooo gree-aat togeeeeth-eeer."

He stopped pumping and paused. "Yeah, well, we're not so gree-aat together now, missy. I think he's seeing someone else. Right. I'm going to put two shades of blond in; a golden color and the blond you had before. Otherwise it'll go that brassy color that's reserved for prostitutes only."

"Oh Leo, I'm sorry. If he has any sense at all he'll realize what he's missing."

"He mustn't have any sense; we split up two months ago and he hasn't realized it yet. Or else he has and he's delighted. I'm fed up; I've had enough of men. I'm just going to turn straight."

"Oh Leo, now that's the most stupid thing I've ever heard . . ."

Holly bounced out of the salon with delight. Without Gerry's presence beside her, a few men looked her way, something that was alien to her and made her feel uncomfortable, so she ran to the safety of her car and prepared herself for her parents' house. So far today was going well. It had been a good move to visit Leo. Even in his heartbreak he worked hard to make her laugh. Holly took note of it.

She pulled up to the curb outside her parents' house in Portmarnock and took a deep breath. To her mother's surprise Holly had called her first thing in the morning to arrange a time to meet up. It was three-thirty now, and Holly sat outside in the car with butterflies in her tummy. Apart from the visits her parents had paid to her over the past two months, Holly had barely spent any proper time with her family. She didn't want all the attention directed at her; she didn't want the intrusive questions about how she was feeling and what she was going to do next being fired at her all day. However, it was time to put that fear aside. They were her family.

Her parents' house was situated directly across the road from Portmarnock beach, the blue flag bearing testament to its cleanliness. She parked the car and stared across the road to the sea. She had lived here from the day she was born till the day she moved out to live with Gerry. She had loved waking up to the sound of the sea lapping against the rocks and the excited call of the seagulls. It was wonderful having the beach as your front garden, especially during the summer. Sharon had lived around the corner, and on the hottest days of the year the girls would venture across the road in their summer's best and keep an eye out for the best-looking boys. Holly and Sharon were the complete opposite of each other. Sharon with her brown hair, fair skin and huge chest. Holly with her blond hair, sallow skin and small chest. Sharon would be loud, shouting to the boys and calling them over. Holly would just stay quiet and flirt with her eyes, fixing them on her favorite boy and not moving them till he noticed. Holly and Sharon really hadn't changed all that much since.

She didn't intend to stay long, just to have a little chat and collect the envelope that she had decided could possibly be from Gerry. She was tired of punishing herself about what could be inside it, so she was determined to end her silent torture of herself.

She took a deep breath, rang the doorbell and placed a smile on her face for all to see.

"Hi, love! Come in, come in!" said her mother with the welcoming, loving face that Holly just wanted to kiss every time she saw her.

"Hi, Mum. How are you?" Holly stepped into the house and was comforted by the familiar smell of home. "You on your own?"

"Yes, your father's out with Declan buying paint for his room."

"Don't tell me you and Dad are still paying for everything for him?"

"Well, your father might be, but I'm certainly not. He's working nights now so at least he has a bit of pocket money these days. Although we don't see a penny of it being spent on anything for here." She chuckled and brought Holly to the kitchen, where she put the kettle on.

Declan was Holly's youngest brother and the baby of the family, so her mum and dad still felt like they had to spoil him. If you could see their "baby": Declan was a twenty-two-year-old child studying film production at college and constantly had a video camera in his hand.

"What job has he got now?"

Her mother rolled her eyes to heaven. "He's joined some band. The Orgasmic Fish, I think they call themselves, or something like that. I'm sick to death of hearing about it, Holly. If he goes on one more time about who was there at their gigs promising to sign them up and how famous they're going to be, I'll go mad."

"Ah, poor Deco, don't worry, he'll eventually find something."

"I know, and it's funny, because of all you darling children, he's the least I worry about. He'll find his way."

They brought their mugs into the sitting room and settled down in front of the television. "You look great, love, I love the hair. Do you think Leo would ever do mine for me, or am I too old for his styles?"

"Well, as long as you don't want Jennifer Aniston's hairstyle, you'll have no problems." Holly explained the story about the woman in the salon and they both rolled around laughing.

"Well, I don't want the Joan Collins look, so I'll just stay clear of him."

"That might be wise."

"Any luck with a job yet?" Her mother's voice was casual but Holly could tell she was just dying to know.

"No, not yet, Mum. To be honest I haven't even started looking; I don't quite know what I want to do."

"You're right," her mother nodded. "Take your time and think about what you like, or else you'll end up rushing into a job you hate, like the last time." Holly was surprised to hear this. Although her family had always been supportive of her over the years, she found herself moved by the abundance of their love.

The last job Holly had had was working as a secretary for an unforgiving little slimeball in a solicitor's office. She had been forced to leave her job when the little creep failed to understand that she needed time off work to be with her dying husband. Now she had to go looking for a new one. For a new job, that is. At the moment it seemed unimaginable to go to work in the morning.

Holly and her mother relaxed, falling in and out of conversation for a few hours until Holly finally built up the courage to ask for the envelope.

"Oh, of course, love, I completely forgot about it. I hope it's nothing important, it's been there for a long time."

"I'll find out soon enough."

They said their good-byes and Holly couldn't get out of the house quickly enough.

Perching herself on the grass overlooking the golden sand and sea, Holly ran her hands over the envelope. Her mother hadn't described it very well, for it was not an envelope at all but a thick brown package. The address had been typed onto a sticker so she couldn't even guess the origin. And above the address were two words thick and bold—THE LIST.

Her stomach did a little dance. If it wasn't from Gerry, then Holly had to finally accept the fact that he was gone, gone completely from her life, and she had to start thinking about existing without him. If it *was* from him she would be faced with the same future but at least she could hold on to a fresh memory. A memory that would have to last her a lifetime.

Her trembling fingers gently tore at the seal of the package. She turned it upside down and shook the contents out. Out fell ten separate tiny little envelopes, the kind you would expect to find on a bouquet of flowers, each with a different month written on them. Her heart missed a few beats as she saw the familiar handwriting on a loose page underneath the pile of envelopes.

It was from Gerry.

Five

HOLLY HELD HER BREATH, AND with tears in her eyes and a pounding heart, she read the familiar handwriting knowing that the person who had sat down to write to her would never be able to do so again. She ran her fingers over his words knowing that the last person to have touched the page was him.

> *My darling Holly,*
>   *I don't know where you are or when exactly you are reading this. I just hope that my letter has found you safe and healthy. You whispered to me not long ago that you couldn't go on alone. You can, Holly.*
>   *You are strong and brave and you can get through this. We shared some beautiful times together and you made my life . . . you made my life. I have no regrets. But I am just a chapter in*

your life, there will be many more. Remember our wonderful
memories, but please don't be afraid to make some more.

Thank you for doing me the honor of being my wife. For
everything, I am eternally grateful.

Whenever you need me, know that I am with you.

Love Forever,
Your husband and best friend,
Gerry

PS, I promised a list, so here it is. The following
envelopes must be opened exactly when labeled and must be
obeyed. And remember, I'm looking out for you, so I will
know . . .

Holly broke down, sadness sweeping over her. Yet she felt
relief at the same time; relief that Gerry would somehow continue
to be with her for another little while. She leafed through the
small white envelopes and searched through the months. It was
April now. She had missed March, and so she delicately picked out
that envelope. She opened it slowly, wanting to savor every
moment. Inside was a small card with Gerry's handwriting on it.
It read:

Save yourself the bruises and buy yourself a bedside
lamp!

PS, I love you . . .

Her tears turned to laughter as she realized her Gerry was back!
Holly read and reread his letter over and over in an attempt to
summon him back to life again. Eventually, when she could no

longer see the words through her tears, she looked out to the sea. She had always found the sea so calming, and even as a child she would run across the road to the beach if she was upset and needed to think. Her parents knew that when she went missing from the house they would find her here by the sea.

She closed her eyes and breathed in and out along with the gentle sighing of the waves. It was as though the sea were taking big deep breaths, pulling the water in while it inhaled and pushing it all back up onto the sand as it exhaled. She continued to breathe along with it and felt her pulse rate slow down as she became calmer. She thought about how she used to lie by Gerry's side during his final days and listen to the sound of his breathing. She had been terrified to leave him to answer the door, to fix him some food or to go to the toilet, just in case that was the time he chose to leave her. When she would return to his bedside she would sit frozen in a terrified silence while she listened for his breathing and watched his chest for any movement.

But he always managed to hang on. He had baffled the doctors with his strength and determination to live; Gerry wasn't prepared to go without a fight. He kept his good humor right up until the end. He was so weak and his voice so quiet, but Holly had learned to understand his new language as a mother does her babbling child just learning to talk. They would giggle together late into the night, and other nights they would hold each other and cry. Holly remained strong for him throughout, as her new job was to be there for him whenever he needed her. Looking back on it, she knew that she needed him more than he needed her. She needed to be needed so she could feel she wasn't just idly standing by, utterly helpless.

On the second of February at four o'clock in the morning,

Holly held Gerry's hand tightly and smiled at him encouragingly as he took his last breath and closed his eyes. She didn't want him to be afraid, and she didn't want him to feel that she was afraid, because at that moment she wasn't. She had felt relief, relief that his pain was gone, and relief that she had been there with him to witness the peace of his passing. She felt relieved to have known him, to love him and to be loved by him, and relief that the last thing he saw was her face smiling down on him, encouraging him and assuring him it was OK to let go.

The days after that were a blur to her now. She had occupied herself by making the funeral arrangements and by meeting and greeting his relatives and old school friends that she hadn't seen for years. She had remained so solid and calm through it all because she felt that she could finally think clearly. She was just thankful that after months his suffering was over. It didn't occur to her to feel the anger or bitterness that she felt now for the life that had been taken away from her. That feeling didn't arrive until she went to collect her husband's death certificate.

And that feeling made a grand appearance.

As she sat in the crowded waiting room of her local health clinic waiting for her number to be called, she wondered why on earth Gerry's number had been called so early in his life. She sat sandwiched between a young couple and an elderly couple. The picture of what she and Gerry had once been and a glimpse of the future that could have been. And it all just seemed unfair. She felt squashed between the shoulders of her past and her lost future, and she felt suffocated. She realized she shouldn't have had to be there.

None of her friends had to be there.

None of her family had to be there.

In fact, the majority of the population of the world didn't have to be in the position she was in right now.

It didn't seem fair.

Because it just wasn't fair.

After presenting the official proof of her husband's death to bank managers and insurance companies, as if the look on her face weren't enough proof, Holly returned home to her nest and locked herself away from the rest of the world, which contained hundreds of memories of the life she had once had. The life she had been very happy with. So why had she been given another one, and a far worse one at that?

That was two months ago and she hadn't left the house until today. And what a welcome she had been given, she thought, smiling down at the envelopes. Gerry was back.

Holly could hardly contain her excitement as she furiously dialed Sharon's number with trembling hands. After reaching a few wrong numbers she eventually calmed herself and concentrated on dialing the correct number.

"Sharon!" she squealed as soon as the phone was picked up. "You'll never guess what! Oh my God, I can't believe it!"

"Eh no . . . it's John, but I'll get her for you now." A very worried John rushed off to get Sharon.

"What, what, what?" panted a very out-of-breath Sharon. "What's wrong? Are you OK?"

"Yes I'm fine!" Holly giggled hysterically, not knowing whether to laugh or cry and suddenly forgetting how to structure a sentence.

John watched as Sharon sat down at her kitchen table looking very confused while she tried with all her strength to make sense of the rambling Holly on the other end. It was something about Mrs. Kennedy giving Holly a brown envelope with a bedside lamp in it. It was all very worrying.

"*Stop!*" shouted Sharon, much to Holly and John's surprise. "I cannot understand a word you are saying, so please," Sharon spoke very slowly, "slow down, take a deep breath and start from the very beginning, preferably using words from the English language."

Suddenly she heard quiet sobs from the other end.

"Oh, Sharon," Holly's words were quiet and broken, "he wrote me a list. Gerry wrote me a list."

Sharon froze in her chair while she digested this information.

John watched his wife's eyes widen and he quickly pulled out a chair and sat next to her and shoved his head toward the telephone so he could hear what was going on.

"OK, Holly, I want you to get over here as quickly but as *safely* as you can." She paused again and swatted John's head away as if he were a fly so she could concentrate on what she had just heard. "This is . . . great news?"

John stood up from the table insulted and began to pace the kitchen floor trying to guess what it could be.

"Oh it is, Sharon," sobbed Holly. "It really is."

"OK, make your way over here now and we can talk about it."

"OK."

Sharon hung up the phone and sat in silence.

"What? What is it?" demanded John, unable to bear being left out of this obviously serious event.

"Oh sorry, love. Holly's on the way over. She . . . em . . . she said that, eh . . . ."

"*What?* For Christ's sake?"

"She said that Gerry wrote her a list."

John stared at her, studied her face and tried to decide if she was serious. Sharon's worried blue eyes stared back at him and he realized she was. He joined her at the table and they both sat in silence and stared at the wall, lost in thought.

Six

"Wow," was all Sharon and John could say as the three of them sat around the kitchen table in silence staring at the contents of the package that Holly had emptied as evidence. Conversation between them had been minimal for the last few minutes as they all tried to decide how they felt. It went something like this:

"But how did he manage to . . ."

"But why didn't we notice him . . . well . . . God."

"When do you think he . . . well, I suppose he was on his own sometimes . . ."

Holly and Sharon just sat looking at each other while John stuttered and stammered his way through trying to figure out just when, where and how his terminally ill friend had managed to carry out this idea all alone without anyone finding out.

"Wow," he eventually repeated after coming to the conclusion that Gerry had done just that. He had carried it out alone.

"I know," Holly agreed. "So the two of you had absolutely no idea then?"

"Well, I don't know about you, Holly, but it's pretty clear to me that John was the mastermind behind all of this," Sharon said sarcastically.

"Ha-ha," John replied dryly. "Well, he kept his word anyway, didn't he?" John looked to both of the girls with a smile on his face.

"He sure did," Holly said quietly.

"Are you OK, Holly? I mean, how do you feel about all this, it must be . . . weird," asked Sharon again, clearly concerned.

"I feel fine." Holly was thoughtful. "Actually I think it's the best thing that could have happened right now! It's funny, though, how amazed we all are considering how much we all went on about this list. I mean, I should have been expecting it."

"Yeah, but we never expected any of us to ever do it!" said John.

"But why not?" questioned Holly. "This was the whole reason for it in the first place! To be able to help your loved ones after you go."

"I think Gerry was the only one who took it really seriously."

"Sharon, Gerry is the only one of us who is gone, who knows how seriously anyone else would have taken it?"

There was a silence.

"Well, let's study this more closely then," perked up John, suddenly starting to enjoy himself. "There's how many envelopes?"

"Em . . . there's ten," counted Sharon, joining in with the spirit of their new task.

"OK, so what months are there?" John asked. Holly sorted through the pile.

"There's March, which is the lamp one I already opened, April, May, June, July, August, September, October, November and December."

"So there's a message for every month left in the year," Sharon said slowly, lost in thought. They were all thinking the same thing, Gerry had planned this knowing he wouldn't live past February. They all took a moment to ponder this, and eventually Holly looked around at her friends with happiness. Whatever Gerry had in store for her was going to be interesting, but he had already succeeded in making her feel almost normal again. While she was laughing with John and Sharon as they guessed what the envelopes contained, it was as though he were still with them.

"Hold on!" John exclaimed very seriously.

"What?"

John's blue eyes twinkled. "It's April now and you haven't opened it yet."

"Oh, I forgot about that! Oh no, should I do it now?"

"Go on," encouraged Sharon.

Holly picked up the envelope and slowly began to open it. There were only eight more to open after this and she wanted to treasure every second before it became another memory. She pulled out the little card.

> *A Disco Diva must always look her best. Go shopping for an outfit, as you'll need it for next month!*
> *PS, I love you . . .*

"Ooooh," John and Sharon sang with excitement, "he's getting cryptic!"

Seven

HOLLY LAY ON HER BED like a demented woman, switching the lamp on and off with a smile on her face. She and Sharon had gone shopping in Bed Knobs and Broomsticks in Malahide, and both girls had eventually agreed on the beautifully carved wooden stand and the cream shade, which matched the cream and wooden furnishings of the master bedroom (of course they had chosen the most ridiculously expensive one, it would have been wrong to spoil tradition). And although Gerry hadn't physically been there with her as she bought it, she felt that they had made the purchase together.

She had drawn the curtains of her bedroom in order to test her new merchandise. The bedside lamp had a softening effect on the room, making it appear warmer. How easily this could have ended their nightly arguments, but perhaps neither of them wanted to end them. It had become a routine, something familiar that made them feel closer. How she would give anything to have one of those little arguments now. And she would gladly get out of her cozy bed for him, she would gladly walk on the cold floor for him, and she would gladly bruise herself on the bedpost while fumbling in the dark for the bed. But that time was gone.

The sound of Gloria Gaynor's "I Will Survive" snapped her back to the present as she realized her mobile phone was ringing.

"Hello?"

"G'day, mate, I'm hooooome!" shrieked a familiar voice.

"Oh my God, Ciara! I didn't know you were coming home!"

"Well, neither did I actually, but I ran out of money and decided to surprise you all!"

"Wow, I bet Mum and Dad were surprised all right."

"Well, Dad did drop the towel with fright when he stepped out of the shower."

Holly covered her face with her hand. "Oh Ciara, you didn't!" she warned.

"No hugs for Daddy when I saw him!" Ciara laughed.

"Oh yuck, yuck, yuck. Change the subject, I'm having visions," Holly said.

"OK, well, I was calling to tell you that I was home, obviously, and that Mum's organizing dinner tonight to celebrate."

"Celebrate what?"

"Me being alive."

"Oh, OK. I thought you might have an announcement or something."

"That I'm alive."

"O . . . K. So who's going?"

"The whole family."

"Did I mention that I'm going to the dentist to have all my teeth pulled out? Sorry, I can't make it."

"I know, I know, I said the same thing to Mum, but we haven't all been together for ages. Sure when's the last time you've even seen Richard and Meredith?"

"Oh, good ol' Dick, well, he was in flying form at the funeral. Had lots of wise and comforting things to say to me like, 'Did you not consider donating his brain to medical science?' Yes, he's such a fantastic brother all right."

"Oh gosh, Holly, I'm sorry. I forgot about the funeral." Her sister's voice changed. "I'm sorry I couldn't make it."

"Ciara, don't be silly, we both decided it was best you stay," Holly said briskly. "It's far too expensive to be flying back and forth from Australia, so let's not bring it back up, OK?"

"OK."

Holly quickly changed the subject. "So when you say the whole family do you mean . . . ?"

"Yes, Richard and Meredith are bringing our adorable little niece and nephew. And Jack and Abbey are coming you'll be pleased to know, Declan will be there in body but probably not in mind, Mum, Dad and me of course, and you *will* be there."

Holly groaned. As much as Holly moaned about her family she had a great relationship with her brother Jack. He was only two years older than her so they had always been close when growing up, and he had always been very protective of her. Their mother had called them her "two little elves" because they were always getting up to mischief around the house (this mischief was usually aimed at their eldest brother, Richard). Jack was similar to Holly in both looks and personality, and she considered him to be the most normal of her siblings. It also helped that she got along with his partner of seven years, Abbey, and when Gerry was alive the four of them often met up for dinner and drinks. When Gerry was alive . . . God, that didn't sound right.

Ciara was a whole different kettle of fish altogether. Jack and Holly were convinced she was from the planet Ciara, population: one. Ciara had the look of her father, long legs and dark hair. She also had various tattoos and piercings on her body as a result of her travels around the world. A tattoo for every country, her dad used to joke. A tattoo for every man, Holly and Jack were convinced.

Of course this carry-on was all frowned upon by the eldest of the family, Richard (or Dick as he was known to Jack and Holly). Richard was born with the serious illness of being an eternal old man. His life revolved around rules and regulations and obedience. When he was younger he had one friend and they had a fight when they were ten, so after that Holly could never remember him bringing anyone home, having any girlfriends or ever going out to socialize. She and Jack thought it was a wonder where he met his equally joyless wife, Meredith. Probably at an anti-happiness convention.

It's not as though Holly had the *worst* family in the world, it's just that they were such a strange mix of people. These huge clashes of personalities usually led to arguments at the most inappropriate times, or as Holly's parents preferred to call them, "heavy discussions." They *could* get along, but that was with everyone really trying and being on their best behavior.

Holly and Jack often met up for lunch or for drinks just to catch up on each other's lives; they had an interest in each other. She enjoyed his company and considered him to be not only a brother but a real friend. Lately they hadn't seen much of each other. Jack understood Holly well and knew when she needed her space.

The only time Holly caught up on her younger brother Declan's life was when she called the house looking for her parents and he would answer. Declan wasn't a great conversationalist. He was a twenty-two-year-old "boy" who didn't quite yet feel comfortable in the company of adults, so Holly never really knew that much about him. A nice boy, he just had his head up in the clouds a bit.

Ciara, her twenty-four-year-old little sister, had been away for the entire year and Holly had missed her. They were never the kind of sisters to swap clothes and giggle about boys, their tastes differed so much. But as the only two girls in a family of brothers, they formed a bond. Ciara was closer to Declan; both of them dreamers. Jack and Holly had always been inseparable as children and friends as adults. That left Richard. He was out on his own in the family, but Holly suspected he liked that feeling of being separated from those in his family he couldn't quite understand. Holly was dreading his lectures on all-things-boring, his insensitive questioning of her life and just the whole feeling of being frustrated by comment after comment at the dinner table. But it was a welcome-home dinner for Ciara and Jack would be there; Holly could count on him.

So was Holly looking forward to tonight? Absolutely not.

Holly reluctantly knocked on the door to her family home and immediately heard the pounding of tiny feet flying toward the door followed by a voice that should not belong to a child.

"Mummy! Daddy! It's Aunty Holly, it's Aunty Holly!"

It was Nephew Timothy, Nephew Timothy.

His happiness was suddenly crushed by a stern voice. (Although it was unusual for her nephew to be happy about

Holly's arrival; things must be especially boring in there.) "Timo-thy! What did I tell you about running in the house! You could fall and hurt yourself, now go stand in the corner and think about what I said. Do I make myself clear?"

"Yes, Mummy."

"Ah come on, Meredith, will he hurt himself on the carpet or on the comfy padded couch?"

Holly laughed to herself; Ciara was definitely home. Just as Holly was contemplating escape, the door swung open and there stood Meredith. She looked even more sour-faced and unwelcom-ing than usual.

"Holly." She nodded her head in acknowledgment.

"Meredith," Holly imitated.

Once in the living room Holly looked around for Jack, but to her disappointment he was nowhere to be seen. Richard stood in front of the fireplace dressed in a surprisingly colorful sweater; perhaps he was letting his hair down tonight. He stood with his hands in his pockets rocking back and forth from his heels to the balls of his toes like a man ready to give a lecture. His lecture was being aimed at their poor father, Frank, who sat uncomfortably in his favorite armchair looking like a chastised schoolboy. Richard was so lost in his story he didn't see Holly enter the room. Holly blew her poor father a kiss from across the room, not wanting to be brought into their conversation. Her father smiled at her and pretended to catch her kiss.

Declan was slumped on the couch wearing his ripped jeans and *South Park* T-shirt, puffing furiously on a cigarette while Meredith invaded his space and warned him of the dangers of smoking. "Really? I didn't know that," he said, sounding worry-ingly interested while stabbing out his cigarette. Meredith's face looked satisfied until Declan winked at Holly, reached for the box again and immediately lit up another one. "Tell me some more, please, I'm just dying to know." Meredith stared back at him in disgust.

Ciara was hiding behind the couch throwing pieces of popcorn at the back of poor Timothy's head. He stood facing the wall in the corner of the room and was too afraid to turn around. Abbey was pinned to the floor and being bossed around by little five-year-old Emily and an evil-looking doll. She caught Holly's eye and mouthed "Help" to her.

"Hi Ciara." Holly approached her sister, who jumped up and gave her a big hug, squeezing Holly a bit tighter than usual. "Nice hair."

"You like it?"

"Yeah, pink is really your color."

Ciara looked satisfied. "That's what I tried to tell them," she said, squinting her eyes and staring at Richard and Meredith. "So how's my big sis?" Ciara asked softly, rubbing Holly's arm affectionately.

"Oh, you know," Holly smiled weakly, "I'm hanging in there."

"Jack is in the kitchen helping your mum with the dinner if you're looking for him, Holly," Abbey announced, widening her eyes and mouthing "Help me" again.

Holly raised her eyebrows at Abbey. "Really? Well isn't he great helping out Mum?"

"Oh, Holly, didn't you know how much Jack just loves cooking, he just *loves* it. Can't get enough of it," she said sarcastically.

Holly's dad chuckled to himself, which stopped Richard in his tracks. "What's so funny, Father?"

Frank shifted in his seat nervously. "I just find it remarkable that all this happens in just one tiny little test tube."

Richard let out a disapproving sigh at his father's stupidity. "Yes, but you have to understand these are so minuscule, Father, it's rather fascinating. The organisms combine with the . . ." And away he went while his father settled back down in his chair and tried to avoid eye contact with Holly.

Holly tiptoed quietly into the kitchen, where she found her brother at the table with his feet up on a chair munching on some food. "Ah, here he is, the naked chef himself."

Jack smiled and stood up from his chair. "There's my favorite sister." He scrunched up his nose. "I see you got roped into coming to this thing as well." He walked toward her and held out his arms to offer her one of his big bear hugs. "How are you?" he said quietly into her ear.

"I'm OK, thanks." Holly smiled sadly and kissed him on the cheek before turning to her mother. "Darling Mother, I am here to offer my services at this extremely stressful and busy time of your life," Holly said, planting a kiss on her mother's flushed cheek.

"Oh, aren't I just the luckiest woman in the world having such caring children like you," Elizabeth said sarcastically. "Tell you what; you can just drain the water from the potatoes there."

"Mum, tell us about the time when you were a little girl during the famine and the spuds were gone," Jack said, putting on an exaggerated Irish accent.

Elizabeth hit him across the head playfully with the tea towel. "Ah, sure 'tis years before my time, son."

"Sure 'tis true," said Jack.

"No, you t'aren't at all," joined in Holly.

They both stopped and stared at her. "Since when is there such a word as t'aren't?" laughed her mum.

"Ah, shut up the both of you." Holly joined her brother at the table.

"I hope you two won't be getting up to any mischief tonight. I would like this to be an argument-free zone for a change."

"Mother, I am shocked the thought even crossed your mind." Jack winked across to Holly.

"All right," she said, not believing a word of it. "Well, sorry my babies, but there's nothing else to be done here. Dinner will be ready in a few minutes."

"Oh." Holly was disappointed.

Elizabeth joined her children at the table and the three of them stared at the kitchen door all thinking the same thing.

"No, Abbey," squealed Emily loudly, "you're not doing what I tell you," and she burst into tears. This was shortly followed by a loud guffaw from Richard; he must have cracked a joke because he was the only one laughing.

"But I suppose it's important that we all stay here and keep an eye on the dinner," Elizabeth added.

"OK everyone, dinner is being served," announced Elizabeth, and everyone made their way to the dining room. There was an awkward moment like at a child's birthday party while everyone scuffled to sit beside their best friend. Eventually Holly was satisfied with her position at the table and settled down with her mother on her left at the end of the table and Jack to her right. Abbey sat with a scowl on her face between Jack and Richard. Jack would have some making up to do when he got home. Declan sat opposite Holly and wedged in between him was an empty seat where Timothy should be sitting, then Emily and Meredith, then Ciara. Holly's father got a raw deal sitting at the head of the table between Richard and Ciara, but he was such a calm man he was the best one for the job.

Everyone oohed and aahed as Elizabeth brought out the food and the aroma filled the room. Holly had always loved her mother's cooking, she was never afraid to experiment with new flavors and recipes, a trait that had not been passed down to her daughter. "Hey, poor little Timmy must be starving out there," Ciara exclaimed to Richard. "He must have done his time by now."

She knew she was skating on thin ice but she loved the danger of it, and more important, she loved to wind Richard up. After all, she had to make up for lost time, she had been away for a year.

"Ciara, it's important that Timothy know when he has done something wrong," explained Richard.

"Yeah, but couldn't you just tell him?"

The rest of the family tried hard not to laugh.

"He needs to know that his actions will lead to serious consequences so he will not repeat them."

"Ah well," she said, raising her voice a few octaves, "he's missing all this yummy food. Mmm-mmm-mmm," she added, licking her lips.

"Stop it, Ciara," Elizabeth snapped.

"Or you'll have to stand in the corner," Jack added sternly.

The table erupted with laughter, bar Meredith and Richard of course.

"So Ciara, tell us about your adventures in Australia," Frank moved swiftly on.

Ciara's eyes lit up. "Oh, I had the most amazing time, Dad, I would definitely recommend going there to anyone."

"Awful long flight, though," Richard said.

"Yeah it is, but it's so worth it."

"Did you get any more tattoos?" Holly asked.

"Yeah, look." With that, Ciara stood up at the table and pulled down her trousers, revealing a butterfly on her behind.

Mum, Dad, Richard and Meredith protested in outrage while the others sat in convulsions of laughter. This carried on for a long time. Finally, when Ciara had apologized and Meredith had removed her hands from Emily's eyes, the table settled down.

"They are revolting things," Richard said in disgust.

"I think butterflies are pretty, Daddy," said Emily with big innocent eyes.

"Yes, some butterflies are pretty, Emily, but I'm talking about tattoos. They can give you all sorts of diseases and problems." Emily's smile faded.

"Hey, I didn't exactly get this done in a dodgy place sharing needles with drug dealers, you know. The place was perfectly clean."

"Well, that's an oxymoron if ever I heard one," Meredith said with disgust.

"Been in one recently, Meredith?" Ciara asked a bit too force-fully.

"Well, em . . . n-n-n-no," she stuttered, "I have never been in one, thank you very much, but I am sure they are." Then she turned to Emily. "They are dirty, horrible places, Emily, where only dangerous people go."

"Is Aunt Ciara dangerous, Mummy?"

"Only to five-year-old little girls with red hair," Ciara said, stuffing her face.

Emily froze.

"Richard dear, do you think that Timmy might want to come in now for some food?" Elizabeth asked politely.

"It's Timothy," Meredith interrupted.

"Yes, Mother, I think that would be OK."

A very sorry little Timothy walked slowly into the room with his head down and took his place silently beside Declan. Holly's heart leapt out to him. How cruel to treat a child like that, how cruel to stop him from being a child . . . her sympathetic thoughts diminished immediately as she felt his little foot kick her shin underneath the table. They should have left him out there.

"So Ciara, come on, give us the gossip, do anything wild and wonderful out there?" Holly pushed for more information.

"Oh yeah, I did a bungee jump actually, well, I did a few. I have the photo here." She reached into her back pocket and everyone looked away just in case she was planning to reveal any more bits of her anatomy. Thankfully she only took out her wallet; she passed the photo around the table and continued explaining.

"The first one I did was off a bridge and my head hit the water when I fell . . ."

"Oh Ciara, that sounds dangerous," her mother said with her hands across her face.

"Oh no, it wasn't dangerous at all," she reassured her.

The photograph was passed to Holly and she and Jack burst out laughing. Ciara dangled upside down from a rope with her face contorted in the middle of a scream from pure terror. Her hair (it was blue at that time) was shooting out in all directions as though she had been electrocuted.

"Attractive photo, Ciara. Mum, you must get that framed for over the fireplace," Holly joked.

"Yeah!" Ciara's eyes lit up as the thought hit her. "That would be a cool idea."

"Sure darling, I'll just take down the one of you making your

Holy Communion and replace it with that," Elizabeth said sarcastically.

"Well, I don't know which one would be scarier," said Declan.

"Holly, what are you doing for your birthday?" asked Abbey, leaning across toward her. She was clearly dying to get out of the conversation she was having with Richard.

"Oh, that's right!" shouted Ciara. "You're gonna be thirty in a few weeks!"

"I'm not doing anything big at all," she warned everyone. "I don't want any surprise party or anything, *please*."

"Oh, you have to . . . ," said Ciara.

"No, she doesn't have to if she doesn't want to," her father interrupted, and he winked supportively at Holly.

"Thank you, Dad. I'm just going to have a girly night out clubbing or something. Nothing mad, nothing wild."

Richard tutted as the photograph reached him and passed it on to his father, who chuckled to himself over the sight of Ciara.

"Yes, I agree with you, Holly," said Richard, "those birthday celebrations are always a bit embarrassing. Grown adults acting like children, doing 'Rock the boat' on the floor and drinking far too much. You're quite right."

"Well, I actually quite enjoy those parties, Richard," Holly shot back, "but I just don't feel in the celebratory mood this year, that's all."

There was silence for a moment before Ciara piped up, "A girly night it is then."

"Can I tag along with the camera?" asked Declan.

"For what?"

"Just for some footage of clubs and stuff for college."

"Well, if it'll help . . . but as long as you know I won't be going to all the trendy places that you like."

"No, I don't mind where you g . . . OW!" he shouted and stared menacingly at Timothy.

Timmy stuck his tongue out at him and the conversation continued on. After the main course had finished, Ciara disappeared out of the room and arrived with a bulging bag in her hand and announced, "Presents!!"

Timmy and Emily cheered. Holly hoped that Ciara had remembered to get them something.

Her father received a colorfully painted boomerang that he pretended to throw down at his wife, Richard was given a T-shirt with the map of Australia on it, which he immediately began to teach to Timmy and Emily at the table, Meredith quite comically wasn't given anything, Jack and Declan were given T-shirts with perverted pictures and a caption saying "I've been to the bush," Holly's mum received a collection of old Aboriginal recipes and Holly was touched by the dream catcher made from brightly colored feathers and sticks. "So all your dreams come true," Ciara had whispered in her ear before kissing her on the cheek.

Thankfully Ciara had bought sweets for Timmy and Emily, but they looked strangely like the sweets you could buy from the local shop. These were briskly taken away by Richard and Meredith, who claimed they would rot their teeth.

"Well, give them back then so I can rot my own," Ciara demanded.

Timmy and Emily looked around sadly at everyone's presents and were immediately chastised by Richard for not concentrating on the map of Australia. Timmy made a face at Holly and a warm feeling returned to her heart. As long as the kids kept on acting like they deserved their harsh treatment, it made it easier for Holly to deal with. In fact, she may even have bordered on enjoying watching them being given out to.

"Right, we better hit the road, Richard, or the children will fall asleep at the table," announced Meredith. The children, though, were wide awake and kicking Holly and Declan repeatedly under the table.

"Well, before everybody goes disappearing," Holly's father announced loudly over the chatter. The table grew silent. "I would like to propose a toast to our beautiful daughter Ciara, as this is her welcome-home dinner." He smiled at his daughter and Ciara lapped up all the attention. "We missed you, love, and we're glad you're home safely," Frank finished. He lifted his glass into the air, "To Ciara!"

"To Ciara!" everyone repeated, and they finished off what was in their glasses.

As soon as the door closed behind Richard and Meredith everyone began to leave one by one. Holly stepped into the chilly air and walked to her car alone. Her mum and dad stood at the door waving her off but she still felt lonely. Usually she left dinner parties with Gerry, and if not *with* him then she was returning home *to* him. But not tonight or the next night or the night after that.

Eight

HOLLY STOOD IN FRONT OF the full-length mirror and inspected herself. She had carried out Gerry's orders and had purchased a new outfit. What for, she didn't know, but several times every day she had to drag herself away from opening the envelope for May. There were only two days left until she could, and the anticipation left her no room to think of anything else.

She had settled on wearing an all-black outfit to suit her current mood. Black fitted trousers slimmed her legs and were tailored perfectly to sit over her black boots. A black corset that made her look like she had a bigger chest finished the outfit off perfectly. Leo had done a wonderful job on her hair, tying it up and allowing strands to fall in loose waves around her shoulders. Holly ran her fingers through her hair and smiled at the memory of her time at the hairdresser's. She had arrived at the salon with her face flushed and out of breath. "Oh, I'm so sorry, Leo, I got caught on the phone and didn't realize the time."

"Don't worry, love, whenever you make an appointment I have the staff trained to pencil it in for half an hour later. *Colin!*" he yelled, clicking his fingers in the air. Colin dropped everything and ran.

"God, are you taking horse tranquilizers or something? The length of your hair already, and I just cut it a few weeks ago."

He pumped vigorously on the chair, raising Holly higher. "Anything special tonight?" he asked, attacking the chair.

"The big three-oh," she said, biting her lip.

"What's that, your local bus route?"

"No! I'm the big three-oh!"

"Of course I knew that, love, *Colin!*" he yelled again, snapping his fingers in the air.

With that, Colin appeared from the staff room behind Holly with a cake in his hand, followed by a row of hairdressers joining Leo in a chorus of "Happy Birthday." Holly was dumbfounded. "Leo!" was all she could say. She battled the tears that were welling in her eyes and failed miserably. By this stage the entire salon had joined in and Holly was just overwhelmed by their show of love. When it was over everyone applauded and normal business resumed.

Holly couldn't speak.

"Christ Almighty, Holly, one week you're in here laughing so hard you practically fall off your chair and the next visit you're crying!"

"Oh, but that was just so special, Leo, thank you," she said, drying her eyes and giving him a huge hug and a kiss.

"Well, I had to get you back after you mortified me," he said, shrugging her off, uncomfortable with the sentimentality.

Holly laughed, remembering Leo's surprise fiftieth birthday party. The theme had been "feathers and lace" as she recalled. Holly had worn a beautiful tight-fitting lace dress and Gerry, who was always game for a laugh, had worn a pink feather boa to match his pink shirt and tie. Leo claimed to have been excruciatingly embarrassed, but everyone knew he was secretly delighted with all the attention. The next day, Leo had rung every guest who had attended the party and left a threatening message on their machine. Holly had been terrified to make an appointment with Leo for weeks after that in case he butchered her. Word had it that business was very slow for Leo that week.

"Well, you enjoyed the stripper that night anyway," Holly teased.

"Enjoyed? I went out with him for a month after that. The bastard."

A slice of cake arrived in front of each customer and everyone turned to thank her.

"Don't know why they're thanking you," Leo muttered under his breath, "I'm the one who bloody bought it."

"Don't worry, Leo, I'll make sure your tip covers the cost."

"Are you mad? Your tip wouldn't cover the cost of my bus fare home."

"Leo, you live next door."

"Exactly!"

Holly pouted her lip and pretended to sulk. Leo laughed. "Thirty years old and you're still acting like a baby. Where are you off to tonight?"

"Oh, nowhere mad. I just want a low-key, nice quiet night out with the girls."

"That's what I said at my fiftieth. Who's going?"

"Sharon, Ciara, Abbey and Denise, haven't seen her for ages."

"Ciara home?"

"Yeah, her and her pink hair."

"Merciful hour! She'll stay away from me if she knows what's good for her. Right missus, you look fab, you'll be the belle of the ball—have fun!"

Holly stopped daydreaming and returned her gaze to her reflection in her bedroom mirror. She didn't feel thirty. But then again, what was being thirty supposed to feel like? When she was younger, thirty seemed so far away, she thought that a woman of that age would be so wise and knowledgeable, so settled in her life with a husband and children and a career. She had none of those things. She still felt as clueless as she had felt when she was twenty, only with a few more gray hairs and crow's-feet around her eyes. She sat down on the edge of the bed and continued to stare at herself. There was nothing about being thirty worth celebrating.

The doorbell rang and Holly could hear the excited chatter and giggles of the girls outside. She tried to perk herself up, took a deep breath and plastered a smile on her face.

"Happy Birthday!" they all yelled in unison.

She stared back at their happy faces and was immediately cheered up by their enthusiasm. She ushered them into the living room and waved hello to the camera being held by Declan.

"No, Holly, you're supposed to ignore him!" hissed Denise, and she dragged Holly by the arm onto the couch, where they all surrounded her and immediately started thrusting presents in her face.

"Open mine first!" squealed Ciara, knocking Sharon out of the way so hard that she toppled off the couch. Sharon froze in horror, unsure of how to react, then she burst into giggles.

"OK, calm down, everyone," said the voice of reason (Abbey), struggling to help up a hysterical Sharon. "I think we should pop open the bubbly first and *then* open the pressies."

"OK, but as long as she opens mine first," pouted Ciara.

"Ciara, I promise to open yours first." Holly spoke to her as though she were addressing a child.

Abbey raced into the kitchen and returned with a tray full of champagne flutes. "Anyone for champers, sweetie darlings?"

The flutes were a wedding gift and one of the glasses had Gerry and Holly's names inscribed on it, which Abbey had tactfully removed from the set. "OK, Holly, you can do the honors," Abbey said, handing her the bottle.

Everyone ran for cover and ducked as Holly began to remove the cork. "Hey, I'm not that bad, everyone!"

"Yeah, she's an old pro at this by now," said Sharon, appearing from behind the couch with a cushion on her head.

The girls all cheered as they heard the pop and crawled out from their hiding places. "The sound of heaven," Denise said dramatically, holding her hand up to her heart.

"OK, now open my present!" Ciara screamed again.

"Ciara!" they all shouted. "After the toast," added Sharon.

Everyone held up their glasses.

"OK, here's to my bestest friend in the whole world who has had such a difficult year, but all throughout, she's been the bravest and the strongest person I've ever met. She's an inspiration to us all. Here's to her finding happiness for the next thirty years of her life! To Holly!"

"To Holly," they all chorused. Everyone's eyes were sparkling with tears as they took a sip of their drink, except of course for Ciara, who had knocked back her glass of champagne and was scrambling to give her present to Holly first.

"OK, first you have to wear this tiara because you are our princess for the night, and second here's my present from me to you!"

The girls helped Holly put on the sparkling tiara that luckily went perfectly with her black glittery corset, and at that moment, surrounded by her friends, she felt like a princess.

Holly carefully removed the tape from the neatly wrapped parcel.

"Oh, just rip it open!" said Abbey to everyone's surprise.

Holly looked at the box inside, confused. "What is it?"

"Read it!" Ciara said excitedly.

Holly began to read aloud from the box, "It's a battery-operated . . . oh my God! Ciara! You naughty girl!" Holly and the girls laughed hysterically.

"Well, I'll definitely need this," Holly laughed, holding the box up to the camera.

Declan looked like he was about to throw up.

"Do you like it?" Ciara asked, searching for approval. "I wanted to give it to you at dinner that time but I didn't think it would be appropriate . . ."

"Gosh! Well, I'm glad you saved it till now!" Holly laughed, giving her sister a hug.

"OK, me next," Abbey said, putting her parcel on Holly's lap. "It's from me and Jack, so don't expect anything like Ciara's!"

"Well, I would worry if Jack gave me something like that," she said, opening Abbey's present. "Oh, Abbey, it's beautiful!" Holly said, holding up the sterling silver–covered photo album.

"For your new memories," Abbey said softly.

"Oh, it's perfect," she said, wrapping her arms around Abbey and squeezing her. "Thank you."

"OK, well, mine is less sentimental, but as a fellow female I'm sure you will appreciate it," said Denise, handing her an envelope.

"Oh brilliant! I've always wanted to go here," Holly exclaimed as she opened it. "A weekend of pampering in Haven's health and beauty clinic!"

"God, you sound like you're on *Blind Date,*" teased Sharon.

"So let us know when you want to make an appointment, it's valid for a year, and the rest of us can book the same time. Make a holiday out of it!"

"Oh, that's a great idea, Denise, thank you!"

"OK, last but not least!" Holly winked at Sharon. Sharon fidgeted with her hands nervously while she watched Holly's face.

It was a large silver photo frame with a photograph of Sharon, Denise and Holly at the Christmas Ball two years ago. "Oh, I'm wearing my 'spensive white dress!" sobbed Holly playfully.

"*Before* it was ruined," pointed out Sharon.

"God, I don't even remember that being taken!"

"I don't even remember being there," mumbled Denise.

Holly continued to stare at the photo sadly while she walked over to the fireplace.

That had been the last ball that she and Gerry had been to, as he had been too ill to attend last year's.

"Well, this will take pride of place," Holly announced, walking over to the mantelpiece and placing it beside her wedding photo.

"OK, girls, let's get some serious drinking done!" screamed Ciara, and everyone dived to safety, as another bottle of champagne was popped open.

Two bottles of champagne and several bottles of red wine later, the girls stumbled out of the house and piled into a taxi. Through the giggling and shouting someone managed to explain to the taxi driver where they were going. Holly insisted on sitting in the passenger seat of the taxicab and having a heart-to-heart with John the driver, who probably wanted to kill her by the time they reached town.

"Bye John!" they all shouted to their new best friend before falling out onto the curb in Dublin city, where they watched him drive off at a high speed. They had decided (while drinking their third bottle of wine) to chance their luck in Dublin's most stylish club, Boudoir. The club was reserved for the rich and famous only, and it was a well-known fact that if you weren't rich and famous, you then had to have a member's card to be granted access. Denise walked up to the door coolly waving her video store membership card in the bouncers' faces. Believe it or not, they stopped her.

The only famous faces they saw overtaking them to get into the club, as they fought with the bouncers to get in, were a few newsreaders from the national TV station who Denise smiled at, and she hilariously kept repeating "good evening" very seriously to their faces. Unfortunately after that, Holly remembered no more.

Holly awoke with her head pounding. Her mouth was as dry as Gandhi's sandal and her vision was impaired. She leaned up on one elbow and tried to open her eyes, which were somehow glued together. She squinted around the room. It was bright, very bright, and the room seemed to be spinning. Something very odd was going on. Holly caught sight of herself in the mirror ahead and startled herself. Had she been in an accident last night? She ran out of energy and collapsed flat on her back again. Suddenly the house alarm began wailing and she lifted her head slightly from the pillow and opened one eye. Oh, take whatever you want, she thought, just as long as you bring me a glass of water before you go. After a while she realized it wasn't the alarm but the phone ringing beside her bed.

"Hello?" she croaked.

"Oh good, I'm not the only one," said a desperately ill voice on the other end.

"Who are you?" croaked Holly again.

"My name is Sharon, I think," came the reply, "although don't ask me who Sharon is because I don't know. The man beside me in bed seems to think I know him." Holly heard John laughing loudly in the background.

"Sharon, what happened last night? Please enlighten me."

"Alcohol happened last night," said Sharon drowsily, "lots and lots of alcohol."

"Any other information?"

"Nope."

"Know what time is it?"

"Two o'clock."

"Why are you ringing me at this hour of the morning?"

"It's the afternoon, Holly."

"Oh. How did that happen?"

"Gravity or something. I was out that day in school."

"Oh God, I think I'm dying."

"Me too."

"I think I'll just go back to sleep, maybe when I wake up, the ground will have stopped moving."

"Good idea, oh and Holly, welcome to the thirties club."

Holly groaned, "I have not started as I mean to go on. From now on I will be a sensible, mature thirty-year-old woman."

"Yeah, that's what I said too. Good night."

"'Night." Seconds later Holly was asleep. She awoke at various stages during the day to answer the phone, conversations that all seemed part of her dreams. And she made many trips to the kitchen to rehydrate herself.

Eventually at nine o'clock that night Holly succumbed to her stomach's screaming demands for food. As usual there was nothing in the fridge, so she decided to treat herself to a Chinese take-away. She sat snuggled up on the couch in her pajamas watching the very best of Saturday night TV while stuffing her face. After the trauma of being without Gerry for her birthday the previous day, Holly was surprised to notice that she felt very content with herself. It was the first time since Gerry had died that she was at ease with her own company. There was a slight chance she could make it without him.

Later that night Jack called her on her mobile. "Hey sis, what are you doing?"

"Watching TV, having Chinese," she said.

"Well, you sound in good form. Unlike my poor girlfriend who's suffering here beside me."

"I'm never going out with you again, Holly," she heard Abbey scream weakly in the background.

"You and your friends perverted her mind," he joked.

"Don't blame me, she was doing just fine all by herself as far as I remember."

"She says she can't remember anything."

"Neither can I. Maybe it's something that happens as soon as you hit thirty, I was never like this before."

"Or maybe it's just an evil plan you all hatched so you wouldn't have to tell us what you got up to."

"I wish it was . . . oh, thanks for the pressie by the way, it's beautiful."

"Glad you like it. It took me ages to find the right one."

"Liar."

He laughed.

"Anyway, I was ringing you to ask if you're going to Declan's gig tomorrow night."

"Where is it?"

"Hogan's pub."

"No way. There is no way I'm ever setting foot in a pub again, especially to listen to some loud rock band with screeching guitars and noisy drums," Holly told him.

"Oh, it's the old 'I'm never drinking again' excuse, is it? Well, don't drink then. Please come, Holly. Declan's really excited about it and no one else will come."

"Ha! So I'm the last resort, am I? Nice to know you think so highly of me."

"No you're not. Declan would love to see you there and we hardly got a chance to talk at dinner, we haven't gone out for ages," he pleaded.

"Well, we're hardly going to have a heart-to-heart with the Orgasmic Fish banging out their tunes," she said sarcastically.

"Well, they're actually called Black Strawberries now, which has a nice sweet ring to it I think," he laughed.

Holly held her head in her hands and groaned, "Oh, please don't make me go, Jack."

"You're going."

"OK, but I'm not staying for the whole thing."

"Well, we can discuss that when we get there. Declan will be chuffed when I tell him, the family never usually goes to these things."

"OK then, about eightish?"

"Perfect."

Holly hung up and sat stuck to the couch for another few hours. She felt so stuffed, she couldn't move. Maybe that Chinese wasn't such a good idea after all.

Nine

HOLLY ARRIVED AT HOGAN'S PUB feeling a lot fresher than the day before, but her reactions were still a little slower than usual. Her hangovers seemed to be gradually getting worse as she got older, and yesterday took the gold medal for the hangover of all hangovers. She had gone for a long walk along the coast from Malahide to Portmarnock earlier that day and the crisp fresh breeze helped to clear her fuzzy head. She had called into her parents' for Sunday dinner, where they presented her with a beautiful Waterford crystal vase for her birthday. It had been a wonderful, relaxing day with her parents and she almost had to drag herself off the comfortable couch to go to Hogan's.

Hogan's was a popular three-story club situated in the center of town, and even on a Sunday the place was jammed. The first floor was a trendy nightclub that played all the latest music from the charts. It was where the young, beautiful people went to show off their latest fashions. The ground floor was a traditional Irish pub for the older crowd (it usually contained old men perched up on their bar stools and stooped over their pints contemplating life). A few nights a week there was a traditional Irish music band that played all the old favorites, which was popular with the young and old. The basement was dark and dingy and it was where bands usually played, the clientele was purely students and Holly seemed to be the oldest person in there. The bar consisted of a tiny counter in the corner of the long hall, and it was surrounded by a huge crowd of young students dressed in scruffy jeans and ripped T-shirts, pushing one another violently in order to be served. The bar staff also looked like they should be in school and were rushing around at a hundred miles per hour with sweat dripping from their faces.

The basement was stuffy with no ventilation or air-conditioning at all, and Holly was finding it difficult to breathe in the smoky air. Practically everyone around her seemed to be smoking a cigarette, and her eyes were already stinging her. Holly dreaded to think what it might be like in an hour's time, although she seemed to be the only one who was bothered by it. She waved at Declan to let him know she was there but decided not to make her way over, as he was surrounded by a crowd of girls. She wouldn't want to cramp his style. Holly had missed out on the whole student scene when she was younger. She had decided not to go to college after school and instead began working as a secretary, where she moved from job to job every few months, ending with the awful job she left so she could spend time with Gerry while he was sick. She doubted she would have stayed at it that much longer anyway. Gerry had studied marketing at Dublin City

University but he never socialized much with his college friends; instead he chose to go out with Holly, Sharon and John, Denise and whoever she was with at the time. Looking around at everyone, Holly didn't feel like she had missed anything special.

Finally Declan managed to tear himself away from his female fans and make his way over to Holly.

"Well hello, Mr. Popular, I feel privileged you chose me to speak to next." All the girls stared Holly up and down and wondered what the hell Declan saw in this older woman.

Declan laughed and rubbed his hands together cheekily. "I know! This band business is great, looks like I'll be getting a bit of action tonight," he said cockily.

"As your sister it's always a pleasure to be informed of that," Holly replied sarcastically. She found it impossible to maintain a conversation with Declan, as he refused eye contact with her and instead scoured the crowds.

"OK, Declan, just go, why don't you, and flirt with these beauties instead of being stuck here with your old sister."

"Oh no, it's not that," he said defensively. "It's just that we were told there might be a record company guy coming to see us play tonight."

"Oh cool!" Holly's eyes widened with excitement for her brother. This obviously meant a lot to him, and she felt guilty for never taking an interest in it before. She looked around and tried to spot someone who looked like a record company guy. What would he look like? It's not as if he would be sitting in the corner with a notebook and pen scribbling furiously. Finally her eyes fell upon a man who seemed much older than the rest of the crowd, more her own age. He was dressed in a black leather jacket, black slacks and a black T-shirt and stood with his hands on his hips staring at the stage. Yes, he was definitely a record company guy, as he had stubble all around his jaw and looked like he hadn't been to bed for days. He must have stayed up all night every night this week attending concerts and gigs and probably slept all day. He probably smelled bad as well. Or else he was just a weirdo who liked to go to student nights and ogle all the young girls. Also a possibility.

"Over there, Deco!" Holly raised her voice over the noise and pointed at the man. Declan looked excited and his eyes followed to where her finger pointed. His smile faded as he obviously recognized the man. "No, it's just *Danny!*" he yelled, and he wolf-whistled to grab his attention.

Danny twirled around trying to find his caller and nodded his head in recognition and made his way over. "Hey man," Declan said, shaking his hand.

"Hi Declan, how are you set?" The man looked stressed.

"Yeah, OK," Declan nodded unenthusiastically. Somebody must have told Declan that acting like you didn't care was cool.

"Sound check go OK?" He pressed him for more information.

"There were a few problems but we sorted them out."

"So everything's OK?"

"Sure."

"Good." His face relaxed and he turned to greet Holly. "Sorry for ignoring you there, I'm Daniel."

"Nice to meet you, I'm Holly."

"Oh sorry," Declan interrupted. "Holly, this is the owner; Daniel, this is my sister."

"Sister? Wow, you look nothing alike."

"Thank God," Holly mouthed to Daniel so Declan couldn't see, and he laughed.

"Hey Deco, we're on!" yelled a blue-haired boy at him.

"See you two later," and he ran off.

"Good luck!" yelled Holly after him. "So you're a Hogan," she said, turning to face Daniel.

"Well, no actually, I'm a Connolly," he smiled. "I just took over the place a few weeks ago."

"Oh." Holly was surprised. "I didn't know they sold the place. So are you going to change it to Connolly's then?"

"Can't afford all the lettering on the front, it's a bit long."

Holly laughed. "Well, everyone knows the name Hogan's at this stage; it would probably be stupid to change it."

Daniel nodded in agreement. "That was the main reason actually."

Suddenly Jack appeared at the entrance and Holly waved him over. "I'm so sorry I'm late, did I miss anything?" he said, giving her a hug and a kiss.

"Nope, he's just about to go on now. Jack, this is Daniel, the owner."

"Nice to meet you," Daniel said, shaking his hand.

"Are they any good?" Jack asked him, nodding his head in the direction of the stage.

"To tell you the truth, I've never even heard them play," Daniel said worriedly.

"That was brave of you!" laughed Jack.

"I hope not too brave," he said, turning to face the front as the boys took to the stage.

"I recognize a few faces here," Jack said, scanning the crowd. "Most of them are under eighteen as well."

A young girl dressed in ripped jeans and a belly top walked slowly by Jack with an unsure smile on her face. She placed her finger over her lip as though telling him to be quiet. Jack smiled and nodded back.

Holly looked at Jack questioningly. "What was that about?"

"Oh, I teach her English at the school. She's only sixteen or seventeen. She's a good girl, though." Jack stared after her as she walked by, then added, "But she better not be late for class tomorrow."

Holly watched the girl down a pint with her friends, wishing she had had a teacher at school like Jack; all the students seemed to love him. And it was easy to see why; he was a lovable kind of person. "Well, don't tell *him* they're under eighteen," Holly said under her breath, nodding her head in the direction of Daniel.

The crowd cheered and Declan took on his moody persona as he lifted his guitar strap over his shoulder. The music started and after that there was no chance of carrying on any kind of conversation. The crowd began to jump up and down, and once too often Holly's foot was stomped on. Jack just looked at her and laughed, amused at her obvious discomfort. *"Can I get you two a drink?"* Daniel yelled, making a drinking motion with his hand. Jack asked for a pint of Budweiser and Holly settled for a 7UP. They watched Daniel battle through the moshing crowd and climb behind the bar to fix the drinks. He returned minutes later with their drinks and a stool for Holly. They turned their attention back to the stage and watched their brother perform. The music really wasn't Holly's type of thing, and it was so loud and noisy it was difficult for her to tell if they were actually any good. It was a far cry from the soothing sounds of her favorite Westlife CD, so perhaps she wasn't in the right position to judge the Black Strawberries. The name said it all, though, really.

After four songs Holly had had enough, and she gave Jack a

hug and a kiss good-bye. *"Tell Declan I stayed till the end!"* she yelled. *"Nice meeting you, Daniel! Thanks for the drink!"* she screamed and made her way back to civilization and cool fresh air. Her ears continued to ring all the way home in the car. It was ten o'clock by the time she got there. Only two more hours till May. And that meant she could open another envelope.

Holly sat at her kitchen table nervously drumming her fingers on the wood. She gulped back her third cup of coffee and uncrossed her legs. Staying awake for just two more hours had proved more difficult than she thought; she was obviously still tired from overindulging at her party. She tapped her feet under the table with no particular rhythm, and then crossed her legs again. It was 11:30 p.m. She had the envelope on the table in front of her and she could almost see it sticking its tongue out and singing "Na-na na-na-na."

She picked it up and ran it over in her hands. Who would know if she opened it early? Sharon and John had probably forgotten there was even an envelope for May, and Denise was probably conked out after the stress of her two-day hangover. She could just as easily lie if they ever asked her if she cheated, then again they probably wouldn't even care. No one would know and no one would care.

But that wasn't true.

Gerry would know.

Each time Holly held the envelopes in her hand she felt a connection with Gerry. The last two times she opened them she had felt as though Gerry were sitting right beside her and laughing at her reactions. She felt like they were playing a game together even though they were in two different worlds. But she could *feel* him, and he would know if she cheated, he would know if she disobeyed the rules of their game.

After another cup of coffee Holly was bouncing off the walls. The small hand of the clock seemed to be auditioning for a part in *Baywatch* with its slow-motion run around the dial, but eventually it struck midnight. Once again she slowly turned the envelope over and treasured every moment of the process. Gerry sat opposite her at the table. "Go on; open it!"

She carefully tore open the seal and ran her fingers along it, knowing the last thing that had touched it was Gerry's tongue. She slid the card out of its pouch and opened it.

> *Go on, Disco Diva! Face your fear of karaoke at Club Diva this month and you never know, you might be rewarded . . .*
>
> *PS, I love you . . .*

She felt Gerry watching her and the corners of her lips lifted into a smile and she began to laugh. Holly kept repeating *"no way!"* whenever she caught her breath. Finally she calmed down and announced to the room, "Gerry! You bastard! There is absolutely no way I am going through with this!"

Gerry laughed louder.

"This is *not* funny. You know how I feel about this, and I refuse to do it. Nope. No way. Not doing it."

"You have to do it, you know," laughed Gerry.

"I do not have to do this!"

"Do it for me."

"I am not doing it for you, for me or for world peace. I hate karaoke!"

"Do it for me," he repeated.

The sound of the phone caused Holly to jump in her seat. It

was Sharon. "OK, it's five past twelve, what did it say? John and I are dying to know!"

"What makes you think I opened it?"

"Ha!" Sharon snorted. "Twenty years of friendship qualifies me as being an expert on you; now come on, tell us what it says."

"I'm not doing it," Holly stated bluntly.

"What? You're not telling us?"

"No, I'm not doing what he wants me to do."

"Why, what is it?"

"Oh, just Gerry's *pathetic* attempt at being *humorous*," she snapped at the ceiling.

"Oh, I'm intrigued now," Sharon said, "tell us."

"Holly, spill the beans, what is it?" John was on the downstairs phone.

"OK . . . Gerry wants me . . . to . . . singatakaraoke," she rushed out.

"Huh? Holly, we didn't understand a word you said," Sharon gave out.

"No, I did," interrupted John. "I think I heard something about a karaoke. Am I right?"

"Yes," Holly replied like a bold little girl.

"And do you have to sing?" inquired Sharon.

"Ye-eess," she replied slowly. Maybe if she didn't say it, it wouldn't have to happen.

The other two burst out laughing so loud, Holly had to quickly remove the phone from her ear. "Phone me back when the two of you shut up," she said angrily, hanging up.

A few minutes later they called back.

"Yes?"

She heard Sharon snort down the phone, relapse into a fit of the giggles and then the line went dead.

Ten minutes later she phoned back.

"Yes?"

"OK." Sharon had an overly serious "let's get down to business" tone in her voice. "I'm sorry about that, I'm fine now. Don't look at me, John," Sharon said away from the phone. "I'm sorry, Holly, but I just kept thinking about the last time you—"

"Yeah, yeah, yeah," she interrupted, "you don't need to bring it back up. It was *the most embarrassing day of my life,* so I just happen to remember it. That's why I'm not doing it."

"Oh, Holly, you can't let a stupid thing like that put you off!"

"Well, if that wouldn't put a person off, then they're clinically insane!"

"Holly, it was only a little fall . . ."

"Yes, thank you! I remember it just fine! Anyway I can't even sing, Sharon; I think I established that fact marvelously the last time!"

Sharon was very quiet.

"Sharon?"

Still silence.

"Sharon, you still there?"

There was no answer.

"Sharon, are you laughing?" Holly gave out.

She heard a little squeak and the line went dead.

"What wonderfully supportive friends I have," she muttered under her breath.

"Oh Gerry!" Holly yelled. "I thought you were supposed to be helping me, not turning me into a nervous wreck!"

She got very little sleep that night.

Ten

"HAPPY BIRTHDAY, HOLLY! OR SHOULD I say happy belated birthday?" Richard laughed nervously. Holly's mouth dropped open in shock at the sight of her older brother standing on her doorstep. This was a rare occurrence; in fact, it may have been a first. She opened and closed her mouth like a goldfish, completely unsure of what to say. "I brought you a potted mini Phalaenopsis orchid," he said, handing her a potted plant. "They have been shipped fresh, budding, and are ready to bloom." He sounded like an advertisement. Holly was even more stunned as she fingered the tiny pink buds. "Gosh, Richard, orchids are my favorite!"

"Well, you have a nice big garden here anyway, nice and"—he cleared his throat—"green. Bit overgrown, though . . ." He trailed off and began that annoying rocking thing he did with his feet.

"Would you like to come in or are you just passing through?" Please say no, please say no. Despite the thoughtful gift, Holly was in no mood for Richard's company.

"Well yes, I'll come in for a little while so." He wiped his feet for a good two minutes at the door before stepping into the house. He reminded Holly of her old math teacher at school, dressed in a brown knitted cardigan with brown trousers that stopped just at the top of his neat little brown loafers. He hadn't a hair on his head out of place and his fingernails were clean and perfectly manicured. Holly could imagine him measuring them with a little ruler every night to see that they didn't outgrow the required European standard length for fingernails, if such a thing existed.

Richard never seemed comfortable in his own skin. He looked like he was being choked to death by his tightly knotted (brown) tie, and he always walked as if he had a barge pole shoved up his backside. On the rare occasions that he smiled, the smile never managed to reach his eyes. He was the drill sergeant of his own body, screaming at and punishing himself every time he lapsed into human mode. But he did it to himself, and the sad thing was that he thought he was better off than everyone else for it. Holly led him into the living room and placed the ceramic pot on top of the TV for the time being.

"No, no, Holly," he said, wagging a finger at her as though she were a naughty child. "You shouldn't put it there, it needs to be in a cool, draft-free location away from harsh sunlight and heat vents."

"Oh, of course." Holly picked the pot back up and searched around the room in panic for a suitable place. What had he said? A draft-free, warm location? How did he always manage to make her feel like an incompetent little girl?

"How about that little table in the center, it should be safe there."

Holly did as she was told and placed the pot on the table, half expecting him to say "good girl." Thankfully he didn't.

Richard took his favorite position at the fireplace and surveyed the room. "Your house is very clean," he commented.

"Thank you, I just, eh . . . cleaned it."

He nodded as if he already knew.

"Can I get you a tea or coffee?" she asked, expecting him to say no.

"Yes, great," he said, clapping his hands together, "tea would be splendid. Just milk, no sugar."

Holly returned from the kitchen with two mugs of tea and placed them down on the coffee table. She hoped the steam rising from the mugs wouldn't murder the poor plant.

"You just need to water it regularly and feed it during the months of spring." He was still talking about the plant. Holly nodded, knowing full well she would not do either of those things.

"I didn't know you had green fingers, Richard," she said, trying to lighten the atmosphere.

"Only when I'm painting with the children. At least that's what Meredith says," he laughed, cracking a rare joke.

"Do you do much work in your garden?" Holly was anxious to keep the conversation flowing; as the house was so quiet, every silence was amplified.

"Oh yes, I love to work in the garden." His eyes lit up. "Saturdays are my garden days," he said, smiling into his mug of tea.

Holly felt as though a complete stranger were sitting beside her. She realized she knew very little about Richard and he equally knew very little about her. But that was the way Richard had always liked to keep things, he had always distanced himself from the family even when they were younger. He never shared exciting news with them or even told them how his day went. He was just full of facts, facts and more facts. The first time the family had even heard of Meredith was the day they both came over for dinner to announce their engagement. Unfortunately at that stage it was too late to convince him not to marry the flame-haired green-eyed dragon. Not that he would have listened anyway.

"So," she announced, far too loudly for the echoing room, "anything strange or startling?" Like why are you here?

"No, no, nothing strange, everything is ticking over as normal." He took a sip of tea then a while later added, "Nothing startling either, for that matter. I just thought I would pop in and say hello while I was in the area."

"Ah, right. It's unusual for you to be over this side of the city." Holly laughed. "What brings you to the dark and dangerous world of the north side?"

"Oh, you know, just a little business," he mumbled to himself. "But my car's parked on the other side of the River Liffey of course!"

Holly forced a smile.

"Just joking of course," he added. "It's just outside the house . . . it will be safe, won't it?" he asked seriously.

"I think it should be OK," Holly said sarcastically. "There doesn't seem to be anyone suspicious hanging around the cul-de-sac in broad daylight today." Her humor was lost on him. "How's Emily and Timmy, sorry, I mean Timothy?" That was an honest mistake for once.

Richard's eyes lit up. "Oh, they're good, Holly, very good. Worrying, though." He looked away and surveyed her living room.

"What do you mean?" Holly asked, thinking that perhaps Richard might open up to her.

"Oh, there isn't one thing in particular, Holly. Children are a worry in general." He pushed the rim of his glasses up his nose and looked her in the eye. "But I suppose you're glad you will never have to worry about all this children nonsense," he said, laughing.

There was a silence.

Holly felt like she had been kicked in the stomach.

"So have you found a job yet?" he continued on.

Holly sat frozen on her chair in shock; she couldn't believe he had the audacity to say that to her. She was insulted and hurt and she wanted him out of her house. She really wasn't in the mood to be polite to him anymore and she certainly couldn't be bothered explaining to his narrow little mind that she hadn't even begun looking for a job yet as she was still grieving the death of her husband. "Nonsense" that he wouldn't have to experience for another fifty years.

"No," she spat out.

"So what are you doing for money? Have you signed on the dole?"

"No, Richard," she said, trying not to lose her temper, "I haven't signed on the dole, I get *widow's* allowance."

"Ah, that's a great, handy thing, isn't it?"

"Handy is not quite the word I would use, devastatingly depressing is more like it."

The atmosphere was tense. Suddenly he slapped his leg with his hand, signaling the end of the conversation. "I better motor on so and get back to work," he announced, standing up and exaggerating a stretch as though he had been sitting down for hours.

"OK then." Holly was relieved. "You better leave while your

car is still there." Once again her humor was lost on him; he was peering out the window to check.

"You're right; it's still there, thank God. Anyway, nice to see you and thank you for the tea," he said to a spot on the wall above her head.

"You're welcome and thank you for the orchid," Holly said through gritted teeth. He marched down the garden path and stopped midway to look at the garden. He nodded his head disapprovingly and shouted to her, "You really must get someone to sort this mess out," and drove off in his brown family car.

Holly fumed as she watched him drive off and banged the door shut. That man made her blood boil so much she felt like knocking him out. He just hadn't a clue . . . about anything.

Eleven

"OH SHARON, I JUST *HATE* him," Holly moaned to her friend on the phone later that night.

"Just ignore him, Holly, he can't help himself, he's an idiot," she replied angrily.

"But that's what annoys me even more. Everyone says he can't help himself or it's not his fault. He's a grown man, Sharon. He's thirty-six years old. He should bloody well know when to keep his mouth shut. He says those things deliberately," she fumed.

"I really don't think he does it deliberately, Holly," she said soothingly. "I genuinely think he called around to wish you a happy birthday . . ."

"Yeah! And what's that about?" Holly ranted. "Since *when* has he ever called around to my house to give me a birthday present? *Never!* That's when!"

"Well, thirty is more of a big deal than any other . . ."

"Not in his eyes it's not! He even said so at dinner a few weeks ago. If I recall, his exact words were," she mimicked his voice, "I don't agree with silly celebrations blah-blah-blah, I'm a sap blah-blah-blah. He really is a Dick."

Sharon laughed at her friend sounding like a ten-year-old. "OK, so he's an evil monster of a being who deserves to burn in hell!"

Holly paused. "Well, I wouldn't go that far, Sharon . . ."

Sharon laughed. "Oh, I just can't please you at all, can I?"

Holly smiled weakly. Gerry would know exactly how she was feeling, he would know exactly what to say and he would know exactly what to do. He would give her one of his famous hugs and all her problems would melt away. She grabbed a pillow from her bed and hugged it tight. She couldn't remember the last time she hugged someone, *really* hugged someone. And the depressing thing was that she couldn't imagine ever embracing anyone the same way again.

"Helloooo? Earth to Holly? You still there or am I talking to myself again?"

"Oh sorry, Sharon, what did you say?"

"I said, have you given any more thought to this karaoke business?"

"Sharon!" Holly yelped. "No more thought is required on that subject!"

"OK, calm down, woman! I was just thinking that we could hire out a karaoke machine and we could set it up in your living room. That way, you'll be doing what he wants minus the embarrassment! What do you think?"

"No, Sharon, it's a great idea but it won't work; he wants me to do it in Club Diva, wherever that is."

"Ah! So sweet! Because you're his Disco Diva?"

"I think that was the general idea," Holly said miserably.

"Ah! That's a lovely idea, although Club Diva? Never heard of it."

"Well, that's that settled then, if no one knows where it is, then I just can't do it, can I?" Holly said, satisfied she had found a way out.

They both said their good-byes and as soon as Holly had hung up, the phone rang again.

"Hi, sweetheart."

"Mum!" Holly said accusingly.

"Oh God, what have I done now?"

"I received a little visit from your evil son today and I'm not very happy."

"Oh, I'm sorry, dear, I tried to call you earlier to tell you he was on his way over but I kept getting that bloody answering machine, do you ever turn your phone on?"

"That is not the point, Mum."

"I know, I'm sorry. Why, what did he do?"

"He opened his mouth. There lies the problem in itself."

"Oh no, and he was so excited about giving you that present."

"Well, I'm not denying that the present was very nice and thoughtful and all of those wonderful things, but he said some of the most insulting things without batting an eyelid!"

"Do you want me to talk to him for you?"

"No, it's OK; we're big boys and girls now. But thanks anyway. So what are you up to?" Holly was anxious to change the subject.

"Ciara and I are watching a Denzel Washington film. Ciara thinks she's going to marry him someday," Elizabeth laughed.

"I am, too!" Ciara shouted in the background.

"Well, sorry to burst her little bubble, but he's already married."

"He's married, honey." Elizabeth passed on the message.

"Hollywood marriages . . . ," Ciara mumbled in the background.

"Are the two of you on your own?" Holly asked.

"Frank is down the pub and Declan is in college."

"College? But it's ten o'clock at night!" Holly laughed. Declan was probably out somewhere doing something illegal and using college as an excuse. She didn't think her mum would be so gullible to believe that, especially after having four other children.

"Oh, he's a very hard worker when he puts his mind to it, Holly, he's working on some project. I don't know what it is; I don't listen half the time."

"Mmm," Holly replied, not believing a word of it.

"Anyway, my future son-in-law is back on television so I must be off," Elizabeth laughed. "Would you like to come around and join us?"

"Thanks but no, I'm OK here."

"All right, love, but if you change your mind you know where we are. Bye, dear."

Back to her empty, silent house.

Holly woke up the next morning still fully dressed and lying on her bed. She could feel herself slipping into her old habits again. All her positive thoughts of the past few weeks were melting away bit by bit every day. It was so bloody tiring trying to be happy all the time and she just didn't have the energy anymore. Who cared if the house was a mess? Nobody but her was going to see it, and she certainly didn't care one way or the other. Who cared if she didn't wear makeup or wash for a week? She certainly had no intention of impressing anyone. The only guy she was seeing regularly was the pizza delivery boy, and she had to tip him to make him smile. *Who bloody cared?* Her phone vibrated beside her, signaling a message. It was from Sharon.

CLUB DIVA NO 36700700
THINK BOUT IT. WUD B FUN.
DO IT 4 GERRY?

Gerry's bloody dead, she felt like texting back. But ever since she had begun opening the envelopes he didn't feel dead to her. It was as though he were just away on holiday and writing her letters, so he wasn't *really* gone. Well, the very least she could do was ring the club and suss out the situation. That didn't mean she had to go through with it.

She dialed the number and a man answered. She couldn't think of anything to say so she quickly hung up again. Oh, come on, Holly, she told herself, it's really not that difficult, just say a friend is interested in singing.

Holly braced herself and pressed redial.

The same voice answered, "Club Diva."

"Hi, I was wondering if you do karaoke nights there?"

"Yes we do, they are on a . . . ," she heard him leafing through some pages, "yeah sorry, they're on a Thursday."

"Thursday?"

"No sorry, sorry, hold on . . ." He leafed through some pages again. "No, they're on a Tuesday night."

"Are you sure?"

"Yes, they are definitely on a Tuesday."

"OK, em, well, I was wondering if, em . . ." Holly took a deep breath and began the sentence again. "My friend might be interested in singing and she was wondering what she would have to do?"

There was a long pause on the other end.

"Hello?" Was this person stupid?

"Yeah sorry, I don't actually organize the karaoke nights, so . . ."

"OK." Holly was losing her temper. It had taken a lot to summon up the courage to actually make the call and some underqualified unhelpful little twit wasn't going to ruin it for her. "Well, is there anyone there who might have a clue?"

"Eh, no, there isn't, the club isn't actually open yet, it's very early in the morning still," came the sarcastic response.

"Well, thank you very much, you've been a terrific help," she said, matching his sarcasm.

"Excuse me, if you can just bear with me for a moment, I'll try and find out for you." Holly was put on hold and was forced to listen to "Greensleeves" for the next five minutes.

"Hello? Are you still there?"

"Barely," she said angrily.

"OK, I'm very sorry about the delay but I just made a phone call there. What's your friend's name?"

Holly froze, she hadn't planned on this. Well, maybe she could just give her name and then get "her friend" to call back and cancel if she changed her mind.

"Em, her name is Holly Kennedy."

"OK, well, it's actually a karaoke competition on Tuesday nights. It goes on for a month and every week two people out of ten are chosen till the last week of the month, where the six people sing again in the final."

Holly gulped. She didn't want to do this.

"But unfortunately," he continued, "the names have all been entered a few months in advance, so you can tell your friend Holly that maybe she could try again at Christmas. That's when the next competition is on."

"Oh, OK."

"By the way, the name Holly Kennedy rings a bell. Would that be Declan Kennedy's sister?"

"Eh, yeah, why, do you know her?" said a shocked Holly.

"I wouldn't say I know her, I just met her briefly here the other night with her brother."

Was Declan going around and introducing girls as his sister? The sick and twisted little . . . No, that couldn't be right, what on earth?

"Declan played a gig in Club Diva?"

"No no," he laughed, "he played with his band downstairs in the basement."

Holly quickly tried to digest the information until finally it clicked.

"Is Club Diva in Hogan's?"

He laughed again, "Yeah, it's on the top floor. Maybe I should advertise a bit more!"

"Is that Daniel?" Holly blurted out and then kicked herself for being so stupid.

"Eh, yeah, do I know you?"

"Em, no! No you don't! Holly just mentioned you in conversation, that's all." Then she realized how that sounded. "Very briefly in conversation," she added. "She said you gave her a stool." Holly began hitting her head softly on the wall.

Daniel laughed again. "Oh, OK, well, tell her if she wants to sing in the karaoke at Christmas I can put her name down now for her. You wouldn't believe the amount of people that want to sign up."

"Really," Holly said weakly. She felt like a fool.

"Oh, by the way, who am I speaking to?"

Holly paced her bedroom floor. "Em, Sharon, you're speaking to Sharon."

"OK, Sharon, well, I have your number on caller ID so I'll call you if anyone backs out."

"OK, thanks a lot."

And he hung up.

And Holly leapt into bed, throwing the duvet over her head as she felt her face going purple with embarrassment. She hid under the covers, cursing herself for being such a bimbo. Ignoring the phone ringing, she tried to convince herself she hadn't been a complete idiot. Eventually, after she had persuaded herself she could show her face in public again (it took a long time), she crawled out of bed and hit the button on her answering machine.

"Hi Sharon, I must have just missed you. It's Daniel here from Club Diva." He paused and then, laughing, added, "In Hogan's. Em, I was just looking through the list of names in the book and it seems somebody already entered Holly's name a few months back, in fact it's one of the first entries. Unless it's another Holly Kennedy . . ." He trailed off. "Anyway, call me back when you get a chance so we can sort it out. Thanks."

Holly sat shocked on the edge of her bed, unable to move for the next few hours.

Twelve

SHARON, DENISE AND HOLLY SAT by the window in Bewley's Café overlooking Grafton Street. They often met up there to watch the world go by; Sharon always said it was the best window-shopping she could ever do as she had a bird's-eye view of all her favorite stores.

"I can't believe Gerry organized all this!" gasped Denise when she heard the news. She flicked her long brown hair behind her shoulders and her bright blue eyes sparkled back at Holly enthusiastically.

"It'll be a bit of fun, won't it?" Sharon said excitedly.

"Oh God." Holly had butterflies in her stomach just over the thought of it. "I still really, really, *really* don't want to do it, but I feel I have to finish off what Gerry started."

"That's the spirit Hol!" said Denise, "and we'll all be there to cheer you on!"

"Now hold on a minute, Denise," Holly said, changing the celebratory tone. "I just want you and Sharon there, no one else. I don't want to make a big deal out of this at all. Let's keep it between us."

"But Holly!" Sharon protested. "It is a big deal! No one ever thought you'd do karaoke again after last time . . ."

"Sharon!" warned Holly. "One must not speak of such things. One is still scarred from that experience."

"Well, I think one is a daft cow for not getting over it," mumbled Sharon.

"So when's the big night?" Denise changed the subject, sensing bad vibes.

"Next Tuesday," Holly groaned, bending forward and banging her head playfully on the table. The surrounding customers stared at her curiously.

"She's just out for the day," Sharon announced to the room, pointing at Holly.

"Don't worry, Holly; that gives you seven days exactly to transform yourself into Mariah Carey. No problem at all," Denise said, smiling at Sharon.

"Oh please, we would have a better chance teaching Lennox Lewis how to do ballet," said Sharon.

Holly looked up from banging her head. "Well, thanks for the encouragement, Sharon."

"Ooh, but imagine Lennox Lewis in a pair of tights, that tight little arse dancing around . . . ," Denise said dreamily.

Holly and Sharon stopped growling at each other to stare at their friend.

"You've lost the plot, Denise."

"What?" Denise said, defensively snapping out of her fantasy. "Just imagine those big muscular thighs . . ."

"That would snap your neck in two if you went near him," Sharon finished for her.

"Now *there's* a thought," Denise said, widening her eyes.

"I can see it all now," Holly joined in, staring off into space. "The death pages would read: 'Denise Hennessey has tragically died, crushed to death by the most tremendous thunder thighs after briefly catching a glimpse of heaven . . . '"

"I like that," Denise agreed. "Ooh, and what a way to die! Give me a slice of that heaven!"

"OK, you," Sharon interrupted, pointing her finger at Denise, "keep your sordid little fantasies to yourself, please. And you," she pointed at Holly, "stop trying to change the subject."

"Oh, you're just jealous, Sharon, because your husband couldn't snap a matchstick between his skinny little thighs," teased Denise.

"Excuse me, but John's thighs are perfectly fine, I just wish mine could be more like his," Sharon finished.

"Now you!" Denise pointed at Sharon. "Keep your sordid little fantasies to yourself."

"Girls, girls!" Holly snapped her fingers in the air. "Let's focus on me now, focus on me." She gracefully motioned with her hands, bringing them toward her chest.

"OK, Ms. Selfish, what are you planning on singing?"

"I have no idea, that's why I called this emergency meeting."

"No it's not, you told me you wanted to go shopping," Sharon said.

"Oh really?" Denise said, looking at Sharon and raising an eyebrow. "I thought you were both coming to visit me on my lunch break."

"You are both correct," Holly asserted. "I am shopping for ideas and I need you both."

"Ha-ha! Good answer," they both agreed for once.

"OK, OK!" Sharon exclaimed excitedly. "I think I've got an idea. What was that song we sang for the whole two weeks in Spain and we couldn't get it out of our heads and it used to bug the hell out of us?"

Holly shrugged her shoulders. If it bugged the hell out of them it was hardly a very good choice.

"I don't know, I wasn't invited on that holiday," muttered Denise.

"Oh, you know the one, Holly!"

"I can't remember."

"Oh, you have to!"

"Sharon, I don't think she can remember," Denise frustratedly said to Sharon.

"Oh, what is it?" Sharon put her face in her hands, irritated. Holly shrugged her shoulders at Denise again. "OK, I've got it!!" she announced happily, and began to sing loudly in the café. " 'Sun, sea, sex, sand, come on boy give me your hand!' "

Holly's eyes widened and her cheeks flushed with embarrassment as people at the surrounding tables turned to stare. She turned to Denise for support in silencing Sharon.

" 'Ooh ooh ooh *so sexy, so sexy!*' " Denise joined in with Sharon. Some people stared in amusement but most in loathing while Denise and Sharon warbled their way through the tacky European dance song that had been a hit a few summers previously. Just as they were about to sing the chorus for the fourth time (neither of them could remember the verses), Holly silenced them.

"Girls, I can't sing that song! Besides, the verses are rapped by a guy!"

"Well, at least you wouldn't have to sing too much," chuckled Denise.

"No way! I am not rapping at a karaoke competition!"

"Fair enough," nodded Sharon.

"OK, well, what CD are you listening to at the moment?" Denise got serious again.

"Westlife?" she looked at them hopefully.

"Then sing a Westlife song," Sharon encouraged. "That way, at least you'll know all the words."

Sharon and Denise began to laugh uncontrollably. "You might not get the tune right," Sharon forced out between hacking laughs.

"But at least you'll know the words!" Denise managed to finish for her before the two of them doubled over at the table.

First Holly was angry, but looking at the both of them crouched over, holding their stomachs in hysterics, she had to giggle. They were right, Holly was completely tone-deaf and hadn't a note in her head. Finding a song she could actually sing was going to prove impossible. Finally after the girls settled down again, Denise looked at her watch and moaned about having to get back to work. They left Bewley's (much to the other customers' delight). "The miserable sods will probably throw a party now," Sharon had mumbled, passing their tables.

The three girls linked arms and walked down Grafton Street, heading toward the clothes store where Denise was manager. The day was sunny with just a light chill in the air; Grafton Street was busy as usual with people running around on their lunch breaks while shoppers slowly meandered up the street, taking full advantage of the lack of rain. At every stretch of the road there was a busker fighting for attention from the crowds, and Denise and Sharon embarrassingly did a quick Irish dance as they passed a man playing the fiddle. He winked at them and they threw some money into his tweed cap on the ground.

"Right, you ladies of leisure, I better head back to work," Denise said, pushing the door to her shop open. As soon as her staff saw her they scarpered from gossiping at the counter and immediately began to fix the clothes rails. Holly and Sharon tried not to laugh. They said their good-byes and both headed up to Stephen's Green to collect their cars.

"'Sun, sea, sex, sand,'" Holly quietly sang to herself. "Oh shit, Sharon! You've got that stupid song in my head now," she complained.

"You see, there you go with that 'shit Sharon' thing again. So negative, Holly." Sharon began humming the song.

"Oh, shut up!" Holly laughed, hitting her on the arm.

Thirteen

I T WAS FOUR O'CLOCK BY the time Holly eventually got out of
town and started heading home to Swords. Evil Sharon convinced Holly to go shopping after all, which resulted in her splashing out on a ridiculous top she was far too old to wear. She really
needed to watch her spending from now on; her funds were running low, and without regular income she could sense tense times
ahead. She needed to start thinking about getting a job, but she
was finding it hard enough to get out of bed in the morning as it
was, another depressing nine-to-five job wasn't going to help matters. But it would help pay the bills. Holly sighed loudly, all these
things she had to handle all by herself. The thought of it was just
depressing her, and her problem was that she spent too much time
on her own thinking about it. She needed people around her, like
today with Denise and Sharon, as they always succeeded in taking

her mind off things. She phoned her mum and checked if it was all right for her to call around.

"Of course you can, love, you're always welcome here." Then she lowered her voice to a whisper, "Just as long as you know that Richard is here." Christ! What was with all the little visits all of a sudden?

Holly had contemplated heading straight home when she heard that but convinced herself she was being silly. He was her brother, and as annoying as he was, she couldn't go on avoiding him forever.

She arrived to an extremely loud and crowded house and it felt like old times again, hearing screams and shouts in every room. Her mum was setting an extra place at the table just as she walked in. "Oh, Mum, you should have told me you were having dinner," Holly said, giving her a hug and a kiss.

"Why, have you eaten already?"

"No, actually I'm starving, but I hope you didn't go to too much trouble."

"No trouble at all, dear, it just means that poor Declan will have to go without food for the day, that's all," she said, teasing her son who was taking his seat. He made a face at her.

The atmosphere was so much more relaxed this time around, or maybe it had just been Holly who was uptight during the last family dinner.

"So, Mr. Hard Worker, why aren't you in college today?" she said sarcastically.

"I've been in college all morning," he replied, making a face, "and I'm going back in at eight o'clock, actually."

"That's very late," said her father, pouring gravy all over his plate. He always ended up with more gravy than food on his plate.

"Yeah, but it was the only time I could get to book the editing suite."

"Is there only one editing suite, Declan?" piped up Richard.

"Yeah." Ever the conversationalist.

"And how many students are there?"

"It's only a small class, there are just twelve of us."

"Don't they have the funds for any more?"

"For what, students?" Declan teased.

"No, for another editing suite."

"No, it's only a small college, Richard."

"I suppose the bigger universities would be better equipped for things like that, they're better all-round."

And there was the dig they were all waiting for.

"No, I wouldn't say that, the facilities are top of the range, there's just fewer people so therefore less equipment. And the lecturers aren't inferior to university lecturers, they're a bonus because they work in the industry as well as lecturing. In other words, they practice what they preach. It's not just textbook stuff."

Good for you, Declan, Holly thought, and winked across the table at him.

"I wouldn't imagine they get paid well doing that, so they probably have no choice but to lecture as well."

"Richard, working in film is a very good job; you're talking about people who have spent years in college studying for degrees and master's . . ."

"Oh, you get a degree for that, do you?" Richard was amazed. "I thought it was just a little course you were doing."

Declan stopped eating and looked at Holly in shock. Funny how Richard's ignorance still amazed everyone.

"Who do you think makes all those gardening programs you

watch, Richard?" Holly interjected. "They're not just a crowd of people who are doing a little course."

The thought had clearly never crossed his mind that there was a skill involved.

"Great little programs they are," he agreed.

"What's your project on, Declan?" Frank asked.

Declan finished chewing his food before he spoke. "Oh, it's kind of too messy to go into, but basically it's on club life in Dublin."

"Ooh, will we be in it?" Ciara broke her unusual silence and asked excitedly.

"Yeah, I might just show the back of your head or something," he joked.

"Well, I can't wait to see it," Holly said encouragingly.

"Thanks." Declan put his knife and fork down and started laughing. "Hey, what's this I hear about you singing in a karaoke competition next week?"

"What?" Ciara yelled, her eyes nearly popping out of her head.

Holly pretended not to know what he was talking about.

"Ah come on, Holly!" he persisted. "Danny told me!" He turned to the rest of the table and explained, "Danny is the owner of the place where I did the gig the other night and he told me Holly has entered a karaoke competition in the club upstairs."

Everyone oohed and aahed and talked about how great it was. Holly refused to give in. "Declan, Daniel's just playing games with you. Sure everyone knows I can't sing! Now come on," she addressed the rest of the table. "Honestly, if I was singing in a karaoke competition I *think* I would tell you all." She laughed as if the thought were so ridiculous. In fact, the thought *was* so ridiculous.

"Holly!" he laughed. "I saw your name on the list! Don't lie!"

Holly put her knife and fork down, she suddenly wasn't hungry anymore.

"Holly, why didn't you tell us you're going to sing in a competition?" her mother asked.

"Because I can't sing!"

"Then why are you doing it?" Ciara burst out laughing.

She might as well tell them, she figured; otherwise Declan would beat it out of her and she didn't like lying to her parents. It's just a shame Richard would have to hear it too.

"OK, it's a really complicated story, but basically Gerry entered my name in months ago because he really wanted me to do it, and as much as I *don't* want to do it, I feel I have to go through with it. It's stupid, I know."

Ciara stopped laughing abruptly.

Holly felt paranoid with her family staring at her, and she nervously tucked her hair behind her ears.

"Well, I think that's a wonderful idea," her dad suddenly announced.

"Yes," added her mum, "and we'll all be there to support you."

"No, Mum, you really don't have to, it's no big deal."

"There's no way my sister is singing in a competition without me being there," declared Ciara.

"Here, here," said Richard. "We'll all go so. I've never been to a karaoke before, it should be . . . ," he searched his brain for the right word, ". . . fun."

Holly groaned and closed her eyes, wishing she had gone straight home from town. Declan was laughing hysterically. "Yes, Holly, it'll be . . . hmmm . . . ," he said, scratching his chin, ". . . fun!"

"When is it on?" Richard said, taking out his diary.

"Eh . . . Saturday," Holly lied, and Richard began writing it down.

"It is not!" Declan burst out. "It's next Tuesday, you liar!"

"Shit!" cursed Richard, much to everyone's surprise. "Has anyone got any Tipp-Ex?"

Holly could not stop going to the toilet. She was nervous and had gotten practically no sleep the night before. And she looked just the way she felt. There were huge bags under her bloodshot eyes, and her lips were bitten.

The big day had arrived, her worst nightmare, singing in public.

Holly wasn't the kind of person who even sang in the shower, for fear of cracking all the mirrors. But man, was she spending time in the toilet today. There was no better laxative than fear, and Holly felt like she had lost a stone in just one day. Her friends and family had been as supportive as ever, sending her good luck cards. Sharon and John had even sent her a bouquet of flowers, which she placed on the draft-free, heat-vent-free coffee table beside her half-dead orchid. Denise had "hilariously" sent her a sympathy card.

Holly dressed in the outfit Gerry had told her to buy in April and cursed him all throughout. There were far more important things to worry about right now than irrelevant little details like how she looked. She left her hair down so it could cover her face as much as possible and piled on the waterproof mascara as though it could prevent her from crying. She could foresee the night ending in tears. She tended to have psychic powers when it came to facing the shittiest days of her life.

John and Sharon collected Holly in the taxi and she refused to talk to them, cursing everyone for forcing her to do this. She felt physically sick and couldn't sit still. Every time the taxi stopped at a red light she contemplated jumping out and running for dear life, but by the time she built up the courage the lights would go green again. Her hands fidgeted nervously and she kept opening and closing her bag, pretending to Sharon she was searching for something just to keep herself occupied.

"Relax, Holly," Sharon said soothingly, "everything will be fine."

"Fuck off," she snapped.

They continued on in silence for the rest of the journey, even the taxi driver didn't speak. They finally reached Hogan's, and John and Sharon had a hell of a time trying to stop her ranting (something about preferring to jump in the River Liffey) and persuading her to go inside. Much to Holly's horror, the club was absolutely jammed, and she had to squeeze by everyone to make her way to her family, who had saved a table (right beside the toilet as requested).

Richard was sitting awkwardly on a stool looking out of place in a suit. "So tell me about these rules, Father, what will Holly have to do?" Holly's dad explained the "rules" of karaoke to Richard and her nerves began to build even more.

"Gosh, that's terrific, isn't it?" Richard said, staring around the club in awe. Holly didn't think he had ever been in a nightclub before.

The sight of the stage terrified Holly; it was much bigger than she had expected and there was a huge screen on the wall for the crowd to see the words of the songs. Jack was sitting with his arm draped around Abbey's shoulders; they both gave her a supportive smile. Holly scowled at them and looked away.

"Holly, the funniest thing just happened earlier on," Jack said, laughing. "Remember that guy Daniel we met last week?"

Holly just stared at him, watching his lips moving but not giving a damn about what he said. "Well, me and Abbey got here first to keep the table and we were having a kiss and your man came over and whispered in my ear that you were gonna be here tonight. He thought we were going out and that I was doing the dirt!" Jack and Abbey laughed hysterically.

"Well, I think that's disgusting," Holly said and turned away.

"No," Jack tried to explain, "he didn't know that we were brother and sister. I had to explain . . ." Jack trailed off as Sharon shot him a warning look and silenced him.

"Hi, Holly," Daniel said, approaching her with a clipboard in his hand, "OK, the order of tonight is the following: First up is a girl called Margaret, then a guy called Keith and then you're up after him. Is that OK?"

"So I'm third."

"Yeah, after . . ."

"That's all I need to know," Holly snapped rudely. She just wanted to get out of this stupid club and wished that everyone would just stop annoying her and leave her alone to wish evil thoughts on them all. She wished the ground would open and swallow her up, that a natural disaster would occur and everyone would have to evacuate the building. In fact, that was a good idea; she searched around frantically for a button to raise the fire alarm, but Daniel was still talking away to her.

"Look, Holly, I'm really sorry to disturb you again, but could you tell me which of your friends is Sharon?" He looked like he was afraid she was going to bite her head off. So he should be, she thought, squinting her eyes.

"Her over there." Holly pointed to Sharon. "Hold on, why?"

"Oh, I just wanted to apologize for the last time we spoke." He started to walk toward Sharon.

"Why?" Holly said with panic in her voice, making him turn around again.

"Oh, we just had a minor disagreement on the phone last week." He looked at her confused as to why he had to explain himself to her.

"You know, you really don't need to do that, she's probably forgotten about it completely by now," she stammered. This was the last thing she needed.

"Yeah, but I would still like to apologize," and he headed over to her. Holly leapt from her stool.

"Sharon, hi, I'm Daniel, I just wanted to apologize about the confusion on the phone last week."

Sharon looked at him as though he had ten heads. "Confusion?"

"You know, on the phone?"

John placed his arm protectively around her waist.

"On the phone?"

"Eh . . . yes, on the phone." He nodded.

"What's your name again?"

"Em, it's Daniel."

"And we spoke on the phone?" Sharon said with a smile appearing on her face.

Holly gestured wildly to her behind Daniel's back. Daniel cleared his throat nervously. "Yes, you called the club last week and I answered, does that ring a bell?"

"No, sweetie, you've got the wrong girl," Sharon said politely.

John threw Sharon a dirty look for calling him sweetie; if it had been up to him he would have told Daniel where to go. Daniel brushed his hand through his hair and appeared to be more confused than anyone else and began to turn around to face Holly.

Holly nodded her head frantically to Sharon.

"Oh . . . ," Sharon said, looking like she finally remembered. "Oh Daniel!" she yelled, a bit overenthusiastically. "God, I am so sorry, my brain cells seem to be going a bit dead." She laughed like a madwoman. "Must be too much of this," she laughed, picking up her drink.

Relief washed over Daniel's face. "Good, I thought it was me going mad there for a minute! OK, so you remember us having that conversation on the phone?"

"Oh, *that* conversation we had on the phone. Listen, don't worry about it," she said, waving her hand dismissively.

"It's just that I only took over the place a few weeks ago and I wasn't too sure of the exact arrangements for tonight."

"Oh, don't worry . . . we all need our time . . . to adjust . . . to things . . . you know?" Sharon looked at Holly to see if she had said the right thing or not.

"OK then, well, it's nice to finally meet you in person," Daniel laughed. "Can I get you a stool or anything?" he said, trying to be funny.

Sharon and John sat on their stools and stared back at him in silence, not knowing what to say to this strange man.

John watched with suspicion as Daniel walked away.

"What was that all about?" Sharon asked Holly as soon as he was out of earshot.

"Oh, I'll explain it to you later," said Holly as she turned to face the stage. Their karaoke host for the evening was just stepping up onstage.

"Good evening, ladies and gentlemen!" he announced.

"Good evening!" shouted Richard, looking excited. Holly rolled her eyes up to heaven.

"We have an exciting night ahead of us . . ." He went on and on and on in his DJ voice while Holly danced nervously from foot to foot. She desperately needed the toilet again.

"So first up tonight we have Margaret from Tallaght, who is going to sing the theme to *Titanic*, 'My Heart Will Go On,' by Celine Dion. Please put your hands together for the wonderful Margaret!" The crowd went wild. Holly's heart raced. The hardest song in the world to sing, typical.

When Margaret began to sing, the room became so quiet you could almost hear a pin drop. Holly looked around the room and watched everyone's faces. They were all staring at Margaret in amazement, including Holly's family, the traitors. Margaret's eyes were closed and she sang with such passion it seemed she had lived every line of the song. Holly hated her and contemplated tripping her up on her way back to her seat.

"Wasn't that incredible?" the DJ announced. The crowd cheered again, and Holly prepared herself not to hear that sound after her own song. "Next up we have Keith, you may remember him as last year's winner, and he's singing 'America,' by Neil Diamond. Give it up for Keith!" Holly didn't need to hear any more and rushed into the toilet.

She paced up and down the toilet and tried to calm herself, her knees were knocking, her stomach was twisted in knots and she felt the beginnings of vomit rising to her mouth. She looked at herself in the mirror and tried to take big deep breaths. It didn't work, as it only made her feel dizzy. The crowd applauded outside and Holly froze. She was next.

"Wasn't Keith terrific, ladies and gentlemen?"

Lots of cheers again.

"Perhaps Keith is going for the record of winning two years in a row, well, it doesn't get any better than that!"

It was about to get a lot worse.

"Next we have a newcomer to the competition. Her name is Holly and she's singing . . ."

Holly ran to the cubicle and locked herself in. There was no way in this world they were getting her out of there.

"So ladies and gentlemen, please put your hands together for Holly!"

There was a huge applause.

Fourteen

I T WAS THREE YEARS AGO when Holly had taken to the stage
for her debut karaoke performance. Coincidentally it had been
three years *since* Holly had taken to the stage to do karaoke.

A huge crowd of her friends had gone to their local pub in
Swords to celebrate the thirtieth birthday of one of the lads. Holly
had been extremely tired, as she had been working overtime for
the previous two weeks. She really wasn't in the mood to go out
partying. All she wanted was to go home, have a nice long bath,
put on the most unsexy pair of pajamas she owned, eats lots of
chocolate and snuggle up on the couch in front of the TV with
Gerry.

After standing on an overcrowded DART all the way from
Blackrock to Sutton Station, Holly was definitely not in the
mood to go through the whole ordeal again in an overcrowded,

stuffy pub. On the train, half her face had been squashed up against the window and the other half lodged underneath the sweaty armpit of a very unhygienic man. Right behind her a man was breathing alcoholic fumes rather loudly down her neck. It didn't help matters that every time the train swayed he "accidentally" pressed his big beer belly up against her back. She had suffered through this indignity every day going to work and coming home for two weeks and she could take it no longer. She wanted her pajamas.

Finally she arrived at Sutton Station and the very clever people there thought it was a great idea to all get *on* the train while people tried to get off. It took her so long to fight her way through the crowd to get *off* the train that by the time she reached the platform she saw her feeder bus drive off, packed with happy little people smiling out the window at her. And because it was after six o'clock, the coffee shop had closed and she was left standing in the freezing cold waiting for another half an hour till the next bus arrived. This experience only strengthened her desire to cuddle up in front of the TV.

But a good evening at home was not to be. Her beloved husband had other plans. She arrived home tired and extremely pissed off to a crowded house and thumping music. People she didn't even know were wandering around her living room with cans of beer in their hands and slumping themselves on the couch she had intended to live on for the next few hours. Gerry stood at the CD player acting DJ and trying to look cool. At that moment in time she had never seen him look so uncool in her life.

"What is wrong with you?" Gerry asked her after seeing her storming upstairs to the bedroom.

"Gerry, I am tired, I am pissed off, I am not in the mood to go out tonight, and you didn't even ask me if it was all right to invite all these people over. And by the way, *who are they?*" she yelled.

"They're friends of Conor's and by the way, *this is my house too!*" he yelled back.

Holly placed her fingers on her temples and began to gently massage her head; she had an incredible headache and the music was driving her crazy.

"Gerry," she said quietly, trying to stay calm, "I'm not saying that you can't invite people over. It would be fine if you had planned it in advance and told me. *Then* I wouldn't care, but today of all days when I am so so tired," her voice became weaker and weaker with every word, "I just wanted to relax in my own house."

"Oh, every day's the same with you," he snapped. "You never want to do anything anymore anyway. Every night you're the same. You come home in your cranky moods and bitch at me about everything!"

Holly's jaw dropped.

"Excuse me! I have been working hard!"

"And so have I, but you don't see me biting your head off every time I don't get my own way."

"Gerry, this isn't about me getting my own way, this is about you inviting the whole street into our h—"

"It's Friday," he yelled, silencing her. *"It's the weekend!* When is the last time you went out? Leave your work behind and let your hair down for a change. Stop acting like such a *granny!*" And he stormed out of the bedroom and slammed the door.

After spending a long time in the bedroom hating Gerry and dreaming of a divorce, she managed to calm down and think rationally about what he had said. And he was right. OK, he wasn't right in the way he had phrased it, but she *had* been cranky and bitchy all month and she knew it.

Holly was the type of person who finished work at 5 p.m. and had her computer switched off, lights off, desk tidied and was running for her train by 5:01 p.m. whether her employers liked it or not. She never took her work home and never stressed about the future of the business because, quite frankly, she didn't care, and she phoned in sick as many Monday mornings as possible without running the risk of being fired. But due to a momentary lapse of concentration when looking for new employment, she had found herself accepting an office job that forced her to take paperwork home, to agree to work late and to worry about the business, which she was not happy with *at all*. How she even managed to stay there for an entire month was anybody's guess, but nevertheless, Gerry had been right. Ouch, it even hurt to think it. She hadn't gone out with him or her friends for weeks and she fell asleep the minute her head hit the pillow every night. Come to think of it, that was probably Gerry's main problem, never mind the bitchiness.

But tonight would be different. She intended to show her neglected friends and husband that she was still the irresponsible, fun and frivolous Holly who could drink them all under the table and yet manage to walk the white line all the way home. This show of antics began by preparing home cocktails, God only knows what was in them, but they worked their little magic and at eleven o'clock they all danced down the road to the pub where a karaoke was taking place. Holly demanded to be first up and heckled the karaoke host until she got her way. The pub was jammed and that night there was a rowdy crowd who were out on a stag night. It was as though a film crew had arrived in the pub hours earlier and worked away setting the scene for disaster. They couldn't have done a better job.

The DJ gave Holly a huge buildup after believing her lies of being a professional singer. Gerry lost all power of speech and sight from laughing so hard but she was determined to show him that she could still let her hair down. He needn't plan that divorce yet. Holly decided to sing "Like a Virgin" and dedicated it to the man who was getting married the next day. As soon as she started singing, Holly had never heard so many boos in her whole life and at such a loud volume. But she was so drunk she didn't care and continued on singing to her husband, who seemed to be the only one without a moody face.

Eventually when people began to throw things at the stage and when the karaoke host himself encouraged them to boo even louder, Holly felt that her work there had been done. When she handed him back the microphone there was a cheer so loud that people from the pub next door came running in. It was all the more people to see Holly trip down the steps in her stilettos and fall flat on her face. They all watched as her skirt went flying over her head to reveal the old underwear that had once been white was now gray, and that she hadn't bothered to change when she got home from work.

Holly was taken to hospital to see to her broken nose.

Gerry lost his voice from laughing so loudly and Denise and Sharon helped matters by taking photographs of the scene of the crime, which Denise then chose as the cover for the invitations to her Christmas party, with the heading "Let's get pissed!"

Holly vowed *never* to do karaoke again.

Fifteen

"HOLLY KENNEDY? ARE YOU HERE?" the karaoke host's voice boomed. The crowd's applause died down into a loud chatter as everyone looked around in search of Holly. Well, they would be a long time looking, she thought as she lowered the toilet seat and sat down to wait for the excitement to settle so they could move on to their next victim. She closed her eyes, rested her head on her hands and prayed for this moment to pass. She wanted to open her eyes and be safely at home a week from now. She counted to ten, praying for a miracle, and then slowly opened her eyes again.

She was still in the toilet.

Why couldn't she, at least just this once, suddenly find magical powers? It always happened to the American girls in the films and it just wasn't fair . . .

Holly had known this would happen; from the moment she opened that envelope and read Gerry's third letter, she foresaw tears and humiliation. Her nightmare had come true.

Outside, the club sounded very quiet and a sense of calm engulfed her as she realized they were moving on to the next singer. Her shoulders relaxed and she unclenched her fists, her jaw relaxed and air flowed more easily into her lungs. The panic was over, but she decided to wait until the next singer began his song before she made a run for it. She couldn't even climb out the window because she wasn't on the ground floor, well, not unless she wanted to plummet to her own death. Another thing her American friend would be able to do.

Outside the cubicle Holly heard the toilet door open and slam. Uh-oh, they were coming to get her. Whoever *they* were.

"Holly?"

It was Sharon.

"Holly, I know you're in there, so just listen to me, OK?"

Holly sniffed back the tears that were beginning to well.

"OK, I know that this is an absolute nightmare for you and I know you have a major phobia about this kind of thing, but you need to relax, OK?"

Sharon's voice was so soothing, Holly's shoulders once again relaxed.

"Holly, I hate mice, you know that."

Holly frowned, wondering where this little pep talk was going.

"And my worst nightmare would be to walk out of here to a room full of mice. Now could you imagine me?"

Holly smiled at the thought and remembered the time when Sharon moved in with Gerry and Holly for two weeks after she had caught a mouse in her house. John, of course, was granted conjugal visits.

"Yeah, well I would be right here where you are now and nothing in the whole world would bring me out."

She paused.

"What?" the DJ's voice said into the microphone and then started laughing, "Ladies and gentlemen, it appears that our singer is currently in the toilets." The entire room erupted in laughter.

"Sharon!" Holly's voice trembled in fear. She felt as though the angry mob were about to break down the door, strip her of her clothes and carry her over their heads to the stage for her execution. Panic took over for the third time. Sharon rushed her next sentence. "Anyway, Holly, all I'm saying is that you don't have to do this if you don't want to. Nobody here is forcing you . . ."

"Ladies and gentlemen, let's let Holly know that she's up next!" yelled the DJ. "Come on!" Everybody began to stamp their feet and chant her name.

"OK, well, at least nobody who cares about you is forcing you to do this," stammered Sharon, now under pressure from the approaching mob. "But if you don't do this, I know you will never be able to forgive yourself. Gerry wanted you to do this for a reason."

"HOLLY! HOLLY! HOLLY!"

"Oh Sharon!" Holly repeated again, panicking. Suddenly the walls of the cubicle felt like they were closing in on her; beads of sweat formed on her forehead. She had to get out of there. She burst through the door. Sharon's eyes widened at the sight of her distraught friend, who looked like she had just seen a ghost. Her eyes were red and puffy with black lines of mascara streaming down her face (that waterproof stuff never works) and her tears had washed all her makeup away.

"Don't mind them, Holly," Sharon said coolly, "they can't make you do anything you don't want to do."

Holly's lower lip began to tremble.

"Don't!" Sharon said, gripping her by the shoulders and looking her in the eye. "Don't even think about it!"

Her lip stopped trembling but the rest of her didn't. Finally Holly broke her silence. "I can't sing, Sharon," she whispered, her eyes wide with terror.

"I know that!" Sharon said laughing. "And your family knows that! Screw the rest of them! You are never gonna see any of their ugly mugs *ever again!* Who cares what they think? I don't, do you?"

Holly thought about it for a minute. "No," she whispered.

"I didn't hear you, what did you say? Do you care what they think?"

"No," she said, a little stronger.

"Louder!" Sharon shook her by the shoulders.

"No!" she yelled.

"Louder!"

"NOOOOOOOOO! I DON'T CARE WHAT THEY THINK!" Holly screamed so loud the crowd began to quiet down outside. Sharon looked a little shaken, was probably a little deaf, and stood frozen in her place for a while. The two of them smiled at each other and then began to giggle at their stupidity.

"Just let this be another silly Holly day so we can laugh about it a few months from now," Sharon pleaded with her.

Holly took one last look at her reflection in the mirror, washed away her smudged mascara lines, took a deep breath and charged toward the door like a woman on a mission. She opened the door to her adoring fans, who were all facing it and chanting her name. They all began to cheer when they saw her, so she took an extremely theatrical bow and headed toward the stage to the sound of claps and laughter and a yell from Sharon saying, "Screw them!"

Holly had everybody's attention now whether she liked it or not. If she hadn't run into the toilet, the people who were chatting down the back of the club probably wouldn't have noticed her singing, but now she had attracted even more attention.

She stood with her arms folded on the stage and stared at the audience in shock. The music started without her even noticing and she missed the first few lines of the song. The DJ stopped the track and put it back to the start.

There was complete silence. Holly cleared her throat and the sound echoed around the room. Holly stared down at Denise and Sharon for help and her whole table held their thumbs up at her. Ordinarily Holly would have laughed at how corny they all looked, but right then it was strangely comforting. Finally the music began again and Holly held the microphone tightly in her two hands and prepared to sing. With an extremely shaky and timid voice she sang: "What would you do if I sang out of tune? Would you stand up and walk out on me?"

Denise and Sharon howled with laughter at the wonderful choice of song and gave her a big cheer. Holly struggled on, singing dreadfully and looking like she was about to burst into tears. Just when she felt like she was about to hear boos again her family and friends joined in with the chorus. "Ooh, I'll get by with a little help from my friends; yes, I'll get by with a little help from my friends."

The crowd turned to her table of family and friends and laughed and the atmosphere warmed a little more. Holly prepared herself for the high note coming up and yelled at the top of her lungs, "Do you *neeeed* anybody?" She even managed to give herself a fright with the volume and a few people helped her out to sing, "I need somebody to love."

"Do you *neeeed* anybody?" she repeated and held the microphone out to the crowd to encourage them to sing, and they all sang, "I need somebody to love," and gave themselves a round of applause. Holly felt less nervous now and battled her way through the rest of the song. The people down the back continued on chatting, the bar staff carried on serving drinks and smashing glasses until Holly felt like she was the only one listening to herself.

When she had finally finished singing, a few polite tables up front and her own table to the right were the only people to acknowledge her. The DJ took the microphone from her hand and managed to say between laughs, "Please give it up for the incredibly brave Holly Kennedy!"

This time her family and friends were the only people to cheer. Denise and Sharon approached her with cheeks wet from tears of laughter.

"I'm so proud of you!" Sharon said, throwing her arms around Holly's neck. "It was awful!"

"Thanks for helping me, Sharon," she said as she hugged her friend.

Jack and Abbey cheered and Jack shouted, "Terrible! Absolutely terrible!"

Holly's mother smiled encouragingly at her, knowing she had passed her special singing talent down to her daughter, and Holly's father could barely look her in the eye he was laughing so much. All Ciara could manage was to repeat over and over again, "I never knew anyone could be so bad."

Declan waved at her from across the room with a camera in

his hand and gave her the thumbs-down. Holly hid in the corner at the table and sipped on her water while she listened to everyone congratulating her on being so desperately bad. Holly couldn't remember the last time she had felt so proud.

John shuffled over to Holly and leaned against the wall beside her, where he watched the next act onstage in silence. Eventually he plucked up the courage to speak and said, "Gerry's probably here, you know," and looked at her with watery eyes.

Poor John, he missed his best friend too. She gave him an encouraging smile and looked around the room. He was right. Holly *could* feel Gerry's presence. She could feel him wrapping his arms around her and giving her one of the hugs she missed so much.

After an hour the singers had finally finished and Daniel and the DJ headed off to tot up the votes. Everyone had been handed a voting slip as they paid at the door and Holly couldn't bring it upon herself to write her own name down, so she gave her slip to Sharon. It was pretty obvious that Holly wasn't going to win, but that had never been her intention. And on the off chance that she did win, she shuddered at the thought of having to return in two weeks' time to repeat the whole experience. She hadn't learned a thing from it, only that she hated karaoke even more. Last year's winner, Keith, had brought along at least thirty of his friends, which meant that he was a sure winner, and Holly doubted very much that her "adoring fans" in the crowd would vote for her.

The DJ played a pathetic CD of a drumroll as the winners were about to be announced. Daniel took to the stage once again in his black leather jacket and black slacks uniform and was greeted by wolf whistles and screams from the girls. Worryingly, the loudest of these girls was Ciara. Richard looked excited and crossed his fingers at Holly. A very sweet but incredibly naïve gesture, she thought; he obviously didn't understand the "rules" properly.

There was a bit of embarrassment as the drumroll began to skip and the DJ rushed over to his equipment to shut it down. The winners were announced undramatically, in dead silence. "OK, I'd like to thank everyone for taking part in tonight's competition, you provided us all with some terrific entertainment." That last part was directed at Holly and she slithered down her seat with embarrassment. "OK, so the two people that will be going through to the final are," Daniel paused for dramatic effect, "Keith and Samantha!"

Holly jumped up with excitement and danced around in a huddle with Denise and Sharon. She had never felt such relief in her life. Richard looked on very confused, and the rest of Holly's family congratulated her on her victorious loss.

"I voted for the blond one," Declan announced with disappointment.

"That's just because she had big tits," Holly laughed.

"Well, we all have our own individual talents," Declan agreed.

Holly wondered what hers were as she sat back down. It must be a wonderful feeling to win something, to know that you have a talent. Holly had never won anything in her life; she didn't play any sports, couldn't play an instrument, now that she thought about it, she didn't have *any* hobbies or special interests. What would she put down on her CV when she eventually got around to applying for a job? "I like to drink and shop" wouldn't go down very well. She sipped her drink thoughtfully. Holly had lived her life being interested only in Gerry; in fact, everything she did revolved around him. In a way, being his wife was all she was good at; being his partner was all she knew. Now what did she have? No job, no husband and she couldn't even sing in a karaoke competition properly, never mind win it.

Sharon and John seemed engrossed in a heated discussion, Abbey and Jack were gazing into each other's eyes like love-struck teenagers as usual, Ciara was snuggling up to Daniel, and Denise was . . . Actually, where was Denise?

Holly looked around the club and spotted her sitting on the stage swinging her legs and striking a very provocative pose for the karaoke host. Holly's parents had left hand in hand just after her name wasn't announced as a winner, which left . . . Richard. Richard sat squashed beside Ciara and Daniel, looking around the room like a lost puppy and taking a sip from his drink every few seconds out of paranoia. Holly realized she must have looked like him . . . a complete loser. But at least this loser had a wife and two children to go home to, unlike Holly, who had a date with a microwave dinner.

Holly moved over and sat on the high stool opposite Richard and struck up a conversation.

"You enjoying yourself?"

He looked up from his drink, startled that someone had spoken to him. "Yes, thank you, I'm having fun, Holly."

If that was him having fun Holly dreaded to think what he looked like when he wasn't.

"I'm surprised you came, actually, I didn't think this would be your scene."

"Oh, you know . . . you have to support the family." He stirred his drink.

"So where's Meredith tonight?"

"Emily and Timothy," he said, as if that explained it all.

"You working tomorrow?"

"Yes," he said suddenly, knocking back his drink, "so I best be off. You were a great sport tonight, Holly." He looked around awkwardly at his family, debating whether to interrupt them and say good-bye but eventually deciding against it. He nodded to Holly and off he went, maneuvering his way through the thick crowd.

Holly was once again alone. As much as she wanted to grab her bag and run home, she knew she should sit this one out. There would be plenty of times in the future when she would be alone like this, the only singleton in the company of couples, and she needed to adapt. She felt awful, though, and she also felt angry with the others who didn't even notice her. Then she cursed herself for being so childish, she couldn't have asked for more supportive friends and family. Holly wondered whether this had been Gerry's intention. Did he think that this situation was what she needed? Did he think that this would help her? Perhaps he was right, because she was certainly being tested. It was forcing her to become braver in more ways than one. She had stood on a stage and sung to hundreds of people, and now she was stuck in a situation where she was surrounded by couples. They were all around her. Whatever his plan was, she was being forced to become braver without him. Just sit it out, she told herself.

Holly smiled as she watched her sister nattering away to Daniel. Ciara was nothing like her at all, she was so carefree and confident and never seemed to worry about anything. For as long as Holly could remember, Ciara had never managed to hold down a job or a boyfriend, her brain was always somewhere else, lost in the dream of visiting another far-off country. Holly wished she could be more like her, but she was such a home-bird and could never imagine herself moving away from her family and friends and leaving the life she had made for herself here. At least she could never leave the life she once had.

She turned her attention to Jack, who was still lost in a world with Abbey. She even wished she could be more like him; he absolutely loved his job as a secondary school teacher. He was the cool English teacher that all the teenagers respected, and whenever Holly and Jack passed one of his students on the street they always greeted him with a big smile and a "Hiya, sir!" All the girls fancied him and all the boys wanted to be like him when they got older. Holly sighed loudly and drained her drink. Now she was bored.

Daniel looked over. "Holly, can I get you a drink?"

"Ah no, it's OK, thanks, Daniel, I'm heading home soon anyway."

"Ah Hol!" protested Ciara. "You can't go home so early! It's your night!"

Holly didn't feel like it was her night. She felt like she had gate-crashed a party and didn't know anyone there.

"No, I'm all right, thanks," she assured Daniel again.

"No, you're staying," Ciara insisted. "Get her a vodka and Coke and I'll have the same again," she ordered Daniel.

"Ciara!" Holly exclaimed, embarrassed at her sister's rudeness.

"No, it's OK!" Daniel assured her. "I asked," and he headed off to the bar.

"Ciara, that was so rude," Holly gave out to her sister.

"What? It's not like he has to pay for it, he owns the bloody place," she said defensively.

"That still doesn't mean you can go around demanding free drinks . . ."

"Where's Richard?" Ciara interrupted.

"Gone home."

"Shit! How long ago?" She jumped down from her seat in a panic.

"I dunno, about five or ten minutes. Why?"

"He's supposed to be driving me home!" She threw everyone's coats into a pile on the floor while she rooted around for her bag.

"Ciara, you'll never catch him now, he's gone far too long."

"No, I will. He's parked ages away and he'll have to drive back down this road to get home. I'll get him while he's passing." She finally found her bag and legged it out the door yelling, "Bye, Holly! Well done, you were shite!" and disappeared out the door.

Holly was once again alone. Great, she thought, watching Daniel carrying the drinks back to the table, now she was stuck talking to him all by herself.

"Where's Ciara gone?" Daniel asked, placing the drinks on the table and sitting down opposite Holly.

"Oh, she said to say she's really sorry but she had to chase my brother for a lift." Holly bit her lip guiltily, knowing full well that Ciara hadn't even given Daniel a second thought as she raced out the door. "Sorry for being so rude to you earlier as well." Then she started laughing, "God, you must think we're the rudest family in the world. Ciara's a bit of a motormouth; she doesn't mean what she says half the time."

"And you did?" he smiled.

"At the time, yes," she laughed again.

"Hey, it's fine, just means there's more drink for you," he said, sliding the shot glass across the table to her.

"Ugh, what is this?" Holly wrinkled her nose up at the smell.

Daniel looked away awkwardly and cleared his throat. "I can't remember."

"Oh, come on!" Holly laughed. "You just ordered it! It's a woman's right to know what she's drinking, you know!"

Daniel looked at her with a smile on his face. "It's called a BJ.

You should have seen the barman's face when I asked for one. I don't think he knew it was a shot!"

"Oh, God," Holly said. "What's Ciara doing drinking this? It smells awful!"

"She said she found it easy to swallow." He started laughing again.

"Oh, I'm sorry, Daniel, she really is ridiculous sometimes." Holly shook her head over her sister.

Daniel stared past Holly's shoulder with amusement. "Well, it looks like your friend is having a good night anyway."

Holly swirled around and saw Denise and the DJ wrapped around each other beside the stage. Her provocative poses had obviously worked.

"Oh no, not the horrible DJ who forced me to come out of the toilet," Holly groaned.

"That's Tom O'Connor from Dublin FM," Daniel said. "He's a friend of mine."

Holly covered her face in embarrassment.

"He's working here tonight because the karaoke went out live on the radio," he said seriously.

"What?" Holly nearly had a heart attack for the twentieth time that night.

Daniel's face broke into a smile. "Only joking; just wanted to see the look on your face."

"Oh my God, don't do that to me," Holly said, putting her hand on her heart. "Having the people in here hear me was bad enough, never mind the entire city as well." She waited for her heart to stop pounding while Daniel stared at her with an amused look in his eye.

"If you don't mind me asking, if you hate it so much, why did you enter?" he asked carefully.

"Oh, my hilarious husband thought it would be funny to enter his tone-deaf wife into a singing competition."

Daniel laughed. "You weren't *that* bad! Is your husband here?" he asked, looking around. "I don't want him thinking I'm trying to poison his wife with that awful concoction." He nodded toward the shot glass.

Holly looked around the club and smiled. "Yeah, he's definitely here . . . somewhere."

Sixteen

HOLLY SECURED HER BEDSHEET ONTO the washing line with a peg and thought about how she had bumbled around for the remainder of May trying to get her life into some sort of order. Days went by when she felt so happy and content and *confident* that her life would be OK, and then as quickly as the feeling came it would disappear again, and she would feel her sadness setting in once more. She tried to find a routine she could happily fall into so that she felt like she belonged in her body and her body belonged in this life, instead of wandering around like a zombie watching everybody else live theirs while she waited around for hers to end. Unfortunately the routine hadn't turned out exactly as she hoped it would. She found herself immobile for hours in the sitting room, reliving every single memory that she and Gerry had shared. Sadly, she spent most of that time thinking about every argument they had had, wishing she could take them back, wishing she could take back every horrible word she had ever said to him. She prayed that Gerry had known her words had only been spoken out of anger and that they had not reflected her true feelings. She tortured herself for the times she had acted selfishly, going out with her friends for the night when she was mad at him instead of staying home with him. She chastised herself for walking away from him when she should have hugged him, when she held grudges for days instead of forgiving him, when she went straight to sleep some nights instead of making love to him. She wanted to take back every moment she knew he had been so angry with her and hated her. She wished all her memories could be of the good times, but the bad times kept coming back to haunt her. They had all been such a waste of time.

And nobody had told them that they were short on time.

Then there were her happy days, when she would walk around in a daydream with nothing but a smile on her face, catching herself giggling as she walked down the street when a joke of theirs would suddenly pop into her head. That was her routine. She would fall into days of deep dark depression, then finally build up the strength to be positive and to snap out of it for another few days. But the tiniest and simplest thing would trigger off her tears again. It was a tiring process, and most of the time she couldn't be bothered battling with her mind. It was far stronger than any muscle in her body.

Friends and family came and went, sometimes helping her with her tears, other times making her laugh. But even in her laughter there was something missing. She never seemed to be truly happy; she just seemed to be passing time while she waited for something else. She was tired of just existing; she wanted to live. But what was the point in living when there was no life in it? These questions went through her mind over and over until she reached the point of not wanting to wake up from her dreams— they were what felt real.

Deep down, she knew it was normal to feel like this, she didn't particularly think she was losing her mind. She knew that people said that one day she would be happy again and that this feeling would just be a distant memory. It was getting to that day that was the hard part.

She read and reread Gerry's original letter over and over, ana-lyzing each word and each sentence, and each day she came up with a new meaning. But she could sit there till the cows came home trying to read between the lines and guess the hidden mes-sage. The fact was that she would never *really* know *exactly* what he meant because she would never speak to him *ever again*. It was this thought that she had the most difficulty trying to come to terms with, and it was killing her.

Now May had gone and June had arrived, bringing bright long evenings and the beautiful mornings that came with them. And with these bright sunny days June brought clarity. There was no hiding indoors as soon as it got dark, and there were no lie-ins until the afternoon. It seemed as though the whole of Ireland had come out of hibernation, taken a big stretch and a yawn and suddenly started living again. It was time to open all the windows and air the house, to free it of the ghosts of the winter and dark days, it was time to get up early with the songbirds and go for a walk and look people in the eye and smile and say hello instead of hiding under layers of clothes with eyes to the ground while running from destination to destina-tion and ignoring the world. It was time to stop hiding in the dark and to hold your head up high and come face-to-face with the truth.

June also brought another letter from Gerry.

Holly had sat out in the sun, reveling in the new brightness of life, and nervously yet excitedly read the fourth letter. She loved the feel of the card and the bumps of Gerry's handwriting under her finger as it ran over the dried ink. Inside, his neat handwriting had listed the items that belonged to him that remained in the house, and beside each of his possessions he explained what he wanted Holly to do with them and where he wished for them to be sent. At the bottom it read:

> *PS, I love you, Holly, and I know you love me. You don't need my belongings to remember me by, you don't need to keep them as proof that I existed or still exist in your mind. You don't need to wear my sweater to feel me around you; I'm already there . . .* always *wrapping my arms around you.*

That had been difficult for Holly to come to terms with. She almost wished he would ask her to do karaoke again. She would have jumped from an airplane for him; run a thousand miles, *anything* except empty out his wardrobes and rid herself of his presence in the house. But he was right and she knew it. She couldn't hang on to his belongings forever. She couldn't pretend to herself that he was coming back to collect them. The physical Gerry was gone; he didn't need his clothes.

It was an emotionally draining experience. It took her days to complete. She relived a million memories with every garment and piece of paper she bagged. She held each item near to her before saying good-bye. Every time an item left her fingers it was like saying good-bye to a part of Gerry all over again. It was difficult; so difficult and at times too difficult.

She informed her family and friends of what she was about to do, and although they all offered their assistance and support time and again, Holly knew she had to do this alone. She needed to take her time. Say a proper good-bye because she wouldn't be getting anything back. Just like Gerry, his belongings couldn't return. Despite Holly's wishes of wanting to be alone, Jack had called around a few times to offer some brotherly support and Holly had appreciated it. Every item had a history and they would talk and laugh about the memories surrounding it. He was there for her when she cried and he was there when she finally clapped her hands together, ridding her skin of the dust that remained. It was a difficult job but one that needed to be done. And one that was made easier by Gerry's help. Holly didn't need to worry about making all the big decisions, Gerry had already made them for her. Gerry was helping her, and for once, Holly felt like she was helping him too.

She laughed as she bagged the dusty cassettes of his favorite rock band from his school days. At least once a year Gerry came across the old shoe box during his efforts to control the mess that grew inside his closet. He would blast the heavy metal music from every speaker in the house to torment Holly with its screeching guitars and badly produced sound quality. She always told him she couldn't wait to see the end of those tapes. The relief didn't wash over her as she once hoped it would.

Her eyes rested upon a crumpled ball lying in the back corner of the wardrobe—Gerry's lucky football jersey. It was still covered in grass and mud stains, fresh from its last victorious day on the pitch. She held it close to her and inhaled deeply; the smell of beer and sweat was faint, but still there. She put it aside to be washed and passed on to John.

So many objects, so many memories. Each was being labeled and packed away in bags just as it was in her mind. To be stored in an area that would sometime be called upon to teach and help in future life. Objects that were once so full of life and importance but that now lay limp on the floor. Without him they were just *things*.

Gerry's wedding tuxedo, his suits, shirts and ties that he would moan about having to wear every morning before going to work. The fashions of the years gone by, eighties shiny suits and shell tracksuits bundled away. A snorkel from their first time scuba diving, a shell that he picked from the ocean floor ten years ago, his collection of beer mats from every pub in every country they had visited. Letters and birthday cards from friends and family sent to him over the years. Valentine's Day cards from Holly. Childhood teddies and dolls put aside to be sent back to his parents. Records of bills, his golf clubs for John, books for Sharon, memories, tears and laughter for Holly.

His entire life bundled into twenty refuse sacks.

His and her memories bundled away into Holly's mind.

Each item unearthed dust, tears, laughter and memories. She bagged the items, cleared the dust, wiped her eyes and filed away the memories.

Holly's mobile began to ring and she dropped the laundry basket onto the grass under the washing line and ran through the patio doors into the kitchen to answer the phone.

"Hello?"

"I'm gonna make you a star!" Declan's voice screeched hysterically on the other end and he broke into uncontrollable laughter.

Holly waited for him to calm down while she searched her

brain and tried to figure out what he could be talking about. "Declan, are you drunk?"

"Maybe jus a li'l bit, but that's completely irrevelant," he hiccuped.

"Declan, it's ten o'clock in the morning!" Holly laughed. "Have you been to bed yet?"

"Nope," he hiccuped again, "I'm on the train home now and will be in bed in 'proximately three hours."

"Three hours! Where are you?" Holly laughed again. She was enjoying this, as it reminded her of when she used to call Jack at all hours of the morning from all sorts of locations after misbehaving on a night out.

"I'm in Galway. The 'wards were on last night," he said, as if she should know.

"Oh, sorry for my ignorance, but what awards were you at?"

"I told you!"

"No you didn't."

"I told Jack to tell you, the bastard—" He stumbled over his words.

"Well, he didn't," she interrupted him, "so now you can tell me."

"The student media 'wards were on last night and I won!" he yelled, and Holly heard what sounded like the entire carriage celebrating with him. She was delighted for him.

"And the prize is that it's gonna be aired on Channel 4 next week! Can you believe it!" There were more cheers this time and Holly could barely make out what he was saying. "You're gonna be famous, sis!" was the last thing she heard before the line went dead. What was this odd feeling she detected running through her body? Was it . . . no it couldn't . . . could it be that Holly was experiencing a sensation of happiness?

She rang around her family to share the good news but learned that they had all received a similar phone call. Ciara had stayed on the phone for ages chattering like an excited schoolgirl about how they were going to be on TV, and eventually her story ended with her marrying Denzel Washington. It was decided that the family would gather in Hogan's pub next Wednesday to watch the documentary being aired. Daniel had kindly offered Club Diva as the venue so they could watch it on the big wall screen. Holly was excited for her brother and rang Sharon and Denise to let them know the good news.

"Oh, this is brill news, Holly!" Sharon whispered excitedly.

"Why are you whispering?" Holly whispered back.

"Oh, old wrinkly face here decided it would be a great idea to ban us from accepting personal calls," moaned Sharon, referring to her boss. "She says we spend more time chatting on the phone to friends than doing business, so she's been patrolling our desks all morning. I swear I feel like I'm back at school again with the old hag keeping her eye on us." Suddenly she spoke up and became businesslike. "May I take your details please?"

Holly laughed. "Is she there?"

"Yes absolutely," Sharon continued.

"OK, well, I won't keep you very long then. The details are that we're all meeting up in Hogan's on Wednesday night to watch it, so you're welcome to come."

"That's great . . . OK." Sharon pretended to take her details.

"Brilliant, we'll have fun. Sharon, what will I wear?"

"Hmm . . . brand-new or secondhand?"

"No, I really can't afford anything new; even though you forced me to buy that top a few weeks ago, I'm refusing to wear it on the grounds that I am no longer eighteen. So probably something old."

"OK . . . red."

"The red top I wore to your birthday?"

"Yes, exactly."

"Yeah, maybe."

"What's your current state of employment?"

"To be honest I haven't even started looking yet." Holly chewed the inside of her mouth and frowned.

"And date of birth?"

"Ha-ha, shut up, you bitch," Holly laughed.

"I'm sorry, we only give motor insurance to ages twenty-four and older. You're too young, I'm afraid."

"I wish. OK, I'll speak to you later."

"Thank you for calling."

Holly sat at the kitchen table wondering what she should wear next week; she wanted something new. She wanted to look sexy and gorgeous for a change, and she was sick of all her old clothes. Maybe Denise had something in her shop. She was about to call when she received a text message from Sharon.

HAG RITE BHIND ME

TLK 2 U L8R XXX

Holly picked up the phone and called Denise at work.

"Hello, 'Casuals,'" answered a very polite Denise.

"Hello, Casuals, Holly here. I know I'm not supposed to call you at work but I just wanted to tell you that Declan's documentary won some student award thingy and it's gonna be aired on Wednesday night."

"Oh, that's so cool, Holly! Are we gonna be in it?" she asked excitedly.

"Yeah, I think so. So we're all meeting up at Hogan's to watch it that night. You up for that?"

"Oooh, of course! I can bring my new boyfriend too," she giggled.

"What new boyfriend?"

"Tom!"

"The karaoke guy?" Holly asked in shock.

"Yeah, of course! Oh Holly, I'm so in love!" she giggled childishly again.

"In love? But you only met him a few weeks ago!"

"Oh I don't care; it only takes a minute . . . as the saying goes."

"Wow, Denise . . . I don't know what to say!"

"Tell me how great it is!"

"Yeah . . . wow . . . I mean . . . of course . . . it's really great news."

"Oh, try not to sound too enthusiastic, Holly," she said sarcastically. "Anyway, I can't wait for you to meet him, you'll absolutely love him. Well, not as much as I do, but you'll certainly really *really* like him." She rambled on about how great he was.

"Denise, are you forgetting that I met him already?" Holly interrupted her in the middle of a story about how Tom had saved a child from drowning.

"Yeah, I know you have, but I would rather you meet him when you're not acting like a demented woman hiding in toilets and shouting into microphones."

"Look forward to it then . . ."

"Yeah, cool, it's gonna be great! I've never been to my own premiere before!" she said excitedly.

Holly rolled her eyes at her friend's dramatics and they said their good-byes.

. . .

Holly barely got any housework done that morning, as she spent most of the time talking on the phone. Her mobile was burning and it was giving her a headache. She shuddered at the thought. Every time she had a headache it reminded her of Gerry. She hated to hear her loved ones complaining of headaches and migraines and would immediately launch herself at them, warning them of the dangers and how they should take it more seriously and go see their doctors. She ended up petrifying everyone with her stories and they eventually stopped telling her when they felt ill.

She sighed loudly; she was turning into such a hypochondriac even her doctor was sick of the sight of her. She went running to her in a panic over the tiniest little things, if she had a pain in her leg or a cramp in her stomach. Last week she was convinced there was something wrong with her feet; her toes just didn't look quite right. Her doctor had examined them seriously and then had immediately started to scribble her prescription down on a slip of paper while Holly watched in terror. Eventually she handed her the piece of paper, and scrawled messily in that handwriting only doctors can perfect, was: "Buy bigger shoes."

It may have been funny, but it cost her forty euro.

Holly had spent the last few minutes on the phone listening to Jack ranting and raving about Richard. Richard had paid him a little visit, too. Holly wondered whether he was just trying to bond with his siblings after years of hiding from them. Well, it was too little too late for most of them, it seemed. It was certainly very difficult trying to hold a conversation with someone who hadn't yet mastered the art of politeness. Oh, stop stop stop! she silently screamed to herself. She needed to stop worrying, stop thinking, stop making her brain go on overdrive, and she certainly needed to stop talking to herself. She was driving herself crazy.

She finally finished hanging out the washing more than two hours later and added another load into the machine and turned it on. She switched the radio on in the kitchen and blared the television from the living room and went back to work. Perhaps that would drown out the whinging little voice in her head.

Seventeen

HOLLY ARRIVED AT HOGAN'S AND pushed her way through the old men in the pub to make her way upstairs to Club Diva. The traditional band was in full swing and the crowd was joining in on all their favorite Irish songs. It was only seven-thirty, so Club Diva wasn't officially open yet. Looking around at the empty club, Holly saw a completely different venue from the one she had been so terrified in a few weeks earlier. She was the first to arrive and settled herself at a table right in front of the big screen so she would have a perfect view of her brother's documentary, not that the place would be so crowded that anyone would stand in her way.

A smashing glass over by the bar made her jump and she looked up to see who had joined her in the room. Daniel emerged from behind the bar with a dustpan and brush in his hand. "Oh, hiya, Holly, I didn't realize anyone had come in." He stared at her in surprise.

"It's just me, I came early for a change." She walked over to the bar to greet him. He looked different tonight, she thought, inspecting him.

"God, you're really early," he said, looking at his watch, "the others probably won't be here for another hour or so."

Holly looked confused and glanced at her watch. "But it's seven-thirty, the show starts at eight, doesn't it?"

Daniel looked confused, "No, I was told nine o'clock, but I could be wrong . . ." He reached for that day's paper and looked at the TV page. "Yep, nine o'clock, Channel 4."

Holly rolled her eyes. "Oh no, I'm sorry, I'll wander around town for a bit and come back later so," she said, hopping off her stool.

"Hey, don't be silly." He flashed his pearly whites. "The shops are all closed by now and you can keep me company, that's if you don't mind . . ."

"Well, I don't mind if you don't mind . . ."

"I don't mind," he said firmly.

"Well then, I'll stay so," she said, happily hopping back onto her stool again. Daniel leaned his hands against the taps in a typical barman's pose. "So now that that's settled, what can I get you?" he said, smiling.

"Well, this is great, no queuing or shouting my order across the bar or anything," she joked. "I'll have a sparkling water, please."

"Nothing stronger?" He raised his eyebrows. His smile was infectious; it seemed to reach from ear to ear.

"No, I better not or I'll be drunk by the time everyone gets here."

"Good thinking," he agreed and reached behind him to the fridge to retrieve the bottled water. Holly realized what it was that made him look so different; he wasn't wearing his trademark black. He was wearing faded blue jeans and an open light blue shirt with a white T-shirt underneath that made his blue eyes twinkle even more than usual. The sleeves of his shirt were rolled up to just below his elbows. Holly could see his muscles through the light fabric. She quickly averted her eyes as he slid the glass toward her.

"Can I get you anything?" she asked him.

"No thanks, I'll take care of this one."

"No, please," Holly insisted. "You've bought me plenty of drinks, it's my turn."

"OK, I'll have a Budweiser then, thanks." He leaned against the bar and continued to stare at her.

"What? Do you want me to get it?" Holly laughed, jumping off her stool and walking around the bar. Daniel stood back and watched her with amusement.

"I always wanted to work behind a bar when I was a kid," she said, grabbing a pint glass and pulling down on the tap. She was enjoying herself.

"Well, there's a spare job if you're looking for one," Daniel said, watching her work closely.

"No thanks, I think I do a better job on the other side of the bar," she laughed, filling the pint glass.

"Mmm . . . well, if you're ever looking for a job, you know where to come," Daniel said after taking a gulp of his pint. "You did a good job."

"Well, it's not exactly brain surgery," she smiled, bouncing across to the other side of the bar. She took out her purse and handed him money. "Keep the change," she laughed.

"Thanks," he smiled, turning to open the cash register, and she scorned herself for checking out his bum. It was nice, though, firm but not as nice as Gerry's, she decided.

"Has your husband deserted you again tonight?" he teased, walking around the bar to join her. Holly bit her lip and wondered how to answer him. Now wasn't really the time to talk about something so depressing to someone who was only making chitchat, but she didn't want the poor man to keep asking her every time he saw her. He would soon realize the truth, which would cause him even more embarrassment.

"Daniel," she said softly, "I don't mean to make you uncomfortable, but my husband passed away."

Daniel stopped in his tracks and his cheeks blushed slightly. "Oh Holly, I'm sorry, I didn't know," he said sincerely.

"It's OK, I know you didn't." She smiled to show him it was all right.

"Well, I didn't meet him the other night, but if someone had told me, I would have gone to the funeral to pay my respects." He sat beside her at the bar.

"Oh no, Gerry died in February, Daniel, he wasn't here the other night."

Daniel looked confused. "But I thought you told me he was here . . ." He trailed off, thinking he had misheard.

"Oh yeah." Holly looked down at her feet with embarrassment. "Well, he wasn't here," she said, looking around the club, "but he was here," she put her hand on her heart.

"Ah, I see," he said, finally understanding. "Well then, you were even braver the other night than I thought, considering the circumstances," he said gently. Holly was surprised by how at ease he seemed. Usually people stuttered and stammered their way through a sentence and either wandered off or changed the subject. She felt relaxed in his presence, though, as if she could talk openly without fear of crying. Holly smiled, shaking her head, and briefly explained the story of the list.

"So that's why I ran off after Declan's gig that time," Holly laughed.

"It wasn't because they were so terrible by any chance?" Daniel joked, then he looked lost in thought. "Ah yes, that's right, that was the thirtieth of April."

"Yeah, I couldn't wait any longer to open it," Holly explained.

"Hmmm . . . when's the next one?"

"July," she said excitedly.

"So I won't be seeing you on the thirtieth of June then," he said dryly.

"Now you're getting the gist," she laughed.

"I have arrived!" announced Denise to the empty room as she swanned in, dolled up to the nines in the dress she had worn to the ball last year. Tom strolled in behind her, laughing and refusing to take his eyes off her.

"God, *you're* dressed up," Holly remarked, staring her friend up and down. In the end Holly had decided to just wear a pair of jeans, black boots and a very simple black top. She hadn't been in the mood to get all dressed up after all, especially as they were only sitting in an empty club, but Denise hadn't quite grasped that concept.

"Well, it's not every day I get to go to my own premiere, is it?" she joked.

Tom and Daniel greeted each other with hugs. "Baby, this is Daniel, my best friend," Tom said, introducing Denise to Daniel. Daniel and Holly raised their eyebrows at each other and smiled, both registering the use of the word "baby."

"Hi, Tom." Holly shook his hand after Denise had introduced her and he kissed her on the cheek. "I'm sorry about the last time I met you, I wasn't feeling very sane that night." Holly blushed at the memory of the karaoke.

"Oh, that's no problem," Tom smiled kindly. "If you hadn't entered then I wouldn't have met Denise, so I'm glad you did," he added, turning to face Denise. Daniel and Holly shared a mutually pleased look for their friends, and Holly settled down on her stool feeling very comfortable with these two new men.

After a while Holly discovered she was enjoying herself; she wasn't just pretending to laugh or finding things mildly amusing, she was genuinely happy. The thought of that made her even happier, as did the knowledge that Denise had finally found someone she really loved.

Minutes later the rest of the Kennedy family arrived, along with Sharon and John. Holly ran down to greet her friends. "Hiya, hun," Sharon said, giving her a hug. "You here long?"

Holly started laughing. "I thought it was on at eight o'clock so I came at half seven."

"Oh no." Sharon looked worried.

"Oh, don't worry, it was fine. Daniel kept me company," she said, pointing over to him.

"Him?" John said angrily, "Watch yourself with him, Holly, he's a bit of an oddball. You should have heard the stuff he was saying to Sharon the other night."

Holly giggled to herself and quickly excused herself from their company to join her family. "Meredith not with you tonight?" she boldly asked Richard.

"No, she's not," he snapped back rudely and headed over to the bar.

"Why does he bother coming to these things at all?" she moaned to Jack while he held her head to his chest and rubbed her hair, playfully consoling her.

"OK, everyone!" Declan stood on a stool and announced to the group, "Because Ciara couldn't decide what to wear tonight, we're all late and *my* documentary is about to start any minute. So if you can just all shut up and sit down that would be great."

"Oh, Declan." Holly's mother admonished him for his rudeness.

Holly searched around the room for Ciara and spotted her glued to Daniel's side at the bar. She laughed to herself and settled down to watch the documentary. As soon as the announcer introduced it, everybody cheered, but they were quickly hushed by an angry Declan, who didn't want them to miss a thing.

The words "Girls and the City" appeared over a beautiful nighttime shot of Dublin city, and Holly became nervous. The words "The Girls" appeared over a black screen and was followed by a shot of Sharon, Denise, Abbey and Ciara all squashed beside each other in the back of a taxi. Sharon was speaking:

"Hello! I'm Sharon and this is Abbey, Denise and Ciara."

Each of the girls posed for their close-up as they were introduced.

"And we're heading to our best friend Holly's house because it's her birthday today . . ."

The scene changed to the girls surprising Holly with shouts of "Happy Birthday" at her front door. It returned to Sharon in the taxi.

"Tonight it's gonna be just us girls and NO men . . ."

The scene switched to Holly opening the presents and holding the vibrator up to the camera and saying, "Well, I'll definitely need this!" Then it returned to Sharon in the taxi saying:

"We are gonna do lots and *lots* of drinking . . ."

Now Holly was popping open the champagne, then the girls were knocking back shots in Boudoir, and eventually it showed Holly with the crooked tiara on her head, drinking out of a champagne bottle with a straw.

"We are gonna go clubbing . . ."

There was then a shot of the girls in Boudoir doing some very embarrassing moves on the dance floor. Sharon was shown next, speaking sincerely.

"But nothing too mad! We're gonna be good girls tonight!"

The next scene showed the girls protesting wildly as they were escorted out of the club by three bouncers.

Holly's jaw dropped open and she stared in shock over at Sharon, who was equally surprised. The men just laughed their hearts out and slapped Declan on the back, congratulating him for exposing their partners. Holly, Sharon, Denise, Abbey and even Ciara slithered down in their seats with humiliation.

What on earth had Declan done?

Eighteen

THERE WAS COMPLETE SILENCE IN the club as everyone stared at the screen in anticipation. Holly held her breath; she was nervous now about what was going to appear. Perhaps the girls would be reminded of what exactly they had all conveniently succeeded in forgetting about that night. The truth terrified her. After all, how drunk must they all have been to completely forget the events of that night? Unless somebody was lying, in which case they should be even more nervous right now. Holly looked around at the girls. They were all chewing on their fingernails. Holly crossed her fingers.

A new title appeared on the screen, "The Gifts." "Open mine first," shrieked Ciara from the television, thrusting her present toward Holly and shoving Sharon off the couch and onto the ground. Everyone in the club laughed while they watched Abbey dragging a horrified Sharon to her feet. Ciara left Daniel's side and tiptoed over to the rest of the girls for security. Everyone oohed and aahed, as one by one Holly's birthday presents were unveiled. A lump formed in Holly's throat as Declan zoomed in on the two photographs on the mantelpiece while Sharon's toast was made.

Once again a new title took over the screen, "Journey to the City," and showed the girls scrambling over one another to get into the seven-seater taxi. It was obvious they were pretty pissed by now. Holly was shocked; she had actually thought she was quite sober at that stage. "Oh, John," Holly moaned drunkenly to the taxi driver from the passenger seat, "I'm thirty today, can you believe it?"

John the taxi driver, who couldn't give a flying flute what age she was, glanced over at her and laughed, "Sure you're only a young one still, Holly." His voice was low and gravelly. The camera zoomed in on Holly's face and she cringed at the sight of herself. She looked so drunk, so *sad*.

"But what am I gonna do, John?" she whinged. "I'm thirty! I have no job, no husband, no children and I'm thirty! Did I tell you that?" she asked, leaning toward him. Behind her Sharon giggled. Holly thumped her.

In the background you could hear the girls all chattering excitedly to one another. Actually it sounded like they were talking over one another; it was hard to see how any type of conversation was going on.

"Ah, enjoy yourself tonight, Holly, don't get caught up in silly emotions on your birthday. Worry about all that shite tomorrow, love." John sounded so caring, Holly made a note to call him and thank him.

The camera stayed with Holly as she leaned her head against

the window and remained silent, lost in thought for the rest of the journey. Holly couldn't get over how lonely she looked. She didn't like it. She looked around the room in embarrassment and caught Daniel's eye. He winked at her in encouragement. Well, if she needed winks for encouragement, she thought, then everybody must have been thinking the same thing. She smiled weakly and turned back around to face the screen in time to see herself screaming to the girls on O'Connell Street.

"OK, girls. We are going to Boudoir tonight and *no one* is going to stop us from getting in, *especially* not any *silly bouncers* who *think* they own the place," and she marched off in what she thought at the time was a straight line. All the girls cheered and followed after her.

The scene immediately jumped to the two bouncers outside Boudoir shaking their heads. "Not tonight, girls, sorry."

Holly's family howled with laughter.

"But you don't understand," Denise said calmly to the bouncers. "Do you not know who we are?"

"No," they both said and stared over their heads, ignoring them.

"Huh!" Denise put her hands on her hips and pointed to Holly. "But this is the very, very extremely famous . . . em . . . Princess Holly from the royal family of . . . Finland." On camera Holly frowned at Denise.

Her family once again howled with laughter. "You couldn't write a script better than this," Declan laughed.

"Oh, she's royalty, is she?" the bouncer with a mustache smirked.

"Indeed she is," Denise said seriously.

"Finland got a royal family, Paul?" Mustache Man turned to Paul.

"Don't think so, boss," was the reply.

Holly fixed the crooked tiara on her head and gave them both a royal wave. "You see?" Denise said, satisfied. "You men will be very embarrassed if you don't let her in."

"Supposing we let her in then, you'll have to stay outside," Mustache Man said and motioned for the people behind them in the queue to pass by and enter the club. Holly gave them a royal wave as they passed.

"Oh, no no no no," Denise laughed. "You don't understand. I am her . . . lady-in-waiting, so I need to be with her at all times."

"Well then, you won't mind waiting till she comes out at closing time then," Paul smirked.

Tom, Jack and John all started laughing and Denise slithered down even further in her seat.

Finally Holly spoke. "Oh, one *must* have a drink. One is *dreadfully* thirsty."

Paul and Mustache Man snorted and tried to keep a straight face while still staring over their heads.

"No, honestly, girls, not tonight, you need to be a member."

"But I am a member of the royal family!" Holly said sternly. "Off with your heads!" she commanded, pointing at the both of them.

Denise quickly forced Holly's arm down. "Honestly, the princess and I will be no trouble at all, just let us in for a few drinks," she pleaded.

Mustache Man stared down at the two of them then raised his eyes to the sky. "All right then, go on in," he said, stepping aside.

"God bless you," Holly said, making the sign of the cross at them as she passed.

"What is she, a princess or a priest?" laughed Paul as she entered the club.

"She's out of her mind," laughed Mustache Man, "but it's the best excuse I've heard while I've been on the job," and the two of them sniggered. They regained their composure as Ciara and her entourage approached the door.

"Is it OK if my film crew follow me in?" Ciara said confidently in a brilliant Australian accent.

"Hold on while I check with the manager." Paul turned his back and spoke into the walkie-talkie. "Yeah, that's no problem, go ahead," he said, holding the door open for her.

"That's that Australian singer, isn't it?" Mustache Man said to Paul.

"Yeah, good song that."

"Tell the boys inside to keep an eye on the princess and her lady," said Mustache Man. "We don't want them bothering that singer with the pink hair."

Holly's father choked on his drink from laughing, and Elizabeth rubbed his back for him while giggling herself.

As Holly watched the image of the inside of Boudoir on the screen she remembered being disappointed by the club. There had always been a mystery as to what "Boudoir" looked like. The girls had read in a magazine that there was a water feature inside that Madonna had apparently jumped into one night. Holly had imagined a huge waterfall cascading down the wall of the club that continued to flow in little bubbling streams all around the club while all the glamorous people sat around it and occasionally dipped their glasses into it to fill them with more champagne. But instead of her champagne waterfall, what Holly got was an oversized fish bowl in the center of the circular bar. What that had to do with anything she didn't know. Her dreams were shattered. The room wasn't as big as Holly thought it would be, and it was decorated in rich reds and gold. On the far side of the room was a huge gold curtain acting as a partition, which was blocked by another menacing-looking bouncer.

At the top of the room the main attraction was a massive king-size bed, which was tilted on a platform toward the rest of the club. On top of the gold silk sheets were two skinny models dressed in no more than gold body paint and tiny gold thongs. It was all a bit too tacky.

"Look at the size of those thongs!" gasped Denise in disgust. "I have a plaster on my baby finger bigger than those."

Beside her in Club Diva, Tom chuckled and began to nibble on Denise's baby finger. Holly looked away and returned her gaze to the screen.

"Good evening and welcome to the twelve o'clock news, I'm Sharon McCarthy." Sharon stood in front of the camera with a bottle in her hand serving as a microphone, and Declan had angled the camera so that she could get Ireland's famous news-readers in the shot.

"Today on the thirtieth birthday of Princess Holly of Finland, her royal self and her lady-in-waiting finally succeeded in being granted access to the famous celebrity hangout Boudoir. Also present is Australian rock chick Ciara and her film crew and . . ." She held her finger to her ear as though she were receiving more information. "News just in, it appears that Ireland's favorite news-reader Tony Walsh was seen smiling just moments ago. Here beside me I have a witness to the fact. Welcome, Denise." Denise posed seductively at the camera. "Denise, tell me, where were you when this event was taking place?"

"Well, I was just over there beside his table when I saw it happening." Denise sucked in her cheekbones and smiled at the camera.

"Can you explain to us what happened?"

"Well, I was just standing there minding my own business when Mr. Walsh took a sip of his drink and then shortly afterward he smiled."

"Gosh, Denise, this is fascinating news. Are you sure it was a smile?"

"Well, it could have been trapped wind causing him to make a face, but others around me also thought it was a smile."

"So there were others who witnessed this?"

"Yes, Princess Holly beside me here saw the whole thing."

The camera panned across to Holly where she stood drinking from a champagne bottle with a straw. "So Holly, can you tell us, was it wind or a smile?"

Holly looked confused then rolled her eyes. "Oh wind, sorry, I think it's this champagne that's doing it to me."

Club Diva erupted in laughter. Jack as usual laughed the loudest. Holly hid her face in shame.

"OK then . . . ," Sharon said, trying not to laugh. "So you heard it here first. The night when Ireland's grimmest presenter was seen smiling. Back to you at the studio." Sharon's smile faded as she looked up and saw Tony Walsh standing beside her, not surprisingly without a smile on his face.

Sharon gulped and said, "Good evening," and the camera was switched off. Everyone in the club was laughing at this stage, including the girls. Holly was finding the whole thing just so ridiculous that she had to laugh.

The camera was switched back on and this time it was focused on the mirror in the ladies' toilet. Declan was filming from outside through a slit in the doorway and Denise and Sharon's reflections were clearly visible.

"I was only having a laugh," Sharon huffed, fixing her lipstick.

"Don't mind the miserable sod, Sharon, he just doesn't want the camera in his face all night, especially on his night off. I can understand that."

"Oh, you're on his side, I suppose," Sharon said grumpily.

"Ah shut up, you moany old whore," Denise snapped.

"Where's Holly?" Sharon asked, changing the subject.

"Don't know, last time I saw her she was doing a few funky moves on the dance floor," said Denise. The two of them looked at each other and laughed.

"Ah . . . our poor little Disco Diva," said Sharon sadly. "I hope she finds someone gorgeous out there tonight and snogs the face off him."

"Yeah," agreed Denise. "Come on then, let's go find her a man," she said, putting her makeup back in her bag.

Just after the girls left the toilet another toilet flushed from the cubicle. The door opened and out stepped Holly. Holly's big smile faded quickly when she saw her face on the screen. Through the crack in the door you could see Holly's reflection in the mirror; her eyes were red from crying. She blew her nose and stared miserably at herself in the mirror for a while. She took a deep breath and opened the door and carried on downstairs to her friends. Holly hadn't remembered crying that night; in fact, she thought she had gotten through it very well. She rubbed her face while she worried about what else was coming up next that she couldn't remember.

Finally the scene changed and the words "Operation Gold Curtain" came up. Denise screamed, "Oh my God, Declan, you bastard!" very loudly and rushed off to the toilet to hide.

She had obviously remembered something.

Declan chuckled and lit himself another cigarette.

"OK, girls," Denise was announcing. "It is now time for Operation Gold Curtain."

"Huh?" Sharon and Holly announced groggily from the couch where they had collapsed in a drunken stupor.

"Operation Gold Curtain," Denise exclaimed excitedly, trying to drag them to their feet. "It's time to infiltrate the VIP bar!"

"You mean this isn't it?" Sharon said sarcastically, looking around the club.

"No! That's where the real celebs go!" Denise said excitedly, pointing at the gold curtain, which was blocked by possibly the biggest and tallest man on the planet.

"I don't really care where the celebs are, to be honest, Denise," piped up Holly. "I'm fine here where I am," and she snuggled into the cozy couch.

Denise groaned and rolled her eyes. "Girls! Abbey and Ciara are in there, why aren't we?"

Jack looked curiously across at his girlfriend. Abbey shrugged her shoulders weakly and held her face in her hand. None of this was jogging anybody's memory except of course Denise's, and she had fled the room. Jack's smile suddenly faded and he slid down in his chair and crossed his arms. It was obviously all right for his sister to act the fool but his girlfriend was a different matter. Jack placed his feet up on the chair in front of him and quieted down for the rest of the documentary.

Once Sharon and Holly had heard that Abbey and Ciara were in the room, they sat up attentively and listened to Denise's plan. "OK, girlies, here's what we're gonna do!"

Holly turned away from the screen and nudged Sharon. Holly couldn't remember doing or saying any of these things at all; she was beginning to think Declan had hired look-alike actors as a horrible practical joke. Sharon turned to face her with wide worried eyes and shrugged. Nope, she wasn't there that night either. The camera followed the three girls as they very suspiciously approached the gold curtain and loitered around like idiots. Sharon finally built up the courage to tap the giant on the shoulder, causing him to turn around and provide Denise with enough time to escape under the curtain. She got down on her hands and knees and stuck her head through to the VIP bar while her bum and legs stuck out from the other side of the curtain.

Holly kicked her in the bum to hurry her along.

"I can see them!" Denise hissed loudly. "Oh my God! They're speaking to that Hollywood actor guy!" She took her head back out from under the curtain and looked at Holly with excitement. Unfortunately, Sharon was running out of things to say to the giant bouncer and he turned his head just in time to catch Denise.

"No no no no no!" Denise said calmly again. "You don't understand! This is Princess Holly of Sweden!"

"Finland," Sharon corrected her.

"Sorry, Finland," Denise said, remaining on her knees. "I am bowing to her. Join me!"

Sharon quickly got on her knees and the two of them began to worship Holly's feet. Holly looked around awkwardly as everyone in the club began to stare, and she once again gave them the royal wave. Nobody seemed very impressed.

"Oh Holly!" her mother said, trying to catch her breath after laughing so hard.

The big burly bouncer turned his back and spoke into his walkie-talkie. "Boys, got a situation with the princess and the lady."

Denise looked at both the girls in panic and mouthed, "Hide!"

The girls jumped to their feet and fled. The camera searched through the crowds for the girls but couldn't find them.

From her seat in Club Diva, Holly groaned loudly and held her head in her hands as it finally clicked with her what was about to happen.

Nineteen

Paul and Mustache Man rushed upstairs to the club and met up at the gold curtain with the very big man. "What's going on?" Mustache Man asked him.

"Those girls you told me to keep my eye on tried to crawl through to the other side," the big man said seriously. You could tell by looking at him that his previous job involved killing people if they tried to crawl over to the other side. He was taking this breach of security very seriously.

"Where are they?" Mustache Man asked.

The big man cleared his throat and looked away. "They're hiding, boss."

Mustache Man rolled his eyes. "They're hiding?"

"Yes, boss."

"Where? In the club?"

"I think so, boss."

"You think so?"

"Well, they didn't pass us on our way in, so they must still be here," Paul piped up.

"OK," Mustache Man sighed. "Well, let's start looking then, get someone to keep an eye on the curtain."

The camera secretly followed the three bouncers as they patrolled the club looking behind couches, under tables, behind curtains; they even got someone to check the toilets. Holly's family laughed hysterically at the scene unfolding before their eyes.

There was a bit of commotion at the top of the club and the bouncers headed toward the noise to sort it out. A crowd was beginning to gather around and the two skinny dancers dressed in gold body paint had stopped dancing and were staring with horrified expressions at the bed. The camera panned across to the king-size bed that was tilted for display. Underneath the gold silk sheets there appeared to be three pigs fighting under a blanket. Sharon, Denise and Holly rolled around screaming at one another, trying to make themselves as flat as possible so they wouldn't be noticed. The crowd thickened, and soon enough the music was shut down. The three big lumps under the bed stopped squirming and suddenly froze, not knowing what was going on outside.

The bouncers counted to three and pulled the covers off the bed. Three very startled-looking girls appearing like deer caught in headlights stared back at them and lay there as flat as they could on their backs with their arms stiffly by their sides.

"*One* just had to get forty winks before *one* left," Holly said with her royal accent and the other girls burst out laughing.

"Come on, Princess, the fun's over," said Paul. The three men accompanied the girls outside, assuring them that they would never again be allowed back into the club.

"Can I just tell my friends that we're gone?" Sharon asked.

The men tutted and looked away.

"Excuse me? Am I talking to myself? I asked you if it was OK if I go in and tell my friends that we had to leave?"

"Look, stop playing around, girls," Mustache Man said angrily. "Your friends aren't in there. Now off you go, back to your beds."

"Excuse me," Sharon said angrily, "I have two friends in the VIP bar; one of them has pink hair and the other one . . ."

"Girls!" he raised his voice. "She does not want anyone bothering her. She is no more your friend than the man on the moon. Now clear off before you get yourselves into more trouble."

Everyone in the club howled with laughter.

The scene changed to "The Long Journey Home," and all the girls were in the taxi. Abbey sat like a dog with her head hanging out of the open window by order of the taxi driver. "You're not throwing up in my cab. You either stick your head out the window or you walk home." Abbey's face was almost purple and her teeth were chattering, but she wasn't going to walk all the way home. Ciara sat with her arms crossed and with a huff on her face, angry with the girls for forcing her to leave the club so early but more embarrassingly for blowing her cover as a famous rock singer. Sharon and Denise had fallen asleep with their heads resting on each other.

The camera turned around to focus on Holly, who was sitting in the passenger seat once again. But this time she wasn't talking the ear off the taxi driver; she rested her head on the back of the seat and stared straight ahead out into the dark night. Holly knew what she was thinking as she watched herself. Time to go home to that big empty house alone again.

"Happy Birthday, Holly," Abbey's tiny little voice trembled.

Holly turned around to smile at her and came face-to-face with the camera. "Are you *still* filming with that thing? Turn it off!" and she knocked the camera out of Declan's hand. The end.

As Daniel went to turn the lights up in the club, Holly slipped quickly away from the gang and escaped through the nearest door. She needed to collect her thoughts before everyone started talking about it. She found herself in a tiny storeroom surrounded by mops and buckets and empty kegs. What a stupid place to hide, she thought. She sat down on a keg and thought about what she had just seen. She was in shock. She felt confused and angry at Declan; he had told her that he was making a documentary about club life. She distinctly remembered him not mentioning anything about making a show of her and her friends. And he had literally made a show of them. If he had asked her politely if he could do it, that would be a different matter. Although she still wouldn't have agreed to do it.

But the last thing she wanted to do right now was to scream at Declan in front of everyone. Apart from the fact that the documentary had completely humiliated her, Declan had actually filmed it and edited it very well. If it had been anyone else but her on the TV, Holly would have thought it very deserving of the award. But it *was* her, so therefore it *didn't* deserve to win . . . Parts of it had been funny, she agreed, and she didn't mind so much the bits of her and her friends being so silly, it was more the sneaky shots of her unhappiness that bothered her.

Thick salty tears trickled down her face and she wrapped her arms around her body to comfort herself. She had seen on television how she truly felt. Lost and alone. She cried for Gerry, she cried for herself with big, thick, heaving sobs that hurt her ribs whenever she tried to catch her breath. She didn't want to be alone anymore, and she didn't want her family seeing the loneliness she tried so hard to hide from them. She just wanted Gerry back and didn't care about anything else. She didn't care if he came back and they fought every day, she didn't care if they were broke and had no house and no money. She just wanted him. She heard the door open behind her and felt big strong arms wrapping themselves around her frail body. She cried as though months of built-up anguish were all tumbling out at once.

"What's wrong with her? Didn't she like it?" she heard Declan ask worriedly.

"Just leave her be, son," her mum said softly, and the door was closed behind them again as Daniel stroked her hair and rocked her softly.

Finally after crying what felt like all the tears in the world, Holly stopped and let go of Daniel. "Sorry," she sniffed, drying her face with the sleeves of her top.

"There's no need to be sorry," he said, gently removing her hand from her face and handing her a tissue.

She sat in silence while trying to compose herself.

"If you're upset about the documentary, then there's no need," he said, sitting down on a crate of glasses opposite her.

"Yeah right," she said sarcastically, wiping her tears again.

"No really," he said honestly, "I thought it was really funny. You all looked like you were having a great time." He smiled at her.

"Pity that's not how I felt," she said sadly.

"Maybe that's not how you felt, but the camera doesn't pick up on feelings, Holly."

"You don't have to try to make me feel better." Holly was embarrassed at being consoled by a stranger.

"I'm not *trying* to make you feel better, I'm just saying it like it is. Nobody but you noticed whatever it is that's upsetting you. I didn't see anything, so why should anyone else?"

Holly felt mildly better. "Are you sure?"

"I'm sure I'm sure," he said, smiling. "Now you really have to stop hiding in all the rooms in my club, I might take it personally," he laughed.

"Are the girls OK?" Holly asked, hoping it was just her being stupid after all. There was loud laughter from outside.

"They're fine, as you can hear," he said, nodding toward the door. "Ciara's delighted everyone will think she's a star, Denise has finally come out of the toilet and Sharon just can't stop laughing. Although Jack's giving Abbey a hard time about throwing up on the way home."

Holly giggled.

"So you see, nobody even noticed what you saw."

"Thanks, Daniel." She took a deep breath and smiled at him.

"You ready to go face your public?" he asked.

"Think so." Holly stepped outside to the sounds of laughter. The lights were up and everyone was sitting around the table and happily sharing jokes and stories. Holly joined the table and sat beside her mum. Elizabeth wrapped her arm around her daughter and gave her a kiss on the cheek.

"Well, I thought it was great," announced Jack enthusiastically. "If only we could get Declan to go out with the girls all the time, then we'd know what they get up to, eh John?" He winked over at Sharon's husband.

"Well, I can assure you," Abbey spoke up, "that what you saw is not a regular girls' night out."

The boys weren't having any of it.

"So is it OK?" Declan asked Holly, afraid he had upset his sister.

Holly threw him a look.

"I thought you would like it, Hol," he said worriedly.

"I might have liked it if I had *known* what you were doing," she snapped back.

"But I wanted it to be a surprise," he said genuinely.

"I hate surprises," she said, rubbing her stinging eyes.

"Let that be a lesson to you, son," Frank warned his son. "You shouldn't go around filming people without them knowing what you're doing. It's illegal."

"I bet they didn't know that when they chose him for the award," Elizabeth agreed.

"You're not gonna tell them, are you, Holly?" Declan asked worriedly.

"Not if you're nice to me for the next few months," Holly said, slyly twisting her hair around her finger. Declan made a face; he was stuck and he knew it. "Yeah whatever," he said, waving her away.

"To tell you the truth, Holly, I have to admit I thought it was quite funny," giggled Sharon. "You and your Operation Gold Curtain," she thumped Denise playfully on the leg.

Denise rolled her eyes. "Oh, I can tell you all something—I am *never* drinking again."

Everyone laughed and Tom wrapped his arm around her shoulders.

"What?" she said innocently. "I really mean it."

"Speaking of drink, would anyone like one?" Daniel stood up from his chair. "Jack?"

"Yeah, a Budweiser, thanks."

"Abbey?"

"Em . . . a white wine, please," she said politely.

"Frank?"

"A Guinness, thanks, Daniel."

"I'll have the same," said John.

"Sharon?"

"Just a Coke, please. Holly, you want the same?" she said, looking at her friend. Holly nodded.

"Tom?"

"JD and Coke, please, Dan."

"Me too," said Declan.

"Denise?" Daniel tried to hide his smile.

"Em . . . I'll have a . . . gin and tonic, please."

"Ha!" everyone jeered her.

"What?" She shrugged her shoulders as though she didn't care. "One drink is hardly going to kill me . . ."

Holly was standing over the sink with her sleeves rolled up to her elbows scrubbing the pots when she heard the familiar voice.

"Hi, honey."

She looked up and saw him standing at the open patio doors. "Hello, you," she smiled.

"Miss me?"

"Of course."

"Have you found that new husband yet?"

"Of course I have, he's upstairs in bed asleep," she laughed, drying her hands.

Gerry shook his head and tutted, "Shall I go up and suffocate him for sleeping in our bed?"

"Ah, give him another hour or so," she joked, looking at her watch, "he needs his rest."

He looked happy, she thought, fresh-faced and still as beautiful as she remembered. He was wearing her favorite blue top, which she had bought him one Christmas. He stared at her from under his long eyelashes with his big brown puppy eyes.

"Are you coming in?" she asked, smiling.

"No, I just popped by to see how you are. Everything going OK?" He leaned against the door ledge with his hands in his pockets.

"So, so," she said, weighing her hands in the air. "Could be better."

"I hear you're a TV star now," he grinned.

"A very reluctant one," she laughed.

"You'll have men falling all around you," he assured her.

"Falling all around me is right," she agreed. "The problem is they keep missing the target," she said, pointing to herself. He laughed. "I miss you, Gerry."

"I haven't gone far," he said softly.

"You leaving me again?"

"For the time being."

"See you soon," she smiled.

He winked at her and disappeared.

Holly woke up with a smile on her face and felt like she had slept for days.

"Good morning, Gerry," she said, happily staring up at the ceiling.

The phone rang beside her. "Hello?"

"Oh my God, Holly, just take a look at the weekend papers," Sharon said in a panic.

Twenty

HOLLY IMMEDIATELY LEAPT OUT OF bed, threw on a tracksuit and drove to her nearest newsagent. She reached the newspaper stand and began to leaf through the pages in search of what Sharon had been raving about. The man behind the counter coughed loudly and Holly looked up at him. "This is not a library, young lady, you'll have to buy that," he said, nodding at the newspaper in her hand.

"I know that," she said, irritated by his rudeness. Honestly, how on earth was anyone supposed to know which paper they wanted to buy if they didn't even know which paper had what they were looking for? She ended up picking up every single newspaper from the stand and slammed them down on the counter, smiling sweetly at him.

The man looked startled and started to scan them into the register one by one. A queue began to form behind her.

She stared longingly at the selection of chocolate bars displayed in front of her and looked around to see if anyone was looking at her. *Everyone* was staring. She quickly turned back to face the counter. Finally her arm jumped up and grabbed the two king-size chocolate bars nearest to her on the shelf from the bottom of the pile. One by one the rest of the chocolate began to slide onto the floor. The teenager behind her snorted and looked away laughing as Holly bent down with a red face and began to pick them up. So many had fallen she had to make several trips up and down. The shop was silent, apart from a few coughs from the impatient queue behind her. She sneakily added another few packets of sweets to her pile. "For the kids," she said loudly to the newsagent, hoping everyone behind her would also hear.

He just grunted at her and continued scanning the items. Then she remembered she needed to get milk, so she rushed from the queue to the end of the shop to retrieve a pint of milk from the fridge. A few women tutted loudly as she made her way back to the top of the queue, where she added the milk to her pile. The newsagent stopped scanning to stare at her; she stared back blankly at him.

"Mark," he yelled.

A spotty young teenager appeared from one of the shopping aisles with a pricing gun in his hand. "Yeah?" he said grumpily.

"Open the other till, will ya, son, we might be here for a while." He glared at her.

Holly made a face at him.

Mark dragged his body over to the second till, all the time staring at Holly. What? she thought defensively; don't blame me for having to do your job. He took over the till and the entire queue behind her rushed over to the other side. Satisfied that no one was staring at her anymore, she grabbed a few packets of crisps from below the counter and added them to her purchases. "Birthday party," she mumbled.

In the queue beside her, the teenager asked for a packet of cigarettes quietly.

"Got any ID?" Mark asked loudly.

The teenager looked around in embarrassment with a red face. Holly snorted at him and looked away.

"Anything else?" the newsagent asked sarcastically.

"No thank you, that will be all," she said through gritted teeth. She paid her money and fumbled with her purse, trying to put all the change back in.

"Next," the newsagent nodded to the customer behind her.

"Hiya, can I have twenty Benson and—"

"Excuse me," Holly interrupted the man. "Could I have a bag, please," she said politely, staring at the huge pile of groceries in front of her.

"Just a moment," he said rudely, "I'll deal with this gentleman first. Yes sir, cigarettes is it?"

"Please," the customer said, looking at Holly apologetically.

"Now," he said, returning to her, "what can I get you?"

"A bag." She clenched her jaw.

"That'll be twenty cents please."

Holly sighed loudly and reached into her bag, searching through the mess to find her money again. Another queue formed behind her.

"Mark, take over the till again, will you?" he said snidely.

Holly took the coin out of her purse and slammed it down on the counter and began to fill the bag with her items.

"Next," he said again, looking over her shoulder. Holly felt under pressure to get out of the way and began stuffing the bag full in panic.

"I'll wait till the lady here is ready," the customer said politely.

Holly smiled at him appreciatively and turned to leave the shop. She walked away grumbling to herself till Mark, the boy behind the counter, startled her by yelling, "Hey, I know you! You're the girl from the telly!"

Holly swirled around in surprise and the plastic handle broke from the weight of all the newspapers. Everything fell onto the floor and her chocolate, sweets and crisps went rolling in all directions.

The friendly customer got down on his knees to help her gather her belongings while the rest of the shop watched in amusement and wondered who the girl from the telly was.

"It is you, isn't it?" the boy laughed.

Holly smiled up weakly at him from the floor.

"I knew it!" He clapped his hands together with excitement. "You're cool!" Yeah, she really felt cool, on her knees on the floor of a shop searching for bars of chocolate. Holly's face went red and she nervously cleared her throat. "Em . . . excuse me, could I have another bag, please?"

"Yeah, that'll be—"

"There you go," the friendly customer interrupted him, placing a twenty-cent coin down on the counter. The newsagent looked perplexed and continued serving the customers.

"I'm Rob," the man said, helping her put all her chocolate back into the bag, and held his hand out.

"I'm Holly," she said, a little embarrassed by his overfriendliness as she took his hand. "And I'm a chocoholic."

He laughed.

"Thanks for the help," she said gratefully, getting to her feet.

"No problem." He held the door open for her. He was good-looking, she thought, a few years older than her, and had the oddest colored eyes, a kind of a gray-green color. She squinted at him and took a closer look.

He cleared his throat.

She blushed, suddenly realizing she had been staring at him like a fool. She walked out to her car and placed the bulging bag in the backseat. Rob followed her over. Her heart did a little flip.

"Hi again," he said. "Em . . . I was wondering if you would like to go for a drink?" Then he laughed, glancing at his watch. "Actually, it's a bit too early for that, how about a coffee?"

He was a very confident man and he rested himself coolly against the car opposite Holly, his hands sat in the pockets of his jeans with his thumbs resting outside, and those weird eyes just stared back at her. However, he didn't make her feel uncomfortable; in fact, he was acting very relaxed, as though asking a stranger out for coffee was the most natural thing in the world. Was this what people did these days?

"Em . . ." Holly thought about it. What harm could it do to go for a coffee with a man who had been so polite to her? The fact that he was absolutely gorgeous also helped. But regardless of his beauty, Holly really craved company and he seemed like a nice, decent man to talk to. Sharon and Denise were at work and Holly couldn't keep calling over to her mother's house, Elizabeth had work to do too. Holly really needed to start meeting new people. Many of Gerry and Holly's other friends had been Gerry's friends from work and from various other walks of life, but once he had died all those "friends" of theirs hadn't been much of a familiar feature around her house. At least she knew who her true friends were.

She was just about to say yes to Rob when he glanced down at her hand and his smile faded. "Oh sorry, I didn't realize . . ." He backed away from her awkwardly, as if she had some kind of disease. "I have to rush off anyway." He smiled quickly at her and took off down the road.

Holly stared after him, confused. Had she said something wrong? Had she taken too long to decide? Had she broken one of the silent rules of this new meeting-people game? She looked down at the hand that had caused him to run away from her and saw her wedding ring sparkle back at her. She sighed loudly and rubbed her face tiredly.

Just then the teenager from the shop walked by with a gang of friends and a cigarette in his mouth and snorted at her.

She just couldn't win.

Holly slammed the door of her car and looked around. She wasn't in the mood to go home, she was sick of staring at the walls all day every day and talking to herself. It was still only ten o'clock in the morning and it was beautifully sunny and warm outside. Across the road her local café, the Greasy Spoon, was setting up tables and chairs outside. Her stomach grumbled. A nice big Irish breakfast was exactly what she needed. She took her sunglasses from the glove compartment of her car, carried her newspapers with both hands and wandered across the road. A plump lady was cleaning the tables. Her hair was tied back tightly in a large bun and a bright red-and-white checked apron covered her flowery dress. Holly felt like she had walked straight into a country kitchen.

"Been a while since these tables have seen sunlight," she said happily to Holly as she approached the café.

"Yeah, it's a beautiful day, isn't it?" Holly said, and the two of them stared up at the clear blue sky. It was funny how good weather in Ireland always seemed to be the conversation of the day with everyone. It was such a rare sight that everyone felt blessed when it finally arrived.

"You want to sit out here, love?"

"Yes I do, might as well make the most out of it, it'll probably be gone in an hour," Holly laughed, taking a seat.

"You need to think positively, love." She busied herself around Holly. "Right, I'll get you the menu," she said, turning to leave.

"No, it's OK," Holly called after her, "I know what I want. I'll have the Irish breakfast."

"No problem, love." She smiled, and her eyes widened when she saw the pile of newspapers on the table. "You thinking of starting your own newsagents?" she chuckled.

Holly looked down at the pile and laughed at the sight of the *Arab Leader* lying on the top. She had grabbed every single paper and hadn't even thought to check what they were. She doubted very much the *Arab Leader* contained any articles about the documentary.

"Well, to tell you the truth, love," the woman said, cleaning the table beside her, "you'd be doing us all a favor if you put that miserable ol' bastard out of business." She glared across the road to the newsagent. Holly laughed as the woman waddled back into the café.

Holly just sat there for a while watching the world go by. She loved catching snippets of people's conversations as they walked by; it gave her a sneaky peak into the lives of others. She loved to guess what people did for a living, where they were headed to as they rushed by, where they lived, if they were married or single . . . Sharon and Holly loved going for coffee in Bewley's café overlooking Grafton Street, as it was the best place for people-spotting.

They would create little scenarios in their heads to pass the time, but Holly seemed to be doing this very regularly these days. Just another demonstration of how her mind was caught in other people's lives instead of focusing on her own. For example, the new story she was creating involved the man walking down the path holding hands with his wife. Holly decided that he was secretly gay and the man headed toward them was his lover. Holly watched their faces as they approached each other, wondering if they would make eye contact. They went one better than that and Holly tried not to giggle as the three of them stopped just in front of her table.

"Excuse me? Have you got the time?" the lover asked the secretly gay man and his wife.

"Yes, it's a quarter past ten," the secretly gay man answered him, looking at his watch.

"Thanks a lot," the lover said, touching his arm, and walked on.

Now it was as clear as day to Holly that that had been secret code for a rendezvous later. She continued her people-spotting for a little while longer until she eventually got bored and decided to live her own life for a change.

Holly flicked through the pages of the tabloids and came to a small article in the review section that caught her eye.

"GIRLS AND THE CITY" A HIT IN THE RATINGS
by Tracey Coleman

For any of you unfortunate people who missed out on the outrageously funny TV documentary "Girls and the City" last Wednesday, do not despair, because it will be back on our screens soon.

The hilarious fly-on-the-wall documentary, directed by Irishman Declan Kennedy, follows five Dublin girls out for a night on the town. They lift the lid on the mysterious world of celebrity life in trendy club Boudoir and provide us with thirty minutes of stomach-aching laughter.

The show proved to be a success when first aired on Channel 4 last Wednesday, the latest TAM ratings revealing 4 million people tuned in in the UK. The show is to be repeated again Sunday night at 11 p.m. on Channel 4. This is must-see TV, so don't miss it!

Holly tried to keep her cool as she read through the article. It was obviously great news for Declan but disastrous for her. Having that documentary aired once was bad enough, never mind a second time. She really needed to have a serious talk with Declan about this. She had let him off lightly the other night because he had been so excited and she didn't want to make a scene, but at this stage she had enough problems on her plate without having to worry about this too.

She flicked through the rest of the papers and saw what it was Sharon was ranting about. Every single tabloid had an article about the documentary and one had even printed a photograph of Denise, Sharon and Holly from a few years ago. How they got their hands on it she did not know. Thank God the broadsheets contained some real news, or Holly would have really worried about the world. However, she wasn't too happy with the use of the words "mad girls," "drunken girls," and the explanation from one of the papers of how they were "well up for it." What did that even mean?

Holly's food finally arrived and she stared at it in shock, wondering how on earth she was going to get through it all. "That'll fatten you up, love," the plump lady said, placing it on the table. "You need a bit of meat on your bones, you're far too skinny," she warned her, waddling off again. Holly felt pleased at the compliment.

The plate was piled high with sausages, bacon, eggs, hash browns, black and white pudding, baked beans, fried potatoes, mushrooms, tomatoes and five slices of toast. Holly looked around her with embarrassment, hoping no one would think she was a complete pig. She saw that annoying teenager heading toward her with his gang of friends again and she picked up her plate and ran inside. She hadn't had much of an appetite lately, but she finally felt ready to eat, and she wasn't going to let some stupid spotty teenager ruin it for her.

Holly must have stayed in the Greasy Spoon much longer than she thought, because by the time she reached her parents' house in Portmarnock it was almost two o'clock. Against Holly's prediction the weather hadn't gotten worse, and the sun was still sitting high in the cloudless blue sky. Holly looked across at the crowded beach in front of the house, and it was difficult to tell where the sky ended and the sea began. Busloads of people were continuously being dropped off across the road, and there was a lovely smell of suntan lotion in the air. There were gangs of teenagers hanging around the grassy area with CD players blaring out the latest tunes. The sound and the smell brought back every happy memory from when Holly was a child.

Holly rang the doorbell for the fourth time and still no one answered. She knew somebody had to be home because the bedroom windows were wide open upstairs. Her mum and dad would never leave them wide open if they weren't home, especially with throngs of strangers wandering around the area. She walked across the grass and pressed her face against the living room window to see if there was any sign of life. She was just about to give up and wander over to the beach when she heard the screaming match between Declan and Ciara.

"CIARA, GET THE DAMN DOOR!"

"NO, I SAID! I . . . AM . . . BUSY!" she yelled back.

"WELL, SO AM I!"

Holly rang the doorbell again just to add fuel to the fire.

"DECLAN!" Ouch, that was a bloodcurdling scream.

"GET IT YOURSELF, YOU LAZY COW!"

"HA! *I'M* LAZY?!"

Holly took out her mobile phone and rang the house.

"CIARA, ANSWER THE PHONE!"

"NO!"

"Oh, for Christ's sake," Holly snapped loudly and hung up the phone. She dialed Declan's mobile number.

"Yeah?"

"Declan, open the goddamn fucking door now or I'll kick it in," Holly growled.

"Oh, sorry Holly, I thought Ciara had answered it," he lied.

He opened the door in his boxer shorts and Holly stormed in. "Jesus Christ! I hope you two don't carry on like that *every* time the doorbell rings."

He shrugged his shoulders noncommittally. "Mum and Dad are out," he said lazily and headed up the stairs.

"Hey, where are you going?"

"Back to bed."

"No you are not," Holly said calmly. "You are going to sit down here with me," she said, patting the couch, "and we're gonna have a nice long chat about 'Girls and the City.'"

"No," Declan moaned. "Do we have to do this now? I'm really, really tired." He rubbed his eyes with his fists.

Holly had no sympathy for him. "Declan, it's two o'clock in the afternoon, how can you still be tired?"

"Because I only got home a few hours ago," he said cheekily, winking at her. Now she definitely had no sympathy for him, she was just plain jealous.

"Sit!" she said, ordering him onto the couch.

He moaned again and dragged his weary body over to the couch, where he collapsed and stretched out along the entire thing, leaving no room for Holly. She rolled her eyes and dragged her dad's armchair closer to Declan.

"I feel like I'm with a shrink," he laughed, crossing his arms behind his head and staring up at her from the couch.

"Good, because I'm really going to pick your brains."

Declan whinged again, "Oh Holly, do we have to? We just talked about this the other night."

"Did you honestly think that was all I was going to say? 'Oh, I'm sorry, Declan, but I didn't like the way you publicly humiliated me and my friends, see you next week'?"

"Obviously not."

"Come on, Declan," she said, softening her tone, "I just want to understand why you thought it would be such a great idea not to tell me you were filming me and my friends."

"You *knew* I was filming," he said defensively.

"For a documentary about *club life!*" Holly raised her voice with frustration at her younger brother.

"And it *was* about club life," Declan laughed.

"Oh, you think you're so bloody clever," she snapped at him, and he stopped laughing. She counted to ten and breathed slowly to prevent herself from attacking him.

"Come on, Declan," she said quietly. "Do you not think that I am going through enough right now without having to worry about this as well? And without even asking me? I cannot for the life of me understand why you would do it!"

Declan sat up on the couch and became serious for a change. "I know, Holly, I know you've been through hell, but I thought this would cheer you up. I wasn't lying when I said I was going to film the club because that's what I had planned on doing. But when I brought it back to college to begin the edit, everyone thought that it was just so funny that I couldn't *not* show it to people."

"Yeah, but you put it on TV, Declan."

"I didn't know that was the prize, honestly," he said, wide-eyed. "Nobody knew, not even my lecturers! How could I say no to it when I won?"

Holly gave up and ran her fingers through her hair.

"I honestly thought you would like it," he smiled. "I even checked with Ciara and *even she* said you'd like it. I'm sorry if I upset you," he eventually mumbled.

Holly continued nodding her head through his explanation, realizing he genuinely had had good intentions, however misguided. Suddenly she stopped. What had he just said? She sat up alert in her seat. "Declan, did you just say that Ciara knew about the tape?"

Declan froze in his seat and tried to think of a way to back himself out of it. Coming up with nothing, he threw himself back onto the couch and covered his head with a cushion, knowing he had just started World War III.

"Oh Holly, don't say anything to her, she'll kill me!" came his muffled reply.

Holly bounded out of her seat and stormed upstairs, thumping her feet on every step to show Ciara she was *really* mad. She yelled threats at Ciara all the way up and pounded on her bedroom door.

"Don't come in!" yelled Ciara from inside.

"You are in so much trouble, Ciara!" Holly screamed. She opened the door and burst her way in, putting on her most terrifying face.

"I told you not to come in!" wailed Ciara. Holly was about to start screaming all sorts of insulting things at her sister but stopped herself when she saw Ciara sitting on the floor with what looked like a photo album on her lap and tears streaming down her face.

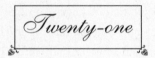

Twenty-one

"OH CIARA, WHAT'S WRONG?" HOLLY said soothingly to her younger sister. Holly was worried; she couldn't remember the last time she had seen her cry, in fact, she didn't know Ciara even knew *how* to cry. Whatever had reduced her strong sister to tears must be something serious.

"Nothing's wrong," Ciara said, snapping the photo album shut and sliding it under her bed. She seemed embarrassed to be caught crying, and she wiped her face roughly, trying to look like she didn't care.

Downstairs on the couch, Declan peeped his head out from under the cushion. It was eerily quiet up there; he hoped they hadn't done anything stupid to each other. He tiptoed upstairs and listened outside the door.

"Something *is* wrong," Holly said, crossing the room to join her sister on the floor. She wasn't sure how to deal with Ciara like this. This was a complete role reversal; ever since they'd been kids it was always Holly who had done all the crying. Ciara was supposed to be the tough one.

"I'm fine," Ciara snapped.

"OK," Holly said, looking around, "but if there's something on your mind that's upsetting you, you know you can talk to me about it, don't you?"

Ciara refused to look at her and just nodded her head. Holly began to stand up to leave her sister in peace when all of a sudden Ciara burst into tears. Holly quickly sat back down and wrapped her arms protectively around her younger sister. Holly stroked Ciara's silky pink hair while her sister cried quietly.

"Do you want to tell me what's wrong?" she asked softly.

Ciara gurgled some sort of reply and sat up to slide the photo album back out from under the bed. She opened it with trembling hands and flicked a few pages.

"Him," she said sadly, pointing to a photograph of her and some guy Holly didn't recognize. Holly barely recognized her sister. She looked so different and so much younger. The photograph was taken on a beautiful sunny day on a boat overlooking the Sydney Opera House. Ciara was sitting happily on the man's knee with her arms wrapped around his neck, and he was staring at her with a huge smile on his face. Holly couldn't get over how Ciara looked. She had blond hair, which Holly had never seen on her sister before, and a great big smile on her face. Her features looked much softer and she didn't look like she was going to bite someone's head off for a change.

"Is that your boyfriend?" Holly asked carefully.

"Was," Ciara sniffed, and a tear landed on the page.

"Is that why you came home?" she asked softly, wiping a tear from her sister's face.

Ciara nodded.

"Do you want to tell me what happened?"

Ciara gasped for breath. "We had a fight."

"Did he . . ." Holly chose her words carefully. "He didn't hurt you or anything, did he?"

Ciara shook her head. "No," she spluttered, "it was just over something really stupid and I said I was leaving and he said he was glad . . ." She trailed off as she started sobbing again.

Holly held her in her arms and waited till Ciara was ready to talk again.

"He didn't even come to the airport to say good-bye to me."

Holly rubbed Ciara's back soothingly as if she were a baby who had just drunk her bottle. She hoped Ciara wouldn't throw up on her. "Has he called you since?"

"No, and I've been home for two months, Holly," she wailed. She looked up at her older sister with such sad eyes Holly almost felt like crying. She didn't like the sound of this guy at all for hurting her sister. Holly smiled at her encouragingly. "Then do you think that maybe he's not the right kind of person for you?"

Ciara started crying again. "But I love Mathew, Holly, and it was only a stupid fight. I only booked the flight because I was angry, I didn't think he would let me go . . ." She stared for a long time at the photograph.

Ciara's bedroom windows were wide open and Holly listened to the familiar sound of the waves and the laughter coming from the beach. Holly and Ciara had shared this room while they grew up, and a weird sense of comfort embraced her as she smelled the same smells and listened to the familiar noises.

Ciara began to calm down beside her. "Sorry, Hol."

"Hey, you don't need to be sorry at all," she said, squeezing her hand. "You should have told me all this when you came home instead of keeping it all inside."

"But this is only minor compared to what's happened to you. I feel stupid even crying about it." She wiped her tears, angry with herself.

Holly was shocked. "Ciara, this *is* a big deal. Losing someone you love is always hard, no matter if they're alive or . . ." She couldn't finish the sentence. "Of course you can tell me anything."

"It's just that you've been so brave, Holly, I don't know how you do it. And here I am crying over a stupid boyfriend I only went out with for a few months."

"Me? Brave?" Holly laughed. "I wish."

"Yes you are," Ciara insisted. "Everyone says so. You've been so strong through everything. If I were you, I'd be lying in a ditch somewhere."

"Don't go giving me ideas, Ciara." Holly smiled at her, wondering who on earth had called her brave.

"You're OK, though, aren't you?" Ciara said worriedly, studying her face.

Holly looked down at her hands and slid her wedding ring up and down her finger. She thought about that question for a while and the two girls became lost in their own thoughts. Ciara, suddenly calmer than Holly had ever seen her, sat by her side patiently awaiting Holly's reply.

"Am I OK?" Holly repeated the question to herself. She looked ahead at the collection of teddy bears and dolls that their parents had refused to throw out. "I'm lots of things, Ciara," Holly explained, continuing to roll her ring around on her finger. "I'm lonely, I'm tired, I'm sad, I'm happy, I'm lucky, I'm unlucky; I'm a million different things every day of the week. But I suppose OK is one of them."

She looked to her sister and smiled sadly.

"And you're brave," Ciara assured her. "And calm and in control. And organized."

Holly shook her head slowly. "No Ciara, I'm not brave. You're the brave one. You were always the brave one. As for being in control, I don't know what I'm doing from one day to the next."

Ciara's forehead creased and she shook her head wildly. "No, I am far from being brave, Holly."

"Yes you are," Holly insisted. "All those things that you do, like jumping out of airplanes and snowboarding off cliffs . . ." Holly trailed off as she tried to think of more crazy things her little sister did.

Ciara shook her head in protest. "Oh no, my dear sister. That's not brave, that's *foolish*. Anybody can bungee jump off a bridge. You could do it." Ciara nudged her.

Holly's eyes widened, terrified at the thought, and she shook her head.

Ciara's voice softened. "Oh, you would *if you had to*, Holly. Trust me, there's nothing brave about it."

Holly looked at her sister and matched her tone. "Yes, and if your husband died you would cope *if you had to*. There's nothing brave about it. There's no choice involved."

Ciara and Holly stared at each other, aware of the other's battle.

Ciara was the first to speak. "Well, I guess you and I are more alike than we thought." She smiled at her big sister and Holly wrapped her arms around her small frame and hugged her tightly. "Well, who would have thought?"

Holly thought her sister looked like such a child with her big innocent blue eyes. She felt like they were both children again, sitting on the floor where they used to play together during their childhood and where they would gossip when they were teenagers.

They sat in silence listening to the sounds outside.

"Was there something you were going to scream at me about earlier on?" Ciara asked quietly with an even more childish voice. Holly had to laugh at her sister for trying to take advantage.

"No, forget about it, it was nothing," Holly replied, staring out at the blue sky. From outside the door, Declan wiped his brow and breathed a sigh of relief; he was in the clear. He tiptoed silently back into his bedroom and hopped back into bed. Whoever this Mathew was, he owed him big-time. His phone beeped, signaling a message, and he frowned as he read the message: Who the hell was Sandra? Then a grin crept across his face as he remembered the night before.

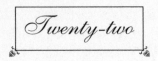

Twenty-two

I**T WAS EIGHT O'CLOCK WHEN** Holly finally drove up her driveway, and it was still bright. She smiled, the world never felt quite so depressing when it was bright. She had spent the day with Ciara chatting about her adventures in Australia. Ciara had changed her mind at least twenty times in the space of a few hours about whether or not she should call Mathew in Australia. By the time Holly left, Ciara was adamant she would never speak to him again, which probably meant she had already called him by now.

She walked up the path to the front door and stared at the garden curiously. Was it her imagination or did it look a little tidier? It was still a complete mess with weeds and overgrown shrubs sprouting up everywhere, but something about it looked different.

The sound of a lawnmower started and Holly spun around to

face her neighbor, who was out working in his garden. She waved over to thank him, presuming it was he who had helped her, and he held his hand up in response.

It had always been Gerry's job to do the garden. He wasn't necessarily a keen gardener, it was just that Holly was an incredibly unkeen gardener, so somebody had to do the dirty work. It had been agreed between them that there was no way in the world Holly was going to waste her day off toiling in the sand. As a result, their garden was simple; just a small patch of grass surrounded by a few shrubs and flowers. As Gerry knew very little about gardening, he often planted flowers during the wrong season or put them in the wrong place; they just ended up dying. But even their patch of grass and few shrubs now looked like nothing more than an overgrown field. When Gerry died, the garden had died along with him.

This thought now reminded Holly of the orchid in her house. She rushed inside and filled a jug with water and poured it over the extremely thirsty-looking plant. It didn't look very healthy at all and she promised herself not to let it die under her care. She threw a chicken curry into the microwave and sat down to wait at the kitchen table. Outside on the road she could still hear the kids playing happily. She always used to love when the bright evenings came; Mum and Dad would let them all play outside longer, which meant she wouldn't have to go to bed till later than usual, and that had always been a treat for them all. Holly thought back over her day and decided it had been a good one, apart from one isolated incident . . .

She looked down at the rings on her wedding finger and she immediately felt guilty. When that man had walked away from her, Holly had felt so awful. He had given her that look as if she were about to initiate an affair when that was the last thing in the world she would ever do. She felt guilty for even *considering* accepting his invitation to go for a coffee.

If Holly had left her husband because she absolutely couldn't stand him anymore, she could understand being able to eventually become attracted to someone else. But her husband had died when they were both still very much in love, and she couldn't just fall out of love all of a sudden solely because he wasn't around anymore. She still *felt* married, and going for a coffee would have seemed like she was betraying her husband. The very thought disgusted her. Her heart, soul and mind still belonged with Gerry.

Holly continued to twist her rings around on her finger. At what point should she take her wedding ring off? Gerry was gone almost five months now, so when was the appropriate time to remove her ring and tell herself she wasn't married anymore? Where was the rulebook for widows that explained when exactly the ring should be taken off? And when it finally did come off, where would she put it, where *should* she put it? In the bin? Beside her bed so she could be reminded of him every single day? She plagued herself with question after question. No, she wasn't quite ready to give up her Gerry yet; as far as she was concerned, he was still living.

The microwave beeped as her dinner was ready. She took the dish out and threw it straight into the bin. She had lost her appetite.

Later that night Denise rang her in a tizzy. "Switch Dublin FM on quick!" Holly raced to the radio and flicked the switch. "I'm Tom O'Connor and you're listening to Dublin FM. If you've just joined us, we are talking about bouncers. In light of the amount of persuasion it took the 'Girls and the City' girls to blag their way in to the club Boudoir, we wanna know what your thoughts on bouncers are. Do you like them? Do you not? Do you agree or understand why they are the way they are? Or are they too strict? The number to call is . . ."

Holly picked the phone back up, forgetting Denise had still been on the other end.

"Well?" Denise said, giggling.

"What the hell have we started, Denise?"

"Oh I know," she giggled again. It was obvious she was loving every minute of it. "Did you see the papers today?"

"Yeah, it's all a bit silly, really. I agree it was a good documentary, but the stuff they were writing was just stupid," Holly said.

"Oh honey, I love it! And I love it even more because I'm in it!" she laughed.

"I bet you do," Holly responded.

They both remained quiet while they listened to the radio. Some guy was giving out about bouncers and Tom was trying to calm him down.

"Oh, listen to my baby," Denise said. "Doesn't he sound so sexy?"

"Em . . . yeah," Holly mumbled. "I take it you two are still together?"

"Of course." Denise sounded insulted by the question. "Why wouldn't we be?"

"Well, it's been a while now, Denise, that's all." Holly quickly tried to explain so she wouldn't hurt her friend's feelings. "And you always said you couldn't be with a man for over a week! You always talk about how much you hate being tied down to one person."

"Yes, well, I said I *couldn't* be with a man for over a period of a week, but I never said I *wouldn't*. Tom is different, Holly," Denise said breathily.

Holly was surprised to hear this coming from Denise, the girl who wanted to remain single for the rest of her life. "Oh, so what's so different with Tom then?" Holly rested the phone between her ear and her shoulder and settled down in the chair to examine her nails.

"Oh, there's just this *connection* between us. It's like he's my soul mate. He's so thoughtful, always surprising me with little gifts and taking me out for dinner and spoiling me. He makes me laugh *all the time,* and I just love being with him. I haven't gotten sick of him like all the other guys. *Plus* he's good-looking."

Holly stifled a yawn, Denise tended to say this after the first week of going out with all her new boyfriends and then she would quickly change her mind. But then again, perhaps Denise meant what she said this time; after all, they had been together for over several weeks now. "I'm very happy for you," Holly added genuinely.

The two girls began listening to a bouncer speaking on the radio with Tom.

"Well, first of all I just want to tell you that for the past few nights we have had I don't know how many princesses and ladies queuing up at our door. Since that bloody program was aired people seem to think we're going to let them in if they're royalty! And I just want to say, girls, it's not going to work again, so don't bother!"

Tom kept laughing and tried to hold himself together. Holly flicked the switch off on the radio.

"Denise," Holly said seriously, "the world is going mad."

. . .

The next day Holly dragged herself out of bed to go for a stroll in the park. She needed to start doing some exercise before she turned into a complete slob, and she also needed to start thinking about job-hunting. Everywhere she went she tried to picture herself working in that environment. She had definitely ruled out clothes stores (the possibility of having a boss like Denise had talked her out of that one), restaurants, hotels and pubs, and she certainly didn't want another nine-to-five office job, which left . . . nothing. Holly decided she wanted to be like the woman in the film she saw the night before; she wanted to work in the FBI so she could run around solving crimes and interrogating people and then eventually fall in love with her partner, whom she had hated when they first met. However, seeing as though she neither lived in America nor had any police training, the chances of that happening didn't seem too hopeful. Maybe there was a circus she could join somewhere . . .

She sat down on a park bench opposite the playground and listened to the children's screams of delight. She wished she could go in and play on the slide and be pushed on the swings instead of sitting here and watching. Why did people have to grow up? Holly realized she had been dreaming of going back to her youth all weekend.

She wanted to be irresponsible, she wanted to be looked after, to be told that she didn't have to worry about a thing and that someone else would take care of everything. How easy life would be without having grown-up problems to worry about. And then she could grow up all over again and meet Gerry all over again and force him to go to the doctor months earlier and then she would be sitting beside Gerry here on the bench watching their children playing. What if, what if, what if . . .

She thought about the stinging remark Richard had made about never having to bother with all that children nonsense. It angered her just thinking about it. She wished so much that she could be worrying about all that children nonsense right now. She wished she could have a little Gerry running around the playground while she shouted at him to be careful and do other mummy things like spit on a tissue and wipe his pudgy little dirty face.

Holly and Gerry had just started talking about having children a few months before he was diagnosed. They had been so excited about it and used to lie in bed for hours trying to decide names and create scenarios in their heads of what it would be like to be parents. Holly smiled at the thought of Gerry being a father; he would have been terrific. She could imagine him being incredibly patient while helping them with their homework at the kitchen table. She could imagine him being overprotective if his daughter ever brought a boy home. Imagine if, imagine if, imagine if . . . Holly needed to stop living her life in her head, remembering old memories and dreaming impossible dreams. It would never get her anywhere.

Well, think of the devil, Holly thought to herself, seeing Richard leaving the playground with Emily and Timmy. He looked so relaxed, she thought, watching him in surprise as he chased the children around the park. They looked like they were having fun, not a very familiar sight. She sat up on the bench and zipped up her extra layer of thick skin in preparation for their conversation.

"Hello, Holly!" Richard said happily, spotting her and walking across the grass to her.

"Hello!" Holly said, greeting the kids as they ran over to her and gave her a big hug. It made a nice change. "You're far from home," she said to Richard. "What brings you all the way over here?"

"I brought the children to see Grandma and Granddad, didn't I?" he said, ruffling Timmy's head.

"*And* we had McDonald's," Timmy said excitedly and Emily cheered.

"Oh yummy!" Holly said, licking her lips. "You lucky things. Isn't your daddy the best?" she said, laughing. Richard looked pleased.

"Junk food?" Holly questioned her brother.

"Ah." He waved his hand dismissively and sat down beside her. "Everything in moderation, isn't that right, Emily?"

Five-year-old Emily nodded her head as though she had completely understood her father. Her big green eyes were wide and innocent and her nodding head was sending her strawberry blond ringlets bouncing. She was eerily like her mother and Holly had to look away. Then she felt guilty and looked back and smiled . . . then had to look away again. There was something about those eyes and that hair that scared her.

"Well, one McDonald's meal isn't going to kill them," Holly agreed with her brother.

Timmy grabbed at his throat and pretended to choke. His face went red as he made gagging noises and he collapsed on the grass and lay very still. Richard and Holly laughed. Emily looked like she was going to cry.

"Oh dear," Richard joked. "Looks like we were wrong, Holly, the McDonald's did kill Timmy."

Holly looked at her brother in shock for calling his son Timmy but she decided not to mention it, it was obviously just a slip of the tongue. Richard got up and threw Timmy over his shoulder. "Well, we better go bury him now and have a funeral." Timmy giggled as he dangled upside down on his father's shoulder.

"Oh, he's alive!" Richard laughed.

"No, I'm not," giggled Timmy.

Holly watched in amusement at the family scene before her. It had been a while since she had witnessed anything like this. None of her friends had any children and Holly was very rarely around them. There was obviously something seriously wrong with her if she was doting on Richard's children. And it wasn't the wisest decision to become broody when there was no man in your life.

"OK, we best be off," laughed Richard. "Bye, Holly."

"Bye, Holly," the children cheered, and Holly watched Richard walk off with Timmy slung over his right shoulder as little Emily skipped and danced along beside her father while gripping his hand.

Holly stared in amusement at the stranger walking off with two children. Who was this man who claimed to be her brother? Holly certainly had never met *that* man before.

Twenty-three

BARBARA FINISHED SERVING HER CUSTOMERS, and as soon as they left the building she ran into the staff room and lit up a cigarette. The travel agent's had been so busy all day that she had had to work through her lunch break. Melissa, her work mate, had called in sick that morning, although Barbara knew very well she had partied too hard the night before and any sickness she might have had was only self-inflicted. So she was stuck in this boring job all by herself today. And of course it was the busiest day they'd had in ages. As soon as November came with those horrible depressing dark nights and dark mornings and piercing winds and sheets of rain, everyone came running in the door booking holidays to beautiful hot sunny countries. Barbara shuddered as she heard the wind rattle the windows and made a note to herself to check for any special holiday deals.

With her boss finally out to run some errands, Barbara was really looking forward to her cigarette break. Of course, just her luck, the bell over the door sounded just then and Barbara cursed the customer entering the shop for disturbing her precious break. She puffed on the cigarette furiously, almost making herself dizzy, reapplied her glossy red lipstick and sprayed perfume all around the room so her boss wouldn't notice the smoke. She left the staff room expecting to see a customer sitting behind the counter, but instead the old man was still slowly making his way to the counter. Barbara tried not to stare and began pressing random buttons on the keypad.

"Excuse me?" she heard the man's weak voice call to her.

"Hello sir, how can I help you?" she said for the hundredth time that day. She didn't mean to be rude by staring at him, but she was surprised at how young the man actually was. From far away his slumped figure looked elderly. His body was hunched and the walking stick in his hand seemed to be the only thing preventing him from collapsing on the floor in front of her. His skin was very white and pasty, as though he hadn't seen the sun for years, but he had big brown puppy eyes that seemed to smile at her. She couldn't help but smile back at him.

"I was hoping to book a holiday," he said quietly, "but I was wondering if you could help me choose a place."

Usually Barbara would have silently screamed at the customer for making her do this unbelievably impossible task. Most of her customers were so fussy that she could be sitting there for hours with them flicking through brochures and trying to persuade them where to go when the truth was she really couldn't give a toss where they went. But this man seemed pleasant, so she was glad to help. She surprised herself.

"No problem, sir, why don't you take a seat there and we'll search through the brochures." She pointed to the chair in front of her and looked away again so she didn't have to watch his struggle to sit down.

"Now," she said, full of smiles, "is there any country in particular that you would like to go to?"

"Em . . . Spain . . . Lanzarote, I think."

Barbara was glad; this was going to be a lot easier than she thought.

"And is it a summer holiday you're looking for?"

He nodded slowly.

They worked their way through the brochures and finally the man found a place that he liked. Barbara was happy that he took her advice into account, unlike some of her other customers, who just ignored every single bit of her knowledge. She should know what was best for them, it being her job and all.

"OK, any month in particular?" she said, looking at the prices.

"August?" he asked, and those big brown eyes looked so deep into Barbara's soul she just wanted to jump over the counter and give him a big hug.

"August is a good month," she agreed with him. "Would you like a sea view or a pool view? The sea view is an extra thirty euro," she added quickly.

He stared into space with a smile on his face as though he were already there. "A sea view, please."

"Good choice. Can I take your name and address, please?"

"Oh . . . this isn't actually for me . . . it's a surprise for my wife and her friends."

Those brown eyes looked sad.

Barbara cleared her throat nervously. "Well, that's very thoughtful of you, sir," she felt she had to add. "Could I have their names then, please?"

She finished taking his details and he settled the bill. She began to print the arrangements from the computer to give to him.

"Oh, do you mind if I leave the details here with you? I want to surprise my wife and I would be afraid of leaving papers around the house in case she finds them."

Barbara smiled; what a lucky wife he had.

"I won't be telling her till July, so do you think it could be kept quiet till then?"

"That's no problem at all, sir, usually the flight times aren't confirmed till a few weeks before anyway, so we would have no reason to call her. I'll give the other staff strict instructions not to call the house."

"Thank you for your help, Barbara," he said, smiling sadly with those puppy eyes.

"It's been a pleasure, Mr. . . . . Clarke?"

"It's Gerry." He smiled again.

"Well, it's been a pleasure, Gerry, I'm sure your wife will have a wonderful time. My friend went there last year and she loved it." Barbara felt the need to reassure him his wife would be fine.

"Well, I better head back home before they think I've been kidnapped. I'm not even supposed to be out of bed, you know." He laughed again and a lump formed in Barbara's throat.

Barbara jumped to her feet and ran around the other side of the counter to hold the door open for him. He smiled appreciatively as he walked past her and she watched as he slowly climbed into the taxi that had been waiting outside for him. Just as Barbara was about to close the door her boss walked in and it banged against his head. She looked over at Gerry, who was still waiting in the taxi to move out onto the road and he laughed and gave her the thumbs-up.

Her boss threw her a look for leaving the counter unattended and marched into the staff room. "Barbara," he yelled, "have you been smoking in here again?" She rolled her eyes and turned to face him.

"God, what's wrong with you? You look like you're about to burst into tears."

It was the first of July and Barbara sat grumpily behind the counter of Swords Travel Agents. Every day she had worked this summer had been a beautiful sunny day, and the last two days she had off it had pissed down with rain. Today was typically the complete opposite. It was the hottest day of the year, all her customers kept bragging as they strolled in, wearing their little shorts and skimpy tops, filling the room with the smell of coconut sun cream. Barbara squirmed in her chair in her uncomfortable and incredibly itchy uniform. She felt like she was back at school again. She banged on the fan once more as it suddenly stalled.

"Oh, leave it, Barbara," Melissa moaned. "That'll only make it worse."

"As if that could be possible," she grumbled, and spun around in her chair to face the computer, where she pounded on the keypad.

"What is it with you today?" Melissa laughed.

"Oh, nothing much," Barbara said through gritted teeth, "it's just the hottest day of the year and we're stuck in this *crappy* job in this *stuffy* room with *no air-conditioning* in these horrible *itchy uniforms*." She shouted each word toward her boss's office, hoping he would hear. "That's all."

Melissa sniggered. "Look, why don't you go outside for a few minutes to get some air and I'll deal with this next customer," she said, nodding to the woman making her way in.

"Thanks, Mel," Barbara said, relieved at finally being able to escape. She grabbed her cigarettes. "Right, I'm going to get some fresh air."

Melissa looked down at Barbara's hand and rolled her eyes. "Hello, can I help you?" she smiled at the woman.

"Yes, I was wondering if Barbara still works here?"

Barbara froze just as she was reaching the door and contemplated whether to run outside or go back to work. She groaned and headed back to her seat. She looked at the woman behind the counter; she was pretty, she decided, but her eyes looked like they were going to pop out of her head as she stared frantically from one girl to the other.

"Yes, I'm Barbara."

"Oh good!" The lady looked relieved and she dived onto the stool in front of her. "I was afraid you might not work here anymore."

"She wishes," Melissa muttered under her breath and received an elbow in the stomach from Barbara.

"Can I help you?"

"Oh God, I really hope you can," the lady said a bit hysterically and rooted through her bag. Barbara raised her eyebrows over at Melissa and the two of them tried to hold in their laughs.

"OK," she said, eventually pulling out a crumpled envelope from her bag. "I received this today from my husband and I was wondering if you could explain it to me."

Barbara frowned as she stared at the crumpled piece of paper on the counter. A page had been torn out of a holiday brochure and written on it were the words: "Swords Travel Agents. Attn: Barbara."

Barbara frowned again and looked at the page more closely. "My friend went there two years ago on holiday, but other than that it means nothing to me. Did you not get any more information?"

The lady shook her head vigorously.

"Well, can't you ask your husband for more information?" Barbara was confused.

"No, he's not here anymore," she said sadly, and tears welled in her eyes. Barbara panicked; if her boss saw her making someone cry she would really be given her marching orders. She was on her last warning as it was.

"OK then, can I take your name and maybe it will come up on the computer."

"It's Holly Kennedy." Her voice shook.

"Holly Kennedy, Holly Kennedy." Melissa repeated her name after listening in on their conversation, "that name rings a bell. Oh, hold on, I was about to call you this week! That's weird! I was under strict instructions from Barbara not to ring you until July for some reason . . ."

"Oh!" Barbara interrupted her friend, finally realizing what was going on. "You're Gerry's wife?" she asked hopefully.

"Yes!" Holly threw her hands to her face in shock. "He was in here?"

"Yes he was," Barbara smiled encouragingly. "He was a lovely man," she said, reaching out to Holly's hand on the counter.

Melissa stared at the two of them, not knowing what was going on. Barbara's heart went out to the lady across the counter, she was so young and it must be so hard for her right now. But

Barbara was delighted to be the bearer of good news. "Melissa, can you get Holly some tissues, please, while I explain to her exactly why her husband was here?" She beamed across the counter at Holly.

She let go of Holly's hand to tap away at the computer and Melissa returned with a box of tissues. "OK, Holly," she said softly. "Gerry has arranged a holiday for you and a Sharon McCarthy and a Denise Hennessey to go to Lanzarote for one week, arriving on the twenty-eighth of July to return home on the third of August."

Holly's hands flew to her face in shock and tears poured from her eyes.

"He was adamant that he find the perfect place for you," Barbara continued, delighted at her new role. She felt like one of those female television hosts who spring surprises on their guests. "That's the place you're going to," she said, tapping the crumpled page in front of her. "You'll have a fab time, believe me, my friend was there two years ago like I said already, and she just loved it. There are loads of restaurants and bars around and . . ." She trailed off, realizing Holly probably didn't give a damn about whether she had a good time or not.

"When did he come in?" Holly asked, still in shock.

Barbara, glad to help in her new role, happily tapped away on the computer. "The booking was made on the twenty-eighth of November."

"November?" Holly gasped. "He shouldn't even have been out of bed then! Was he on his own?"

"Yes, but there was a taxi waiting outside for him the whole time."

"What time of day was this?" Holly asked quickly.

"I'm sorry but I really can't remember. It was quite a long time ago—"

"Yes, of course, I'm sorry," Holly interrupted.

Barbara completely understood. If that was her husband, well, if she ever met someone worth becoming her husband, she would also want to know every single detail. Barbara told her as much as she could remember until Holly could think of no more questions to ask.

"Oh, thank you, Barbara, thank you so much." Holly reached over the counter and gave her a big hug.

"No problem at all." She hugged her back, feeling satisfied with her good deed of the day. "Come back and let us know how you get on," she smiled. "Here's your details." She handed her a thick envelope and watched her walk out of the room. She sighed, thinking the crappy job might not be so crappy after all.

"What on earth was that all about?" Melissa was dying to find out. Barbara began to explain the story.

"OK, girls, I'm taking my break now. Barbara, no smoking in the staff room." Their boss closed and locked his door and then turned around to face them. "Christ Almighty, what *are* you two crying about now?"

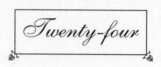

Twenty-four

Holly eventually arrived at her house and waved to Sharon and Denise, who were sitting on her garden wall bathing in the sun. They jumped up as soon as they saw her and rushed over to greet her.

"God, you both got here quick," she said, trying to inject energy into her voice. She felt completely and utterly drained, and she really wasn't in the mood to have to explain everything to the girls right now. But she would have to.

"Sharon left work as soon as you called and she collected me from town," Denise explained, studying Holly's face and trying to assess how bad the situation was.

"Oh, you didn't have to do that," Holly said lifelessly as she put the key in the door.

"Hey, have you been working in your garden?" Sharon asked, looking around and trying to lighten the atmosphere.

"No, my neighbor's been doing it, I think." Holly pulled the key from the door and searched through the bunch for the correct one.

"You think?" Denise tried to keep the conversation going while Holly battled with yet another key in the lock.

"Well, it's either my neighbor or a little leprechaun lives down the end of my garden," she snapped, getting frustrated with the keys. Denise and Sharon looked at each other and tried to figure out what to do. They motioned to each other to stay quiet, as Holly was obviously stressed and finding it difficult to remember which key went in the door.

"Oh, fuck it!" Holly yelled and threw her keys on the ground. Denise jumped back, just managing to keep the heavy bunch from slamming into her ankles.

Sharon picked them up. "Hey, hun, don't worry about it," she said lightheartedly. "This happens to me all the time, I swear the bloody things jump around on the key ring deliberately just to piss us off."

Holly smiled wearily, thankful that somebody else could take control for a while. Sharon slowly worked her way through the keys, talking calmly to her in a singsong voice as though speaking to a child. The door finally opened and Holly rushed in to turn the alarm off. Thankfully she remembered the number, the year Gerry and she had met, and the year they got married.

"OK, why don't you two make yourselves comfortable in the living room and I'll follow you in a minute." Sharon and Denise did as they were told while Holly headed into the toilet to splash cold water on her face. She needed to snap out of this daze, take control of her body and be as excited about this holiday as Gerry had intended. When she felt a little more alive she joined the girls in the living room.

She pulled the footrest over to the couch and sat opposite the girls.

"OK, I'm not going to drag this one out. I opened the envelope for July today and this is what it said." She rooted in her bag for the small card that had been attached to the brochure and handed it to the girls. It read:

> *Have a good Holly day!*
> *PS, I love you . . .*

"Is that it?" Denise wrinkled up her nose, unimpressed. Sharon nudged her in the ribs. "Ow!"

"Well, Holly, I think it's a lovely note," Sharon lied. "It's so thoughtful and it's . . . a lovely play on words."

Holly had to giggle. She knew Sharon was lying because she always flared her nostrils when she wasn't telling the truth. "No, you fool!" she said, hitting Sharon over the head with a cushion.

Sharon began to laugh. "Oh good, because I was beginning to worry there for a second."

"Sharon, you are always so supportive you make me sick sometimes!" Holly exclaimed. "Now this is what else was inside." She handed them the crumpled page that was torn from the brochure.

She watched with amusement as the girls tried to figure out Gerry's writing and Denise finally held her hand up to her mouth. "Oh my God!" she gasped, sitting forward on her seat.

"What what what?" Sharon demanded and leaned forward with excitement. "Did Gerry buy you a holiday?"

"No." Holly shook her head seriously.

"Oh." Sharon and Denise both sat back in their seats with disappointment.

She allowed an uncomfortable silence to gather between them before she spoke again.

"Girls," she said with a smile beginning to spread across her face, "he bought *us* a holiday!"

The girls opened a bottle of wine.

"Oh, this is incredible," Denise said after the news had sunk in. "Gerry's such a sweetie."

Holly nodded, feeling proud of her husband, who had once again managed to surprise them all.

"So you went down to this Barbara person?" Sharon asked.

"Yes, and she was the sweetest girl," Holly smiled. "She sat with me for ages, telling me about the conversation they had that day."

"That was nice." Denise sipped her wine. "When was it by the way?"

"He went in at the end of November."

"November?" Sharon looked thoughtful. "That was after the second operation."

Holly nodded. "The girl said he was pretty weak when he went in."

"Isn't it funny that none of us had any idea at all?" Sharon said, still astonished by the whole thing.

They all nodded silently.

"Well, it looks like we're all off to Lanzarote!" Denise cheered and she held her glass up. "To Gerry!"

"To Gerry!" Holly and Sharon joined in.

"Are you sure Tom and John won't mind?" Holly asked, suddenly aware that the girls had partners to think of.

"Of course John won't mind!" Sharon laughed. "He'll probably be delighted to be rid of me for a week!"

"Yeah, and me and Tom can go away for a week another time, which actually suits me fine," agreed Denise. "Because that way we're not stuck together for two weeks on our first holiday together!" she laughed.

"Sure you two practically live together anyway!" Sharon said, nudging her.

Denise gave a quick smile but didn't answer and the two of them dropped the subject. That annoyed Holly, because they were always doing that. She wanted to hear how her friends were getting on in their relationships but nobody seemed to tell her any of the juicy gossip out of fear of hurting her. People seemed to be afraid to tell her about how happy they were or about the good news in their lives. Then again they also refused to moan about the bad things. So instead of being informed of what was really going on in her friends' lives she was stuck with this mediocre chitchat about . . . nothing, really, and it was starting to bother her. She couldn't be shielded from other people's happiness forever, what good would that do her?

"I have to say that leprechaun really is doing a great job on your garden, Holly," Denise cut into her thoughts as she looked out the window.

Holly blushed. "Oh I know. I'm sorry for being a bitch earlier, Denise," she apologized. "I suppose I should really go next door and thank him properly."

After Denise and Sharon had headed off home Holly grabbed a bottle of wine from under the stairs and carried it next door to her neighbor. She rang the bell and waited.

"Hi Holly," Derek said, opening the door. "Come in, come in."

Holly looked past him and into the kitchen and saw the family sitting around the table eating dinner. She backed away from the door slightly.

"No, I won't disturb you, I just came by to give you this"—she handed him the bottle of wine—"as a token of my thanks."

"Well Holly, this is really thoughtful of you," he said, reading the label. Then he looked up with a confused expression on his face. "But thanks for what, if you don't mind me asking?"

"Oh, for tidying up my garden," she said, blushing. "I'm sure the entire estate was cursing me for ruining the appearance of the street," she laughed.

"Holly, your garden certainly isn't a worry to anyone, we all understand, but I haven't been tidying it for you, I'm sorry to say."

"Oh." Holly cleared her throat, feeling very embarrassed. "I thought you had been."

"No, no." He shook his head.

"Well, you wouldn't by any chance know who has been?" she laughed like an idiot.

"No, I have no idea," he said, looking very confused. "I thought it was you, to be honest. How odd."

Holly wasn't quite sure what to say next.

"So perhaps you would like to take this back," he said awkwardly, thrusting the wine bottle toward her.

"Oh no, that's OK," she laughed again, "you can keep that as thanks for . . . not being neighbors from hell. Anyway, I'll let you get back to dinner." She ran off down the driveway with her face burning with embarrassment. What kind of fool wouldn't know who was tidying her own garden?

She knocked on a few more doors around the estate and to her continued embarrassment nobody seemed to know what she was talking about. Everyone seemed to have jobs and lives, and remarkably enough they didn't spend their days monitoring her garden. She returned to her house even more confused. As she walked in the door the phone was ringing and she ran to answer it.

"Hello?" she panted.

"What were you doing, running a marathon?"

"No, I was chasing leprechauns," Holly explained.

"Oh, cool."

The oddest thing was that Ciara didn't even question her.

"It's my birthday in two weeks."

Holly had completely forgotten. "Yeah, I know," she said matter-of-factly.

"Well, Mum and Dad want us all to go out for a family dinner . . ."

Holly groaned loudly.

"Exactly," and she screamed away from the phone, "Dad, Holly said the same thing as me."

Holly giggled as she heard her father cursing and grumbling in the background.

Ciara returned to the phone and spoke loudly so her father could hear, "OK, so my idea is to go ahead with the family dinner but to invite friends as well so that it can actually be an enjoyable night. What do you think?"

"Sounds good," Holly agreed.

Ciara screamed away from the phone, "Dad, Holly agrees with my idea."

"That's all very well," Holly heard her dad yelling, "but I'm not paying for all those people to eat."

"He has a point." Holly added, "Tell you what, why don't we have a barbecue? That way Dad can be in his element and it won't be so expensive."

"Hey, that's a cool idea!" Ciara screamed away from the phone once again, "Dad, what about having a barbecue?"

There was a silence.

"He's loving that idea," Ciara giggled. "Mr. Super Chef will once again cook for the masses."

Holly also giggled at the thought. Her dad got so excited when they had barbecues; he took the whole thing so seriously and stood by the barbecue constantly while watching over his wonderful creations. Gerry had been like that too. What was it with men and barbecues? Probably it was the only thing that the two of them could actually cook, either that or they were closet pyromaniacs.

"OK, so will you tell Sharon and John, Denise and her DJ bloke, and will you ask that Daniel guy to come too? He's yummy!" she laughed hysterically.

"Ciara, I hardly know the guy. Ask Declan to ask him, he sees him all the time."

"No, because I want you to subtly tell him that I love him and want to have his babies. Somehow I don't think Declan would feel very comfortable doing that."

Holly groaned.

"Stop it!" Ciara gave out, "He's *my* birthday treat!"

"OK," she gave in, "but why do you want all my friends there, what about your friends?"

"Holly, I've lost contact with all my friends, I've been away for so long. And all my other friends are in Australia and the stupid bastards haven't bothered to call me," she huffed.

Holly knew to whom she was referring. "But don't you think this would be a great opportunity to catch up with your old friends? You know, invite them to a barbecue; it's a nice, relaxed atmosphere."

"Yeah right, what would I have to tell them when they start asking questions? Have you a job? Eh . . . no. Have you a boyfriend? Eh . . . no. Where do you live? Eh . . . actually I still live with my parents. How pathetic would I sound?"

Holly gave up. "OK, whatever . . . anyway, I'll call the others and . . ."

Ciara had already hung up.

Holly decided to get the most awkward phone call out of the way first and she dialed the number to Hogan's.

"Hello, Hogan's."

"Hi, can I speak to Daniel Connelly, please?"

"Yeah, hold on." She was put on hold and "Greensleeves" belted out into her ear.

"Hello?"

"Hi, Daniel?"

"Yeah, who's this?"

"It's Holly Kennedy." She danced nervously around her bedroom, hoping he would recognize the name.

"Who?" he yelled as the noise in the background became louder.

Holly dived onto her bed in embarrassment. "It's Holly Kennedy? Declan's sister?"

"Oh Holly, hiya, hold on a second while I go somewhere quieter."

Holly was stuck listening to "Greensleeves" again and she danced around her bedroom and started singing along.

"Sorry Holly," Daniel said, picking up the phone again and laughing. "You like 'Greensleeves'?"

Holly's face went scarlet and she hit herself across the head. "Em, no, not really." She couldn't think of what else to say, then she remembered why she was ringing.

"I was just ringing to invite you to a barbecue."

"Oh great, yeah, I would love to go."

"It's Ciara's birthday on Friday week; you know my sister, Ciara?"

"Eh . . . yes, the one with the pink hair."

Holly laughed. "Yeah, stupid question, everyone knows Ciara. Well, she wanted me to invite you to the barbecue and to subtly tell you that she wants to marry you and have your babies."

Daniel started laughing. "Yes . . . that was very subtle all right."

Holly wondered whether he was interested in her sister, if she was his type.

"She's twenty-five on Friday week," Holly felt like adding for some unknown reason.

"Oh . . . right."

"Em, well, Denise and your friend Tom are coming as well, and Declan will be there with his band of course, so you'll know plenty of people."

"Are you going?"

"Of course!"

"Good, I'll know even more people then, won't I?" he laughed.

"Oh great, she'll be delighted you're coming."

"Well, I would feel rude for not accepting an invitation from a princess."

At first Holly thought he was flirting and then she realized he was referring to the documentary, so she mumbled some sort of incoherent answer. He was just about to hang the phone up when a thought suddenly popped into her head, "Oh, there's just one more thing."

"Go for it," he said.

"Is that position behind the bar still available?"

Twenty-five

THANK GOD IT WAS A BEAUTIFUL day, Holly thought, as she locked her car and walked around to the back of her parents' house. The weather had drastically changed that week and it had rained and rained continuously. Ciara was in hysterics about what would become of her barbecue and she had been hell to be with all week. Luckily for everyone's sake the weather had returned to its former splendor. Holly already had a good tan from lying out in the sun all month, one of the perks of not having a job, and she felt like showing it off today by wearing a cute little denim skirt she had bought in the summer sales and a simple tight white T-shirt that made her look even browner.

Holly was proud of the present she had bought Ciara and she knew Ciara would love it. It was a butterfly belly button ring that had a little pink crystal in each wing. She had chosen it so it would coordinate with Ciara's new butterfly tattoo and her pink hair, of course. She followed the sounds of laughter and was glad to see that the garden was full with family and friends. Denise had already arrived with Tom and Daniel, and they had all flaked out on the grass. Sharon had arrived without John and she was sitting chatting to Holly's mum, no doubt discussing Holly's progress in life. Well, she was out of the house, wasn't she? That was a miracle in itself.

Holly frowned as she noted Jack was once again not present. Ever since he had helped her carry out the task of cleaning out Gerry's wardrobe, he had been unusually distant. Even when they were children Jack had always been great at understanding Holly's needs and feelings without her having to point them out to him, but when she had told him that she needed space after Gerry's death, she didn't mean she wanted to be *completely* ignored and isolated. It was so out of character for him not to be in contact for so long. Nerves fluttered through Holly's stomach and she prayed that he was all right.

Ciara was standing in the middle of the garden screaming at everyone and loving being the center of attention. She was dressed in a pink bikini top to match her pink hair and blue denim cutoffs.

Holly approached her with her present, which was immediately grabbed from her hand and ripped open. She needn't have bothered wrapping it so neatly.

"Oh Holly, I love it!" Ciara exclaimed and threw her arms around her sister.

"I thought you would," Holly said, glad she had chosen the right thing, because otherwise her beloved sister would no doubt have let her know about it.

"I'm gonna wear it now actually," Ciara said, ripping out her current belly button ring and piercing the butterfly through her skin.

"Ugh," Holly shuddered. "I could have gone without seeing that, thank you very much."

There was a beautiful smell of barbecued food in the air and Holly's mouth began to water. She wasn't surprised to see all the men huddled around the barbecue with her dad in pride of place. Hunter men must provide food for women.

Holly spotted Richard and she marched over. Ignoring the small talk she just charged right in. "Richard, did you tidy my garden?"

Richard looked up from the barbecue with a confused expression on his face. "Excuse me, did I what?" The rest of the men stopped their conversation and stared.

"Did you tidy my garden?" she repeated with her hands on her hips. She didn't know why she was acting so angry with him, just a force of habit probably, because if he had tidied it he had done her a huge favor. It was just annoying to keep returning home to see another section of her garden cleared and to not know who was doing it.

"When?" Richard looked around at the others frantically, as though he had been accused of murder.

"Oh, I don't know when," she snapped. "During the days for the past few weeks."

"No, Holly," he snapped back. "Some of us have to work, you know."

Holly glared at him and her father interjected. "What's this, love, is someone working on your garden?"

"Yes, but I don't know who," she mumbled, rubbing her forehead and trying to think again. "Is it you, Dad?"

Frank shook his head wildly, hoping his daughter hadn't finally lost the plot.

"Is it you, Declan?"

"Eh . . . think about it, Holly," he said sarcastically.

"Is it you?" she turned to the stranger standing next to her father.

"Um . . . no, I just flew into Dublin . . . um . . . for the . . . um, weekend," he replied nervously with an English accent.

Ciara started laughing. "Let me help you, Holly. *Is anybody here working on Holly's garden?*" she yelled to the rest of the party. Everybody stopped what they were doing and shook their heads with blank expressions on their faces.

"Now wasn't that much easier?" Ciara cackled.

Holly shook her head with disbelief at her sister and joined Denise, Tom and Daniel on the far side of the garden.

"Hi, Daniel." Holly leaned over to greet Daniel with a kiss on the cheek.

"Hi, Holly, long time no see." He handed her a can from beside him.

"You still haven't found that leprechaun?" Denise laughed.

"No," Holly said, stretching her legs out in front of her and resting back on her elbows. "But it is just *so* odd!" She explained the story to Tom and Daniel.

"Do you think maybe your husband organized it?" Tom blurted out, and Daniel threw his friend a look.

"No," Holly said, looking away, angry that a stranger knew her private business, "it's not part of that." She scowled at Denise for telling Tom.

Denise just held her hands up helplessly and shrugged.

"Thanks for coming, Daniel." Holly turned to him, ignoring the other two.

"No problem at all, I was glad to come."

It was weird seeing him out of his usual wintery clothes; he was dressed in a navy vest and navy combat shorts that went just below his knees with a pair of navy trainers. She watched his biceps as he took a slug of his beer. She had had no idea he was that fit.

"You're very brown," she commented, trying to think of an excuse for being caught staring at his biceps.

"And so are you," he said, purposely staring at her legs.

Holly laughed and tucked them up underneath her. "A result of unemployment, what's your excuse?"

"I was in Miami for a while last month."

"Ooh, lucky you, did you enjoy it?"

"Had a great time," he nodded, smiling. "Have you ever been?"

She shook her head. "But at least us girls are heading off to Spain next week. Can't wait." She rubbed her hands together excitedly.

"Yes I heard that. I'd say that was a nice surprise for you." He gave her a smile, his eyes crinkling at the corners.

"You're telling me." Holly shook her head, still not quite believing it.

They chatted together for a while about his holiday and their lives in general and Holly gave up eating her burger in front of him, as she could find no easy way of eating it without tomato ketchup and mayonnaise dribbling down her mouth every time it was her turn to speak.

"I hope you didn't go to Miami with another woman or poor Ciara will be devastated," she joked, and then kicked herself for being so nosy.

"No, I didn't," he said seriously. "We broke up a few months ago."

"Oh, I'm sorry to hear that," she said genuinely. "Were you together long?"

"Seven years."

"Wow, that's a long time."

"Yeah." He looked away and Holly could tell he didn't feel comfortable talking about it, so she quickly changed the subject.

"By the way, Daniel," Holly lowered her voice to a hushed tone and Daniel moved his head closer. "I just wanted to thank you so much for looking out for me the way you did after the documentary. Most men run away when they see a girl cry; you didn't, so thank you." Holly smiled gratefully.

"No problem at all, Holly. I don't like to see you upset." Daniel returned the smile.

"You're a good friend," Holly said, thinking aloud.

Daniel looked pleased. "Why don't we all go out for drinks or something before you go away?"

"Maybe I can get to know as much about you as you know about me." Holly laughed. "I think you know my whole life story by this stage."

"Yeah, I'd like that," Daniel agreed, and they arranged a time to meet.

"Oh, by the way, did you give Ciara that birthday present?" Holly asked excitedly.

"No," he laughed. "She's been kind of . . . busy."

Holly turned around to look at her sister and spotted her flirting with one of Declan's friends, much to Declan's disgust. Holly laughed at her sister. So much for wanting Daniel's babies.

"I'll call her over, will I?"

"Go on," Daniel said.

"Ciara!" Holly called. "Got another pressie for you!"

"Ooh!" Ciara screamed with delight and abandoned a very disappointed-looking young man.

"What is it?" She collapsed on the grass beside them.

Holly nodded over at Daniel. "It's from him."

Ciara excitedly turned to face him.

"I was wondering if you would like a job working behind the bar at Club Diva?"

Ciara's hands flew to her mouth. "Oh Daniel, that would be brill!"

"Have you ever worked behind a bar?"

"Yeah, loads of times." She waved her hand dismissively.

Daniel raised his eyebrows; he was looking for a bit more information than that.

"Oh, I've done bar work in practically every country I've been to, honestly!" she said excitedly.

Daniel smiled. "So do you think you'll be able for it?"

"Ooh, would I ever!" she squealed and threw her arms around him.

Any excuse, Holly thought, as she watched her sister practically strangling Daniel. His face started to turn red and he made "rescue me" faces toward Holly.

"OK, OK, that's enough, Ciara," she laughed, dragging her off Daniel. "You don't want to kill your new boss."

"Oh sorry," Ciara said, backing off. "This is *so* cool! I have a *job*, Holly!" she squealed again.

"Yes, I heard," Holly said.

Suddenly the garden became very quiet and Holly looked around to see what was happening. Everyone was facing the conservatory and Holly's parents appeared at the door with a large birthday cake in their hands singing "Happy Birthday." Everyone else joined in and Ciara jumped up, lapping up all the attention. As her parents stepped outside, Holly spotted someone following behind them with a huge bouquet of flowers. Her parents walked toward Ciara and placed the birthday cake on the table before her and the stranger behind slowly removed the bouquet from his face.

"Mathew!" Ciara gasped.

Holly grabbed Ciara's hand as her face went white.

"I'm sorry for being such a fool, Ciara." Mathew's Australian accent echoed around the garden. Some of Declan's friends smirked loudly, obviously feeling uncomfortable at this open show of emotion. He actually looked like he was acting out a scene from an Australian soap, but then again drama always seemed to work for Ciara. "I love you! Please take me back!" he announced, and everyone turned to stare at Ciara to see what she would say.

Her lower lip started to tremble and she ran over to Mathew and jumped onto him, wrapping her legs around his waist and her arms around his neck.

Holly was overcome with emotion and tears welled in her eyes at the sight of her sister being reunited with the man she loved. Declan grabbed his camera and began filming.

Daniel wrapped his arm around Holly's shoulders and gave her an encouraging squeeze. "I'm sorry, Daniel," Holly said, wiping her eyes, "but I think you've just been dumped."

"Not to worry," he laughed. "I shouldn't mix business with pleasure anyway." He seemed relieved.

Holly continued to watch as Mathew spun Ciara around in his arms.

"Oh, get a room!" Declan yelled with disgust, and everyone laughed.

. . .

Holly smiled at the jazz band as she passed and looked around the bar for Denise. They had arranged to meet up in the girls' favorite bar, Juicy, known for its extensive cocktail menu and relaxing music. Holly had no intentions of getting drunk tonight, as she wanted to be able to enjoy her holiday as much as she could the next day. She intended on being bright-eyed and bushy-tailed for her week of relaxation, thanks to Gerry. She spotted Denise snuggling up to Tom on a comfortable large black leather couch in a conservatory area that overlooked the River Liffey. Dublin was lit up for the night and all its colors were reflected in the water. Daniel sat opposite Denise and Tom sucking fiercely on a strawberry daiquiri, eyes surveying the room. Nice to see Tom and Denise were ostracizing everyone again.

"Sorry I'm late," Holly apologized, approaching her friends. "I just wanted to finish packing before I came out."

"You're not forgiven," Daniel said quietly into her ear as he gave her a welcoming hug and kiss.

Denise looked up at Holly and smiled, Tom waved slightly and they returned their attention to each other.

"I don't know why they even bother inviting other people out. They just sit there staring into each other's eyes ignoring everyone else. They don't even talk to each other! And then they make you feel like you've interrupted them if you strike up a conversation. I think they've got some weird telepathic conversation going on there," Daniel said, sitting down again and taking another sip from his glass. He made a face at the sweet taste. "And I really need a beer."

Holly laughed. "Oh, so all round it sounds like you've been having a fantastic night."

"Sorry," Daniel apologized. "It's just been so long since I've spoken to another human being, I've forgotten my manners."

Holly giggled. "Well, I've come to rescue you." She picked up the menu and surveyed the choice of drinks before her. She chose a drink with the lowest alcohol content and settled down in the cozy chair. "I could fall asleep here," she remarked, snuggling further down into the chair.

Daniel raised his eyebrows. "Then I would *really* take it personally."

"Don't worry, I won't," she assured him. "So, Mr. Connelly, you know absolutely *everything* about me. Tonight I am on a mission to find out about you, so be prepared for my interrogation."

Daniel smiled. "OK, I'm ready."

Holly thought about her first question. "Where are you from?"

"Born and reared in Dublin." He took a sip of the red cocktail and winced again. "And if any of the people I grew up with saw me drinking this stuff and listening to jazz, I'd be in trouble."

Holly giggled.

"After I finished school I joined the army," he continued.

Holly raised her eyes, impressed. "Why did you decide to do that?"

He didn't even think about it. "Because I hadn't a clue what I wanted to do with my life, and the money was good."

"So much for saving innocent lives," Holly laughed.

"I only stayed with the army for a few years."

"Why did you leave?" Holly sipped on her lime-flavored drink.

"Because I realized I had urges to drink cocktails and listen to jazz music and they wouldn't permit it in the army barracks," he explained.

Holly giggled. "Really, Daniel."

He smiled. "Sorry, it just wasn't for me. My parents had moved down to Galway to run a pub and the idea of that appealed to me. So I moved down to Galway to work there and eventually my parents retired, I took over the pub, decided a few years ago that I wanted to own one of my own, worked really hard, saved my money, took out the biggest mortgage ever and moved back to Dublin and bought Hogan's. And here I am talking to you."

Holly smiled. "Well, that's a wonderful life story, Daniel."

"Nothing special, but a life all the same." He returned her smile.

"So where does the ex come into all this?" Holly asked.

"She's right in between running the pub in Galway and leaving to come to Dublin."

"Ah . . . I see," Holly nodded, understanding. She drained her glass and picked up the menu again. "I think I'll have Sex on the Beach."

"When? On your holidays?" Daniel teased.

Holly thumped him playfully on the arm. Not in a million years.

Twenty-six

"WE'RE ALL GOING ON OUR summer Holly days!" the girls sang in the car all the way to the airport. John had offered to drive them to the airport but he was fast regretting it. They were acting like they had never left the country before. Holly couldn't remember the last time she had truly felt so excited. She felt like she was back at school and off on a school tour. Her bag was packed with packets of sweets, chocolate and magazines, and they couldn't stop .singing cheesy songs in the back of the car. Their flight wasn't until 9:00 p.m., so they wouldn't arrive at their accommodation until the early hours of the morning.

They reached the airport and piled out of the car while John lifted their suitcases out of the boot. Denise ran across the road and into the departure lounge as if doing so would get her there any faster, but Holly stood back from the car and waited for Sharon, who was saying her good-byes to her husband.

"You'll be careful now, won't you?" he asked her worriedly. "Don't be doing anything stupid over there."

"John, of course I'll be careful."

John wasn't listening to a word she said. "Because it's one thing messing around over here, but you can't act like that in another country, you know."

"John," Sharon said, wrapping her arms around his neck, "I'm just going for a nice relaxing holiday; you don't need to worry about me."

He whispered something in her ear and she nodded, "I know, I know."

They gave each other a long good-bye kiss and Holly watched her lifelong friends embrace. She felt around in the front pocket of her bag for the August letter from Gerry. She would be able to open it in a few days while lying on the beach. What luxury. The sun, sand, sea *and* Gerry all in one day.

"Holly, take care of my wonderful wife for me, will you?" John asked, breaking into Holly's thoughts.

"I will, John. We're only going for a week, you know." Holly laughed and gave him a hug.

"I know, but after seeing what you girls get up to on your nights out, I'm just a little worried," he smiled. "You enjoy yourself, Holly, you deserve the rest."

John watched them as they dragged their luggage across the road and into the departure lounge.

Holly paused as she entered the door and took in a deep breath. She loved airports. She loved the smell, she loved the noise, and she loved the whole atmosphere as people walked around happily tugging their luggage, looking forward to going on their holidays or heading back home. She loved to see people arriving and being greeted with a big cheer by their families and she loved to watch them all giving each other emotional hugs. It was a perfect place for people-spotting. The airport always gave her a feeling of anticipation in the pit of her stomach as though she were about to do something special and amazing. Queuing at the boarding gate, she felt like she was waiting to go on a roller coaster ride at a theme park, like an excited little child.

Holly followed Sharon and they joined Denise halfway down the extremely long check-in queue.

"I told you we should have come earlier," Denise moaned.

"Well then, we would just be waiting at the boarding gate for the same amount of time," reasoned Holly.

"Yeah, but at least there's a bar there," explained Denise, "and it's the only place in this entire stupid building that us smoker freaks can smoke in," she mumbled.

"Good point," Holly thought aloud.

"Now, can I just point out something to you two before we even leave. I'm not going to be doing any crazy drinking or having any wild nights. I just want to be able to relax by the pool or on the beach with my book, enjoy a few meals out and go to bed early," Sharon said seriously.

Denise looked at Holly in shock. "Is it too late to invite someone else, Hol? What do you reckon? Sharon's bags are still packed and John can't be too far down the road."

Holly laughed. "No, I have to agree with Sharon on this one. I just want to go and relax and not do anything too stressful."

Denise pouted like a child.

"Oh, don't worry, pet," Sharon said softly, "I'm sure there will be other kids your age that you can play with."

Denise threw her the finger. "Well, if they ask me if I have anything to declare when we get there, I'm telling everyone my two friends are dry shites."

Sharon and Holly sniggered.

After thirty minutes of queuing they finally checked in and Denise ran around the shop like a madwoman buying a lifetime supply of cigarettes.

"Why is that girl staring at me?" Denise said through gritted teeth, eyeing up the girl at the end of the bar.

"Probably because you're staring at her," Sharon responded, checking her watch. "Only fifteen more minutes."

"No honestly, girls." Denise turned back around to face them. "I'm not being paranoid here, she is definitely staring at us."

"Well then, why don't you go over to her and ask her if she wants to take it outside," Holly joked and Sharon sniggered.

"Oh, here she comes," Denise sang and turned her back to her.

Holly looked up and saw a skinny blond-haired girl with big fake tits heading toward them. "You better get those knuckle-dusters out, Denise, she looks like a dangerous one," Holly teased and Sharon choked on her drink.

"Hi there!" the girl squeaked.

"Hello," Sharon said, trying not to laugh.

"I didn't mean to be rude by staring, but I just had to come over and see if it was really you!"

"It's me all right," Sharon said sarcastically, "in the flesh."

"Oh, I just *knew* it!" the girl squealed and jumped up and down with excitement. Unsurprisingly her chest stayed still. "My friends kept telling me I was wrong but I *knew* it was you! That's them over there." She turned around and pointed to the end of the bar and the other four spice girls twinkled their fingers back. "My name's Cindy . . ."

Sharon choked on her water again.

". . . And I'm just the biggest fan of all of you," she squealed excitedly. "I just love that show that you're all in, I've watched it dozens and dozens of times! You play Princess Holly, don't you?" she said, pointing a manicured nail in Holly's face.

Holly opened her mouth to speak but Cindy kept on talking.

"And you play her lady!" she pointed at Denise. "And *you!*" she squealed even louder, pointing at Sharon, "you were friends with that Australian rock star!"

The girls looked at each other worriedly as she pulled out a chair and sat down at their table.

"You see, I'm an actress myself . . ."

Denise rolled her eyes.

". . . And I would just love to work on a show like yours. When are you making the next one?"

Holly opened her mouth to explain that they weren't actually actresses but Denise beat her to it.

"Oh, we're in discussions right now about our next project," she lied.

"Oh, how fantastic!" Cindy clapped her hands. "What's it about?"

"Well, we can't really say right now, but we have to go to Hollywood for filming."

Cindy looked like she was going to have a heart attack. "Oh my God! Who's your agent?"

"Frankie," Sharon interrupted Denise, "so Frankie and us are all going to Hollywood."

Holly couldn't hold her laugh in.

"Oh, don't mind her, Cindy, she's just excited," explained Denise.

"Wow, and so you should be!" Cindy looked down at Denise's boarding pass on the table and nearly had heart failure. "Wow, you girls are going to Lanzarote too?!"

Denise grabbed her boarding pass and shoved it in her bag, as if that would make a difference.

"I'm going there with my friends. They're just over there," she turned around *again* and waved at them *again* and they waved back *again*. "We're staying in a place called Costa Palma Palace. Where are you guys staying?"

Holly's heart sank. "Oh, I can't quite remember the name, girls, can you?" She looked to Sharon and Denise with wide eyes.

They shook their heads vigorously.

"Oh well, not to worry," she shrugged her shoulders happily, "I'll see you when we land anyway! I better go now and board, I wouldn't want the plane to fly off without me!" She squeaked so loudly that the surrounding tables turned to stare. She gave each of the girls a big hug and tottered off back to her friends.

"Looks like we needed those knuckle-dusters after all," Holly said miserably.

"Oh, it doesn't matter," perked up Sharon, always the optimist. "We can just ignore her."

They all stood up and headed over to the boarding gate. As they made their way to their seats Holly's heart sank once again and she immediately dived into the seat on the far side of the aisle. Sharon sat down beside her and Denise's face was a picture when she realized who she had to sit next to.

"Oh fab! You get to sit beside me!" Cindy squeaked at Denise. Denise threw Sharon and Holly a nasty look and plonked herself beside Cindy.

"See? I told you that you'd find yourself a little friend to play with," Sharon whispered to Denise. Sharon and Holly broke into fits of laughter.

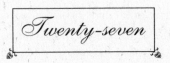

Twenty-seven

Four hours later the plane glided over the sea and landed at Lanzarote Airport, causing everyone to cheer and applaud. No one on the plane was more relieved than Denise.

"Oh, I have the biggest headache," she complained to the girls as they made their way to the luggage reclaim. "That bloody girl just talks and talks and talks." She massaged her temples and closed her eyes, relieved at the peace.

Sharon and Holly spotted Cindy and her crew making their way over to them and they dashed off into the crowd, leaving Denise standing alone with her eyes closed.

They beat their way through the crowd so they had a good view of the luggage. Everybody thought it would be a great idea to stand right next to the conveyer belt and to lean forward so that nobody beside them could see what was coming. They stood there for almost half an hour before the conveyer belt even started moving and a further half an hour later they were still standing there waiting for their bags while the majority of the crowd had headed outside to their coaches.

"You bitches," Denise said, angrily approaching them, dragging her suitcase behind her. "You still waiting for your bags?"

"No, I just find it strangely comforting standing here and watching the same leftover bags going around and around and around. Why don't you go on ahead to the coach and I'll just stay here and continue enjoying myself," Sharon said sarcastically.

"Well, I hope they lost your case," Denise snapped. "Or even better, I hope your bag burst open and all your big knickers and bras are spread all over the conveyer belt for everyone to see."

Holly looked at Denise with amusement. "You feel better now?"

"Not until I have a cigarette," she replied, but she still managed to smile.

"Ooh, there's my bag!" Sharon said happily and swung it off the conveyer belt, managing to whack Holly in the shins.

"*Ow!*"

"Sorry, but must save clothes."

"If they've lost my clothes I'm going to sue them," Holly said angrily. By now everyone else had gone and they were the only people left inside. "Why am I always the last person waiting for my bags?" she asked her friends.

"Murphy's Law," Sharon explained. "Ah, here it is." She grabbed the suitcase and once again whacked it against Holly's already sore shins.

"*Ow! Ow! Ow!*" Holly yelled, rubbing her legs. "Could you at least swing the bloody thing the other way?!"

"Sorry," Sharon looked apologetic, "I only swing one way, darling."

The three of them headed off to meet their holiday rep.

"Stop, Gary! Get off me!" they heard a voice screeching as they rounded a corner. They followed the sound and spotted a young woman dressed in a red holiday rep uniform being attacked by a young man also dressed in a holiday rep uniform. The girls approached her and she straightened herself up.

"Kennedy, McCarthy and Hennessey?" she said in a thick London accent.

The girls nodded.

"Hi, I'm Victoria and I'm your holiday rep for the next week." She plastered a smile on her face. "So follow me and I'll show you to the coach." She winked cheekily at Gary and led the girls outside.

It was two o'clock in the morning, and yet a warm breeze greeted them as they stepped outside. Holly smiled to the girls, who felt it too; now they were really on holiday. When they stepped into the coach everybody cheered and Holly silently cursed them all, hoping this wasn't going to be a cheesy "let's all make friends" holiday.

"Woo-hoo," Cindy sang over to them. She was standing up from her chair and waving at them. "I kept you all a seat back here!"

Denise sighed loudly over Holly's shoulder and the girls trudged down to the backseat of the bus. Holly was lucky to sit next to the window, where she could ignore the rest of them. She hoped Cindy would understand that she wanted to be left alone, the major hint being that Holly had ignored her from the moment she had tottered over to their table.

Forty-five minutes later they reached Costa Palma Palace and the excitement once again returned to Holly's stomach. There was a long driveway in and tall palm trees lined the center of the drive. A large fountain was lit up with blue lights outside the main entrance and to her annoyance everybody on the bus cheered *once again* when they pulled up outside. The girls were booked into a studio apartment, which was a nice neat size containing one bedroom with twin beds, a small kitchen and living area with a sofa bed, a bathroom, of course, and a balcony. Holly stepped onto the balcony and looked out to the sea. Although it was too dark to see anything, Holly could hear the water gently lapping up against the sand. She closed her eyes and listened.

"Cigarette, cigarette, must have cigarette," Denise joined her, ripping the cigarette packet open and inhaling deeply. "Ah! That's much better; I no longer have the desire to kill people."

Holly laughed; she was looking forward to spending time with her friends. "Hol, do you mind if I sleep on the sofa bed? That way I can smoke . . ."

"Only if you keep the door open, Denise," Sharon yelled from inside. "I'm not waking up in the morning to the stink of smoke."

"Thanks," Denise said happily.

At nine o'clock that morning Holly was woken up to the sound of Sharon stirring. Sharon whispered to her she was going down to the pool to save them some sun beds. Fifteen minutes later Sharon returned to the apartment. "The Germans have nicked all the sun beds," she said grumpily. "I'll be down on the beach if you want me." Holly sleepily mumbled some sort of response and fell back asleep again. At ten o'clock Denise jumped on her in bed and they decided to get up and join Sharon at the beach.

The sand was hot and they had to keep moving so as not to burn the soles of their feet. As proud as Holly had been about her tan back in Ireland, it was obvious they had just arrived on the island, as they were the whitest people there. They spotted Sharon sitting under the shade of an umbrella reading her book.

"Oh, this is so beautiful, isn't it?" Denise smiled, looking around.

Sharon looked up from her book and smiled. "Heaven."

Holly looked around to see if Gerry had come to the same heaven. Nope, no sign of him. All around her there were couples, couples massaging sun cream onto each other's bodies, couples walking hand in hand along the beach, couples playing beach tennis, and directly in front of her sun bed, a couple was snuggled up together sunbathing. Holly didn't have any time to be depressed, as Denise had stepped out of her sundress and was hopping around on the hot sand in nothing but a skimpy leopard-skin thong.

"Will one of you put sun cream on me?"

Sharon put her book down and stared at her over the rim of her reading glasses. "I'll do it, but you can put the cream on your tits and bum yourself."

"Damn," Denise joked. "Don't worry about it, I'll go ask someone else then." Denise sat at the end of Sharon's sun bed while Sharon applied the cream. "You know what, Sharon?"

"What?"

"You'll get an awful tan line if you keep that sarong on."

Sharon looked down at herself and pulled the little skirt further down her legs. "What tan? I never get a tan. I've nice Irish skin, Denise. Didn't you know that the color blue was the new brown?"

Holly and Denise laughed. As much as Sharon tried to tan over the years she just ended up getting sunburned and then peeling. She had finally given up trying for a tan and accepted the fact that her skin was meant to be blue.

"Besides, I look like such a blob these days I wouldn't want to scare everyone off."

Holly looked at her friend, annoyed at her for calling herself a blob. She had put a little bit of weight on but was by no means fat.

"Why don't you go up to the swimming pool then and scare all those Germans away?" Denise joked.

"Yeah girls, we really need to get up earlier tomorrow to get a place by the pool. The beach gets boring after a while," Holly suggested.

"Don't vorry. Ve vill get ze Germans," joked Sharon.

The girls relaxed by the beach for the rest of the day, occasionally dipping themselves into the sea to cool down. They ate lunch at the beach bar and generally had a lazy day just as they had planned. Holly gradually felt all the stress and tension working its way out of her muscles, and for a few hours she felt free.

That night they successfully managed to avoid the Barbie Brigade and enjoyed dinner in one of the many restaurants that lined the busy street not far from the complex.

"I can't believe it's ten o'clock and we're heading back to the apartment already," Denise said while staring longingly at the huge choice of bars around them.

People overflowed from the outdoor bars and onto the streets, music vibrating from every building, mixing together to form an unusual eclectic sound. Holly could almost feel the ground pulsing beneath her. Conversation between them stopped as they took in the sights, sounds and smells around them. There was loud laughter, clinking glasses and singing coming from every direction. Neon lights flashed and buzzed, each battling for its own customers. On the street, bar owners fought hard against each other to convince passersby to enter, handing out leaflets, free drinks and concessions.

Tanned young bodies hung out in big groups around the outdoor tables and strolled confidently by them on the street, the smell of coconut sun cream rich in the air. Looking at the average age of the clientele, Holly felt old.

"Well, we can go to a bar for a few drinks if you want," Holly said uncertainly, watching the younger ones dancing around on the street.

Denise stopped walking and scanned the bars in order to choose one.

"All right, beautiful." A very attractive man stopped and flashed his pearly whites at Denise. He had an English accent. "Are you coming in here with me?"

Denise stared at the young man for a while, lost in thought. Sharon and Holly smirked at each other, knowing that Denise wouldn't be going to bed early after all. In fact, Denise might not get to bed at all that night, knowing her.

Finally Denise snapped out of her trance and straightened herself up. "No thank you, I have a boyfriend and I love him!" she announced proudly. "Come on, girls!" she said to Holly and Sharon and walked off in the direction of the hotel.

The two girls remained on the street, mouths open in shock. They couldn't quite believe it. They had to run to catch up with her.

"What are you two gawking at?" Denise smiled.

"You," Sharon said, still shocked. "Who are you and what have you done with my man-eating friend?"

"OK." Denise held her hands up in the air and grinned. "Maybe being single isn't all it's cracked up to be."

Holly lowered her eyes and kicked a stone along the path as they made their way back to their resort. It sure wasn't.

"Well good for you, Denise," Sharon said happily, wrapping her arm around Denise's waist and giving her a little squeeze.

A silence fell between them and Holly listened as the music faded away slowly, leaving only a beat of the bass in the distance.

"That street made me feel so old," Sharon said suddenly.

"Me too!" Denise's eyes widened. "Since when did people start going out so young?"

Sharon began to laugh. "Denise, the people aren't getting younger, *we* are getting older, I'm afraid."

Denise thought about that for a while. "Well, it's not like we're *old* old, for God's sake. I mean, it's not exactly time for us to hang up our dancing shoes and grab our walking sticks. We could stay out all night if we wanted to, we just . . . are tired. We've had a long day . . . oh God, I do sound old." Denise rambled on to herself as Sharon was too busy watching Holly, head down, kicking a stone along the path.

"Holly, are you OK? You haven't said a word in a while." Sharon was concerned.

"Yeah, I was just thinking," Holly said quietly, keeping her head down.

"Thinking about what?" Sharon asked softly.

Holly's head shot up. "Gerry." She looked at the girls. "I was thinking about Gerry."

"Let's go down to the beach," Denise suggested, and they slipped out of their shoes and allowed their feet to sink into the cool sand.

The sky was clear black and a million little stars twinkled down on them; it was as if someone had thrown glitter up into a massive black net. The full moon rested itself low over the horizon, reflecting its beam and showing where the sea met the sky. The girls sat in its path along the shore. The musical water gently lapped before them, calming them, relaxing them. The air was warm but a small cool breeze brushed past Holly, causing her hair to tickle her skin. She closed her eyes, took a deep breath and filled her lungs with fresh air.

"That's why he brought you here, you know," Sharon said, watching her friend relaxing.

Holly's eyes remained closed and she smiled.

"You don't talk about him much, Holly," Denise said casually, making designs with her finger in the sand.

Holly slowly opened her eyes. Her voice was quiet but warm and silky. "I know."

Denise looked up from drawing circles in the sand. "Why not?"

Holly paused for a while and looked out to the black sea. "I don't know how to talk about him." She thought for a while. "I don't know whether to say 'Gerry was' or 'Gerry is.' I don't know whether to be sad or happy when I talk about him to other people. It's like if I'm happy when I talk about him, certain people judge and expect me to be crying my eyes out. When I'm upset when talking about him, it makes people feel uncomfortable." She stared out to the black sea sparkling in the background and her voice was quieter when she spoke again. "I can't tease him in conversation like I used to because it feels *wrong*. I can't talk about things he told me in confidence because I don't want to give his secrets away, because they're *his* secrets. I just don't quite know *how* to remember him in conversation. It doesn't mean I don't remember him up here," she tapped the side of her temples.

The three girls sat cross-legged on the soft sand.

"John and I talk about Gerry all the time." Sharon looked at Holly with glittering eyes. "We talk about the times he made us laugh, which was *a lot*." The girls laughed at the memory. "We even talk about the times we fought. Things we loved about him, things he did that *really* annoyed us."

Holly raised her eyebrows.

Sharon continued, "Because to us, that's just how Gerry was. He wasn't all nice. We remember *all* of him, and there's absolutely *nothing* wrong with that."

There was a long silence.

Denise was the first to speak. "I wish my Tom had known Gerry." Her voice trembled a little.

Holly looked at her in surprise.

"Gerry was my friend too," she said, tears pricking in her eyes. "And Tom didn't even know him at all. So I try to tell him things about Gerry all the time just so he knows that not long ago, one of the nicest men on this earth was *my* friend and I think *everyone* should have known him." Her lip wobbled and she bit down on it hard. "But I can't believe that someone I now love so much, who knows everything else about me, doesn't know a friend that I loved for ten years."

A tear ran down Holly's cheek and she reached out to hug her friend. "Well then, Denise, we'll just have to keep telling Tom about him, won't we?"

They didn't bother meeting up with their holiday rep the next morning, as they had no intention of going on any tours or taking part in any silly sports tournaments. Instead, they got up early and took part in the sun bed dance, running around trying to throw their towels on the sun beds to reserve their positions for the day. Unfortunately, they still hadn't managed to get up early enough. ("Don't those bloody Germans ever sleep?" Sharon had given out.) Finally after Sharon had sneakily thrown a few towels away from some unattended beds, the girls managed to get three beds together.

Just as Holly found herself nodding off she heard piercing screams and a crowd ran by her. For some reason, Gary, one of the holiday reps, thought it would be a really funny idea to dress in drag and be chased around the swimming pool by Victoria. Everyone around the pool cheered them on as the girls rolled their eyes. Eventually Victoria caught Gary and they both managed to fall on top of each other into the swimming pool.

Everyone applauded.

Minutes later as Holly was taking a quiet swim a woman announced into a microphone attached to her head that she was going to begin aqua aerobics in the pool in five minutes. Victoria and Gary, helped by the Barbie Brigade, ran around all the sun beds dragging everyone up and forcing them to take part.

"Ah, would you ever fuck off!" Holly heard Sharon scream at one of the members of the Barbie Brigade as she tried to drag her into the pool. Holly was soon forced out of the pool by the approaching herd of hippopotami who were about to dive in for their aqua aerobics session. They sat through an incredibly annoying half hour session of aerobics with the instructor yelling out the movements into the headpiece. When it was finally over they announced a water polo tournament was about to take place, so the girls immediately jumped up and headed over to the beach for some peace and quiet.

· · ·

"You ever hear from Gerry's parents, Holly?" Sharon asked as she and Holly lounged on their inflatable rafts in the sea.

"Yeah, they send me postcards every few weeks telling me where they are and how they're getting on."

"So they're still on that cruise?"

"Yeah."

"Do you miss them?"

"To be honest, I don't really think they feel like they're part of me anymore. Their son's gone and they have no grandchildren, so I don't think they feel we have any connection anymore."

"That's bullshit, Holly. You were married to their son and that makes you their daughter-in-law. That's a very strong connection."

"Oh, I don't know," she sighed. "I just don't think that's enough for them."

"They're a bit backward, aren't they?"

"Yeah, *very*. They hated me and Gerry 'living in sin' as they said. Couldn't wait for us to get married. And *then* they were even worse when we did! They couldn't understand why I wouldn't change my name."

"Yeah, I remember that," Sharon said. "His mum gave me an earful at the wedding. She said it was the woman's duty to change her name as a sign of respect to her husband. Imagine that? The cheek of her!"

Holly laughed.

"Ah well, you're better off without them being around anyway," Sharon assured her.

"Hello girls." Denise floated out to meet them.

"Hey, where have you been?" Holly asked.

"Oh, I was just chatting to some bloke from Miami. Really nice guy."

"Miami? That's where Daniel went on holiday," she said, lightly running her fingers through the clear blue water.

"Hmmm," Sharon replied, "nice guy, Daniel, isn't he?"

"Yeah, he's a really nice guy," Holly agreed. "Very easy to talk to."

"Tom was telling me he's really been through the wars recently," Denise said, turning to lie on her back.

Sharon's ears pricked up at the sound of gossip, "Why's that?"

"Oh, he was engaged to be married to some chick and it turns out she was sleeping with someone else. That's why he moved to Dublin and bought the pub, to get away from her."

"I know, it's awful, isn't it?" Holly said sadly.

"Why, where did he live before?" Sharon asked.

"Galway. He used to run a pub there," Holly explained.

"Oh," Sharon said, surprised, "he doesn't have a Galway accent."

"Well, he grew up in Dublin and joined the army, then he left and moved to Galway where his family owns a pub, then he met Laura, they were together for seven years, were engaged to be married, but she cheated on him so they broke up and he moved back to Dublin and bought Hogan's." Holly caught her breath.

"Don't know much about him, do you?" Denise teased.

"Well, if you and Tom had paid the slightest bit more attention to us the other night in the pub then maybe I wouldn't know so much about him," Holly replied playfully.

Denise sighed loudly. "God, I really miss Tom," she said sadly.

"Did you tell the guy from Miami that?" Sharon laughed.

"No, I was just chatting to him," Denise said defensively. "To be honest, nobody else interests me. It's really weird, it's like I can't even *see* any other men, and I mean that I don't even *notice* them.

And as we are currently surrounded by hundreds of half-naked men, I think that's saying a lot."

"I think they call it love, Denise." Sharon smiled at her friend.

"Well, whatever it is, I've never felt like this before."

"It's a nice feeling," Holly said more to herself.

They lay in silence for a while, all lost in their own thoughts, allowing the gentle motion of the waves to soothe them.

"Holy shit!" Denise suddenly yelled, causing the other two to jump. "Look how far out we are!"

Holly sat up immediately and looked around. They were out so far from the shore everybody on the beach looked like little ants.

"Oh shit!" panicked Sharon, and as soon as Sharon panicked Holly knew they were in trouble.

"Start swimming, quick!" Denise yelled, and they all lay on their stomachs and started splashing around with all their might. After a few minutes of tirelessly going at it they gave up, out of breath. To their horror they were even farther out than they had been when they started.

It was no use, the tide was moving out too quickly, and the waves were just too strong.

Twenty-eight

"Help!" Denise screamed at the top of her lungs and waved her arms around wildly.

"I don't think they can hear us," Holly said with tears welling in her eyes.

"Oh, could we be any more stupid?" Sharon gave out and continued to rant on about the dangers of rafts in the sea.

"Oh, forget about that, Sharon," Denise snapped. "We're here now so let's all scream together and maybe they'll hear us."

They all cleared their throats and sat up on their rafts as much as they possibly could without causing them to sink under their weight.

"OK, one, two, three . . . HELP!" they all yelled, and waved their arms around frantically.

Eventually they stopped screaming and stared in silence at the dots on the beach to see if it had made any impact. Everything remained as it was.

"Please tell me there aren't any sharks out here," Denise whimpered.

"Oh please, Denise," Sharon snapped viciously, "that is the last thing we need to be reminded of right now."

Holly gulped and stared down into the water. The once clear blue water had darkened. Holly hopped off her raft to see how deep it was, and as her legs dangled, her heart began to pound. Their situation was bad. Sharon and Holly tried to swim for it while dragging their rafts behind them, while Denise continued her bloodcurdling screams.

"Jesus, Denise," Sharon panted, "the only thing that's gonna respond to that is a dolphin."

"Look, why don't you two just stop swimming because you've been at it now for a few minutes and you're still right beside me."

Holly stopped swimming and looked up. Denise stared back at her.

"Oh." Holly tried to hold back her tears. "Sharon, we might as well stop and save our energy."

Sharon stopped swimming and the three of them huddled together on their rafts and cried. There was really nothing more they could do, Holly thought, beginning to panic even more. They had tried shouting for help, but the wind was carrying their voices in the other direction; they had tried swimming, which had been completely pointless, as the tide was too strong. It was beginning to get chilly and the sea was looking dark and ugly. What a stupid situation to get themselves into. Through all her fear and worry, Holly managed to surprise herself by feeling completely humiliated.

She wasn't sure whether to laugh or cry, but the unusual sound of both began to tumble out of her mouth, causing Sharon and Denise to stop crying and stare at her as though she had ten heads.

"At least one good thing came out of this," Holly half laughed and half cried.

"There's a good thing?" Sharon said, wiping her eyes.

"Well, the three of us always talked about going to Africa," she giggled like a madwoman, "and by the looks of things, I would say we're probably halfway there."

The girls looked out to sea to their future destination. "It's a cheaper mode of transport too," Sharon joined in with Holly.

Denise stared at them as if they were mad, and just one look at her lying in the middle of the ocean naked with only a leopard-skin thong on and blue lips was enough to set the girls off laughing.

"What?" Denise looked at them wide-eyed.

"I'd say we're in deep deep trouble here," Sharon giggled.

"Yeah," Holly agreed, "we're in way over our heads."

They lay there laughing and crying for a few minutes more till the sound of a speedboat approaching caused Denise to sit up and start waving frantically again. Holly and Sharon laughed even harder at the sight of Denise's chest bouncing up and down as she waved at the approaching lifeguards.

"It's just like a regular night out with the girls," Sharon giggled, watching Denise being dragged half naked into the boat by a muscular lifeguard.

"I think they're in shock," one lifeguard said to the other as they dragged the remaining hysterical girls onto the boat.

"Quick, save the rafts!" Holly just about managed to blurt out through her laughter.

"Raft overboard!" Sharon screamed.

The lifeguards looked at each other worriedly as they wrapped warm blankets around the girls and sped off back to the shore.

As they approached the beach there appeared to be a large crowd gathering. The girls looked at one another and laughed even harder. As they were lifted off the boat there was a huge applause; Denise turned and curtsied to them all.

"They clap now, but where were they when we needed them," Sharon grumbled.

"Traitors," Holly giggled.

"There they are!" They heard a familiar squeal and saw Cindy and the Barbie Brigade pushing their way through the crowd. "Oh my God!" she squeaked. "I saw the whole thing through my binoculars and called the lifeguards. Are you OK?" She looked to each of them frantically.

"Oh, we're fine," Sharon said rather seriously. "We were the lucky ones. The poor rafts never even had a chance." With that Sharon and Holly cracked up laughing and were ushered away to be looked at by a doctor.

That night the girls realized the seriousness of what had happened to them and their moods drastically changed. They sat in silence throughout dinner, all thinking about how lucky they were to be rescued and kicking themselves for being so careless. Denise squirmed uncomfortably in her chair and Holly noticed she had barely touched her food.

"What's wrong with you?" Sharon said, sucking in a piece of spaghetti, which caused the sauce to splash all over her face.

"Nothing," Denise said, quietly refilling her glass with water.

They sat in silence for another little while.

"Excuse me, I'm going to the toilet." Denise stood up and walked awkwardly into the ladies.

Sharon and Holly frowned at each other.

"What do you think is wrong with her?" Holly asked.

Sharon shrugged, "Well, she's drunk about ten liters of water through dinner, so no wonder she keeps going to the toilet," she exaggerated.

"I wonder if she's mad at us for going a bit funny out there today."

Sharon shrugged again and they continued to eat in silence. Holly had reacted unusually out there in the water, and it bothered her to think about why she had. After the initial panic of thinking she was going to die, Holly became feverishly giddy as she realized that if she did die she knew she would be with Gerry. It bothered her to think that she didn't care whether she lived or died. Those were selfish thoughts. She needed to change her perspective on life.

Denise winced as she sat down.

"Denise, what is wrong with you?" Holly asked.

"I'm not telling either of you or you'll laugh," she said childishly.

"Oh come on, we're your friends, we won't laugh," Holly said, trying to keep the smile off her face.

"I said no." She filled her glass with more water.

"Ah come on, Denise, you know you can tell us anything. We promise not to laugh." Sharon said it so seriously that Holly felt bad for smiling.

Denise studied both their faces, trying to decide whether they could be trusted.

"Oh, OK," she sighed loudly and mumbled something very quietly.

"What?" Holly said, moving in closer.

"Honey, we didn't hear you, you were too quiet," Sharon said, pulling her chair in closer.

Denise looked around the restaurant to make sure nobody was listening and she moved her head into the center of the table. "I said, from lying out in the sea for so long, my bum is sunburnt."

"Oh," Sharon said, sitting back in her chair abruptly.

Holly looked away to avoid eye contact with Sharon, and she counted the bread rolls in the basket to take her mind off what Denise had just said.

There was a long silence.

"See, I said you would both laugh," Denise huffed.

"Hey, we're not laughing," Sharon said shakily.

There was another silence.

Holly couldn't help herself. "Just make sure you put plenty of sun cream on it so that it doesn't peel." The two of them finally broke down.

Denise just nodded her head and waited for them to stop laughing. She had to wait a long time. In fact, hours later as she lay on the sofa bed trying to sleep she still waited.

The last thing she heard before she went to sleep was a smart remark from Holly: "Make sure you lie on your front, Denise." This was followed by more laughter.

"Hey, Holly," Sharon whispered after they had finally calmed down. "Are you excited about tomorrow?"

"What do you mean?" Holly asked, yawning.

"The letter!" Sharon replied, surprised that Holly didn't remember immediately. "Don't tell me that you forgot."

Holly reached her hand under her pillow and felt around for the letter. In one hour she would be able to open Gerry's sixth letter. Of course she hadn't forgotten.

. . .

The next morning Holly awoke to the sound of Sharon throwing up in the toilet. She followed her in and gently rubbed her back and held her hair back.

"You OK?" she asked worriedly after Sharon had eventually stopped.

"Yeah, it's just those bloody dreams I had all night. I dreamt I was on a boat and on a raft and all sorts of things. I think it was just seasickness."

"I had those dreams too. It was scary yesterday, wasn't it?"

Sharon nodded. "I'm never going on a raft again," she smiled weakly.

Denise arrived at the bathroom door already dressed in her bikini. She had borrowed one of Sharon's sarongs to cover up her burned behind and Holly had to bite her tongue to stop herself from teasing her, as she was clearly in a great deal of pain.

When they arrived down at the swimming pool, Denise and Sharon joined the Barbie Brigade. Well, it was the least they could do, seeing as they were the ones who had called for help. Holly couldn't believe that she had fallen asleep before midnight the previous night. She had planned to get up quietly without waking the girls, sneak out to the balcony and read the letter. How she fell asleep in all her excitement was beyond her, but she couldn't listen to the Barbie Brigade any longer. Before Holly was dragged into any conversation she signaled to Sharon that she was leaving, and Sharon gave her an encouraging wink, knowing why she was disappearing. Holly wrapped her sarong around her hips and carried her small beach bag containing the all-important letter.

She positioned herself away from all the excited shouts of children and adults playing and stereo blaring out the latest chart songs. She found a quiet corner and made herself comfortable on her beach towel to avoid more contact with the burning sand. The waves crashed and fell. The seagulls called out to one another in the clear blue sky, flew down, dipped themselves into the cool, crystal water to catch their breakfasts. It was morning and already the sun was hot.

Holly carefully pulled the letter out of her bag as though it were the most delicate thing in the world, and she ran her fingers along the neatly written word, "August." Taking in all the sounds and smells of the world around her she gently tore open the seal and read Gerry's sixth message.

> *Hi Holly,*
>
> *I hope you're having a wonderful holiday. You're looking beautiful in that bikini, by the way! I hope I picked the right place for you, it's the place you and I almost went for our honeymoon, remember? Well, I'm glad you got to see it in the end . . .*
>
> *Apparently, if you stand at the very end of the beach near the rocks across from your hotel, and look around the corner to the left, you'll see a lighthouse. I'm told that's where the dolphins gather . . . not many people know that. I know you love dolphins . . . tell them I said hi . . .*
>
> *PS, I love you, Holly . . .*

With shaking hands, Holly put the card back into the envelope and secured it safely in a pocket of her bag. She felt Gerry's eyes on her as she stood up and quickly rolled up the beach towel. She felt he was here with her. She quickly ran to the end of the beach, which suddenly stopped because of a cliff. She put her trainers on and began to climb the rocks so she could see around the corner.

And there it was.

Exactly where Gerry had described it, the lighthouse sat high on the cliff, bright white as though it were some sort of torch to heaven. Holly carefully climbed over the rocks and made her way around the little cove. She was on her own now. It was completely private. And then she heard the noises. The squeaks of dolphins playing near the shore away from the view of all the tourists on the beaches beside it. Holly collapsed on the sand to watch them play and listen to them talk to one another.

Gerry sat beside her.

He may even have held her hand.

Holly felt happy enough to head back to Dublin, relaxed, de-stressed and brown. Just what the doctor ordered. That didn't stop her from groaning when the plane landed in Dublin Airport to heavy rain. This time the passengers didn't applaud and cheer and the airport seemed like a very different place from the one she had left last week. Once again, Holly was the last person to receive her luggage, and an hour later they trudged gloomily out to John, who was waiting in the car.

"Well, it looks like the leprechaun didn't do any more work in your garden while you were away," Denise said, looking at the garden as John reached Holly's home.

Holly gave her a friends a big hug and a kiss and made her way into her quiet, empty house. There was a horrible musty smell inside and she moved to the kitchen patio doors to let the fresh air circulate.

She froze just as she was turning the key in the door and stared outside.

Her entire back garden had been relandscaped.

The grass was cut. The weeds were gone. The garden furniture had been polished and varnished. A fresh coat of paint gleamed from her garden walls. New flowers had been planted and in the corner, underneath the shade of the great oak tree, sat a wooden bench. Holly looked around in shock; who on earth was doing all this?

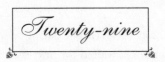

Twenty-nine

I N THE DAYS FOLLOWING HER return from Lanzarote, Holly
kept a low profile. Holly, Denise and Sharon were all keen to
spend the next few days apart from one another. It wasn't something they had talked about, but after living in each other's ears
every day for a whole week, Holly was sure they all agreed it would
be healthy to spend some time apart. Ciara was impossible to get
hold of, as she was either working hard at Daniel's club or spending time with Mathew. Jack was spending his last few precious
weeks of summer freedom down in Cork at Abbey's parents' house
before he had to go back to school, and Declan was . . . well, who
knew where Declan was.

Now she was back, she wasn't exactly bored with her life, but
she wasn't exactly overjoyed either. It just seemed so . . . nothing
and so pointless. She'd had the holiday to look forward to, but now

felt she had no real reason to get out of bed in the morning. And as she was taking a time-out from her friends, she really had nobody else to talk to. There was only so much conversation she could have with her parents. Compared to last week's sweltering heat in Lanzarote, Dublin was wet and ugly, which meant she couldn't even work at maintaining her beautiful tan or appreciate her new back garden.

Some days she never even got out of bed, she just watched television and waited . . . waited for next month's envelope from Gerry, wondering what journey he would take her on next. She knew her friends would disapprove after she'd been so positive on holiday, but when he was alive she'd lived for him, and now that he was gone she lived for his messages. Everything was about him. She had truly believed that her purpose in life had been to meet Gerry and enjoy all their days together for the rest of their lives. What was her purpose now? Surely she had one, or perhaps there had been an error in the administration up above.

Something that she did feel she should do was to catch the leprechaun. After further interrogation of her neighbors she still knew nothing more of her mystery gardener, and she was beginning to think the whole thing had just been an awful mistake. Eventually she had herself convinced that a gardener had made a mistake and that he was working on the wrong garden, so she checked the post every day for a bill that she was going to refuse to pay. But no bill arrived, of that variety anyway. Plenty of others arrived and she was running out of money fast. She had loans up to her eyeballs, electricity bills, phone bills, insurance bills, everything that came through her door was a bloody bill, and she hadn't a clue how she was going to continue paying them all. But she didn't even care; she had become numb to all those irrelevant problems in life. She just dreamed the impossible dreams.

One day Holly realized why the leprechaun hadn't returned. Her garden was only tidied when she wasn't home. So she got out of bed early one morning and drove her car around the corner from her house. She walked back home and settled down on her bed and waited for her mystery gardener to appear.

After three days of Holly repeating this behavior, the rain finally stopped and the sun began to shine again. Holly was about to give up hope of ever solving her mystery when she heard someone approach her garden. She jumped out of bed in a panic, unprepared for what she should do, even though she had spent days planning. She peeped over her windowsill and spotted a young boy who looked about twelve years old walking down her drive tugging a lawnmower along behind him. She threw on Gerry's oversized dressing gown and raced down the stairs not caring what she looked like.

She pulled open the front door, causing the young boy to jump. His arm froze in midair and his finger hovered just over the doorbell. His mouth dropped open at the sight of the woman in front of him.

"*A-ha!*" Holly yelled happily. "I think I caught my little leprechaun!"

His mouth opened and closed like a goldfish's; he was clearly unsure of what to say. Eventually he scrunched up his face as though he were about to cry and screamed, "Da!"

Holly looked up and down the road in search of his father and decided to squeeze as much information out of the boy as she could before the adult reached them.

"So you're the one who's been working on my garden." She folded her arms across her chest.

He shook his head wildly and gulped.

"You don't have to deny it," she said gently, "you've been caught now." She nodded over at the lawnmower.

He turned around to stare at it and yelled again, "Da!" His dad slammed the door of a van and made his way over to her house.

"What's wrong, son?" He wrapped his arm around the boy's shoulders and looked at Holly for an explanation.

Holly wasn't going to fall for this little charade. "I was just asking your son here about your little scam."

"What scam?" He looked angry.

"The one where you work on my garden without my permission and then you expect me to pay for it. I've heard about this kind of thing before." She put her hands on her hips and tried to look like she couldn't be messed with.

The man looked confused. "Sorry, I don't know what you're talking about, missus. We've never worked on your garden before." He stared around at the state of her front garden, thinking the woman was insane.

"Not *this* garden, you landscaped my *back* garden." She smiled and raised her eyebrows, thinking she had caught him.

He laughed back at her. "Landscaped your garden? Lady, are you mad? We cut grass, that's all. See this? This is a lawnmower, nothing else. All it does is cut the bloody grass."

Holly dropped her hands from her hips and slowly placed them in the pockets of her gown. Maybe they were telling the truth. "Are you sure you haven't been in my garden?" she squinted her eyes.

"Lady, I have never even worked on this street before, never mind your garden, and I can guarantee I won't be working in your garden in the future."

Holly's face fell. "But I thought—"

"I don't care what you thought," he interrupted. "In future, you try to get your facts straight before you start terrorizing my kid."

Holly looked at the young boy and saw his eyes fill with tears.

PS, I LOVE YOU / 257

Her hands flew to her mouth with embarrassment. "Gosh, I'm so sorry," she apologized. "Just hold on there a minute."

She rushed into the house to get her purse and squeezed her last fiver into the boy's chubby little hand. His face lit up.

"OK, let's go," his dad said, turning his son around by the shoulders and leading him down the drive.

"Da, I don't wanna do this job anymore," the boy moaned to his dad as they carried on to the next house.

"Ah, don't worry, son, they all won't be as mad as her."

Holly closed the door and studied her reflection in the mirror. He was right; she had turned into a madwoman. Now all she needed was a house full of cats. The sound of the phone ringing pulled Holly's eyes away from her image.

"Hello?" Holly said, answering the phone.

"Hiya, how are you?" Denise asked happily.

"Oh, full of the joys of life," Holly said sarcastically.

"Oh, me too!" she giggled in response.

"Really? What's got you so happy?"

"Oh nothing much, just life in general," she giggled again.

Of course, just life. Wonderful, wonderful, beautiful life. What a silly question.

"So what's happening?"

"I'm calling to invite you out for dinner tomorrow night. I know it's short notice, so if you're too busy . . . cancel whatever it is you have planned!"

"Hold on and let me check my diary," Holly said sarcastically.

"No problem," Denise said seriously and was silent while she waited.

Holly rolled her eyes. "Oh look at that, whaddaya know? I appear to be free tomorrow night."

"Oh goody!" Denise said happily. "We're all meeting at Chang's at eight."

"Who's we?"

"Sharon and John are going and some of Tom's friends too. We haven't been out together for ages, so it'll be fun!"

"OK then, see you tomorrow." Holly hung up feeling angry. Had it completely slipped Denise's mind that Holly was still a grieving widow and that life just wasn't fun for her anymore? She stormed upstairs and opened her wardrobe. Now what piece of old and disgusting clothing would she wear tomorrow night, and how on earth was she going to afford an expensive meal? She could barely even afford to keep her car on the road. She grabbed all her clothes from her wardrobe and flung them across the room, screaming her head off until she finally felt sane again. Perhaps tomorrow she would buy those cats.

Thirty

HOLLY ARRIVED AT THE RESTAURANT at eight-twenty, as she had spent hours trying on different outfits and ripping them off again. Eventually she settled with the outfit that she had been instructed to wear by Gerry for the karaoke just so she could feel closer to him. She hadn't been coping very well over the past few weeks; she had had more downs than ups and was finding it harder to pick herself back up again.

As she was walking toward the table in the restaurant her heart sank.

Couples "R" Us.

She paused halfway there and quickly sidestepped, hiding behind a wall. She wasn't sure she could go through with this. She hadn't the strength to keep battling with her emotions. She looked around to find the easiest escape route; she certainly couldn't leave the way she had come in or they would definitely see her. She spotted the fire escape beside the kitchen door, which had been left open to clear some of the smoke. The moment she stepped out into the cool fresh air she felt free again. She walked across the car park, trying to formulate an excuse to tell Denise and Sharon.

"Hi, Holly."

She froze and slowly turned around, realizing she had been caught. She spotted Daniel leaning against his car smoking a cigarette.

"Hiya, Daniel." She walked toward him. "I didn't know you smoked."

"Only when I'm stressed."

"You're stressed?" They greeted each other with a hug.

"I was trying to figure out whether to join Happy Couples United in there." He nodded toward the restaurant.

Holly smiled. "You too?"

He laughed, "Well, I won't tell them I saw you if that's what you want."

"So you're going in?"

"Have to face the music sometime," he said, grimly stabbing out his cigarette with his foot.

Holly thought about what he'd said. "I suppose you're right."

"You don't have to go in if you don't want to. I don't want to be the cause of you having a miserable night."

"On the contrary, it would be nice to have another loner in my company. There are so very few of our kind in existence."

Daniel laughed and held out his arm. "Shall we?"

Holly linked her arm in his and they slowly made their way into the restaurant. It was comforting to know she wasn't alone in feeling alone.

"By the way, I'm getting out of here as soon as we finish the main course," he laughed.

"Traitor," she answered, thumping him on the arm. "Well, I have to leave early anyway to catch the last bus home." She hadn't had the money to fill the tank in the car for the past few days.

"Well then, we have the perfect excuse. I'll say we have to leave early because I'm driving you home and you have to be home by . . . what time?"

"Half-eleven?" At twelve she planned on opening the September envelope.

"Perfect time." He smiled and they made their way into the restaurant feeling slightly reinforced by each other's company.

"Here they are!" Denise announced as they made their way to the table.

Holly sat beside Daniel, sticking to her alibi like glue. "Sorry we're late," she apologized.

"Holly, this is Catherine and Thomas, Peter and Sue, Joanne and Paul, Tracey and Bryan, John and Sharon you know, Geoffrey and Samantha, and last but not least, this is Des and Simon."

Holly smiled and nodded at all of them.

"Hi, we're Daniel and Holly," Daniel said smartly, and Holly giggled beside him.

"We had to order already, if you don't mind," Denise explained. "But we just ordered loads of different dishes so we can all share them. Is that OK?"

Holly and Daniel nodded.

The woman beside Holly, whose name she couldn't remember, turned to her and spoke loudly, "So Holly, what do you do?"

Daniel raised his eyebrows at Holly.

"Sorry, what do I do when?" Holly answered seriously. She

hated nosy people. She hated conversations that revolved around what people did for a living, especially when those people were complete strangers that she had just met less than a minute ago. She felt Daniel shaking with laughter beside her.

"What do you do for a living?" the woman asked again.

Holly had intended on giving her a funny but slightly rude answer but suddenly stopped herself as all the conversations around the table died down and focused on her. She looked around with embarrassment and cleared her throat nervously, "Em . . . well . . . I'm between jobs right now." Her voice shook.

The woman's lips began to twitch and she scraped a piece of bread from between her teeth rudely.

"What is it that you do?" Daniel asked her loudly, breaking the silence.

"Oh, Geoffrey runs his own business," she said, proudly turning to her husband.

"Oh right, but what is it that *you* do?" Daniel repeated.

The lady seemed disconcerted that her answer hadn't been good enough for him. "Well, I keep myself busy all day every day doing various things. Honey, why don't you tell them about the company?" She turned to her husband again to divert the attention from herself.

Her husband leaned forward in his seat. "It's just a small business." He took a bite out of his bread roll, chewed it slowly, and everyone waited while he swallowed so he could continue.

"Small but successful," his wife added for him.

Geoffrey finally finished eating his bread. "We make car windshields and sell them to the warehouses."

"Wow, that's very interesting," Daniel said dryly.

"So what is it that you do, Dermot?" she said, turning to look at Daniel.

"Sorry, my name is Daniel actually. I'm a publican."

"Right," she nodded and looked away. "Awful weather we're having these days, isn't it?" she addressed the table.

Everyone fell into conversation and Daniel turned to Holly. "Did you enjoy your holiday?"

"Oh, I had a fabulous time," she answered. "We took it easy and relaxed every day, didn't do anything wild and weird."

"Just what you needed," he smiled. "I heard about your near-death experience."

Holly rolled her eyes. "I bet Denise told you that."

He nodded and laughed.

"Well, I'm sure she gave you the exaggerated version."

"Not really, she just told me about how you were surrounded by sharks and had to be airlifted from the sea by a helicopter."

"She didn't!"

"No, not really," he laughed. "Still, that must have been some conversation you were having to not notice you were drifting out to sea!"

Holly's face blushed a little as she recalled that they had been talking about him.

"OK everyone," Denise called. "You're probably wondering why Tom and I invited you all here tonight."

"Understatement of the year," Daniel mumbled, and Holly giggled.

"Well, we have an announcement to make." She looked around at everyone and smiled.

Holly's eyes widened.

"Myself and Tom are getting married!" Denise squealed, and Holly's hands flew up to her mouth in shock. She did *not* see that one coming.

"Oh Denise!" she gasped, and walked around the table to hug them. "That's wonderful news! Congratulations!"

She looked at Daniel's face; it had gone white.

They popped open a bottle of champagne and everyone raised their glasses as Jemima and Jim or Samantha and Sam or whatever their names were made a toast.

"Hold on! Hold on!" Denise stopped them just before they started. "Sharon, did you not get a glass?"

Everyone looked at Sharon, who was holding a glass of orange juice in her hand.

"Here you go," Tom said, pouring her a glass.

"No no no! Not for me, thanks," she said.

"Why not?" Denise huffed, upset that her friend wouldn't celebrate with her.

John and Sharon looked at each other and smiled. "Well, I didn't want to say anything because it's Denise and Tom's special night . . ."

Everyone urged her to speak.

"Well . . . I'm pregnant! John and I are going to have a baby!"

John's eyes began to water and Holly just froze in shock in her seat. She did *not* see that one coming either. Tears filled her eyes as she went over to congratulate Sharon and John. Then she sat down and took deep breaths. This was all too much.

"So let's make a toast to Tom and Denise's engagement and Sharon and John's baby!"

Everyone clinked glasses and Holly ate dinner in silence, not really tasting anything.

"You want to make that time eleven o'clock?" Daniel asked quietly, and she nodded in agreement.

After dinner Holly and Daniel made their excuses to leave and nobody really tried to persuade them to stay.

"How much should I leave toward the bill?" Holly asked Denise.

"Oh, don't worry about it." She waved her hand at her dismissively.

"No, don't be silly, I couldn't let you pay for it. How much, honestly?"

The woman beside her grabbed the menu and started adding up the price of all the meals they had bought. There had been so many and Holly had only picked at her own and had even avoided eating a starter so she could afford it.

"Well, it works out as about fifty each, and that's including all the wine and bottles of champagne."

Holly gulped and stared down at the thirty euro in her hand.

Daniel grabbed her hand and pulled her up. "Come on, let's go, Holly."

She opened her mouth to make the excuse of not bringing as much money as she thought, but when she opened the palm of her hand and looked at the money, there appeared to be an extra twenty.

She smiled at Daniel gratefully and they both headed out to the car.

They sat in the car in silence, both thinking about what had happened that night. She wanted to feel happy for her friends, really she did, but she couldn't shake off the feeling of being left behind. Everyone else's lives were moving on except hers.

Daniel pulled up outside her house. "Do you want to come in for a tea or coffee or anything?" She was sure he would say no and was shocked when he undid his seat belt and accepted her offer. She really liked Daniel, he was very caring and fun to be with, but right now she just wanted to be alone.

"That was some night, wasn't it?" he said, taking a sip of his coffee. Holly just shook her head with disbelief. "Daniel, I have known those girls practically all of my life, and I did *not* see any of that coming."

"Well, if it makes you feel any better, I've known Tom for years too and he didn't mention a thing."

"Although Sharon wasn't drinking when we were away," she hadn't listened to a word Daniel had said, "and she did throw up a few mornings, but she said it was seasickness . . ." She trailed off and her brain went into overdrive as things started to add up.

"Seasickness?" Daniel asked, confused.

"After our near-death experience," she explained.

"Oh, right."

This time neither of them laughed.

"It's funny," he said, settling down into the couch. Oh no, Holly thought; he's never going to leave the house now.

"The lads always said that myself and Laura would be the first to get married," he continued. "I just didn't think that Laura would be getting married before me."

"She's getting married?" Holly asked gently.

He nodded and looked away. "He used to be a friend of mine, too," he laughed bitterly.

"Obviously he's not anymore."

"Nope," he shook his head. "Obviously not."

"Sorry to hear that," she said genuinely.

"Ah well, we all get our fair share of bad luck. You know that better than anyone."

"Huh, fair share," she repeated.

"I know, there's nothing fair about it, but don't worry, we'll have our good luck too."

"You think?"

"I hope."

They sat in silence for another while and Holly watched the clock. It was five past twelve. She really needed to get him out of the house so she could open the envelope.

He read her mind. "So how're the messages from above going?"

Holly sat forward and placed her mug down on the table. "Well, I've another one to open tonight actually. So . . ." She looked at him.

"Oh right," he said, jumping to attention. He sat up quickly and put his mug down on the table. "I better leave you at it so."

Holly bit her lip, feeling guilty at ushering him out so quickly, but she was also relieved he was finally going.

"Thanks a million for the lift, Daniel," she said, following him to the door.

"No problem at all." He quickly grabbed his coat from the banister and headed out the door. They gave each other a quick hug.

"See you soon," she said, feeling like a right bitch, and watched him walk down to his car in the rain. She waved him off and her guilt immediately faded as soon as she closed the door. "Right Gerry," she said as she headed toward the kitchen and picked up the envelope from the table. "What have you got in store for me this month?"

Thirty-one

HOLLY HELD THE TINY ENVELOPE tightly in her hands and glanced up at the clock on the wall over the kitchen table. It was twelve-fifteen. Usually Sharon and Denise would have called her by now, all excited to hear about what was inside the envelope. But so far neither of them had called. It seemed news of an engagement and a pregnancy beat the news of a message from Gerry these days. Holly scorned herself for being so bitter; she wanted to be happy for her friends, she wanted to be back in the restaurant right now celebrating their good news with them like the old Holly would have done. But she couldn't bring herself even to smile for them.

She was jealous of them and their good fortune. She was angry with them for moving on without her. Even in the company of friends she felt alone; in a room of a thousand people she would feel alone. But mostly when she roamed the rooms of her quiet house she felt so alone.

She couldn't remember the last time she'd felt truly happy, when somebody or something caused her to laugh so hard her stomach pained her and her jaw ached. She missed going to bed at night with absolutely nothing on her mind, she missed enjoying eating food instead of it becoming something she just had to endure in order to stay alive, she hated the butterflies she got in her tummy every time she remembered Gerry. She missed *enjoying* watching her favorite television programs instead of their just becoming something she would stare at blankly to pass the hours. She hated feeling like she had no reason to wake up; she hated the feeling when she did wake up. She hated the feeling of having no excitement or anything to look forward to. She missed the feeling of being loved, of knowing Gerry was watching her as she watched television or ate her dinner. She missed sensing his eyes on her as she entered a room; she missed his touches, his hugs, his words of advice, his words of love.

She hated counting down the days till she could read another one of his messages because they were all she had left of him, and after this one there would be only three more. And she hated to think of what her life might be like when there would be no more Gerry. Memories were fine, but you couldn't touch them, smell them or hold them. They were never exactly as the moment had been, and they faded with time.

So damn Sharon and Denise, they could go on with their happy lives, but for the next few months all Holly had was Gerry. She wiped a tear from her face, tears had become such a permanent feature on her face the past few months, and she slowly opened her seventh envelope.

Shoot for the moon, and if you miss you'll still be among the stars.

Promise me you will find a job you love this time!

PS, I love you . . .

Holly read and reread the letter, trying to discover how it made her feel. She had been dreading going back to work for such a long time now, had believed that she wasn't ready to move on, that it was too soon. But now she knew she had no choice. It was time. And if Gerry said it was to be, it would be. Holly's face broke into a smile. "I promise, Gerry," she said happily. Well, it was no holiday to Lanzarote, but at least it was one step further to getting her life back on track. She studied his writing for a long time after reading it, as she always did, and when she was satisfied with the fact she had analyzed every word, she rushed over to the kitchen drawer, took out a notepad and pen and began to write her own list of possible jobs.

LIST OF POSSIBLE JOBS

1. FBI Agent?—Am not American. Do not want to live in America. Have no police experience.

2. Lawyer—Hated school. Hated studying. Do not want to go to college for ten million years.

3. Doctor—Ugghh.

4. Nurse—Unflattering uniforms.

5. Waitress—Would eat all the food.

6. Professional people-spotter—Nice idea, but no one would pay me.

7. Beautician—Bite my nails and wax as rarely as possible. Do not want to see areas of other people's bodies.

8. Hairdresser—Would not like boss like Leo.

9. Retail assistant—Would not like boss like Denise.

10. Secretary—NEVER AGAIN.

11. Journalist—Cont spill properly enuff. Ha-ha, should be comedienne.

12. Comedienne—Reread last joke. Wasn't funny.

13. Actress—Could not possibly outdo my wonderful performance in the critically acclaimed "Girls and the City."

14. Model—Too small, too fat, too old.

15. Singer—Rethink idea of comedienne (number 12).

16. Hotshot businesswoman in control of life— Hmm . . . Must do research tomorrow . . .

Holly finally collapsed onto her bed at three in the morning and dreamed of being a big hotshot advertising woman making a presentation in front of a huge conference table on the top floor of a skyscraper overlooking Grafton Street. Well, he did say aim for the moon . . . She woke up early that morning excited from her dreams of success, had a quick shower, beautified herself and walked down to her local library to look up jobs on the Internet.

Her heels made a loud noise on the wooden floor as she walked across the room to the librarian's desk, which caused several people to look up from their books and stare at her. She continued clattering across the huge room and her face blushed as she realized everyone was watching her. She slowed down immediately and started to tiptoe so as not to attract any more attention. She felt like one of the cartoon characters on TV that hugely exaggerated their tiptoeing, and her face flared up even more when she realized she must have looked like a complete idiot. A couple of schoolkids dressed in their uniforms who were obviously playing truant for the day sniggered together as she made her way past their table. Holly stopped her weird walk halfway between the door and the librarian's desk and tried to decide what to do next.

"Shush!" The librarian scowled over at the schoolkids. More people looked up from their books to watch the woman standing in the middle of the room. She decided to keep on walking and quickened her pace. Her heels clicked loudly on the floor and echoed around the room and the sound got faster and faster as she raced to the desk in order to end this humiliation.

The librarian looked up and smiled and tried to appear surprised to see someone standing at the counter. As if she hadn't heard Holly thudding across the room.

"Hi," Holly whispered quietly, "I was wondering if I could use the Internet."

"Excuse me?" The librarian spoke normally and moved her head closer to Holly so she could hear.

"Oh," Holly cleared her throat, wondering what happened to having to whisper in libraries, "I was wondering if I could use the Internet."

"No problem, they're just over there," she smiled, directing her over to the row of computers on the far side of the room. "It's five euro for every twenty minutes online."

Holly handed over her last ten euro. It was all she had managed to take out of her bank account that morning. She had kept a long line of people waiting behind her at the ATM machine as she worked her way down from one hundred euro to ten as the ATM embarrassingly beeped every time she entered a sum of money to let her know she had "insufficient funds." She couldn't believe that was all she had left, but it had given her even more reason to go job-hunting immediately.

"No no," the librarian said, handing back her money, "you can pay when you finish."

Holly stared across the floor to the computers. She would have to make another big noise just to get there. She took a deep breath and raced over, passing rows and rows of tables. Holly nearly laughed at the sight of everyone; it was almost like dominos as she passed, each head arose from a book to stare at her. Finally she reached the computers and realized that there were none free. She felt like she had just lost a game of musical chairs and that everyone was laughing at her. This was getting ridiculous. She raised her hands angrily at them as if to say, "What are you all looking at?" and they quickly buried their heads in their books again.

Holly stood in the center of the floor between the rows of tables and computers, drummed her fingers on her handbag and looked around. Her eyes nearly popped out of her head as she spotted Richard tapping away on one of the computers. She tiptoed over to him and touched him on the shoulder. He jumped with fright and swirled around in his chair.

"Hiya," she whispered.

"Oh hello, Holly, what are you doing here?" he said uneasily, as though she had caught him doing something naughty.

"I'm just waiting for a computer," she explained. "I'm finally looking for a job," she said proudly. Even saying the words made her feel like less of a vegetable.

"Oh right." He turned to face his computer and shut down the screen. "You can use this one so."

"Oh no, you don't have to rush for me!" she said quickly.

"Not at all. I was just doing some research for work." He stood up from his chair and made room for her to sit down.

"All the way over here?" she said, surprised. "Don't they have computers in Blackrock?" she joked. She wasn't quite sure what exactly it was that Richard did for a living, and it would seem rude to ask him after he'd worked there more than ten years. She knew it involved wearing a white coat, wandering around a lab and dropping colorful substances into test tubes. Holly and Jack had always said he was making a secret potion to rid the world of happiness. She felt bad now for ever saying that. While Holly couldn't imagine ever being truly close to Richard, and he would probably always drive her crazy, she was coming to realize he had his good qualities. Like giving her his space at the library computer, for one.

"My work brings me everywhere," Richard joked awkwardly.

"Shush!" the librarian said loudly. Holly's audience once again looked up from their books. Oh, so *now* she was supposed to whisper, Holly thought angrily.

Richard said a quick good-bye, made his way over to pay at the desk and slipped quietly out of the room.

Holly sat down at the computer and the man beside her smiled strangely at her. She smiled back and glimpsed nosily at his computer screen. She looked away quickly and nearly gagged at the sight of the porn on his screen. He continued to stare at her with a scary smile on his face while Holly ignored him and became engrossed in her job-hunting.

Forty minutes later she shut down the computer happily, made her way to the librarian and placed her ten euro on the desk. The woman tapped away on the computer and ignored the money on the counter. "That's fifteen euro, please."

Holly gulped as she looked down at her note, "But I thought you said it was five for twenty minutes."

"Yes, that's right," she smiled at her.

"But I was only online for forty minutes."

"Actually, you were on for forty-four minutes, which cuts into the extra twenty minutes," she said, consulting her computer.

Holly giggled, "But that's only a few minutes more. It's hardly worth five euro."

The librarian just continued to smile back at her.

"So you expect me to pay?" Holly asked, surprised.

"Yes, that's the rate."

Holly lowered her voice and moved her head closer to the woman. "Look, this is really embarrassing, but I actually only have the ten on me now. Is there any way I can come back with the rest later on today?"

The librarian shook her head. "I'm sorry, but we can't allow that. You need to pay the entire amount."

"But *I don't have* the entire amount," Holly protested.

The lady stared back blankly.

"Fine," Holly huffed, taking out her mobile.

"Sorry, but you can't use that in here." She pointed to the no mobile phones sign on the counter.

Holly looked up slowly at her and counted to five in her head.

"If you *won't* let me use my phone, well then I *can't* phone some-body for help. If I *can't* phone somebody, then they *can't* come down here to give me the money. If they *don't* come down here with the money, well then *I can't pay you.* So we have a little prob-lem here, don't we?" she raised her voice.

The lady shuffled nervously from foot to foot.

"Can I go outside to use the phone?"

The lady thought about the dilemma. "Well, usually we don't allow people to leave the premises without paying, but I suppose I can make an exception." She smiled and then added quickly, "As long as you stand just in front of the entrance there."

"Where you can see me?" Holly said sarcastically.

The lady nervously shuffled papers below the counter and pretended to go back to work.

Holly stood outside the door and thought about who to call. She couldn't call Denise and Sharon. Although they would proba-bly rush home from work for her, she didn't want them to know about her failures in life now that they were both so blissfully happy. She couldn't call Ciara because she was on a day shift at Hogan's pub, and seeing as Holly already owed Daniel twenty euro, she didn't think it would be wise to call her sister away from work for the sake of five euro. Jack was back teaching at the school, Abbey was too, Declan was at college and Richard wasn't even an option.

Tears rolled down her face as she scrolled down through the list of names in her phone book. The majority of people in her phone hadn't even called her since Gerry had died, which meant she had no other friends to call. She turned her back on the librar-ian so she wouldn't see that she was upset. What should she do? How embarrassing her situation was to actually have to call some-body to ask for five euro. It was even more humiliating that she had absolutely nobody to call. But she had to or the snotty librarian would probably call the police on her. She dialed the first number that came into her head.

"Hi, this is Gerry, please leave a message after the beep and I'll get back to you as soon as I can."

"Gerry," Holly said crying, "I need you . . ."

Holly stood outside the door of the library and waited. The librarian kept a close watch on her just in case she ran off. Holly made a face at her and turned her back to her.

"Stupid bitch," she growled.

Finally her mum's car pulled up outside and Holly tried to make herself appear as normal as she could. Watching her mother's happy face driving in and parking in the car park brought back memories. Her mum used to collect her from school every day when she was younger and she was always so relieved to see that familiar car come to rescue her after her hellish day in school. Holly had always hated school, well, she had until she met Gerry. Then she would look forward to going to school each day so they could sit together and flirt down the back of the class.

Holly's eyes filled with tears again and Elizabeth rushed over to her and wrapped her arms around her baby. "Oh, my poor poor Holly, what happened, love?" she said, stroking her hair and casting evil glances in at the librarian as Holly explained the story.

"OK, love, why don't you wait out in the car and I'll go in and deal with her." Holly did as she was told and sat in the car flicking through the radio stations as her mum confronted the school bully.

"Silly cow," her mother grumbled as she climbed back into the car. She looked over at her daughter, who looked so lost. "Why don't we go home and we can relax?"

Holly smiled gratefully and a tear trickled down her face. Home. She liked the sound of that.

Holly snuggled up on the couch with her mum in Portmarnock. She felt like a teenager again. She and her mum used to always cuddle up on the couch and fill each other in on all the gossip in their lives. She wished she could have the same giggling conversations with her now as she used to have then. Her mum broke into her thoughts, "I rang you last night at home, were you out?" She took a sip of her tea.

Oh, the wonders of the magical tea. The answer to all of life's little problems. You have a gossip and you make a cup of tea, you get fired from your job and you have a cup of tea, your husband tells you he has a brain tumor and you have a cup of tea . . .

"Yeah, I went out to dinner with the girls and about a hundred other people I didn't know." Holly rubbed her eyes tiredly.

"How are the girls?" Elizabeth said fondly. She had always gotten along well with Holly's friends, unlike Ciara's friends, who terrified her.

Holly took a sip of her tea. "Sharon's pregnant and Denise got engaged," she said, still staring off into space.

"Oh," Elizabeth squeaked, not sure how to react in front of her obviously distressed daughter. "How do you feel about that?" she asked softly, brushing a hair away from Holly's face.

Holly stared down at her hands and tried to compose herself. She wasn't successful and her shoulders began to tremble and she tried to hide her face behind her hair.

"Oh Holly," Elizabeth said sadly, putting her cup down and moving closer to her daughter. "It's perfectly normal to feel like this."

Holly couldn't even manage to get any words out of her mouth.

The front door banged and Ciara announced to the house, "We're hoooome!"

"Great," Holly sniffed, resting her head on her mum's chest.

"Where is everyone?" Ciara shouted, banging doors closed around the house.

"Just a minute, love," Elizabeth called out, angry that her moment with Holly was ruined.

"I have news!" Ciara's voice got louder as she got nearer to the living room. Mathew burst open the door carrying Ciara in his arms. "Me and Mathew are moving back to Australia!" she yelled happily into the room. She froze as she saw her upset sister in her mum's arms. She quickly jumped down from Mathew's arms, led him out of the room, and closed the door silently behind them.

"Now Ciara's going too, Mum," Holly cried even harder, and Elizabeth cried softly for her daughter.

Holly stayed up late that night talking to her mum about everything that had been bubbling up inside her for the past few months. And although her mother offered many words of kind reassurance, Holly still felt as trapped as before. She stayed in the guest bedroom that night and woke up to a madhouse the following morning. Holly smiled at the familiarity of the sound of her brother and sister running around the house screaming about how they were late for college and late for work, followed by their dad grumbling at them to get a move on, followed by her mum's gentle pleas for everyone to stay silent so as not to disturb Holly. The world went on, simple as that, and there was no bubble big enough to protect her.

At lunchtime Holly's dad dropped her home and squeezed a check for five thousand euro into her hand.

"Oh, Dad, I can't accept this," Holly said, overcome with emotion.

"Take it," he said, gently pushing her hand away. "Let us help you, love."

"I'll pay back every cent," she said, hugging him tightly.

Holly stood at the door and waved her father off down the road. She looked at the check in her hand and immediately a weight was lifted from her shoulders. She could think of twenty things she could do with this check, and for once buying clothes wasn't one of them. Walking into the kitchen she noticed the red light flashing on the answering machine on the table in the hall. She sat on the end of the stairs and hit the button.

She had five new messages.

One was from Sharon ringing to see if she was OK because she hadn't heard from her all day. The second was from Denise ringing to see if she was OK because she hadn't heard from her all day. The two girls had obviously been talking to each other. The third was from Sharon, the fourth was from Denise and the fifth was just somebody hanging up. Holly pressed delete and ran upstairs to change her clothes. She wasn't quite ready to talk to Sharon and Denise yet; she needed to get her life into order first so she could be more of a support for them.

She sat in the spare room in front of her computer and began to type up a CV. She had become an old pro at doing this as she changed her jobs so often. It had been a while since she had to worry about going to interviews, though. And if she did get an interview, who would want to hire someone who hadn't been working for a whole year?

It took her two hours to finally print out something that she thought was at least half decent. In fact, she was really proud of what she had done, she had somehow managed to make herself look intelligent and experienced. She laughed loudly in the room, hoping she would manage to fool her future employers into thinking she was a capable worker. Reading back over her CV she decided that even she would hire herself. She dressed smartly and drove down to the village in the car she had finally managed to fill with petrol. She parked outside the recruitment office and applied lip gloss in her car mirror. There was to be no more time wasting. If Gerry said to find a job, she was going to find a job.

Thirty-two

A COUPLE OF DAYS LATER HOLLY sat out on her new garden furniture in her back garden, sipped on a glass of red wine and listened to the sound of her wind chimes making music in the breeze. She looked around at the neat lines of her newly land-scaped garden and decided that whoever was working on her garden had to be a professional. She breathed in and allowed the sweet scent of the flowers to fill her nostrils. It was eight o'clock and already it was beginning to get dark. The bright evenings were gone, and everybody was once again preparing for hibernation for the winter months.

She thought about the message she had received on her answering machine that day. It had been from the recruitment agency and she was shocked to have received a reply from them so quickly. The woman on the phone said that there had been a great response to her resume and already Holly had two job interviews lined up. Butter-flies fluttered around her stomach at the thought of it. She had never been particularly good at job interviews, but then again she had never been particularly keen on any of the jobs she was being inter-viewed for. This time she felt different; she was excited to get back to work and to try something new. Her first interview was for a job selling advertising space for a magazine that circulated throughout Dublin. It was something she had absolutely no experience in, but she was willing to learn because the idea of it sounded far more interesting than any of her former jobs, which had mostly entailed answering the phone, taking messages and filing. Anything that involved not having to do any of those things was a step up.

The second interview was with a leading Irish advertising company and she knew she had absolutely no hope of being employed there. But Gerry had told her to shoot for the moon . . .

Holly also thought about the phone call she had just received from Denise. Denise had been so excited on the phone she didn't seem to be at all bothered by the fact that Holly hadn't talked to her since they'd gone out for dinner. In fact, Holly didn't think she had even noticed that Holly hadn't returned her phone call. Denise had been all talk about her wedding arrangements and rambled on for almost an hour about what kind of dress she should wear, what flowers she should choose, where she should hold the reception. She started sentences and then forgot to finish them as she jumped from topic to topic. All Holly had to do was make a few noises to let her know she was still listening . . . although she wasn't. The only piece of information she had taken in was that Denise was planning to have the wedding on New Year's Eve, and by the sounds of it Tom wouldn't be having a say in how Denise's special day should be run. Holly was surprised to hear they had set a date so soon, she had just assumed it would be one of those long-winded last-a-few-years kind of engagements, especially as Denise and Tom had only been an item for four months. But Holly didn't worry about that as much as she would have when she was her old self. She was now a regular subscriber to the finding love and holding on to it forever magazine. Denise and Tom were right not to waste time worrying about what people thought if they knew in their hearts it was the right decision.

Sharon hadn't called Holly since the day after she had announced her pregnancy, and Holly knew she would have to call her friend soon before the days passed her by and it was too late. This was an important time in Sharon's life and she knew she should be there for her, but she just couldn't bring herself to do it. She was being a jealous, bitter and incredibly selfish friend, she knew that, but Holly needed to be selfish these days in order to survive. She was still trying to get her head around the fact that Sharon and John were managing to achieve everything that everyone had always assumed Holly and Gerry would do first. Sharon had always said she hated kids, Holly thought angrily. Holly would call Sharon when she was good and ready.

It began to get chilly and Holly took her glass of wine inside to her warm house where she refilled it. All she could do for the next couple of days was wait for her job interviews and pray for success. She went into the sitting room, turned on her and Gerry's favorite album of love songs on the CD player and snuggled up on the couch with her glass of wine, where she closed her eyes and pictured them dancing around the room together.

The following day she was awoken by the sound of a car driving into her driveway. She got out of bed and threw Gerry's dressing gown on, presuming it was her car being returned from the garage. She peeped out of the curtains and immediately jumped back as she saw Richard stepping out of his car. She hoped he hadn't seen her because she really wasn't in the mood for one of his visits. She paced her bedroom floor feeling guilty as she ignored the doorbell ringing for the second time. She knew she was being horrible, but she just couldn't bear sitting down with him for another awkward conversation. She really hadn't anything to talk about anymore, nothing had changed in her life, she had no exciting news, not even any normal news to tell *anybody*, never mind Richard.

She breathed a sigh of relief as she heard him walk away and heard his car door bang shut. She stepped into the shower and allowed the warm water to run over her face and she was once again lost in a world of her own. Twenty minutes later she padded downstairs in her Disco Diva slippers. A scraping noise from outside made her freeze in her step. She pricked her ears up and listened more closely, trying to identify the sound. There it was again. A scraping noise and a rustling like somebody was in her garden . . . Holly's eyes widened as she realized that her leprechaun was outside working in her garden. She stood still, unsure of what to do next.

She crept into the living room, stupidly thinking the person outside would hear her wandering around her house, and she got down on her knees. Peering above the windowsill she gasped as she saw Richard's car still sitting in the driveway. What was even more surprising was the sight of Richard on his hands and knees with a small gardening implement in his hand, digging up the soil and planting new flowers. She crawled away from the window and sat on the carpet in shock, unsure of what to do next. The sound of her car being parked outside the house snapped her back to attention and her brain went on overdrive as she tried to figure out whether to answer the door to her mechanic or not. For some odd reason Richard didn't want Holly to know that he was working on her garden, and she decided she was going to respect that wish . . . for now.

She hid behind the couch as she saw her mechanic approach the door and she had to laugh at how ridiculous this all seemed. She giggled quietly to herself as the doorbell rang and she scurried even further behind the couch as her mechanic walked over to the window and stared in. Her heart beat wildly and she felt as though she were doing something illegal. She covered her mouth and tried to smother her laughs. She felt like such a child again. She had always been hopeless at playing hide-and-seek, whenever she felt her seeker coming near her she would always get an attack of the giggles and her hiding place would be found. Then for the rest of the day she would have to search for everybody else. She wouldn't giggle then because everybody knew that was the boring part that was always given to the youngest child. But she was making up for lost wins in the past because she had succeeded in fooling both Richard and her mechanic, and she rolled around on the carpet laughing at herself as she heard him drop the keys through the letterbox and walk away from the door.

A few minutes later she stuck her head out from around the couch and checked if it was safe to come out. She stood up and brushed the dust off her clothes, telling herself she was too old to be playing silly games. She peeked out from behind the curtain again and saw Richard packing up his gardening equipment.

On second thought, these silly games were fun and she had nothing else to do. Holly kicked off her slippers and shoved her feet into her trainers. As soon as she saw Richard drive down the road she ran outside and hopped into her car. She was going to chase her leprechaun.

She managed to stay three cars behind him all the way, just like they did in the movies, and she slowed down as she saw him pulling over ahead of her. He parked his car and went into the newsagent and returned with a newspaper in his hand. Holly put her sunglasses on, adjusted her baseball cap and peered over the top of the *Arab Leader* that was covering her face. She laughed at herself as she caught sight of her reflection in the mirror. She looked like the most suspicious person in the world. She watched Richard cross the road and head into the Greasy Spoon. She was slightly disappointed; she was hoping for a far juicier adventure than this.

She sat in her car for a few minutes trying to formulate a new plan and jumped with fright as a traffic warden banged on her window.

"You can't park here," he said, motioning toward the car park. Holly smiled back sweetly and rolled her eyes as she backed into a free space. Surely Cagney and Lacey never had this problem.

Eventually her inner child settled down to have a nap and mature Holly took her cap and glasses off and tossed them onto the passenger seat, feeling foolish. Silly games over. Real life starting now.

She crossed the road and looked around inside the café for her brother. She spotted him sitting down with his back to her, hunched over his newspaper and drinking a cup of tea. She marched over happily with a smile on her face. "God, Richard, do you ever go to work?" she joked loudly, causing him to jump. She was about to say more but stopped herself as he looked up at her with tears in his eyes and his shoulders began to shake.

Thirty-three

HOLLY LOOKED AROUND TO SEE if anyone else in the café had noticed and she slowly pulled out a chair and sat down beside Richard. Had she said something wrong? She looked at Richard's face in shock, not knowing what to do or what to say. She could safely say that she had *never* been in this situation before. Tears rolled down his face and he tried with all his might to stop them.

"Richard, what's wrong?" she said, confused, and she placed her hand awkwardly on his arm and patted it.

Richard continued to shake with tears.

The plump lady dressed in a canary yellow apron this time made her way around the counter and placed a box of tissues on the table beside Holly.

"Here you go," she said, handing Richard a tissue. He wiped

his eyes and blew his nose loudly, a big old-man blow, and Holly tried to hide her smile.

"I'm sorry for crying," Richard said, embarrassed, and avoided eye contact with her.

"Hey," she said softly, placing her hand more easily on his arm this time, "there's nothing wrong with crying. It's my new hobby these days, so don't knock it."

He smiled at her weakly. "Everything just seems to be falling apart, Holly," he said sadly, catching a tear with the tissue before it dropped from his chin.

"Like what?" she asked, concerned at her brother's transformation into somebody she didn't know at all. Come to think of it, she had never really known the real Richard. She had seen so many sides to him over the past few months he had her slightly baffled.

Richard took a deep breath and gulped back his tea. Holly looked up at the woman behind the counter and ordered another pot.

"Richard, I've recently learned that talking about things helps," Holly said gently. "And coming from me that's a huge tip, because I used to keep my mouth shut thinking I was super-woman, able to keep all feelings inside." She smiled at him encouragingly. "Why don't you tell me about it."

He looked doubtful.

"I won't laugh, I won't say anything if you don't want me to. I won't tell a soul what you tell me, I'll just listen," she assured him.

He looked away from her and focused on the salt and pepper shakers at the center of the table and spoke quietly, "I lost my job."

Holly remained silent and waited for him to say more. After a while, when she didn't say anything, Richard looked up to face her.

"That's not so bad, Richard," she said softly, giving him a

smile. "I know you loved your job, but you can find another one. Hey, if it makes you feel any better, I used to lose my jobs all the time—"

"I lost my job in April, Holly," he interrupted. Then he spoke angrily, "It is now September. There's nothing for me . . . not in my line of work . . ." He looked away.

"Oh." Holly didn't know quite what to say. After a long silence she spoke again, "But at least Meredith is still working, so you still have a regular income. Just take the time you need to find the right job . . . I know it doesn't feel like it right now, but—"

"Meredith left me last month," he interrupted her again, and this time his voice was weaker.

Holly's hands flew to her mouth. Oh, poor Richard. She had never liked the bitch, but Richard had adored her. "The kids?" she asked carefully.

"They're living with her," he said and his voice cracked.

"Oh Richard, I'm so sorry," she said, fidgeting with her hands, not knowing where to put them. Should she hug him or leave him alone?

"I'm sorry too," he said miserably and continued to stare at the salt and pepper shakers.

"It wasn't your fault, Richard, so don't go telling yourself it was," she protested strongly.

"Wasn't it?" he said, his voice beginning to shake. "She told me I was a pathetic man who couldn't even look after his own family." He broke down again.

"Oh, never mind that silly bitch," Holly said angrily. "You are an excellent father and a loyal husband," she said strongly and realized she meant every word of it. "Timmy and Emily love you because you're fantastic with them, so don't mind what that demented woman says to you." She wrapped her arms around him and hugged her brother while he cried. She felt so angry she wanted to go over to Meredith and punch her in the face. In fact, she had always wanted to do that, but now she even had an excuse.

Richard's tears finally subsided and he pulled away from her and grabbed another tissue. Holly's heart went out to him; he had always tried so hard to be perfect and to create a perfect life and family for himself and it hadn't worked out as he had planned. He seemed to be in a great deal of shock.

"Where are you staying?" she asked, suddenly realizing that he had had no home to go to for the past few weeks.

"In a B&B down the road. Nice place. Friendly people," he said, pouring another cup of tea. Your wife leaves you and you have a cup of tea . . .

"Richard, you can't stay there," Holly protested. "Why didn't you tell any of us?"

"Because I thought we could work it out, but we can't . . . she's made up her mind."

As much as Holly wanted to invite him to stay with her in her house, she just couldn't do it. She had far too much to deal with on her own, and she was sure Richard would understand that.

"What about Mum and Dad?" she asked. "They would love to be able to help you out."

Richard shook his head. "No, Ciara's home now and so is Declan, I wouldn't want to dump myself on them as well. I'm a grown man now."

"Oh Richard, don't be silly." She made a face. "There's the spare room, which is your old room. I'm positive you would be welcome back there." She tried to persuade him. "Sure I even slept there a few nights ago."

He looked up from staring at the table.

"There is absolutely nothing wrong with returning to the house you grew up in every now and again. It's good for the soul." She smiled at him.

He looked uncertain. "Em . . . I don't think that's such a good idea, Holly."

"If it's Ciara you're worried about, then don't. She's heading back to Australia in a few weeks with her boyfriend so the house will be . . . less hectic."

His face relaxed a little.

Holly smiled. "So what do you think? Come on, it's a great idea and this way you won't be throwing your money away on some smelly ol' dump. I don't care how nice you say the owners are."

Richard smiled and it quickly faded again. "I couldn't ask Mother and Father, Holly, I . . . wouldn't know what to say."

"I'll go with you," she promised. "And I'll talk to them for you. Honestly, Richard, they'll be delighted to help out. You're their son and they love you. We all do," she added, placing her hand over his.

"OK," he finally agreed, and she linked her arm in his as they headed out to their cars.

"Oh by the way, Richard, thank you for my garden." Holly smiled at him, then leaned over and kissed him on the cheek.

"You know?" he asked, surprised.

She nodded. "You have a huge talent, and I'm going to pay you every single penny you deserve as soon as I find a job."

Her brother's face relaxed into a shy smile.

They got into their cars and drove back to Portmarnock to the house they'd grown up in.

. . .

Two days later Holly looked at herself in the toilet mirror of the office building where her first job interview was taking place. She had lost so much weight since she had last worn her old suits that she had had to go out and purchase a new one. It was flattering to her new slim figure. The jacket was long and went to just above her knees, and it was fastened tightly by one button at the waist. The trousers were just the right fit and fell perfectly over her boots. The outfit was black with light pink lines going through and she matched it with a light pink top underneath. She felt like a hotshot advertising businesswoman in control of her life, and all she needed to do now was to sound like one. She applied another layer of pink lip gloss and ran her fingers through her loose curls, which she had decided to allow to tumble down her shoulders. She took a deep breath and headed back out to the waiting area.

She took her seat again and glanced down at all the other applicants for the job. They seemed far younger than Holly and they all seemed to have a thick folder of some kind sitting on their laps. She looked around and started to panic . . . sure enough everybody had one of these folders. She stood up from her seat again and headed over to the secretary.

"Excuse me," Holly said, trying to get her attention.

The woman looked up and smiled, "Can I help you?"

"Yes, I was just in the toilet there and I think I must have missed being given a folder." Holly smiled politely at her.

The woman frowned and looked confused. "I'm sorry, what folders were handed out?"

Holly turned around and pointed to the folders sitting on the other applicants' laps and turned to face the secretary with a smile on her face.

The lady smiled and motioned her to come closer with her finger.

Holly tucked her hair behind her ears and moved nearer. "Yes?"

"Sorry honey, but they're actually portfolios that they brought themselves," she whispered to her so that Holly wouldn't be embarrassed.

Holly's face froze. "Oh. Should I have brought one of them with me?"

"Well, do you have one?" the lady asked with a friendly smile.

Holly shook her head.

"Well then, don't worry about it. It's not a requirement, people just bring these things to show off," she whispered to her and Holly giggled.

Holly returned to her seat and continued to worry about this portfolio business. Nobody had said anything to her about any stupid portfolios. Why was she the last to know everything? She tapped her foot and looked around the office while she waited. She got a good feeling from the place, the colors were warm and cozy and the light poured in from the large Georgian windows. The ceilings were high and there was a lovely feeling of space. Holly could sit there all day thinking. She suddenly felt so relaxed that her heart didn't even jump as her name was called. She walked confidently down toward the door of the interview office and the secretary winked at her to wish her good luck. Holly smiled back at her; for some reason she already felt part of the team. She paused just outside the door of the office and took a deep breath.

Shoot for the moon, she whispered to herself, shoot for the moon.

Thirty-four

H OLLY KNOCKED LIGHTLY ON THE door and a deep gruff
voice told her to enter. Her heart did a little flip at the
sound of his voice, feeling as if she had been summoned to the
principal's office at school. She wiped her clammy hands on her
suit and entered the room.

"Hello," she said more confidently than she felt. She walked
across the small room and held out her hand to the man who had
stood up from his chair and was extending his hand to her. He
greeted her with a big smile and a warm handshake. The face
didn't seem to match the grumpy voice at all, thankfully. Holly
relaxed a little at the sight of him, he reminded her of her father.
He looked to be in his late fifties with a big cuddly bear physique,
and she had to stop herself from leaping over the desk to hug him.
His hair was neat and almost a sparkling silver color and she imagined he had been an extremely handsome man in his youth.

"Holly Kennedy, isn't it?" he said, taking his seat and glancing down at her CV in front of him. She sat down in the seat opposite him and forced herself to relax. She had read every interview technique manual she could get her hands on over the past few days and had tried to put it all into practice, from walking into the room to the proper handshake to the way she positioned herself in her chair. She wanted to look like she was experienced, intelligent and highly confident. But she would need more than a firm handshake to succeed in proving that.

"That's right," she said, placing her handbag on the ground beside her and resting her sweaty hands on her lap.

He put his glasses on the end of his nose and flicked through her CV in silence. Holly stared at him intently and tried to read his facial expressions. It wasn't an easy task, as he was one of those people who had a constant frown on his face while he read. Well, it was either that or he wasn't at all impressed by what he was seeing. She glanced around at his desk and waited for him to start speaking again. Her eyes fell upon a silver photo frame with three pretty girls close to her age all smiling happily at the camera. She continued to stare at it with a smile on her face, and when she looked up she realized he had put the CV down and was watching her. She smiled and tried to appear more businesslike.

"Before we start talking about you, I'll explain exactly who I am and what the job entails," he explained.

Holly nodded along with him, intending to look very interested.

"My name is Chris Feeney and I'm the founder and editor of the magazine, or the boss man as everyone likes to call me around here," he chuckled, and Holly was charmed by his twinkling blue eyes.

"Basically we are looking for someone to deal with the advertising aspect of the magazine. As you know, the running of a magazine or any media organization is hugely reliant on the advertising we receive. We need the money for our magazine to be published, so this job is extremely important. Unfortunately, our last man had to leave us in a hurry, so I'm looking for somebody who could begin work almost immediately. How would you feel about that?"

Holly nodded. "That would be no problem at all, in fact I'm eager to begin work as soon as possible."

Mr. Feeney nodded and looked down at her CV again. "I see you've been out of the workforce for over a year now, am I correct in saying that?" He lowered his head and stared at her over the rim of his glasses.

"Yes that's right," Holly nodded. "And I can assure you that was purely out of choice. Unfortunately my husband was ill, and I had to take time off work to be with him."

She swallowed hard; she knew that this would be an issue for every employer. Nobody wanted to employ someone who had been idle for the past year.

"I see," he said, looking up at her. "Well, I hope that he's fully recovered now," he said, smiling warmly.

Holly wasn't sure whether that was a question or not and wasn't sure whether to keep talking. Did he want to hear about her personal life? He continued to look at her and she realized he was waiting for an answer.

She cleared her throat. "Well no, actually, Mr. Feeney, unfortunately he passed away in February . . . he had a brain tumor. That's why I felt it was important to leave my job."

"Gosh." Mr. Feeney put down the CV and took his glasses off.

"Of course I can understand that. I'm very sorry to hear that," he said sincerely. "It must be hard for you being so young and all . . ." He looked down at his desk for a while and then met her eyes again. "My wife lost her life to breast cancer just last year, so I understand how you may be feeling," he said generously.

"I'm sorry to hear that," Holly said sadly, looking at the kind man across the table.

"They say it gets easier," he smiled.

"So they say," Holly said grimly. "Apparently gallons of tea does the trick."

He started to laugh, a big guffaw of a laugh. "Yes! I've been told that one too, and my daughters inform me that fresh air is also a healer."

Holly laughed. "Ah yes, the magic fresh air; it does wonders for the heart. Are they your daughters?" She smiled, looking at the photograph.

"Indeed they are," he said, smiling also. "My three little doctors who try to keep me alive," he laughed. "Unfortunately the garden no longer looks like that anymore, though," he said, referring to the photograph.

"Wow, is that your garden?" Holly said, wide-eyed. "It's beautiful; I presumed it was the Botanic Gardens or somewhere like that."

"That was Maureen's specialty. You can't get me out of the office long enough to sort through that mess."

"Oh, don't talk to me about gardens," Holly said, rolling her eyes, "I'm not exactly Ms. Greenfingers myself, and the place is beginning to look like a jungle." Well, it did look like a jungle, she thought to herself.

They continued to look at each other and smile, and Holly

was comforted to hear a similar story from someone else in her position. Whether she got the job or not, at least she was comforted that she was not entirely alone.

"Anyway, getting back to the interview," Mr. Feeney said. "Have you any experience in working with the media at all?"

Holly didn't like the way he said "at all"; it meant that he had read through her CV and couldn't see any sign of experience for the job.

"Yes I have, actually." She returned to business mode and tried hard to impress him. "I once worked in an estate agents and I was responsible for dealing with the media regarding advertising the new properties that were for sale. So I was on the other end of what this job requires and so I know how to deal with companies who are wishing to buy space."

Mr. Feeney nodded along. "But you have never actually worked on a magazine or newspaper or anything like that?"

Holly nodded her head slowly and racked her brains for something to say. "But I was responsible for printing up a weekly newsletter for a company I worked for . . ." She rambled on and on, grasping at every little straw she could, and realized she was sounding rather pathetic.

Mr. Feeney was too polite to interrupt her as she went through every job she'd ever worked at and exaggerated anything that was in any way related to advertising or media. Eventually she stopped talking as she grew bored at the sound of her own voice, and she twisted her fingers around each other nervously on her lap. She was underqualified for this job and she knew it, but she also knew that she could do it if he would just give her the chance.

Mr. Feeney took off his glasses. "I see. Well Holly, I can see that you have a great deal of experience in the workplace in various different areas, but I notice that you haven't stayed in any of your jobs for a period longer than of nine months . . ."

"I was searching for the right job for me," Holly said, her confidence now totally shattered.

"So how do I know you won't desert me after a few months?" He smiled but she knew he was serious.

"Because this is the right job for me," she said seriously. Holly took a deep breath as she felt her chances slipping away from her, and she wasn't prepared to give up that easily. "Mr. Feeney," she said, moving forward to sit on the edge of her chair. "I'm a very hard worker. When I love something I give it one hundred percent, as I'm extremely committed. I'm a very capable person and what I don't know now I am more than willing to learn so that I can do my best for myself, for you and for the company. If you put your trust in me, I promise I won't let you down." She stopped herself just short of getting down on her knees and begging for the damn job. Her face blushed as she realized what she had just done.

"Well then, I think that's a good note to finish on," Mr. Feeney said, smiling at her. He stood up from his chair and held his hand out. "Thank you very much for taking the time to come down here. I'm sure we'll be in touch."

Holly shook his hand and thanked him quietly, picked her bag up from the ground and felt his eyes burning into her back as she headed toward the door. Just before she stepped outside the door she turned back to face him. "Mr. Feeney, I'll make sure your secretary brings you in a nice hot pot of tea. It'll do you the world of good." She smiled and closed the door to the sound of his loud laughter. The friendly secretary raised her eyebrows at Holly as she passed her desk, and the rest of the applicants held on to their portfolios tightly and wondered what the lady had said to make the interviewer laugh so loudly. Holly smiled to herself as she continued to hear Mr. Feeney laughing and made her way out into the fresh air.

Holly decided to drop in on Ciara at work, where she could have a bite to eat. She rounded the corner and entered Hogan's pub and searched for a table inside. The pub was packed with people dressed smartly on their lunch breaks from work, and some were even having a few sneaky pints before heading back to the office. Holly found a small table in the corner and settled down.

"Excuse me," she called out loudly and clicked her fingers in the air, "can I get some service here please?"

The people at the tables around her threw her looks for being so rude to the staff and Holly continued to click her fingers in the air. "Oi!" she yelled.

Ciara swirled around with a scowl on her face but it broke into a smile when she spotted her sister grinning at her. "Jesus, I was about to smack the head off you," she laughed, approaching the table.

"I hope you don't speak to all your customers like that," Holly teased.

"Not *all* of them," Ciara replied seriously. "You having lunch here today?"

Holly nodded. "Mum told me you were working lunches, I thought you were supposed to be working in the club upstairs?"

Ciara rolled her eyes. "That man has got me working all the hours under the sun, he's treating me like a slave," Ciara moaned.

"Did I hear someone mention my name?" Daniel laughed, walking up behind her.

Ciara's face froze as she realized he had overheard her. "No, no . . . I was just talking about Mathew," she stammered. "He has me up all hours of the night, I'm like his sex slave . . ." She trailed off and wandered over to the bar to get a notepad and pen.

"Sorry I asked," Daniel said, staring at Ciara bewildered. "Mind if I join you?" he asked Holly.

"Yes," Holly teased, but pulled out a stool for him. "OK, what's good to eat here?" she asked, looking through the menu as Ciara returned with pen in hand.

Ciara mouthed "Nothing" behind Daniel's back and Holly giggled.

"The toasted special is my favorite," Daniel suggested, and Ciara shook her head wildly at Holly. Ciara obviously didn't think much of the toasted special.

"What are you shaking your head at?" Daniel said to her, catching her in the act again.

"Oh, it's just that . . . Holly is allergic to onions," Ciara stammered again. This was news to Holly.

Holly nodded her head. "Yes . . . they, eh . . . make my head . . . eh . . . bloat." She blew her cheeks out. "Terrible things are those onions. Fatal in fact. Could kill me someday." Ciara rolled her eyes at her sister, who once again managed to take things way over the top.

"OK, well then, leave the onions out," Daniel suggested and Holly agreed.

Ciara stuck her fingers in her mouth and pretended to gag as she walked away.

"You're looking very smart today," Daniel said, studying her outfit.

"Yes, well, that was the impression I was trying to give. I was just at a job interview," Holly said and winced at the thought of it.

"Oh yeah, that's right," Daniel smiled, then he made a face. "Didn't it go well?"

Holly shook her head. "Well, let's just say I need to buy a smarter-looking suit. I won't be expecting a call from them anytime soon."

"Oh well, not to worry," Daniel said, smiling. "There will be plenty of other opportunities. Still have that job upstairs if you're interested."

"I thought you gave that job to Ciara. Why is she working downstairs now?" Holly said, looking confused.

Daniel made a face. "Holly, you know your sister; we had a bit of a *situation*."

"Oh no!" Holly laughed. "What did she do this time?"

"Some guy at the bar said something to her she didn't quite like so she poured him his pint then served it to him over his head."

"Oh no!" Holly gasped. "I'm surprised you didn't fire her!"

"Couldn't do that to a member of the Kennedy family, could I?" he smiled. "And besides, how would I ever be able to face you again?"

"Exactly." Holly smiled, "You may be my friend, but you 'gotta respect the family.'"

Ciara frowned at her sister as she arrived with her plate of food. "Well, that has to be the worst Godfather impression I've ever heard. *Bon appétit*," she said sarcastically, slamming the plate down on the table and turning on her heel.

"Hey!" Daniel frowned, taking Holly's plate away from her and examining her sandwich.

"What are you doing?" she demanded to know.

"There are onions in it," he said angrily. "Ciara must have given the wrong order again."

"No no, she didn't." Holly jumped to her sister's rescue and grabbed the plate back from his hands. "I'm only allergic to red onions," she blurted out.

Daniel frowned. "How odd. I didn't think there was a huge difference."

"Oh, there is." Holly nodded her head and tried to sound wise, "They may be part of the same family but the red onion . . . contains deadly toxins . . ." She trailed off.

"Toxins?" Daniel said disbelievingly.

"Well, they're toxic to me aren't they?" she mumbled, and bit into the sandwich to shut herself up. She found it difficult to eat her sandwich under Daniel's glare without feeling like a pig, so she finally gave up and left the remains on her plate.

"Not like it?" he asked worriedly.

"No, not at all. I love it, I just had a big breakfast," she lied, patting her empty stomach.

"So have you had any luck with that leprechaun yet?" he teased.

"Well, actually I found him!" Holly laughed, wiping her greasy hands on her napkin.

"Really? Who was it?"

"Would you believe it was my brother Richard?" she laughed.

"Go away! So why didn't he tell you? Did he want it to be a surprise or something?"

"Something like that, I suppose."

"He's a nice guy, Richard," Daniel said, looking thoughtful.

"You think?" Holly said, surprised.

"Yeah, he's a harmless kind of a guy. He has a nice nature."

Holly nodded her head while she tried to digest this information. He cut in on her thoughts, "Have you spoken to Denise or Sharon lately?"

"Just Denise," she said, looking away. "You?"

"Tom has my head done in with all this talk of weddings. Wants me to be his best man. To be honest, I didn't think they would plan it all so soon."

"Me neither," Holly agreed. "How do you feel about it now?"

"Ah," Daniel sighed. "Happy for him in a selfish and bitter kind of way." He laughed.

"Know how you feel," Holly nodded. "You haven't spoken to your ex lately or anything?"

"Who, Laura?" he said, surprised. "Never want to see the woman again."

"Is she a friend of Tom's?"

"Not as friendly as they used to be, thank God."

"So she won't be invited to the wedding then?"

Daniel's eyes widened. "You know, I never even thought of that. God, I hope not, Tom knows what I would do to him if he did invite her."

There was a silence as Daniel contemplated that thought.

"I think I'm meeting up with Tom and Denise tomorrow night to discuss the wedding plans if you feel like coming out," Daniel said.

Holly rolled her eyes. "Gee thanks, well, that just sounds like the best fun ever, Daniel."

Daniel started laughing. "I know, that's why I don't want to go on my own. Call me later if you want to go anyway."

Holly nodded.

"Right, here's the bill," Ciara said, dropping a piece of paper on the table and sauntering off. Daniel watched after her and shook his head.

"Don't worry, Daniel," Holly laughed, "you won't have to put up with her for much longer."

"Why not?" He looked confused.

Uh-oh, Holly thought, Ciara hadn't told him she was moving away. "Oh nothing," she mumbled, rooting through her bag for her purse.

"No really, what do you mean?" he continued.

"Oh, I mean her shift must be nearly over now," she said, pulling her purse out of her bag and looking at her watch.

"Oh . . . listen, don't worry about the bill, I'll take care of that."

"No, I'm not letting you do that," she said, continuing to search through all the receipts and rubbish in her purse for some money. "Which reminds me, I owe you twenty." She placed the money on the table.

"Forget about that." He waved his hand dismissively.

"Hey, are you going to let me pay for anything?" Holly joked, "I'm leaving it here on the table anyway, so you'll have to take it."

Ciara returned to the table and held out her hand for the money.

"It's OK, Ciara, put it on my tab," Daniel said.

Ciara raised her eyebrows at Holly and winked at her. Then she glanced down at the table and spotted the twenty-euro note. "Ooh thanks, sis, I didn't know you were such a good tipper." She pocketed the money and headed over to serve another table.

"Don't worry," Daniel laughed, looking at a shocked Holly. "I'll take it out of her wages."

Holly's heart began to pound as she drove down her estate and spotted Sharon's car outside her house. It had been a long time since Holly had spoken to her and she had left it so long she was embarrassed. She contemplated turning the car around and heading off in the other direction, but she stopped herself. She needed to face the music sometime before she lost another best friend. If it wasn't too late already.

Thirty-five

H OLLY PULLED UP TO HER driveway and took a deep breath before getting out of her car. She should have been to visit Sharon first and she knew it, now things just seemed far worse. She walked toward Sharon's car and was surprised to see John stepping out. There was no Sharon to be seen. Her heart began to pound; she hoped Sharon was OK.

"Hi Holly," John said grimly, banging the car door behind him.

"John! Where's Sharon?!" she asked.

"I just came from the hospital." He walked toward her slowly.

Holly's hands flew to her face and tears filled her eyes. "Oh my God! Is she OK?"

John looked confused. "Yeah, she's just having a checkup, I'm going back to collect her after I leave here."

Holly's hands dropped down by her side. "Oh," she said, feeling stupid.

"You know if you're that concerned about her you should call her." John held his head high and his icy blue eyes stared straight into hers. Holly could see his jawline clenching and unclenching. She held his stare until the force of his gaze caused her to look away.

Holly bit her lip, feeling guilty. "Yeah, I know. Why don't you come inside and I'll make us a cup of tea." At any other time she would have laughed at herself for saying that; she was turning into one of *them*.

She flicked the switch on the kettle and busied herself while John made himself comfortable at the table.

"Sharon doesn't know that I'm here so I would appreciate it if you didn't say anything."

"Oh." Holly felt even more disappointed. Sharon hadn't sent him. She didn't even want to see her; she must have given up on Holly altogether.

"She misses you, you know." John continued to stare straight at her, not blinking for one moment.

Holly carried the mugs over to the table and sat down. "I miss her too."

"It's been a while now, Holly, and you know the two of you used to speak to each other every day." John took the mug from her hand and placed it in front of him.

"Things used to be very different, John," Holly said angrily. Didn't anybody understand what she was going through? Was she the only sane person in the whole entire world these days?

"Look, we all know what you've been through . . . ," John started.

"I know you all *know* what I've been through, John; that's blatantly obvious, but you all don't seem to understand that I'm *still* going through it!"

There was a silence.

"That's not true at all." John's voice was quieter and he fixed his gaze onto the mug he was twirling around on the table before him.

"Yes it is. I can't just move on with my life like you're all doing and pretend that nothing has happened."

"Do you think that that's what we're doing?"

"Well, let's look at the evidence, shall we?" she said sarcastically. "Sharon is having a baby and Denise is getting married—"

"Holly, that's called living," John interrupted, and he looked up from the table. "You seem to have forgotten how to do that. Look, I know that it's difficult for you because I know it's difficult for me. I miss Gerry too. He was my best mate. I lived right next door to him all my life. I went to playschool with the guy, for Christ's sake. We went to primary school together, we went to secondary school together and we played on the same football team. I was his best man at his wedding and he was at mine! Whenever I had a problem I went to Gerry, whenever I wanted to have a bit of fun I went to Gerry. I told him some things that I would never have told Sharon and he told me things he wouldn't have told you. Just because I wasn't married to him doesn't mean that I don't feel like you do. And just because he's dead doesn't mean I have to stop living too."

Holly sat stunned. John twisted his chair around in order to face her properly. The legs of the chair squeaked loudly in the silence. He took a deep breath before he spoke again.

"Yes, it's difficult. Yes, it's horrible. Yes, it's the worst thing that has ever happened to me in my whole life. But I can't just give up. I can't just stop going to the pub because there's two blokes laughing and joking on the stools Gerry and I used to sit on, and I can't stop going to football matches just because it's somewhere we used to go together all the time. I can remember it all right and smile about it, but I can't just stop going there."

Tears welled in Holly's eyes and John continued talking.

"Sharon knows you're hurting and she understands, but you have to understand that this is a hugely important time in her life, too, and she needs her best friend to help her through it. She needs your help just like you need hers."

"I'm trying John," Holly sobbed as hot tears rolled down her cheeks.

"I know you are." He leaned forward and grabbed her hands. "But Sharon needs you. Avoiding the situation isn't going to help anyone or anything."

"But I went for a job interview today," she sobbed childishly.

John tried to hide his smile. "That's great news, Holly. And how did it go?"

"Shite," she sniffed, and John started laughing. He allowed a silence to fall between them before he spoke again.

"She's almost five months pregnant, you know."

"What?" Holly looked up in surprise. "She didn't tell me!"

"She was afraid to," he said gently. "She thought you might get mad at her and never want to speak to her again."

"Well, that was stupid of her to think that," Holly said angrily and wiped her eyes aggressively.

"Oh really?" He raised his eyebrows. "So what do you call all this then?"

Holly looked away. "I meant to call her, I really did. I picked up the phone every day but I just couldn't do it. Then I would say that I'd call the next day, and the next day I would be busy . . . oh, I'm sorry, John. I'm truly happy for the both of you."

"Thank you, but it's not me that needs to hear any of this, you know."

"I know, but I've been so awful! She'll never forgive me now!"

"Oh, don't be stupid, Holly, it's Sharon we're talking about here. She'll have it all forgotten about by tomorrow."

Holly raised her eyebrows at him hopefully.

"Well, maybe not *tomorrow*. Next year perhaps . . . and you'll owe her big-time, but she'll eventually forgive you . . ." His icy eyes warmed and twinkled back at her.

"Stop it!" Holly giggled, hitting him on the arm. "Can I go with you to see her?"

Butterflies fluttered around in Holly's stomach as they pulled up outside the hospital. She spotted Sharon looking around as she stood alone outside, waiting to be collected. She looked so cute Holly had to smile at the sight of her friend. Sharon was going to be a mummy. She couldn't believe she was almost five months pregnant. That meant Sharon had been three months pregnant when they went away on holiday and she hadn't said a word! But more important, Holly couldn't believe that she stupidly hadn't noticed the changes in her friend. Of course she wouldn't have had a bump at only three months; but now, as she looked at Sharon dressed in a polo neck and jeans, she could see the swelling of a tiny bump. And it suited her. Holly stepped out of the car and Sharon's face froze.

Oh no, Sharon was going to scream at her. She was going to tell her she hated her and that she never wanted to see her again and that she was a crappy friend and that . . .

Sharon's face broke into a smile and she held her arms out to her. "Come here to me, you fool," she said softly.

Holly ran into her arms. There, with her best friend hugging her tight, she felt the tears begin again. "Oh Sharon, I'm so sorry, I'm a horrible person. I'm so so so so so so sorry, please forgive me. I never meant to—"

"Oh shut up, you whiner, and hug me." Sharon cried too, her voice cracking, and they squeezed each other for a long time as John looked on.

"Ahem," John cleared his throat loudly.

"Oh come here, you." Holly smiled and dragged him into their huddle.

"I presume this was your idea." Sharon looked at her husband.

"No not at all," he said, winking at Holly, "I just passed Holly on the street and told her I'd give her a lift . . ."

"Yeah right," she said sarcastically, linking arms with Holly as they walked toward the car. "Well, you certainly gave me a lift anyway." She smiled at her friend.

"So what did they say?" Holly asked, squeezing herself forward between the two front seats from the back of the car like an excited little child. "What is it?"

"Well, you'll never believe this, Holly." Sharon twisted around in her chair and matched her friend's excitement. "The doctor told me that . . . and I believe him because apparently he's one of the best . . . anyway he told me . . ."

"Come on!" Holly urged her on, dying to hear.

"He says it's a baby!"

Holly rolled her eyes. "Ha-ha. What I mean is, is it a boy or a girl?"

"It's an it for now. They're not too sure yet."

"Would you want to know what 'it' is if they could tell you?"

Sharon scrunched her nose up. "I don't know actually, I haven't figured that out yet." She looked across at John and the two of them shared a secret smile.

A familiar pang of jealousy hit Holly and she sat quietly while she let it pass until the excitement returned. The three of them headed back to Holly's house. She and Sharon weren't quite ready to leave each other again after just making up. They had so much to talk about. Sitting around Holly's kitchen table, they made up for lost time.

"Sharon, Holly went for a job interview today," John said when he finally managed to get a word in edgewise.

"Ooh really? I didn't know you were job-hunting already!"

"Gerry's new mission for me," Holly smiled.

"Oh, was that what it was this month? I was just dying to know! So how did it go?"

Holly grimaced and held her head in her hands. "Oh it was awful, Sharon. I made a total fool of myself."

"Really?" Sharon giggled. "What was the job?"

"Selling advertising space for that magazine, *X*."

"Ooh, that's cool, I read that at work all the time."

"Don't think I know that one, what kind of magazine is it?" John asked.

"Oh, it kind of has everything in it: fashion, sports, culture, food, reviews . . . everything really."

"And adverts," Holly joked.

"Well, it won't have such good adverts if Holly Kennedy isn't working for them," she said kindly.

"Thanks, but I really don't think I will be working there."

"Why, what was so wrong with the interview? You can't have been that bad." Sharon looked intrigued as she reached for the pot of tea.

"Oh, I think it's bad when the interviewer asks if you have any experience working on a magazine or newspaper and you tell him you once printed up a newsletter for a shitty company." Holly banged her head playfully off the kitchen table.

Sharon burst out laughing. "Newsletter? I hope you weren't referring to that crappy little leaflet that you printed up on the computer to advertise that dive of a company?"

John and Sharon howled with laughter.

"Ah well, it was *advertising* the company . . ." Holly trailed off and giggled, feeling even more embarrassed.

"Remember, you made us all go out and post them around people's houses in the pissing rain and the freezing cold! It took us days to do!"

"Hey, I remember that," John laughed. "Remember, you sent me and Gerry out to post hundreds of them one night?" He kept on laughing.

"Yeah?" Holly was afraid to hear what came next.

"Well, we shoved them in the skip at the back of Bob's pub and went in for a few pints." He kept on laughing at the memory of it and Holly's mouth dropped open.

"You sly little bastards!" she laughed. "Because of you two the company went bust and I lost my job!"

"Oh, I'd say it went bust the minute people took a look at those leaflets, Holly," Sharon teased. "Anyway, that place was a kip. You used to moan about it every day."

"Just one of the jobs Holly moaned about," John joked. But he was right.

"Yeah, well, I wouldn't have moaned about this one," she said sadly.

"There's plenty more jobs out there," Sharon reassured her, "you just need to brush up on your interview skills."

"Tell me about it." Holly stabbed away at the sugar bowl with a spoon.

They sat in silence for a while.

"You published a newsletter," John repeated a few minutes later, still laughing at the thought of it.

"Shut up, you," Holly cringed. "Hey, what else did you and Gerry get up to that I don't know about?" she demanded.

"Ah, a true friend never reveals secrets," John teased, and his eyes danced with the memories.

But something had been unlocked. And after Holly and Sharon threatened to beat some stories out of him, Holly learned more about her husband that night that she never knew. For the first time since Gerry had died, the three of them laughed and laughed all night, and Holly learned how to finally be able to talk about her husband. It used to be that the four of them gathered together; Holly, Gerry, Sharon and John. This time only three of them gathered to remember the one they lost. And with all their talk, he became alive for them all that night. Soon they would be four again, with the arrival of Sharon and John's baby.

Life went on.

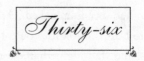

Thirty-six

THAT SUNDAY RICHARD CALLED OUT to visit Holly with the kids. She had told him he was welcome to bring them by whenever it was his day with them. They played outside in the garden while Richard and Holly finished off their dinner and watched them through the patio doors.

"They seem really happy, Richard," Holly said, watching them playing.

"Yes they do, don't they?" He smiled as he watched them chasing each other around. "I want things to be as normal for them as possible. They don't quite understand what's going on, and it's difficult to explain."

"What have you told them?"

"Oh, that Mummy and Daddy don't love each other anymore and that I moved away so that we can be happier. Something along those lines."

"And they're OK with that?"

Her brother nodded slowly. "Timothy is OK but Emily is worried that we might stop loving her and that she will have to move away." He glanced up at Holly, his eyes sad.

Poor Emily, Holly thought, watching her dancing around with her scary-looking doll. She couldn't believe that she was having this conversation with Richard. He seemed like a totally different person these days. Or perhaps it was Holly who had changed; she seemed to have a higher tolerance for him now, she found it easier to ignore his annoying little comments, and there were still many of them. But then again, they now had something in common. They both understood what it was like to feel lonely and unsure of themselves.

"How's everything going at Mum and Dad's house?"

Richard swallowed a forkful of potato and nodded, "Good. They're being extremely generous."

"Ciara bothering you at all?" She felt like she was questioning her child after he returned home from his first day of school, wanting to know if the other kids had bullied him or treated him well. But lately she felt so protective of Richard. It helped her to help him; it gave her strength.

"Ciara is . . . Ciara," he smiled. "We don't see eye to eye on a lot of things."

"Well, I wouldn't worry about that," Holly said, trying to stab a piece of pork with her fork. "The majority of the world wouldn't see eye to eye with her either." Her fork finally made contact with the pork and she sent it flying off her plate and through the air, where it landed on the kitchen counter at the far side of the room.

"And they say pigs don't fly," Richard remarked as Holly crossed the room to retrieve the piece of meat.

Holly giggled, "Hey Richard you made a funny!"

He looked pleased with himself. "I have my moments too, I suppose," he said, shrugging his shoulders. "Although I'm sure you think I don't have many of them."

Holly sat back down in her seat slowly, trying to decide how to phrase what she was going to say. "We're all different, Richard. Ciara is slightly eccentric, Declan is a dreamer, Jack is a joker, I'm . . . well, I don't know what I am. But you were always very controlled. Straight and serious. It's not necessarily a bad thing, we're all just different."

"You're very thoughtful," Richard said after a long silence.

"Pardon?" Holly asked, feeling confused. To cover her embarrassment she stuffed her face with another mouthful of food.

"I've always thought you were very thoughtful," he repeated.

"When?" Holly asked incredulously, through her mouthful.

"Well, I wouldn't be sitting here eating dinner with the kids running around having fun outside if you weren't thoughtful now, but I was actually referring to when we were children."

"I don't think so, Richard," Holly said, shaking her head. "Jack and I were always so awful to you," she said softly.

"You weren't *always* awful, Holly." He gave her an amused smile. "Anyway, that's what brothers and sisters are for, to make each other's lives as difficult as possible for each other as they grow up. It forms a great basis for life, toughens you up. Anyway, I was the bossy older brother."

"So how does that make me thoughtful?" Holly asked, feeling she had completely missed the point.

"You idolized Jack. You used to follow him around all the time and you would do exactly what he told you to do." He started laughing. "I used to hear him telling you to say things to me and you would run into my room terrified and blurt them out and run away again."

Holly looked at her plate feeling embarrassed. She and Jack used to play terrible tricks on him.

"But you always came back," Richard continued. "You would always creep back into my room silently and watch me working at my desk, and I knew that was your way of saying sorry." He smiled at her. "So that makes you thoughtful. None of our siblings had a conscience in that house of ours. Not even me. You were the only one, always the sensitive one."

He continued eating his dinner and Holly sat in silence, trying to absorb all the information he had given her. She didn't remember idolizing Jack, but when she thought about it she supposed Richard was right. Jack was her funny, cool, good-looking big brother who had loads of friends, and Holly used to beg him to let her play with them. She supposed she still felt that way about him; if he called her right now and asked her to go out she would drop everything and go, and she had never even realized that before. However, she was spending far more time with Richard than with Jack these days. Jack had always been her favorite brother; Gerry had always gotten along with Jack the best. It was Jack who Gerry would choose to go out for drinks with during the week, not Richard; it was Jack who Gerry would insist on sitting beside at a family dinner. However Gerry was gone, and although Jack rang her every now and then, he wasn't around as much as he used to be. Had Holly held Jack up on too much of a pedestal? She realized then that she had been making excuses for him every time he didn't call around or phone her when he said he would. In fact, she had been making excuses for him ever since Gerry had died.

Richard had, lately, managed to give Holly a regular intake of food for thought. She watched him remove his serviette from his collar and was interested as he folded it into a neat little square with perfect right angles. He obsessively straightened whatever was on the table so that everything was facing the right way in an orderly fashion. For all Richard's good qualities, which she recognized now, Holly could not live with a man like that at all.

They both jumped as they heard a thump from outside and saw little Emily lying on the ground in floods of tears while a shocked-looking Timmy watched. Richard leapt out of his chair and hurried outside.

"But she just fell, Daddy, I didn't do anything!" she heard Timmy plead with his father. Poor Timmy. She rolled her eyes as she watched Richard dragging him by the arm and ordering him to stand in the corner to think about what he had done. Some people would never really change, she thought wryly.

The next day Holly jumped around the house ecstatically as she replayed the message on the answering machine for the third time.

"Hi Holly," came the gruff voice. "This is Chris Feeney here from magazine X. I'm just calling to say that I was very impressed with your interview. Em . . ." He stalled a bit. "Well, I wouldn't normally say this on an answering machine, but no doubt you'll be delighted to know that I've decided to welcome you as a new member of the team. I would love you to start as soon as possible, so call me on the usual number when you get a chance and we'll discuss it further. Em . . . Good-bye."

Holly rolled around her bed in terrified delight and pressed the PLAY button again. She had aimed for the moon . . . and she had now landed!

Thirty-seven

HOLLY STARED UP AT THE tall Georgian building and her body tingled with excitement. It was her first day of work and she felt good times were ahead of her in this building. It was situated in the center of town, and the busy offices of magazine *X* were on the second floor above a small café. Holly had gotten very little sleep the night before due to nerves and excitement all rolled into one; however, she didn't feel the same dread that she usually felt before starting a new job. She had phoned Mr. Feeney back immediately (after listening to his voice message another three times) and then she had shared the news with her family and friends. They had been ecstatic when they heard the news, and just before she left the house that morning she had received a beautiful bouquet of flowers from her parents congratulating her and wishing her luck on her first day.

She felt like she was starting her first day at school and had gone shopping for new pens, a new notepad, a folder and a new briefcase that made her look extra intelligent. But although she had felt excited when she sat down to eat her breakfast, she had also felt sad. Sad that Gerry wasn't there to share her new start. They had performed a little ritual every time Holly started a new job, which was quite a regular occurrence. Gerry would wake Holly up with breakfast in bed and then he would pack her bag with ham and cheese sandwiches, an apple, a packet of crisps and a bar of chocolate. Then he would drive her into work on her first day, call her on her lunch break to see if the other kids in the office were playing nicely, and return at the end of the day to collect her and bring her home. Then they would sit together over dinner and he would listen and laugh as Holly explained all the different characters in her office and once again grumble about how she hated going to work. Mind you, they only ever did that on her first day, every other day they would tumble out of bed late as usual, race each other to the shower and then wander around the kitchen half asleep, grumbling at each other while they grabbed a quick cup of coffee to help them get started. They would give each other a kiss good-bye and go their separate ways for the day. And then they would start all over again the next day. If Holly had known their time would be so precious, she wouldn't have bothered carrying out all those tedious routines day after day . . .

This morning, however, had been a very different scenario. She awoke to an empty house in an empty bed to no breakfast. She didn't have to fight for her right to use the shower first and the kitchen was quiet without the sound of his fits of morning sneezes. She had allowed herself to imagine that when she woke up Gerry would miraculously be there to greet her because it was tradition and such a special day that it wouldn't feel right without him. But with death there were no exceptions. Gone meant gone.

Now, poised at the entrance, Holly checked herself to see that her fly wasn't undone, her jacket wasn't tucked into her knickers and her shirt buttons were fastened properly. Satisfied that she looked presentable, she made her way up the wooden staircase to her new office. She entered the waiting room area and the secretary she recognized from the interview came from around the desk to meet her.

"Hi Holly," she said happily, shaking her hand, "welcome to our humble abode." She held her hands up to display the room. Holly had liked this woman from the moment she had met her at the interview. She looked to be about the same age as Holly and had long blond hair and a face that seemed to be always happy and smiling.

"I'm Alice by the way, and I work out here in reception as you know. Well, I'll bring you to the boss man now. He's waiting for you."

"God, I'm not late, am I?" Holly asked, worriedly glancing at her watch. She had left the house early to beat the traffic and she had given herself plenty of time to avoid being late on her first day.

"No, you're not at all," Alice said, leading her down to Mr. Feeney's office. "Don't mind Chris and all the other lot, they're all workaholics. They need to get themselves a life, bless them. You wouldn't see me hanging around here anytime after six, that's for sure."

Holly laughed; Alice reminded her of her former self.

"By the way, don't feel that you have to come in early and stay late just because they do. I think Chris actually lives in his office, so you'll never compete with that. The man isn't normal," she said loudly, tapping on his door lightly and leading her in.

"Who's not normal?" Mr. Feeney asked gruffly, standing up from his chair and stretching.

"You." Alice smiled and closed the door behind her.

"See how my staff treat me?" Mr. Feeney laughed, approaching Holly and holding out his hand to greet her. His handshake was once again warm and welcoming, and Holly felt immediately at ease with the atmosphere between the workers.

"Thank you for hiring me, Mr. Feeney," Holly said genuinely.

"You can call me Chris, and there's no need to thank me. Right, why don't you follow me and I'll show you around the place." He started leading her down the hall. The walls were covered by framed covers of every *X* magazine that had been published for the last twenty years.

"There's not much to the place; in here is our office of little ants." He pushed open the door and Holly looked into the huge office. There were about ten desks in all, and the room was packed with people all sitting in front of their computers and talking on the phone. They looked up and waved politely. Holly smiled at them, remembering how important first impressions were. "These are the wonderful journalists who help pay my bills," Chris explained. "That's John Paul the fashion editor; Mary our food woman; and Brian, Steven, Gordon, Aishling and Tracey. You don't need to know what they do, they're just wasters." He laughed and one of the men gave Chris the finger and continued talking on the phone. Holly presumed he was one of the men accused of being a waster.

"Everyone, this is Holly!" Chris yelled, and they smiled and waved again and continued talking on the phone.

"The rest of the journalists are freelancers, so you won't see them hanging around these offices much," Chris explained, leading her to the room next door. "This is where all our computer nerds hide. That's Dermot and Wayne, and they're in charge of layout and design, so you'll be working closely with them and keeping them informed about what advertisements are going where. Lads, this is Holly."

"Hi, Holly." They both stood up and shook her hand and then continued working on their computers again.

"I have them well trained," Chris chuckled, and he headed back out to the hall again. "Down here is the boardroom. We have meetings every morning at eight forty-five."

Holly nodded to everything he was saying and tried to remember the names of everyone he had introduced to her.

"Down those steps are the toilets, and I'll show you your office now."

He headed back down the way they had come and Holly glanced at the walls feeling excited. This was nothing like she had ever experienced before.

"In here is your office," he said, pushing the door open and allowing her to walk in ahead of him.

Holly couldn't stop herself from smiling as she looked around at the small room. She had never had her own office before. It was just big enough to fit a desk and filing cabinet. There was a computer sitting on the desk with piles and piles of folders. Opposite the desk was a bookcase crammed with yet more books, folders and stacks of old magazines. The huge Georgian window practically covered the entire back wall behind her desk, and although it was cold and windy outside, the room had a bright and airy feel to it. She could definitely see herself working here.

"It's perfect," she told Chris, placing her briefcase on the desk and looking around.

"Good," Chris said. "The last guy who was here was extremely organized, and all those folders there will explain very clearly what exactly it is you need to do. If you have any problems or any questions about anything at all, just come ask me. I'm right next door." He knocked on the wall that separated their offices.

"Now I'm not looking for miracles from you, because I know you're new to this, which is why I expect you to ask lots of questions. Our next edition is due out next week, as we put them out on the first day of every month."

Holly's eyes widened; she had a week to fill an entire magazine.

"Don't worry." He smiled again. "I want you to concentrate on November's edition. Familiarize yourself with the layout of the magazine, as we stick to the same style every month, so you will know what kind of pages will need what type of advertisements. This is a lot of work, but if you keep yourself organized and work well with the rest of the team, everything will run smoothly. Again, I ask you to speak to Dermot and Wayne, and they'll fill you in on the standard layout, and if you need anything done, just ask Alice. She's there to help everyone." He stopped talking and looked around. "So that's about it. Any questions?"

Holly shook her head. "No, I think you covered just about everything."

"Right, I'll leave you to it so." He closed the door behind him and Holly sat down at her new desk in her new office. She was slightly daunted by her new life. This was the most impressive job she had ever had, and by the sounds of things she was going to be extremely busy, but she was glad. She needed to keep her mind occupied. However, there was no way on earth she had remembered everyone's name, so she took out her notepad and pen and started to write down the ones she knew. She opened the folders and got to work.

She was so engrossed in her reading that she realized after a while that she had worked through her lunch break. By the sounds of things, no one else from the office had budged an inch. In her other jobs, Holly would stop working at least half an hour before lunchtime just to think about what she was going to eat. Then she would leave fifteen minutes early and return fifteen minutes late due to "traffic," even though she would walk to the shop. Holly would daydream the majority of the day, make personal phone calls, especially abroad, because she didn't have to pay the bill, and would be first in queue to collect her monthly paycheck, which was usually spent within two weeks.

Yes, this was very different from her previous jobs, but she was looking forward to every minute of it.

"Right Ciara, are you sure you've got your passport?" Holly's mum asked her daughter for the third time since leaving the house.

"Yes, Mum," Ciara groaned, "I told you a million billion times, it's right here."

"Show me," Elizabeth said, twisting around in the passenger seat.

"No! I'm not showing it to you. You should just take my word for it, I'm not a baby anymore, you know."

Declan snorted and Ciara elbowed him in the ribs. "Shut up, you."

"Ciara, just show Mum the passport so you can put her mind at rest," Holly said tiredly.

"Fine," she huffed, lifting her bag onto her lap. "It's in here, look Mum . . . no, hold on, actually it's in here . . . no, actually maybe I put it in here . . . oh fuck!"

"Jesus Christ, Ciara," Holly's dad growled, slamming on the brakes and turning the car around.

"What?" she said defensively. "I put it in here, Dad, someone must have taken it out," she grumbled, emptying the contents of her bag in the car.

"Bloody hell, Ciara," Holly moaned as a pair of knickers went flying over her face.

"Ah shut up," she grumbled again. "You won't have to put up with me for much longer."

Everyone in the car went silent as they realized that was true. Ciara would be in Australia for God only knew how long, and they would all miss her; as loud and irritating as she was.

Holly sat squashed beside the window in the backseat of the car with Declan and Ciara. Richard was driving Mathew and Jack (ignoring his protestations), and they were probably already at the airport at this stage. This was their second time returning to the house, as Ciara had forgotten her lucky nose ring and demanded that her dad turn the car around.

An hour after setting off, they reached the airport in what should have been only a twenty-minute drive.

"Jesus, what took you so long?" Jack moaned to Holly when they all finally trudged into the airport with long faces on them. "I was stuck talking to Dick all on my own."

"Oh give it a rest, Jack," Holly said defensively, "he's not that bad."

"Ooh, you've changed your tune," he teased, his face all mock-surprise.

"No I haven't, you're just singing the wrong song," she snapped, and she walked over to Richard, who was standing alone watching the world go by. She smiled at her oldest brother.

"Pet, keep in touch with us a lot more this time, won't you?" Elizabeth cried to her daughter as she hugged her.

"Of course I will, Mum. Oh please, don't cry or you'll get me started too." A lump formed in Holly's throat and she fought back the tears. Ciara had been good company over the last few months and had always succeeded in cheering Holly up when she felt that life just couldn't be worse. She would miss her sister, but she understood that Ciara needed to be with Mathew. He was a nice guy and she was happy that they had found each other.

"Take care of my sister." Holly stood on the tips of her toes to hug the enormous Mathew.

"Don't worry, she's in good hands," he smiled.

"Look after her now, won't you?" Frank smacked him on the back and smiled. Mathew was intelligent enough to know it was more of a warning than a question and gave him a very persuasive answer.

"Bye, Richard," Ciara said, giving him a big hug. "Stay away from that Meredith bitch now. You're far too good for her." Ciara turned to Declan. "You can come over anytime you like, Dec, maybe make a movie or something about me," she said seriously to the youngest of the family and gave him a big hug.

"Jack, look after my big sis," she said, smiling at Holly. "Ooh, I'm gonna miss you," she said sadly, squeezing Holly tightly.

"Me too," Holly's voice shook.

"OK, I'm going now before all you depressing people make me cry," she said, trying to sound happy.

"Don't go using those rope jumps again, Ciara. They're far too dangerous," Frank said, looking worried.

"Bungee jumps, Dad!" Ciara laughed, kissing him and her mother on the cheeks again. "Don't worry, I'm sure I'll find something new to try," she teased.

Holly stood in silence with her family and watched as Ciara

and Mathew walked hand in hand out the door. Even Declan had a tear in his eye but pretended his eyes were watering because he was about to sneeze.

"Just look at the lights, Declan." Jack threw his arm around his baby brother. "They say that helps you sneeze."

Declan stared up at the lights and avoided watching his favorite sister walking away. Frank held his wife close to him as she waved at her daughter constantly while tears rolled down her cheeks.

They all laughed as the alarm went off when Ciara walked through the security scanner and was ordered to empty her pockets, followed by a frisk.

"Every bloody time," Jack laughed. "It's a wonder they agreed to let her into the country at all."

They all waved good-bye as Ciara and Mathew walked on until her pink hair was eventually lost among the crowd.

"OK," Elizabeth said, wiping the tears from her face, "why don't the rest of my babies come back to the house and we can all have lunch."

They all agreed, seeing how upset their mother was.

"I'll let you go with Richard this time," Jack said smartly to Holly and wandered off with the rest of the family, leaving Richard and Holly standing there slightly taken aback.

"So how was your first week at work, darling?" Elizabeth asked Holly as they all sat around the table eating lunch.

"Oh, I love it, Mum," Holly said and her eyes lit up. "It's so much more interesting and challenging than any other job I've done, and all the staff are just so friendly. There's a great atmosphere in the place," she said happily.

"Well, that's the most important thing, isn't it?" Frank said, pleased. "What's your boss like?"

"Oh, he's such a doll. He reminds me so much of you, Dad, I just feel like giving him a big hug and a kiss every time I see him."

"Sounds like sexual harassment in the workplace to me," Declan joked, and Jack sniggered.

Holly rolled her eyes at her brothers.

"Are you doing any new documentaries this year, Declan?" Jack asked.

"Yeah, on homelessness," he said with his mouth full of food.

"Declan." Elizabeth scrunched up her nose at him. "Don't talk with your mouth full."

"Sorry," Declan said and spat the food out on the table.

Jack burst out laughing and nearly choked on his food while the rest of the family looked away from Declan in disgust.

"What did you say you were doing, son?" Frank asked, trying to avoid a family fight.

"I'm doing a documentary on homelessness this year for college."

"Oh very good," he replied, retreating back to a world of his own.

"What member of the family are you using as your subject this time? Richard?" Jack said slyly.

Holly slammed down her knife and fork.

"That's not funny, man," Declan said seriously, surprising Holly.

"God, why is everyone so touchy these days?" Jack asked, looking around. "It was just a joke," he defended himself.

"It wasn't funny, Jack," Elizabeth said sternly.

"What did he say?" Frank asked his wife after snapping out of his trance. Elizabeth just shook her head dismissively and he knew not to ask again.

Holly watched Richard, who sat at the end of the table eating his food quietly. Her heart leapt out to him. He didn't deserve this, and either Jack was being more cruel than usual or else this was the norm and Holly must have been a fool to find it funny before.

"Sorry Richard, I was just joking," Jack said.

"That's OK, Jack."

"So have you found a job yet?"

"No, not yet."

"That's a shame," he said dryly, and Holly glared at him. What the hell was his problem?

Elizabeth calmly picked up her cutlery and plate of food without a word to anyone and quietly made her way into the living room, where she turned the television on and ate her dinner in peace.

Her "funny little elves" weren't making her laugh anymore.

Thirty-eight

HOLLY DRUMMED HER FINGERS ON her desk and stared out the window. She was absolutely flying through her work this week. She didn't know it was possible to actually enjoy *work* so much. She had happily sat through lunch breaks and had even stayed back late to work, and she didn't feel like punching any of her fellow employees in the face yet. But it was only her third week, after all; give her time. The good thing was that she didn't even feel uncomfortable around any of her fellow colleagues. The only people she had real contact with were Dermot and Wayne, the guys from layout and design. The office had developed a lighthearted banter and she would often hear people screaming at each other from office to office. It was all in good humor and she loved it.

She loved feeling like she was a part of the team, as though she were actually doing something that made a real impact on the finished product. She thought of Gerry every single day. Every time she made a deal she thanked him, thanked him for pushing her all the way to the top. She still had her miserable days when she didn't feel worthy of getting out of bed. But the excitement of her job was dragging her out and spurring her on.

She heard the radio go on in Chris's office next door and she smiled. On the hour every hour without fail, he turned on the news. And all the news seeped into Holly's brain subconsciously. She had never felt so intelligent in her life.

"Hey!" Holly yelled, banging on the wall. "Turn that thing down! Some of us are trying to work!"

She heard him chuckle and she smiled. She glanced back down at her work again; a freelancer had written an article on how he traveled around Ireland trying to find the cheapest pint and it was very amusing. There was a huge gap at the bottom of the page and it was up to Holly to fill it. She flicked through her book of contacts and an idea came to her immediately. She picked up the phone and dialed.

"Hogan's."

"Hi, Daniel Connelly, please."

"One moment."

Bloody "Greensleeves" again. She danced around the room to the music while she waited. Chris walked in, took one look at her and closed the door again. Holly smiled.

"Hello?"

"Daniel?"

"Yes."

"Hiya, it's Holly."

"How are you doin', Holly?"

"I'm grand, thanks, you?

"Couldn't be better."

"That's a nice complaint."

He laughed. "How's that snazzy job of yours?"

"Well, actually that's why I'm calling." Holly sounded guilty.

"Oh no!" he laughed. "I have made it company policy not to employ any more Kennedys here."

Holly giggled, "Oh damn, and I was so looking forward to throwing drinks over the customers."

He laughed. "So what's up?"

"Do I remember hearing you say you needed to advertise Club Diva more?" Well, he had actually thought that he was saying it to Sharon, but she knew he wouldn't remember that minor detail.

"I do recall saying that, yes."

"Good, well how would you like to advertise it in magazine X?"

"Is that the name of the magazine you work on?"

"No, I just thought it would be an interesting question, that's all," she joked. "Of course it's where I work!"

"Oh of course, I'd forgotten, that's the magazine that has offices just around the corner from me!" he said sarcastically. "The one that causes you to walk by my front door every day, and yet you still don't call in. Why don't I see you at lunchtime?" he teased. "Isn't my pub good enough for you?"

"Oh, everyone here eats their lunch at their desks," she explained. "So what do you think?"

"I think that's very boring of you all."

"No, I mean what do you think about the ad?"

"Yeah sure, that's a good idea."

"OK, well, I'll put it in the November issue. Would you like it placed monthly?"

"Would you like to tell me how much that would set me back?" he laughed.

Holly totted up the figures and told him.

"Hmm . . . ," he said, thinking. "I'll have to think about it, but I'll definitely go for the November edition."

"Oh, that's great! You'll be a millionaire after this goes to print."

"I better be," he laughed. "By the way, there's a launch party for some new drink coming up next week. Can I put your name down for an invite?"

"Yeah, that would be great. What new drink is it?"

"Blue Rock, it's called. It's a new Alco pop drink that's apparently going to be huge. Tastes like shite but it's free all night so I'll buy the rounds."

"Wow, you're such a good advertisement for it," she laughed. "When is it on?" She took out her diary and made a note of it. "That's perfect, I can come straight after work."

"Well, make sure you bring your bikini to work in that case."

"Make sure I bring my *what?*"

"Your bikini," he laughed. "It has a beach theme."

"But it's winter, you nutter."

"Hey, it wasn't my idea. The slogan is 'Blue Rock, the hot new drink for winter.'"

"Ugghh, how tacky," she groaned.

"And messy. We're getting sand thrown all over the floor, which will be a nightmare to clean up. Anyway, listen, I better get back to work, we're mad busy today."

"OK, thanks, Daniel. Have a think about what you want your ad to say and get back to me."

"Will do."

She hung up and sat quietly for a moment. Finally she stood up and went next door to Chris's office, a thought occurring to her.

"You finished dancing in there?" he chuckled.

"Yeah, I just made up a routine. Came in to show you," she joked.

"What's the problem?" he said, finishing off what he was writing and taking off his glasses.

"No problem; just an idea."

"Take a seat." He nodded to the chair in front of him. Just three weeks ago she had sat there for an interview, and now here she was putting ideas forward to her new boss. Funny how life changed so quickly, but then again she had learned that already . . .

"What's the idea?"

"Well, you know Hogan's around the corner?"

Chris nodded.

"Well, I was just on to the owner and he's going to place an ad in the magazine."

"That's great, but I hope you don't tell me about every time you fill a space, we could be here all year."

Holly made a face. "That's not it, Chris. Anyway, he was telling me that they're having a launch party for a new drink called Blue Rock. A new Alco pop drink. It has a beach theme, all the staff will be in bikinis and that kind of thing."

"In the middle of winter?" he raised his eyebrows.

"It's apparently the hot new drink for winter."

He rolled his eyes. "Tacky."

Holly smiled. "That's what I said. Anyway, I just thought it might be worth finding out about and covering. I know we're supposed to raise ideas in the meetings, but this is happening pretty soon."

"I understand. That's a great idea, Holly. I'll get one of the lads onto it."

Holly smiled happily and stood up from her chair. "By the way, did you get that garden sorted yet?"

Chris frowned. "I've had about ten different people come down to look at it. They tell me it'll cost six grand to do."

"Wow, six grand! That's a lot of money."

"Well, it's a big garden, so they have a point. A lot of work needs to be done."

"What was the cheapest quote?"

"Five and a half grand, why?"

"Because my brother will do it for five," she blurted out.

"Five?" His eyes nearly popped out of his head. "That's the lowest I've heard yet. Is he any good?"

"Remember I told you my garden was a jungle?"

He nodded.

"Well, it's a jungle no longer. He did a great job on it, but the only thing is that he works alone, so it takes him longer."

"For that price I don't care how long it takes. Have you got his business card with you?"

"Eh . . . yeah, hold on and I'll get it." She stole some impressive-looking card stock from Alice's desk, typed up Richard's name and mobile number in fancy writing, and printed it out. She cut it into a small rectangle shape, making it appear like a business card.

"That's great," Chris said, reading it. "I think I'll give him a call now."

"No no," Holly said quickly. "You'll get him easier tomorrow. He's up to his eyeballs today."

"Right so; thanks, Holly." She started to head toward the door and stopped when he called out to her, "Oh, by the way, how are you at writing?"

"It was one of the subjects I learned at school."

Chris laughed. "Are you still on that level?"

"Well, I'm sure I could purchase a thesaurus."

"Good, because I need you to cover that launch thing on Tuesday."

"Oh?"

"I can't get any of the others at such short notice and I can't go to it myself, so I have to rely on you." He shuffled some papers on his desk. "I'll send one of the photographers down with you; get a few shots of the sand and the bikinis."

"Oh . . . OK." Holly's heart raced.

"How does eight hundred words sound?"

Impossible, she thought. As far as she knew, she had only fifty words in her vocabulary. "That's no problem," she said confidently and backed out the door. Shit shit shit shit, she thought to herself; how on earth was she going to pull this one off? She couldn't even spell properly.

She picked up the phone and pressed redial.

"Hogan's."

"Daniel Connelly, please."

"One moment."

"Don't put me on . . ."

"Greensleeves" started.

"Hold," she finished.

"Hello?"

"Daniel, it's me," she said quickly.

"Would you ever leave me alone," he teased.

"No, I need help."

"I know you do, but I'm not qualified for that," he laughed.

"No seriously, I mentioned that launch to my editor and he wants to cover it."

"Oh brilliant. You can forget about that ad so!" he laughed.

"No, not brilliant. He wants *me* to write it."

"That's great news, Holly."

"No it's not, I can't write," she panicked.

"Oh really? That was one of the main subjects in my school."

"Oh Daniel, please be serious for a minute . . ."

"OK, what do you want me to do?"

"I need you to tell me absolutely everything you know about this drink and the launch so I can start writing it now and have a few days to work on it."

"Yes, just one minute, sir," he yelled away from the phone. "Look Holly, I really have to get back to work now."

"Please," she whimpered.

"OK listen, what time do you finish work?"

"Six." She crossed her fingers and prayed for him to help her.

"OK, why don't you come around here at six, and I'll take you somewhere to have a bite?"

"Oh, thank you so much, Daniel." She jumped around her office with relief. "You're a star!"

She hung up the phone happily and breathed a sigh of relief. Maybe there was a chance she could get the article done after all and still manage to keep her job. Then she froze as she went back over the conversation in her head.

Had she just agreed to go on a date with Daniel?

Thirty-nine

HOLLY COULDN'T CONCENTRATE DURING THE last hour of work; she kept on watching the clock, willing the time to go more slowly. For once it was the exact opposite. Why didn't it go this fast when she was waiting to open her messages from Gerry? She opened her bag for the millionth time that day to double-check that Gerry's eighth message was still tucked safely in the inside pocket. As it was the last day of the month she had decided to bring the October envelope with her to work. She wasn't sure why, because she knew she had no intentions of working till midnight, she could easily wait until she got home to open it. But her excitement was just so strong that she couldn't face leaving it sitting on the kitchen table as she headed out to work. She was even more intrigued by this one, as the envelope was slightly larger than the others. Plus, she felt Gerry was closer to her this way. His words were in her handbag and that was the closest she would get to him. She was only hours away from being that much closer to him again, and while she willed the clock to move faster so she could read it, she was also dreading her dinner with Daniel.

At six o'clock on the button she heard Alice switch off her computer and clatter down the wooden stairs to freedom. Holly smiled, remembering that was exactly how she had once felt. But then again, everything was different when you had a beautiful husband to go home to. If she still had Gerry with her she would be racing Alice out the door.

She listened as a few of the others packed up their things and she prayed Chris would dump another load on her desk just so she would have to stay late and cancel dinner with Daniel. She and Daniel had been out together millions of times, so why was she worrying now? But something was niggling her at the back of her mind. There was something in his voice that worried her, and there was something that happened to her stomach when his voice came on the phone that made her feel uneasy about meeting up with him. She felt so guilty and ashamed for going out with him, and she tried to convince herself it was just a business dinner. In fact, the more she thought about it the more she realized that that was exactly what it was. She thought about how she had become one of those people who discussed business over dinner. Usually the only business she discussed over dinner was men and life in general with Sharon and Denise, which was girls' business.

She slowly shut down her computer and packed her briefcase with meticulous care. Everything she did was in slow motion, as though that would prevent her from having to have dinner with Daniel. She hit herself over the head . . . it was a *business* dinner.

"Hey, don't beat yourself up about it." Alice leaned in through Holly's door.

Holly jumped with fright. "Jesus, Alice, I didn't see you there."

"Everything OK?"

"Yeah," she said unconvincingly. "I just have to do something that I really don't want to do. But I kind of want to do it, which makes me not want to do it even more because it seems so wrong even though it's right. You know?" She looked at Alice, who was staring at her with wide eyes.

"I thought I overanalyzed things."

"Oh, don't mind me." Holly perked up, "I'm just going nuts."

"It happens to the best of us," Alice smiled.

"What are you doing back here?" Holly said suddenly, realizing she had heard her legging it out the door earlier. "Does freedom not beckon you?"

"I know," Alice rolled her eyes, "but I forgot we had a meeting at six."

"Oh," Holly was disappointed. Nobody had told her about any meeting today, which wasn't unusual because she wasn't required to be at all of them. But it was unusual for Alice to attend one without Holly being asked.

"Is it about anything interesting?" Holly poked around for information, trying to make herself sound uninterested while she busied herself at her desk.

"It's the astrology meeting."

"Astrology meeting?"

"Yeah, we have it monthly."

"Oh, am I supposed to be there or am I not invited to it?" She tried not to sound bitter but failed miserably, much to her embarrassment.

344 / Cecelia Ahern

Alice laughed. "Of course you're welcome to come, Holly, I was just about to ask you, which is why I'm standing outside your office."

Holly put her briefcase down feeling stupid and followed Alice into the boardroom, where everybody was sitting down and waiting.

"Everyone, this is Holly's first astrology meeting, so let's make her feel welcome," Alice announced.

Holly took her seat while they all jokingly applauded their new member at the table. Chris spoke to Holly: "Holly, I just want you to know that I have absolutely nothing to do with this nonsense and I want to apologize in advance for you being dragged into it."

"Oh shut up, Chris." Tracey waved a hand at her boss as she took her seat at the head of the table with a notepad and pen in her hand.

"OK, who wants to go first this month?"

"Let Holly go first," Alice said generously.

Holly looked around completely baffled. "But Holly doesn't have a clue what's going on."

"Well, what star sign are you?" Tracey asked.

"Taurus."

Everyone oohed and aahed, and Chris held his head in his hands and tried to look like he wasn't enjoying himself.

"Ooh great," Tracey said happily. "We've never had a Taurus before. OK, so are you married or seeing anyone or single or anything?"

Holly blushed as Brian winked over at her and Chris smiled at her encouragingly; he was the only one at the table who knew about Gerry. Holly realized this was the first time she had had to answer this question since Gerry had died, and she was confused as to how to answer. "Em . . . no, I'm not really seeing anyone but . . ."

"OK then," Tracey said, starting to write, "this month Taurus shall look out for someone tall, dark and handsome and . . ." She shrugged and looked up, "Anybody?"

"Because he will have a big impact on her future," Alice helped out.

Brian winked over at her again, obviously finding it very amusing that he was also tall and dark, and obviously blind if he thought he was handsome. Holly visibly shuddered and he looked away.

"OK, the career stuff is easy," Tracey continued. "Taurus will be occupied and satisfied by a new workload that comes their way. Lucky day will be a . . ." she thought for a while, "Tuesday, and lucky color is . . . blue," she decided, looking at the color of Holly's top. "Right, who's next?"

"Hold on a minute," Holly interrupted. "Is this my horoscope for next month?" she asked, shocked.

Everyone around the table laughed. "Have we shattered your dreams?" Gordon teased.

"Completely," she said, sounding crushed. "I love reading my horoscopes. Please tell me this isn't what all magazines do?" she pleaded.

Chris shook his head, "No, not all magazines do it like this, Holly, some of them just hire people who have the talent to make it up themselves without involving the rest of the office." He glared at Tracey.

"Ha-ha, Chris," Tracey said dryly.

"So Tracey, you're not psychic?" Holly asked sadly.

Tracey shook her head, "No, not psychic, but I'm good as an agony aunt and at making up crossword puzzles, thank you very much." She glared at Chris and he mouthed the word "wow" at her.

"Ah, you've all ruined it for me now," Holly laughed, and sat back in her chair feeling deflated.

"OK Chris, you're next. This month Gemini will overwork themselves, never leave their office and eat junk food all the time. They need to find some sort of balance in their lives."

Chris rolled his eyes. "You write that every month, Tracey."

"Well, until you change your lifestyle I can't change what Gemini will do, can I? Besides, I haven't had any complaints so far."

"But I'm complaining!" Chris laughed.

"But you don't count because you don't believe in star signs."

"And I wonder why," he laughed.

They went through everyone's star sign and Tracey finally gave in to Brian's demands that Leo be desired by the opposite sex all month and win the lottery. Hmm . . . wonder what star sign Brian was. Holly looked at her watch and realized she was late for her business meeting with Daniel.

"Oh, sorry everybody, I have to rush off," she said, excusing herself from the table.

"Your tall, dark and handsome man awaits you," Alice giggled. "Send him on to me if you don't want him."

Holly headed outside and her heart beat wildly as she spotted Daniel walking down the road to meet her. The cool autumn months had arrived, so Daniel was back wearing his black leather jacket again, teamed with blue jeans. His black hair was messy and stubble lined his chin. He had that just-out-of-bed look. Holly's stomach lurched again and she looked away.

"Ooh, I told you!" Tracey said excitedly as she walked out the door behind Holly and hurried off down the road happily.

"I'm so sorry, Daniel," she apologized. "I got tied up in a meeting and I couldn't call," she lied.

"Don't worry about it, I'm sure it was important." He smiled at her and she instantly felt guilty. This was Daniel, her friend, not someone she should be avoiding. What on earth was wrong with her?

"So where would you like to go?" he asked.

"How about in there?" Holly said, looking at the small café on the ground floor of her office building. She wanted to go to the least intimate and most casual place possible.

Daniel scrunched up his nose. "I'm a bit hungrier than that if you don't mind. I haven't eaten all day."

They walked along together and Holly pointed out every single café along the way, and Daniel shook his head at each one. Eventually he settled on an Italian restaurant that Holly couldn't say no to. Not because she wanted to go in but because there was nowhere else left to go after she had said no to every other dark, romantic restaurant and Daniel had refused to eat in any of the casual, brightly lit cafés.

Inside it was quiet, with just a few tables occupied by couples staring lovingly into each other's eyes over a candlelit dinner. When Daniel stood up to take his jacket off Holly quickly blew out the candle on their table when he wasn't looking. He was dressed in a deep blue shirt that caused his eyes to seem luminous in the dim restaurant.

"They make you sick, don't they?" Daniel laughed, following Holly's gaze to a couple on the far side of the room who were kissing across the table.

"Actually no," Holly thought aloud. "They make me sad."

Daniel hadn't heard her, as he was busy reading through the menu. "What are you having?"

"I'm going to have a Caesar salad."

"You women and your Caesar salads," Daniel teased. "Aren't you hungry?"

"Not really." She shook her head and blushed as her stomach grumbled loudly.

"I think somebody disagrees with you down there," he laughed. "I don't think you ever eat, Holly Kennedy."

Just not when I'm with you, she thought. "I just don't have a very big appetite, that's all."

"Yeah, well, I've seen rabbits eat more than you do," he laughed.

Holly tried to control the conversation, steering it into safe territory, and they spent the evening talking about the launch party. She wasn't in the mood for discussing their private feelings and thoughts tonight; she wasn't even quite sure what exactly they were right then. Daniel had kindly brought a copy of the press release so that Holly could look through it in advance and get to work on it as soon as possible. He also gave her a list of phone numbers for the people working on Blue Rock so that Holly could get a few quotes. He was extremely helpful, giving her tips on what angle to take and who to talk to for more information. She left the restaurant feeling a lot less panicked about having to write the article; however, she felt a little more panicked about why she had been so uncomfortable with a man that she was certain only wanted to be her friend. She was also still starving after eating only a few lettuce leaves.

She stepped outside of the restaurant for a breath of fresh air while Daniel kindly paid the bill. He was an extremely generous man, there was no denying that, and she was glad of his friendship. It just didn't feel quite right for her to be eating in a small intimate restaurant with anyone other than Gerry. She felt all wrong. She should be at home right now sitting at her kitchen table waiting until twelve o'clock so that she could open her October letter from Gerry.

She froze and tried to hide her face as she spotted a couple walking toward her that she really did not wish to see. She bent over to pretend to tie her shoelace until she realized she had worn her zip-up boots that day and ended up embarrassingly fumbling with the ends of her trousers.

"Holly, is that you?" she heard the familiar voice. She stared at the two pairs of shoes standing in front of her and slowly looked up to meet their eyes.

"Hello there!" She tried to sound surprised while nervously steadying herself to her feet.

"How are you?" the woman asked, giving her a feeble hug. "What are you doing standing out here in the cold?"

Holly prayed that Daniel stayed inside for another while longer. "Oh, you know . . . I was just having a bite to eat," she smiled shakily, pointing at the restaurant.

"Oh, we're just about to go in there," the man said, smiling. "It's a shame we just missed you, we could have eaten together."

"Yes, yes it's a shame . . ."

"Well, good for you anyway," the woman said, patting her on the back. "It's good to get out and do things on your own."

"Well, actually . . ." She glanced at the door again, praying that it wouldn't open. "Yes, it's nice to do that . . ." She trailed off.

"There you are!" Daniel laughed, stepping outside. "I thought you had run off on me." He wrapped his arm loosely around her shoulders.

Holly smiled at him weakly and turned to face the couple.

"Oh sorry, I didn't see you there." Daniel smiled, turning to face them.

The couple stared back at him stonily.

"Eh . . . Daniel, this is Judith and Charles. They're Gerry's parents."

Forty

HOLLY PRESSED DOWN ON HER car horn heavily and cursed at the driver in front of her. She was fuming. She was mad at herself for being caught in such a situation. She was mad at herself for feeling that she *had* been caught in a bad situation when really there was nothing to it. But she was even angrier at herself for feeling like there was more to it because she had really enjoyed Daniel's company all evening. And she shouldn't be enjoying herself because it didn't feel right, but it had felt so right at the time . . .

She held her hand up to her head and massaged her temples. She had a headache and she was overanalyzing things again and the stupid traffic all the way home was driving her insane. Poor Daniel, she thought sadly. Gerry's parents had been so rude to him and had ended the conversation abruptly and charged into the restaurant, refusing to make eye contact with Holly. Oh, why did they have to see her the one time she was happy? They could have come around to the house any day of the week to see her feeling miserable and living the life of the perfect grieving widow. They would have been happy then. But they hadn't, and now they probably thought she was having a great life without their son. Well, screw them, she thought angrily, pushing down on the horn again. Why did it always take people five minutes to move from the traffic lights when they went green?

She stopped at every single set of traffic lights she met, and all she wanted to do was to go home and throw a tantrum in the privacy of her own home. She picked up her mobile and called Sharon, knowing she would understand.

"Hello?"

"Hi John, it's Holly, can I speak to Sharon?" she said.

"Sorry Holly, she's asleep. I would wake her for you but she's been absolutely exhausted—"

"No, don't worry," she interrupted. "I'll call her tomorrow."

"Is it important?" he asked, worried.

"No," she said quietly. "It's not important at all." She hung up and immediately dialed Denise's number.

"Hello?" Denise giggled.

"Hiya," Holly said.

"Are you OK?" Denise giggled again. "Tom, stop!" she whispered, and Holly quickly realized she had called at a bad time.

"Yeah, I'm fine. I just called for a chat but I can hear you're busy there," she forced a laugh.

"OK then, I'll call tomorrow, Hol." She giggled again.

"OK then, b—" Holly didn't even get to finish her sentence as Denise had hung up.

She sat at the traffic light lost in thought until loud beeps behind her caused her to jump and press her foot down on the accelerator.

She decided to go to her parents' house and talk to Ciara, as she would cheer her up. Just as she pulled up outside the house, she remembered Ciara was no longer there and her eyes filled with tears. Once again she had nobody.

She rang the doorbell and Declan answered.

"What's wrong with you?"

"Nothing," she said, feeling sorry for herself. "Where's Mum?"

"In the kitchen with Dad talking to Richard. I'd leave them alone for a bit."

"Oh . . . OK . . ." She felt lost. "What are you up to?"

"I'm just watching what I filmed today."

"Is this for the documentary on homelessness?"

"Yeah, do you wanna watch it?"

"Yeah." She smiled gratefully and settled herself down on the couch. A few minutes into the video and Holly was in tears, but for once they weren't for herself. Declan had done an incisive, heartrending interview with a remarkable man who was living on the streets of Dublin. She realized there were people far worse off than she, and the fact that Gerry's parents had bumped into her and Daniel walking out of a restaurant seemed like such a stupid thing to worry about.

"Oh Declan, that was excellent," she said, drying her eyes when it had finished.

"Thanks," he said quietly, taking the video out of the player and packing it in his bag.

"Are you not happy with it?"

He shrugged his shoulders. "When you end up spending the

day with people like that it's kind of hard to be happy about the fact that what he has to say is *so* bad that it's making a great documentary. So therefore the worse off he is, the better off I am."

Holly listened with interest. "No, I don't agree with that, Declan. I think that you filming this will make a difference to him. People will see it and want to help."

Declan just shrugged. "Maybe. Anyway I'm going to bed now, I'm absolutely knackered." He picked up his bag and kissed her on the top of her head as he passed, which really touched Holly. Her baby brother was growing up.

Holly glanced at the clock on the mantelpiece and noticed it was almost twelve. She reached for her bag and took out the October envelope from Gerry. She dreaded the days when there would be no more letters. After all, there were only two left after this. She ran her fingers over the writing once again and tore the seal open. Holly slid the card out of the envelope and a dried flower that had been pressed between two cards fell onto her lap. Her favorite, a sunflower. Along with it, a small pouch had landed on her lap. She studied it with curiosity and realized it was a packet of sunflower seeds. Her hands shook as she touched the delicate petals, not wanting them to snap between her fingers. His message read:

> *A sunflower for my sunflower. To brighten the dark*
> *October days you hate so much. Plant some more, and be safe*
> *in the knowledge a warm and bright summer awaits.*
> *PS, I love you . . .*
> *PPS, Could you please pass this card on to John?*

Holly lifted the second card that had fallen on to her lap and read the words through her tears and laughter.

To John,

Happy 32nd birthday. You're getting old, my friend, but I hope you have many, many more birthdays. Enjoy life and take care of my wife and Sharon. You're the man now!

Lots of Love, your friend Gerry

PS, Told you I'd keep my promise.

Holly read and reread every single word Gerry had written. She sat on that couch for what seemed like hours and thought about how happy John would be to hear from his friend. She thought about how much her life had changed over the past few months. Her working life had definitely improved significantly, and she was proud of herself for sticking at it; she loved the feeling of satisfaction she got each day when she switched off her computer and left the office. Gerry had pushed her to be brave; he had encouraged her to want a job that meant more to her in life than just a paycheck. She wouldn't have needed to search for those extra things if Gerry were still with her. Life without him was emptier, leaving more room for herself. She'd exchange it all to have Gerry back.

That wasn't an option. She needed to start thinking about herself and her own future. Because there was no one else to share the responsibilities with her anymore.

Holly wiped her eyes and stood up from the couch. She felt a new bounce in her step and she couldn't wipe the grin off her face. She tapped lightly on the kitchen door.

"Come in," Elizabeth called.

Holly stepped in and looked around at her parents and Richard sitting at the table with cups of tea in their hands.

"Oh hello, love," her mum said, happily getting up to give her a hug and a kiss. "I didn't hear you come in."

"I've been here about an hour. I was just watching Declan's documentary." Holly beamed at her family and felt like giving them all a hug.

"It's great, isn't it?" Frank said, standing up to greet his eldest daughter with a hug and a kiss.

Holly nodded and joined them at the table. "Have you found a job yet?" she asked Richard.

He shook his head sadly and looked as though he were going to cry.

"Well, I did."

He looked at her disgusted that she could say such a thing. "Well, I know *you* did."

"No Richard," she smiled. "I mean I got *you* a job."

He looked up at her in surprise. "You what?"

"You heard me," she grinned. "My boss will be calling you tomorrow."

His face fell. "Oh Holly, that's very nice of you indeed, but I have no interest in advertising. My interest is in science."

"And gardening."

"Yes, I like gardening." He looked confused.

"So that's why my boss will be calling you. To ask you to work on his garden. I told him you'll do it for five thousand; I hope that's OK." She smiled at him as his mouth dropped open.

He was completely speechless so Holly kept on talking.

"And here's your business cards," she said, handing him a large pile of cards that she had printed up that day.

Richard and her parents picked up the cards and read them in silence.

Suddenly Richard started laughing, jumped out of his chair pulling Holly with him, and danced her around the kitchen while her parents looked on and cheered.

"Oh, by the way," Richard said, calming down and glancing at the card again, "you spelled 'gardener' wrong. It's not 'gardner,' it is 'gard-en-er.'" He spoke slowly. "See the difference?"

Holly stopped dancing and sighed with frustration.

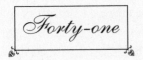

Forty-one

"Ok, this is the last one, I promise, girls!" Denise called as her bra was sent flying over the changing room door.

Sharon and Holly groaned and collapsed onto their chairs again.

"You said that an hour ago," Sharon complained, kicking off her shoes and massaging her swollen ankles.

"Yeah, but I mean it this time. I have a really good feeling about this dress," Denise said, full of excitement.

"You said *that* an hour ago too," Holly grumbled, resting her head back on the chair and closing her eyes.

"Don't you go falling asleep on me now," Sharon warned Holly, and her eyes immediately shot open.

They had been dragged to every single wedding gown boutique in the city and Sharon and Holly were exhausted, irritated and extremely fed up. Whatever excitement they had felt for Denise and her wedding had been drained from their systems as Denise tried on dress after dress. And if Holly heard Denise's irritating squeals one more time she would . . .

"Oooh, I love it!" Denise shrieked.

"OK, here's the plan," Sharon whispered to Holly. "If she walks out of there looking like a meringue sitting on a bicycle pump we are going to tell her she looks beautiful."

Holly giggled. "Oh Sharon, we can't do that!"

"Oooh, wait till you see!" Denise shrieked again.

"On second thought . . ." Holly looked at Sharon miserably.

"OK, are you ready?"

"Yes," Sharon groaned unenthusiastically.

"Ta-da!" She stepped out of the dressing room and Holly's eyes widened.

"Oh, that's so beautiful on you," gushed the sales assistant who had been hovering nearby.

"Oh, stop it!" Denise cried. "You're no help to me at all! You've loved every single one of them."

Holly looked at Sharon uncertainly and tried not to laugh at the look on her face; she looked like there was a bad smell in the air.

Sharon rolled her eyes and whispered, "Hasn't Denise ever heard of a thing called commission?"

"What are you two whispering about?" Denise asked.

"Oh, just about how pretty you look."

Holly frowned at Sharon.

"Oh, do you like it?" Denise squealed again and Holly winced.

"Yes," Sharon said unenthusiastically.

"Are you sure?"

"Yes."

"Do you think Tom will be happy when he looks down the aisle and sees me walking toward him?" Denise even practiced her walk just so the girls could imagine it.

"Yes," Sharon repeated.

"But are you sure?"

"Yes."

"Do you think it's worth the money?"

"Yes."

"Really?"

"Yes."

"It'll be nicer with a tan, won't it?"

"Yes."

"Oh, but does it make my bum look enormous?"

"Yes."

Holly looked at Sharon startled, realizing she wasn't even listening to the questions anymore.

"Oh, but are you sure?" Denise carried on, obviously not even listening to the answers.

"Yes."

"So will I get it?"

Holly expected the sales assistant to start jumping up and down with excitement screaming "Yessss!" but she managed to contain herself.

"No!" Holly interrupted before Sharon said yes again.

"No?" Denise asked.

"No," Holly confirmed.

"Do you not like it?"

"No."

"Is it because it makes me look fat?"

"No."

"Do you not think Tom will like it?"

"No."

"Do you think it's worth the money, though?"

"No."

"Oh." She turned to face Sharon. "Do you agree with Holly?"

"Yes."

The sales assistant rolled her eyes and approached another customer, hoping for better luck with her.

"OK then, I trust you two," Denise said, sadly taking one last look at herself in the mirror. "To be honest I wasn't really that keen on it myself."

Sharon sighed and put her shoes back on. "OK Denise, you said that was the last one. Let's go get something to eat before I drop dead."

"No, I meant it was the last dress I would try on in *this* shop. There's loads more shops to go to yet."

"No way!" Holly protested. "Denise, I am starving to death and at this stage all the dresses are beginning to look the same to me. I need a break."

"Oh, but this is my wedding day, Holly!"

"Yes and . . ." Holly tried to think of an excuse. "But Sharon's pregnant."

"Oh, OK then, we'll get something to eat," Denise said, disappointed, and headed back to the changing room.

Sharon elbowed Holly in the ribs. "Hey, I'm not diseased, you know, just pregnant."

"Oh, it's the only thing that I could think of," Holly said tiredly.

The three of them trudged into Bewley's Café and managed to grab their usual spot by the window overlooking Grafton Street.

"Oh, I hate shopping on Saturdays," Holly moaned, watching as people bumped and crushed one another on the busy street below.

"Gone are the days of shopping midweek, now you're no longer a lady of leisure," Sharon teased, as she picked up a club sandwich and began stuffing her face.

"I know, and I'm *so* tired, but I feel like I've earned the tiredness this time. Unlike before when I just used to stay up late watching insomniac TV," Holly said happily.

"Tell us about the little episode with Gerry's parents," Sharon said with a mouthful of food.

Holly rolled her eyes. "They were just so rude to poor Daniel."

"I'm sorry I was asleep. I'm sure if John had known that's what it was about he would have woken me," Sharon apologized.

"Oh, don't be silly, it wasn't a really big deal. It just felt like it at the time."

"Too right. They can't tell you who to see and who not to see," Sharon gave out.

"Sharon, I'm not seeing him." Holly tried to get the record straight. "I have no intentions of seeing anyone for at least another twenty years. We were just having a business dinner."

"Oooh, a *business* dinner!" Sharon and Denise giggled.

"Well, it was that and it was also nice to have a bit of company." Holly smiled. "And I'm not bitching about you two," she said quickly before they had a chance to defend themselves. "All I'm saying is that when everyone else is busy it's nice to have someone else to chat to. Especially male company, you know? And he's easy to get along with and he makes me feel very comfortable. That's all."

"Yeah, I understand," Sharon nodded. "It's good for you to get out and meet new people anyway."

"So did you find out anything else about him?" Denise leaned forward, her eyes sparkling as she dug for gossip. "He's a bit of a dark horse, that Daniel. Maybe he's hiding some huge secret. Maybe the ghosts of his army past are coming back to torment him," Denise joked.

"Eh . . . no, Denise, I don't think so," Holly laughed. "Unless cleaning his boots in training camp was a traumatizing event. He didn't last much longer than that," she explained.

"I love yummy army men," Denise drooled.

"And DJs," Sharon added.

"Oh, and DJs of course," Denise replied, laughing.

"Well, I told him my view about the army anyway," Holly smiled.

"Oh no, you didn't!" Sharon laughed.

"What's this?" Denise asked.

"So what did he say?" Sharon ignored Denise.

"He just laughed."

"What's this?" Denise asked again.

"Holly's theory about the army," Sharon explained.

"And what is it?" Denise asked, intrigued.

"Oh, that fighting for peace is like screwing for virginity."

The girls burst out laughing.

"Yeah, but you can have hours of endless fun trying," Denise quipped.

"So you haven't mastered it yet?" Sharon asked.

"No, but at every available chance, we try, you know?" Denise replied, and the girls all giggled. "Well, Holly, I'm glad you get along with him, because you're going to have to dance with him at the wedding."

"Why?" She looked at Denise confused.

"Because it's tradition for the best man to dance with the maid of honor at the wedding," her eyes sparkled.

Holly gasped, "You want me to be your maid of honor?"

Denise nodded, full of excitement. "Don't worry, I already asked Sharon and she doesn't mind," she assured Holly.

"Oh, I would love to!" Holly said happily. "But Sharon, are you sure you don't mind?"

"Oh, don't worry about me, I'm happy just being a blown-up bridesmaid."

"You won't be blown up!" Holly laughed.

"Yes I will, I'll be eight months pregnant. I'll need to borrow Denise's marquee to wear as a dress!"

"Oh, I hope you don't go into labor at the wedding." Denise's eyes widened.

"Don't worry, Denise, I won't steal the limelight from you on your day." Sharon smiled, "I won't be due till the end of January so that'll be weeks later."

Denise looked relieved.

"Oh, by the way, I forgot to show you the photograph of the baby!" Sharon said excitedly, rooting through her bag. Finally she pulled out a small photograph of the scan.

"Where is it?" Denise asked, frowning.

"There." Sharon pointed out the area.

"Whoa! That's one big boy," Denise exclaimed, moving the picture closer to her face.

Sharon rolled her eyes. "Denise, that's a leg, you fool, we still don't know the sex yet."

"Oh," Denise blushed. "Well congratulations, Sharon, it looks like you're having a little alien."

"Oh stop it, Denise," Holly laughed. "I think it's a beautiful picture."

"Good." Sharon smiled and looked at Denise and Denise nodded at her, "Because I wanted to ask you something."

"What?" Holly looked worried.

"Well, John and I would love it if you would be our baby's godmother."

Holly gasped with shock for the second time and tears filled her eyes.

"Hey, you didn't cry when I asked you to be maid of honor," Denise huffed.

"Oh Sharon, I would be honored!" Holly said, giving her friend a big hug. "Thank you for asking!"

"Thank you for saying yes! John will be so delighted!"

"Oh, don't you two start crying," Denise moaned, but Sharon and Holly ignored her and continued hugging.

"Hey!" Denise yelled, causing them to jump from their embrace.

"What?!"

Denise pointed out the window: "I can't believe I never noticed that wedding shop over there! Drink up quick and we'll go there next," she said excitedly as her eyes darted from dress to dress.

Sharon sighed and pretended to pass out. "I can't, Denise, I'm pregnant . . ."

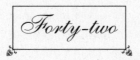

Forty-two

"H<small>EY</small> H<small>OLLY</small>, I <small>WAS JUST</small> thinking," Alice said to Holly as they were reapplying their makeup in the toilets at work before leaving for the day.

"Oh no, did it hurt?" Holly teased.

"Ha-ha," she said dryly. "No, honestly, I was thinking about the horoscope in this month's magazine and I think Tracey may have got it eerily right."

Holly threw her eyes up to heaven. "How?"

Alice put down her lipstick and turned away from the mirror to face Holly. "Well, first there was the thing about the tall, dark, handsome man who you are now seeing . . ."

"I'm not seeing him, we're just friends," Holly explained for the millionth time.

Alice rolled her eyes. "Whatever you say. Anyway, then there was the thing . . ."

"I'm not," Holly repeated.

"Yeah, yeah," Alice said, disbelieving her. "Well then, there's the . . ."

Holly slammed down her makeup bag. "Alice, I am *not* seeing Daniel."

"OK, OK." She held up her hands defensively, "I get it! You're *not* seeing him, but please stop interrupting me and listen!" She waited for Holly to calm down and listen. "OK, so the other thing she said was that your lucky day is Tuesday, which is today . . ."

"Wow, Alice, I think you're on to something here," Holly said sarcastically, applying her lip liner.

"Listen!" Alice said impatiently and Holly shut up. "So she also said that blue was your lucky color. So today being *Tuesday* you have been invited by a *tall, dark, handsome man* to the launch of *Blue* Rock." Alice looked pleased with herself as she summed it all up.

"So what?" Holly said, unimpressed.

"So it's a sign."

"A sign that the color shirt I happened to be wearing that day was blue, which was why Tracey chose that particular color, which I happened to be wearing because everything else I owned was dirty. And she just picked the day off the top of her head. It means *nothing,* Alice."

Alice sighed, "Oh ye of little faith."

Holly laughed. "Well, if I am to believe your little theory, as screwed up as it is, then that also means that Brian is going to win the lotto and he will also become the object of every woman's affections."

Alice bit her lip and looked sheepish.

"What?" Holly asked, knowing something was going through her bizarre little mind.

"Well, Brian won four euro on the scratch card today."

"Whoopdeedoo," Holly laughed. "Well, there's still the problem of at least one human being finding him attractive."

Alice remained silent.

"What now?" Holly demanded.

"Nothing," Alice shrugged and smiled.

"You don't!" Holly said, shocked.

"I don't what?" Her face lit up.

"You don't fancy him, do you? You couldn't possibly!"

Alice shrugged. "He's nice, that's all."

"Oh no!" Holly covered her face with her hands. "You're taking this way too far just to try to prove a point to me."

"I'm not trying to prove anything to you," she laughed.

"Well then, I can't believe you fancy him!"

"Who fancies who?" Tracey asked, walking into the toilet.

Alice shook her head wildly at Holly, begging her not to tell.

"Oh nobody," Holly muttered, staring at Alice in shock. How could Alice fancy the slimeball of all slimeballs?

"Hey, did you hear Brian won money on the lotto scratch card today?" Tracey asked them from the cubicle.

"We were just talking about that," Alice laughed.

"I just might have psychic powers after all, Holly," Tracey giggled and flushed the toilet.

Alice winked at Holly in the mirror and Holly headed out of the bathroom. "Come on, Alice, we better get going to this thing or the photographer will go mad."

"The photographer's already here," Alice explained, applying some mascara.

"Where is he?"

"She."

"Well then, where is she?"

"Ta-da!" Alice announced, taking a camera out of her bag.

"You're the photographer?" Holly laughed. "Well, at least we can both lose our jobs together when this article is published," she called over her shoulder as she headed back to her office.

Holly and Alice pushed their way through the crowds in Hogan's pub and made their way upstairs to Club Diva. Holly gasped as they approached the door. A group of young muscular males dressed in swimwear were banging out some Hawaiian drumbeats to welcome all the guests. Some very skinny female models also dressed in skimpy bikinis greeted the girls at the door by wrapping beautiful multicolored lei around their necks.

"I feel like I'm in Hawaii," Alice giggled, snapping away with her camera. "Oh my God," she exclaimed as they entered the club.

Holly could barely recognize the club; it had been completely transformed. A huge water feature greeted them as they entered. Aqua blue water cascaded down from some rocks, and it looked like a miniature waterfall.

"Oh look, Blue Rock!" Alice laughed. "Very clever."

Holly smiled; so much for her wonderful powers of journalistic observation, she hadn't even copped that the water was actually the drink itself. Then she panicked; Daniel hadn't told her anything about this, which meant she would have to adjust the article so she could hand it in to Chris tomorrow. She looked around the club for Denise and Tom and saw her friend being photographed as she held her hand up to the camera to show off her sparkly engagement ring. Holly laughed at the big celebrity couple.

The bar staff were dressed in their bikinis and swimwear and they lined the entrance with trays of blue drinks in their hands. Holly lifted a drink from the tray and took a sip, trying not to make a face from its overly sweet taste as a photographer snapped her sipping the hot new drink for winter. As Daniel had said, the floors were scattered with sand, making it appear as if they were at a beach party. Each table was sheltered by a huge bamboo umbrella, the bar stools were all big kettle drums and there was a wonderful barbecue smell in the air. Holly's mouth watered as she spotted the waiters carrying trays of barbecued food to the tables. She darted to the nearest table, helped herself to a kebab and took a big bite.

"Oh, so you do eat." Holly found herself facing Daniel. Chewing valiantly, she swallowed her food.

"Em, hello. I haven't had a thing to eat all day so I am absolutely starving. The place looks great," she said, looking around, keen to distract him from the sight of her with a mouthful of kebab.

"Yeah, it worked well all right." He looked pleased. Daniel was slightly more dressed than his staff members; he wore faded blue jeans and a blue Hawaiian shirt with big pink and yellow flowers. He still hadn't shaved and Holly wondered how painful it would be to kiss him with that sharp stubble. Not for her to kiss him, of course. Somebody else . . . and why she was even wondering about it annoyed her.

"Hey Holly! Let me get a photo of you and tall, dark, handsome man," Alice yelled, rushing over with her camera.

Holly was mortified.

Daniel laughed. "You should bring your friends here more often."

"She's not my friend," Holly said through gritted teeth and posed beside Daniel for the photo.

"Hold on a second," Daniel said, covering the camera lens with his hand. He took a napkin from the table and wiped the grease and barbecue sauce from Holly's face. Holly's skin tingled and warmth rushed through her body. She convinced herself it was from her face blushing so much.

"Now it's gone," he said, smiling at her, wrapping his arm around her and facing the camera.

Alice skipped away again and continued to snap all around her. Holly turned to Daniel. "Daniel, once again I'm really sorry about the other night. Gerry's parents were so rude to you, and I'm sorry if you felt uncomfortable."

"Oh, there's no need to apologize again, Holly. In fact, there's no need to apologize *at all*. I only felt uncomfortable for you. They shouldn't be able to tell you who to see and who not to see. Anyway, if you're worried about me then there's no need." He smiled and placed his hands on her shoulders as though he were going to say something more, but someone called him from the bar and he rushed over to sort the problem out.

"But I am *not* seeing you," Holly muttered to herself. If she had to convince even Daniel of that then they certainly had a problem. She hoped he didn't think there was more to the dinner than there really was. He had called her almost every day since that episode. She realized that she looked forward to his calls. There was that niggling thing at the back of her mind again. Holly wandered over to Denise and joined her on the sun bed where she was sipping on the blue concoction.

"Hey Holly, I saved this for you." She pointed to the raft in the corner of the room and the two girls giggled, remembering their big adventure out in the sea while on holiday.

"So what do you think of the hot new drink for winter?" Holly indicated the bottle.

Denise rolled her eyes. "Tacky. I've only had a few and my head is spinning already."

Alice ran over to Holly dragging an enormously muscular man dressed in tiny little shorts. One of his biceps was the size of Alice's waist. She handed the camera to Holly. "Take a picture of the two of us, will you?"

Holly didn't think that these were the kind of photographs Chris was hoping for, but she obliged Alice.

"It's for the screen saver on my computer at work," Alice explained to Denise.

Holly enjoyed herself that evening, laughing and chatting with Denise and Tom while Alice ran around taking photographs of all the half-naked male models. Holly felt guilty for ever being annoyed by Tom all those months ago at the karaoke competition; he was a sweet guy and he and Denise made a lovely couple. Holly barely got to speak to Daniel, as he was too busy running around being the responsible manager. She watched as he gave orders to his staff and they immediately got to work. It was obvious that his staff had great respect for him. He got things done. Every time she spotted him heading over to her group, somebody stopped him in his tracks for an interview or just for a chat. Most of the time, he was stopped by skinny young girls in bikinis. They annoyed Holly, so she looked away.

"I don't know how I'm going to write this article," Holly moaned to Alice as they made their way outside into the cold air.

"Don't worry, Holly, you'll be fine; it's only eight hundred words, isn't it?"

"Yeah, *only*," she said sarcastically. "You see, I already wrote a draft article a few days ago because Daniel gave me all the information. But after seeing all that, I'll have to change it extensively. It already almost killed me trying to get this version done in the first place."

"You're really worried about this, aren't you?"

Holly sighed. "I just can't write, Alice. I was never any good at putting things into words and describing exactly how things are."

Alice looked thoughtful. "Have you got the article in the office?"

Holly nodded.

"Why don't we go over there now? I'll look over it, and maybe I'll make a few changes if it needs it."

"Oh Alice, thank you so much!" Holly said, hugging her with relief.

The following day Holly sat nervously before Chris and watched him read the article. His face remained grumpy as he turned the page. Alice hadn't just made a few changes to the article, she had completely rewritten it, and Holly thought it was incredible. It was funny yet informative and she explained the night exactly as it had been, which Holly was unable to do. Alice was an extremely talented writer and Holly couldn't understand why she was working at reception in a magazine office instead of writing for them.

Finally, Chris finished reading and he slowly took off his reading glasses and looked up at Holly. Holly's hands fidgeted on her lap and she felt like she had just cheated on a school exam.

"Holly, I don't know what you're doing in ad sales," Chris finally said. "You are a fantastic writer, I love it! It's cheeky and funny yet it gets the point across. It's fabulous."

Holly smiled weakly. "Eh . . . thanks."

"You have such a wonderful talent; I can't believe you tried to hide it from me."

Holly's smile stayed glued onto her face.

"How would you feel about writing every now and again?"

Holly's face froze. "Well, Chris, I'm really much more interested in the advertising side of things."

"Oh, of course, and I will pay you more for this too. But if we are ever stuck again, at least I know I have another talented writer on the team. Well done, Holly." He grinned at her and held out his hand.

"Eh . . . thanks," Holly repeated, shaking his hand weakly. "I better get back to work now." She stood up from her chair and walked stiffly out of the office.

"Well, did he like it?" Alice asked loudly, walking down the hall.

"Eh . . . yeah, he loved it. He wants me to write more." Holly bit her lip, feeling guilty for taking all the credit.

"Oh." Alice looked away. "Well, aren't you the lucky one?" She continued walking to her desk.

Forty-three

D ENISE BANGED THE TILL CLOSED with her hip and handed the receipt over the counter to the customer. "Thanks," she smiled, and her smile quickly faded as soon as the customer turned away from the counter. She sighed loudly, staring at the long queue forming in front of the cash register. She would have to stand here at the till all day and she was just dying for a cigarette break. But there was no way she could slip away, so she grumpily grabbed the item of clothing from the next customer, de-tagged it, scanned it, and wrapped it.

"Excuse me, are you Denise Hennessey?" she heard a deep voice ask and she looked up to see where the sexy voice had come from. She frowned as she saw a police officer before her.

She hesitated while trying to think if she had done anything illegal in the past few days, and when she was satisfied that she was crime-free she smiled. "Yes, I am."

"I'm Officer Ryan and I was wondering if you would accompany me to the station, please."

It was more of a statement than a question, and Denise's mouth dropped open in shock. He was no longer the sexy officer, he was the evil-lock-her-up-forever-in-a-tiny-cell-with-a-luminous-orange-jumpsuit-and noisy-flip-flops-and-no-hot-water-or-makeup-type officer. Denise gulped and had an image of herself being beaten up by a gang of tough angry women that didn't care about mascara, in the exercise yard at the prison while the prison guards looked on and made bets over who would win. She gulped, "What for?"

"If you just comply with what I've said, everything will be explained to you down at the station." He started to walk around the counter and Denise backed away slowly and looked at the long line of customers helplessly. Everybody just stared back at her, amused by the scene that was unfolding before them.

"Check his ID, love," one of the customers shouted to her from the end of the queue.

Her voice shook as she demanded to see his ID, which was a completely useless operation, as she had never seen a police ID before nor did she know what a real one would look like. Her hand trembled as she held the ID and studied it closely, but she didn't read a thing. She was too self-conscious of the crowd of customers and staff that had gathered to stare at her with looks of disgust on their faces. They were all thinking the same thing: She was a criminal.

Denise hardened, refusing to go without a fight. "I refuse to go with you until you tell me what this is about."

He walked toward her again. "Ms. Hennessey, if you just work with me here, then there will be no need to use these." He took out a pair of handcuffs from his trousers. "There's no need to make a scene."

"But I didn't do anything!" she protested, starting to panic.

"Well, we can discuss that down at the station, can't we?" He began to get irate.

Denise backed away, she was determined to let her customers and staff know that she hadn't done anything wrong. She would not go with this man to the station until he explained what she had supposedly done wrong. She stopped backing away and crossed her arms across her chest to show how tough she was.

"I said I will *not* go with you until you tell me what this is about."

"OK then," he shrugged, walking toward her. "If you insist." He opened his mouth to speak and she yelled as she felt the cold silver handcuffs being slapped around her wrists. It wasn't exactly the first time she had ever worn a pair of handcuffs, so she wasn't surprised at how they felt, but she was in so much shock she couldn't speak; she just watched everyone's surprised expressions as the officer led her by the arm out of the shop.

"Good luck, love," the customer shouted again as she was led by the queue. "If they send you to Mount Joy tell my Orla I said hi and that I'll be there to visit her at Christmas."

Denise's eyes widened and images of her pacing a cell that she shared with a psycho murderer jumped into her mind. Maybe she would find a little bird with a broken wing and nurse it and teach it to fly to pass the years inside . . .

Her face reddened as they stepped out onto Grafton Street, and the crowds immediately scattered as soon as they saw the garda and a hardened criminal. Denise kept her eyes down to the ground, hoping nobody she knew would spot her being arrested. Her heart beat wildly and she briefly thought of escape. She looked around quickly and tried to figure out an escape route, but she was too slow; she was already being led toward a beat-up-looking minibus, the well-known color blue of the police with blackened-out windows. Denise sat in the front row of seats behind the driver, and although she could sense people behind her, she sat rigidly in her seat, too terrified to turn around and meet her future fellow inmates. She leaned her head against the window and said good-bye to freedom.

"Where are we going?" she asked as they drove past the police station. The female police officer driving the car and Officer Ryan ignored her and stared ahead of them.

"Hey!" she shouted. "I thought you said you were taking me to the station!" They continued to stare straight ahead.

"Hey! Where are we going?!"

No answer.

"I haven't done anything wrong!"

Still no answer.

"I'm innocent goddammit! Innocent, I tell you!"

Denise started kicking the chair in front of her, trying to get their attention. Her blood started to boil when the female officer pushed a cassette into the player and turned the music up. Denise's eyes widened at the choice of song.

Officer Ryan turned around in his chair with a big grin on his face. "Denise, you have been a very naughty girl." He stood up and made his way in front of her. She gulped as he started to gyrate his hips to the song "Hot Stuff."

She was about to give him a great big kick between his legs when she heard whooping and laughing from the back of the bus. She twisted herself around and spotted her sisters, Holly, Sharon and about five other friends picking themselves up from the floor of the minibus. She had been in so much shock she hadn't even noticed them when she got on the bus. She finally figured out what was really happening when her sisters placed a veil on her head while screaming "Happy hen party!" That was the main clue.

"Oh, you bitches!" Denise spat at them, effing and blinding them until she had used every single curse word invented, and even made up a few of her own.

The girls continued to hold their stomachs with laughter.

"Oh, you are so lucky I didn't kick you in the balls!" Denise screamed at the gyrating garda.

"Denise, this is Paul," her sister Fiona giggled, "and he's your stripper for the day."

Denise narrowed her eyes and continued to curse at them. "I almost had a heart attack, I hope you know! I thought I was going to prison. Oh my God, what will my customers think? And my staff! Oh my God, my staff think I'm a criminal." Denise closed her eyes as though she were in pain.

"We told them about it last week," Sharon giggled. "They were all just playing along."

"Oh, the little bitches," Denise repeated. "When I go back to work I'm going to fire the lot of them. But what about the customers?" Denise asked, panicking.

"Don't worry," her sister said. "We told your staff to inform the customers it was your hen party after you left the shop."

Denise rolled her eyes. "Well, knowing *them* they deliberately won't, and if they *don't* then there will be complaints, and if there are complaints I will be *so* fired."

"Denise! Stop *worrying*! You don't think we would have done this without running it by your boss. It's OK!" Fiona explained. "They thought it was *funny*, now *relax* and enjoy the weekend."

"Weekend? What the hell are you girls going to do to me next?! Where are we going for the weekend?" Denise looked around at her friends, startled.

"We're going to Galway, and that's all you need to know," Sharon said mysteriously.

"If I wasn't bloody handcuffed I'd slap you all in the face," Denise threatened.

The girls all cheered as Paul stripped out of his uniform and poured baby oil over his body for Denise to massage into his skin. Sharon unlocked the handcuffs of a gobsmacked Denise.

"Men in uniform are so much nicer out of them . . . ," Denise mumbled, rubbing her wrists as she watched him flex his muscles before her.

"Lucky she's engaged, Paul, or you would be in big trouble!" the girls teased.

"*Big* trouble is right," Denise mumbled again, staring in shock as the rest of the clothes came off. "Oh girls! Thank you so much!" she giggled, her voice a very different tone than before.

"Are you OK, Holly? You've barely said a word since we got into this van," Sharon said, handing her a glass of champagne and keeping a glass of orange juice for herself. Holly turned to look out of the window and stared at the green fields as they flew by. The green hills were dotted with little white specks as the sheep climbed to new heights, oblivious to the wonderful views. Neat stone walls separated each field and you could see the gray lines, jagged like those in jigsaw puzzles, for miles, connecting each piece of land together. Holly had yet to find a few pieces for her own puzzled mind.

"Yeah," she sighed. "I'm OK."

. . .

"Oh, I really have to ring Tom!" Denise groaned, collapsing onto the double bed she and Holly were sharing in the hotel room. Sharon was fast asleep on the single bed beside them and had refused to listen to Denise's hilarious idea of Sharon having to sleep in the double bed on her own due to the size of her rapidly growing bump. She had gone to bed much earlier than the other girls after eventually becoming bored of their drunken behavior.

"I'm under strict orders not to let you ring Tom," Holly yawned. "This is a girls-only weekend."

"Oh please," Denise whimpered.

"No. I am confiscating your phone." She grabbed the mobile from Denise's hand and hid it in the press beside the bed.

Denise looked like she was going to cry. She watched as Holly lay back on the bed and closed her eyes, and she began to formulate a plan. She would wait until Holly was asleep and then she would call Tom. Holly had been so quiet all day it was really starting to irritate Denise. Every time Denise had asked her a question she got nothing but yes or no answers back, and every attempt to strike up a conversation failed. It was obvious that Holly wasn't enjoying herself, but what really annoyed Denise was to see that Holly wasn't even *trying* to enjoy herself, or even *pretending* to be enjoying herself. Denise could understand that Holly was upset and that she had a lot to deal with in her life, but it was her hen party and she couldn't help feeling that Holly was bringing the atmosphere down a bit.

The room was still spinning. Having closed her eyes, Holly was now unable to sleep. It was five o'clock in the morning, which meant that she had been drinking for almost twelve hours, and her head was pounding. Sharon had given in long ago and had done the sensible thing by going to bed early. Her stomach became queasy as the walls spun around and around and around . . . She sat up on the bed and tried to keep her eyes open so she could avoid the feeling of seasickness.

She turned to face Denise on the bed so that they could talk, but the sound of her friend's snores ended all thought of communication between them. Holly sighed and looked around the room. She wanted nothing more than to go home and sleep in her own bed, where she could be surrounded by familiar smells and noises. She felt her way across the bedcovers in the dark for the remote control and flicked on the television. Commercial presentations adorned the screen. Holly watched as they demonstrated a new knife to slice oranges without spraying yourself in the face with the juice. She saw the amazing socks that never got lost in the wash and stayed together at all times.

Denise snored loudly beside her and she kicked Holly in the shins as she changed position. Holly winced and rubbed her leg as she watched with sympathy Sharon's extremely frustrated struggle to lie on her stomach. Eventually she settled on her side and Holly rushed to the toilet and hung her head over the toilet seat, prepared for whatever might come. She wished she hadn't drunk so much, but with all the talk of weddings and husbands and happiness she had needed all the wine in the bar to prevent her from screaming at everyone to shut up. She dreaded to think what the next two days would be like. Denise's friends were twice as bad as Denise. They were loud and hyper and acted exactly the way girls should on a hen weekend, but Holly just didn't have the energy to keep up with them. At least Sharon had the excuse of being pregnant; she could pretend she wasn't feeling well or that she was tired. Holly had no excuse apart from the fact that she had turned into a complete bore, and she was saving that excuse for a time when she really needed it.

It felt like only yesterday that Holly had had her own hen party, but in fact it was more than seven years ago. She had flown over to London with a group of ten girls for the weekend to party hard, but she ended up missing Gerry so much she had to speak to him on the phone every hour. Back then she had been so excited about what was to come and the future had looked so bright.

She was to marry the man of her dreams and live and grow with him for the rest of their lives. For the entire weekend she was away she counted the hours until she could return home. She was so excited on the flight back to Dublin. Although they had been apart for only a few days, it had felt like an eternity. He had been waiting for her at arrivals with a huge board in his hand saying MY FUTURE WIFE. She had dropped her bags when she saw him and run into his arms and hugged him *so* tight. She had never wanted to let go; what a luxury it was for people to be able to hold their loved ones whenever they wanted. The scene at the airport seemed like a scene from a movie now, but it had been real: real feelings, real emotions and real love, because it was real life. Real life had become a nightmare for her.

Yes, she had finally managed to drag herself out of bed every morning, yes, she even managed to get dressed most of the time. Yes, she had succeeded in finding a new job where she had met new people, and yes, she had finally started buying food again and feeding herself. But no, she didn't feel ecstatic about any of these things. They were just formalities, something else to check off on the "things that normal people do" list. None of these things filled the hole in her heart; it was as if her body had become one great jigsaw, just like the green fields with their pretty gray stone walls connecting the whole of Ireland. She had started working on the corners and the edges of her jigsaw because they were the easy bits, and now that they were all in place she needed to do all the bits in between, the hard parts. But nothing she had done so far had managed to fill that hole in her heart; that piece of the jigsaw had yet to be found.

Holly cleared her throat loudly and pretended to have a coughing fit just so the girls would wake up and talk to her. She needed to talk, she needed to cry and she needed to vent all her frustrations and disappointments about her life. But what more could she say to Sharon and Denise that she hadn't said before? What more advice could they give her that they hadn't given her before? She repeated the same old worries over and over. Some-times her friends would succeed in getting through to her and she would feel positive and confident, only to find herself thrown back into despair days later.

After a while Holly tired of staring at the four walls, threw on a tracksuit and made her way back downstairs to the hotel bar.

Charlie groaned with frustration as the table down the back of the bar began to roar with laughter again. He wiped down the bar counter and glanced at his watch. Five-thirty and he was still here working and he couldn't wait to go home. He had thought he was so lucky when the girls from the hen party had eventually gone to bed earlier than expected, and he was about to tidy up and go home when another gang arrived at the hotel after a nightclub had finished in Galway city. And they were still here. In fact, he would have preferred if the girls had stayed up instead of the arrogant crowd sitting down the back. They weren't even residents of the hotel, but he had to serve them because the group included the daughter of the owner of the hotel, who had brought all her friends back to the bar. She and her arrogant boyfriend, and he couldn't stand them.

"Don't tell me you're back for more!" the barman laughed as one of the women from the hen party walked into the room. She walked toward the bar, bumping into the wall many times as she tried to make her way to the high stool. Charlie tried not to laugh. "I just came down for a glass of water," she hiccuped. "Oh my God," she wailed, catching sight of herself in the mirror over the bar. Charlie had to admit that she did look a bit shocking; a bit like the scarecrow in his dad's farm. Her hair looked like straw and was sticking out in all directions, her eyes had black circles around them from smudging her mascara, and her teeth were stained from the red wine.

"There you go," Charlie said, placing a glass of water on a beer mat in front of her.

"Thanks." She dipped her finger into her glass and wiped the mascara from her eyes and rubbed the wine stains from her lips.

Charlie began to laugh and she squinted at his name tag.

"What are you laughing at, Charlie?"

"I thought you were thirsty, but I would have given you a face-cloth if you'd asked for one," he chuckled.

The woman laughed and her features softened. "I find the ice and lemon helps my skin."

"Well, that's a new one." Charlie laughed and continued to wipe down the counter. "Did you girls have fun tonight?"

Holly sighed, "I suppose." *Fun* wasn't a word she often used anymore. She had laughed along with the jokes all night, she had felt excited for Denise, but she didn't feel like she was *completely* there. She felt like the shy girl at school who was always *just there* but never spoke and was never spoken to. She didn't recognize the person she had become; she wanted to be able to stop staring at the clock whenever she went out, hoping the night would soon be over so she could go home and crawl into bed. She wanted to stop wishing time would pass and instead enjoy the moment. She was finding it hard to enjoy moments.

"Are you OK?" Charlie stopped wiping the counter and watched her. He had a horrible feeling she was going to cry, but he was used to it at this stage. A lot of people became emotional when they drank.

"I miss my husband," she whispered, and her shoulders trembled.

The corners of Charlie's lips turned into a smile.

"What's so funny?" She looked at him angrily.

"How long are you here for?" he asked.

"The weekend," she told him, twisting a worn tissue around her finger.

He laughed. "Have you never gone the weekend without seeing him?"

He watched the woman frown. "Only once before," she finally replied, "and that was at my own hen party."

"How long ago was that?"

"Seven years ago." A tear spilled down the woman's face.

Charlie shook his head. "That's a long time ago. Well, if you did it once, you can do it again," he smiled. "Seven years lucky, isn't that what they say?"

Holly snorted into her drink. Lucky her arse.

"Don't worry," Charlie said gently. "Your husband's probably miserable without you."

"Oh God, I hope not." Holly's eyes widened.

"Well then, see?" he replied. "I'm sure he hopes you're not miserable without him either. You're supposed to be enjoying your life."

"You're right," Holly said, perking up. "He wouldn't want me to be unhappy."

"That's the spirit." Charlie smiled and jumped as he saw his boss's daughter coming toward the bar with one of those looks on her face.

"Hey Charlie," she yelled. "I've been trying to get your attention for ages. Maybe if you stopped chatting to the customers at the bar and did a bit of work, me and my friends wouldn't be so thirsty," she said bitchily.

Holly's mouth dropped open with shock. That woman had a nerve speaking to Charlie like that, and her perfume was so strong it made Holly start to cough lightly.

"I'm sorry, do you have a problem?" The woman's head darted toward Holly, and she looked her up and down.

"Yes, actually," Holly slurred, taking a sip of her water. "Your perfume is disgusting and it's making me want to throw up."

Charlie dropped to his knees behind the counter to pretend to look for a lemon to slice and started laughing. He tried to block out the sounds of the two women snapping at each other so he would stop laughing.

"What's the delay here?" a deep voice inquired. Charlie shot to his feet at the sound of her boyfriend's voice. He was even worse. "Why don't you sit down, honey, and I'll bring the drinks over," he said.

"Fine, at least *someone* is polite around here," she snapped, looking Holly up and down once more before storming off to her table. Holly watched her hips go boom-boom-boom as they went from side to side. She must be a model or something, Holly decided. That would explain the tantrums.

"So how are you?" the man beside Holly asked, staring at her chest.

Charlie had to bite his tongue to stop himself from saying anything as he poured a pint of Guinness from the tap and then allowed it to sit on the counter for a while. He had a feeling the woman at the bar wouldn't succumb to Stevie's charms anyway, especially as she seemed to be so head over heels about her husband. Charlie was looking forward to seeing Stevie being ceremoniously dumped.

"I'm fine," Holly replied shortly, staring straight ahead, deliberately avoiding eye contact.

"I'm Stevie," he said, holding out his hand to her.

"I'm Holly," she mumbled and took his hand lightly, not wanting to be overly rude.

"Holly, that's a lovely name." He held her hand for much too long and Holly was forced to look up into his eyes. He had big blue sparkly eyes.

"Eh . . . thanks," she said, embarrassed by his compliment, and her face flushed.

Charlie sighed to himself. Even she had fallen for it, his only hope of satisfaction for the night gone.

"Can I buy you a drink, Holly?" Steve asked smoothly.

"No thanks, I have one here." She sipped on her water again.

"OK, well, I'm just going to bring these drinks down to my table and then I'll be back to buy the lovely Holly a drink." He smiled at her creepily as he walked away. Charlie rolled his eyes as soon as he turned his back.

"Who the hell is that eejit?" Holly asked, looking bewildered, and Charlie laughed, delighted that she hadn't fallen for him. She was a lady with sense even if she was crying because she missed her husband after only one day of separation.

Charlie lowered his voice, "That's Stevie, boyfriend of that blond bitch who was here a minute ago. Her dad owns this hotel, which means I can't exactly tell her where to go, although I would love to. Not worth losing my job over."

"Definitely worth losing your job over, I should think," Holly said, staring at the beautiful woman and thinking nasty thoughts. "Anyway, good night, Charlie."

"You off to bed?"

She nodded. "It's about time; it's after six," she tapped on her watch. "I hope you get home soon," she smiled.

"I wouldn't bet on it," he replied and watched her leave the bar. Stevie followed after her and Charlie, thinking this was suspicious, made his way closer to the door just to make sure she was OK. The blonde, noticing her boyfriend's sudden departure, left her table and arrived at the door with Charlie at the same time. They both stared down the corridor in the direction Holly and Stevie had headed.

The blonde gasped and her hand flew to her mouth.

"Hey!" Charlie called out angrily as he witnessed a distressed Holly pushing a drunken Stevie away from her. Holly angrily wiped her mouth, disgusted with his attempts to kiss her. She backed away from him. "I think you've got the wrong idea here, Stevie. Go back to the bar to your *girlfriend*."

Stevie wobbled slightly on his feet and slowly turned to face his girlfriend and an angry Charlie, who was charging toward them.

"Stevie!" she shrieked. "How could you?!" She ran from the hotel with tears streaming down her face. She was closely followed by a protesting Stevie.

"Uggghh!" Holly said with disgust to Charlie. "I did not want to do that *at all!*"

"Don't worry, I believe you," Charlie said, placing his hand comfortingly on her shoulder. "I saw what happened through the door."

"Ah well, thanks very much for coming to my rescue!" Holly complained.

"Got here too late, sorry. But I must admit, I did enjoy her witnessing that," he laughed, referring to the blonde, and bit his lip feeling guilty.

Holly smiled as she stared down the corridor at Stevie and his frantic girlfriend screaming and fighting with each other.

"Oops," she said, smiling at Charlie.

Holly knocked into everything in the bedroom as she tried to make her way back to her bed in the darkness. "Ouch!" she yelped, stubbing her toe on the bedpost.

"Sshhh!" Sharon said sleepily and Holly grumbled all the way to her bed.

She tapped Denise on the shoulder continuously until she woke up.

"What? What?" Denise moaned sleepily.

"Here." Holly forced a mobile phone in Denise's face. "Phone your future husband, tell him you love him and don't let the girls know."

The next day Holly and Sharon went for a long walk on the beach just outside Galway city. Although it was October, the air had warmth in it and Holly didn't need her coat. She stood in a long-sleeved top and listened to the water gently lapping. The rest of the girls had decided to go for a liquid lunch and Holly's stomach wasn't quite ready for that today.

"Are you OK, Holly?" Sharon approached her from behind and wrapped her arm around her friend's shoulders.

Holly sighed. "Every time someone asks me that question, Sharon, I say, 'I'm fine, thank you,' but to be honest, I'm not. Do people *really* want to know how you feel when they ask how are you? Or are they just trying to be polite?" Holly smiled. "The next time the woman across the road from my house says to me, 'How are you?' I'm going to say to her, 'Well, actually I'm not very well at all, thank you. I'm feeling a bit depressed and lonely. Pissed off at the world. Envious of you and your perfect little family but not particularly envious of your husband for having to live with you.' And then I'll tell her about how I started a new job and met lots of new people and how I'm trying hard to pick myself up but that I'm now at a loss about what else to do. Then I'll tell her how it pisses me off when everyone says time is a healer when at the same time they also say absence makes the heart grow fonder, which really confuses me, because that means that the longer he's gone the more I want him. I'll tell her that nothing is healing at all and that every morning I wake up in my empty bed it feels like salt is being rubbed into those unhealing wounds." Holly took a deep breath. "And then I'll tell her about how much I miss my husband and about how worthless my life seems without him. How uninterested I am in getting on with things without him, and I'll explain how I feel like I'm just waiting for my world to end so that I can join him. She'll probably just say, 'Oh that's good,' like she always does, kiss her husband good-bye, hop into her car and drop her kids at school, go to work, make the dinner and eat the dinner, and go to bed with her husband and she'll have it all done while I'm still trying to decide what color shirt to wear to work. What do you think?" Holly finally finished and turned to Sharon.

"Oooh!" Sharon jumped and her arm flew away from Holly's shoulders.

"Oooh?" Holly frowned. "I say all that and all you can say is 'Oooh'?"

Sharon placed her hand over her bump and laughed. "No, you silly, the baby kicked!"

Holly's mouth dropped open.

"Feel it!" Sharon giggled.

Holly placed her hand over Sharon's swollen belly and felt the tiny little kick. Both their eyes filled with tears.

"Oh Sharon, if only every minute of my life were filled with perfect little moments like this I would never moan again."

"But Holly, nobody's life is filled with perfect little moments. And if it were, they wouldn't be perfect little moments. They would just be normal. How would you ever know happiness if you never experienced downs?"

"Oooh!" they both shrieked again as the baby kicked for a third time.

"I think this little boy is going to be a footballer like his daddy!" Sharon laughed.

"Boy?" Holly gasped. "You're having a boy?"

Sharon nodded happily and her eyes glistened. "Holly, meet baby Gerry. Gerry, meet your godmother Holly."

Forty-four

"HI, ALICE," HOLLY SAID, HOVERING in front of her desk. Holly had been standing there for a few minutes now and Alice hadn't said a word yet.

"Hi," Alice said shortly, refusing to look up at her.

Holly took a deep breath. "Alice, are you mad at me?"

"No," she said shortly again. "Chris wants to see you in his office again. He wants you to write another article."

"*Another* article?" Holly gasped.

"That's what I said."

"Alice, why don't you do it?" Holly said softly. "You're a fantastic writer. I'm sure if Chris knew you could write he would def—"

"He knows," she interrupted.

"What?" Holly was confused. "He knows you can write?"

"Five years ago I applied for a job as a writer, but this was the only job going. Chris said if I hung on then maybe something would come up." Holly wasn't used to seeing the usually chirpy Alice looking so . . . upset wasn't even the word. She was just *angry*.

Holly sighed and made her way into Chris's office. She had a sneaking suspicion she would be writing this one all on her own.

Holly smiled as she flicked through the pages of the November magazine she had worked on. It would be out in the shops tomorrow, the first of November, and she felt so excited. Her first magazine would be on the shelves and she could also open Gerry's November letter. Tomorrow would be a good day.

Although she had only sold the ad space, she felt great pride in being a member of a team that managed to produce something so professional-looking. It was a far cry from that pathetic leaflet she had printed up years ago and she giggled at the memory of mentioning it in her interview. As if it would impress Chris at all. But despite all that she felt she had really proven herself. She had taken her job by the reins and guided it through to success.

"It's nice to see you looking so happy," Alice snapped, strolling tartly into Holly's office and throwing two little scraps of paper onto her desk. "You got two calls while you were out. One from Sharon and one from Denise. Please tell your friends to call you on your lunch break, as it's a waste of time for me."

"OK, thanks," Holly said, glancing at the messages. Alice had scrawled something completely illegible, most likely on purpose. "Hey, Alice!" Holly called after her before she slammed the door behind her.

"What?" she snapped.

"Did you read the article on the launch? The photos and

everything turned out great! I'm really proud," Holly grinned broadly.

"No, I have not!" Alice said, looking disgusted, and she slammed the door behind her.

Holly giggled and chased her out of the office with the magazine in her hand.

"But look at it, Alice! It's so good! Daniel will be so happy!"

"Well whoopdeedoo for you and Daniel," Alice snapped, busying herself with random bits of paper at her desk.

Holly rolled her eyes. "Look, stop being such a baby and read the damn thing!"

"No!" Alice huffed.

"Fine then, you won't see the photo of you with that gorgeous half-naked man then . . ." Holly turned and walked away slowly.

"Give me that!" Alice snapped the magazine from Holly's hand and flicked through the pages. Her jaw dropped as she reached the page of the Blue Rock launch.

At the top of the page it read "Alice in Wonderland," with the photograph of her and the muscular model that Holly had taken.

"Read it out loud," Holly ordered.

Alice's voice shook as she began to read: "A new Alco pop has hit the shelves and our *party correspondent* Alice Goodyear went to find out if the hot new drink for winter was as it claimed to be . . ." She trailed off and her hands flew to her mouth in shock. "Party correspondent?" she squealed.

Holly called Chris out of his office and he came out to join them, a broad grin on his face.

"Well done, Alice; that was a fantastic article you wrote. It was very amusing," he told her with a pat on the shoulder. "So I created a new page called Alice in Wonderland where you will go to all the weird and wonderful things you love to go to and write about them every month."

Alice gasped at them and stuttered, "But Holly . . ."

"Holly can't spell," Chris laughed. "You, on the other hand, are a great writer. One I should have used before now. I'm very sorry, Alice."

"Oh my God!" she gasped, ignoring him. "Thank you so much, Holly!" She threw her arms around her and squeezed her so hard Holly couldn't breathe.

Holly tried to pull Alice's arms away from around her neck and gasped for air. "Alice, this was the hardest secret to keep from anyone ever!"

"It must have been! How on earth didn't I notice this?" Alice looked at Holly, startled, then turned to Chris. "Five years, Chris," she said accusingly.

Chris winced and nodded.

"I waited five years for this," she continued.

"I know, I know." Chris looked like a chastised schoolboy and he scratched his eyebrow awkwardly. "Why don't you step into my office now and we can talk about that."

"I suppose I could do that," Alice replied sternly, but she couldn't hide the glint of happiness in her eyes. As Chris headed toward his office, Alice turned to Holly and winked before doing a quick skip behind him.

Holly made her way back to her own office. Time to get working on the December edition. "Oops!" she said, tripping over a pile of handbags lying outside her door. "What's all this?"

Chris made a face as he stepped out of his office to make Alice a cup of tea for a change. "Oh they're John Paul's handbags."

"John Paul's handbags?" Holly giggled.

"It's for the article he's doing on this season's handbags, or something stupid like that." Chris pretended not to have an interest.

"Oh, they're gorgeous," Holly said, bending down to pick one up.

"Nice, aren't they?" John Paul said, leaning against the door frame of his office.

"Yeah, I love this one," Holly said, sliding it over her shoulder. "Does it suit me?"

Chris made another face. "How can a handbag not suit some-one; it's a handbag for Christ's sake!"

"Well then, you'll have to read the article I'm writing next month, won't you?" John Paul wagged a finger at his boss, "Not all handbags suit everyone, you know." He turned to Holly, "You can have it if you want."

"For keeps?" she gasped. "This must cost hundreds."

"Yeah, but I've got loads of them, you should see the amount of stuff the designer gave me. Trying to sweeten me up with free-bies; the cheek of him!" John Paul pretended to be outraged.

"I bet it works, though," Holly said.

"Absolutely, the first line of my article will be: Everybody go out and buy one, they're fab!" he laughed.

"What else have you got?" Holly tried to peek behind him into the office.

"I'm doing an article on what to wear for all the Christmas parties coming up. A few dresses arrived today. In fact," he looked her up and down and Holly sucked in her belly, "there's one that would look fab on you, come in and try it on."

"Oh goody," Holly giggled. "I'll just have a look, though, John Paul, because to be honest, I have no need for a party dress this year."

Overhearing the exchange, Chris shook his head and yelled from his office, "Does anybody in this bloody office ever do any work?"

"Yes!" Tracey yelled back. "Now shut up and don't be distracting us." Everyone in the office laughed and Holly could swear she saw Chris smile before he slammed his office door shut for dramatic effect.

After searching through John Paul's collection, Holly went back to work and eventually called Denise back.

"Hello? Disgusting, stuffy and ridiculously expensive clothes shop. Pissed off manager speaking, how can I help you?"

"Denise!" Holly gasped. "You can't answer the phone like that!"

Denise giggled, "Oh don't worry, I have caller ID so I knew it was you."

"Hmmm." Holly was suspicious; she didn't think Denise had caller ID on her work phone. "I got a message you called earlier."

"Oh yeah, I was just ringing you to confirm you were going to the ball; Tom is going to buy a table this year."

"What ball?"

"The Christmas ball we go to every year, you dope."

"Oh yeah, the Christmas ball they always hold in the middle of November?" Holly laughed. "Sorry, but I can't make it this year."

"But you don't even know what date it's on yet!" Denise protested.

"Well, I assume it's being held on the same date as every other year, which means I can't make it."

"No, no, it's on the thirtieth of November this year, so you can make it!" Denise said excitedly.

"Oh, the thirtieth . . ." Holly paused and pretended to flick through some pages on her desk very loudly. "No Denise, I can't, sorry. I'm busy on the thirtieth. I have a deadline . . . ," she lied. Well, she did have a deadline, but the magazine would be out in the shops on the first of December, which meant she really didn't need to be in work on the thirtieth at all.

"But we don't have to be there till at least eight o'clock," Denise tried to convince her. "You could even come at nine if it was easier, you would just miss the drinks reception first. It's on a Friday night, Holly, they can't expect you to work late on a Friday . . ."

"Look Denise, I'm sorry," Holly said firmly. "I'm just far too busy."

"Well that makes a change," she muttered under her breath.

"What did you say?" Holly asked, getting slightly angry.

"Nothing," Denise said shortly.

"I heard you; you said that makes a change, didn't you? Well, it just so happens that I take my work seriously, Denise, and I have no plans to lose my job over a stupid ball."

"Fine then," Denise huffed. "Don't go."

"I won't!"

"Fine!"

"Good, well I'm glad that's fine with you, Denise." Holly couldn't help but smile at the ridiculousness of the conversation.

"I'm glad you're glad," Denise huffed.

"Oh, don't be so childish, Denise." Holly rolled her eyes. "I have to work, simple as that."

"Well, that's no surprise, that's all you ever do these days," Denise blurted out angrily. "You never come out anymore; every time I ask you out you're busy doing something apparently much more important, like *work*. At my hen weekend you looked like you were having the worst time of your life, and then you didn't even bother coming out the second night. In fact, I don't know why you bothered to come at all. If you have a problem with me, Holly, I wish you would just say it to my face instead of being such a miserable bore!"

Holly sat in shock and stared at the phone. She couldn't believe Denise had said those things. She couldn't believe Denise could be so stupid and selfish to think that this whole thing was about her and not Holly's own private worries. No wonder she felt like she was going insane, when one of her best friends couldn't even understand her.

"That is the most selfish thing I have ever heard anyone say." Holly tried to control her voice but she knew her anger was spilling out into her words.

"I'm selfish?" Denise squealed. "You're the one who hid in the hotel room on my hen's weekend! *My* hen's weekend! You're supposed to be my maid of honor!"

"I was in the room with Sharon, you know that!" Holly defended herself.

"Oh bullshit! Sharon would have been fine on her own. She's pregnant, not bloody dying. You don't need to be by her side twenty-four-seven!"

Denise went quiet as she realized what she had said.

Holly's blood boiled, and as she spoke her voice shook with rage, "And you wonder why I don't go out with you. Because of stupid, insensitive remarks like that. Did you ever think for one moment that it might be hard for me? The fact that all you talk about are your bloody wedding arrangements and how happy you are and how excited you are and how you can't wait to spend the rest of your life with Tom in wedded bliss. In case you hadn't noticed, Denise, I didn't get that chance because my husband *died.* But I am very happy for you, really I am. I'm delighted you're happy and I'm not asking for any special treatment at all, I'm just asking for a bit of patience and for you to understand that *I will not get over this in a few months!* As for the ball, I have no intention of going to a place that Gerry and I had been going to together for the past ten years. You might not understand this, Denise, but funnily enough I would find it *a bit difficult,* to say the least. So don't book a ticket for me, I am perfectly happy staying at home," she yelled and slammed the phone down. She burst into tears and lay her head down on the desk as she sobbed. She felt lost. Her best friend couldn't even understand her. Maybe she was going mad. Maybe she should be over Gerry already. Maybe that's what normal people did when their loved ones died. Not for the first time she thought she should have bought the rule book for widows to see what the recommended time for grieving was so she wouldn't have to keep on inconveniencing her family and friends.

Her weeping eventually died down into little sobs and she listened to the silence around her. She realized that everyone must have heard everything she'd said and she felt so embarrassed she was afraid to go to the bathroom for a tissue. Her head was hot and her eyes felt swollen from all her tears. She wiped her teary face on the end of her shirt.

"Shit!" she swore, swiping some papers off her desk as she realized she had smudged foundation, mascara and lipstick all along the sleeve of her 'spensive white shirt. She sat up to attention as she heard a light rapping sound on her door.

"Come in," her voice shook.

Chris entered her office with two cups of tea in his hands.

"Tea?" he offered, raising his eyebrows at her, and she smiled weakly, remembering the joke they had shared on the day of her interview. He placed the mug down in front of her and relaxed in the chair opposite.

"Having a bad day?" he asked as gently as his gruff voice could.

She nodded as tears rolled down her face. "I'm sorry, Chris." She waved a hand as she tried to compose herself. "It won't affect my work," she said shakily.

He waved his hand dismissively. "Holly, I'm not worried about that, you're a great worker."

She smiled, grateful for the compliment. At least she was doing something right.

"Would you like to go home early?"

"No thanks, work will keep my mind off things."

He shook his head sadly. "That's not the way to go about it, Holly. I should know that, of all people. I've buried myself inside these walls and it doesn't help things. Not in the long run anyway."

"But you seem happy," her voice trembled.

"Seeming and being are not one and the same. I *know* you know that."

She nodded sadly.

"You don't have to put on a brave face all the time, you know." He handed her a tissue.

"Oh, I'm not brave at all." She blew her nose.

"Ever hear the saying that you need to be scared to be brave?"

Holly thought about that. "But I don't feel brave, I just feel scared."

"Oh, we all feel scared at times. There's nothing wrong with that and there will come a day when you will stop feeling scared.

Look at all you've done!" He held his hands up displaying her office. "And look at all this!" He flicked through the pages of the magazine. "That's the work of a very brave person."

Holly smiled, "I love the job."

"And that's great news! But you need to learn to love more than your job."

Holly frowned. She hoped this wasn't one of those get-over-one-man-by-sleeping-under-another type chats.

"I mean learn to love yourself, learn to love your new life. Don't just let your entire life revolve around your job. There's more to it than that."

Holly raised her eyebrows at him. Talk about the pot calling the kettle black.

"I know I'm not the greatest example of that," he nodded. "But I'm learning too . . ." He placed his hand on the table and started to brush away imaginary crumbs while he thought about what to say next. "I heard you don't want to go to this ball."

Holly cringed at the fact he had heard her phone conversation.

Chris continued. "There were a million places I refused to go to when Maureen died," he said sadly. "We used to go for walks in the Botanic Gardens every Sunday, and I just couldn't go there anymore after I lost her. There were a million little memories contained in every flower and tree that grew in there. The bench we used to sit on, her favorite tree, her favorite rose garden, just everything about it reminded me of her."

"Did you go back?" Holly asked, sipping the hot tea, feeling it warm her insides.

"A few months ago," he said sadly. "It was a difficult thing to do but I did it and now I go every Sunday again. You have to confront things, Holly, and think of things positively. I say to myself, this is a place we used to laugh in, cry in, fight in, and when you go there and remember all those beautiful times you feel closer to your loved one. You can celebrate the love you had instead of hiding from it."

He leaned forward in his chair and stared directly into her eyes. "Some people go through life searching and *never* find their soul mates. They *never* do. You and I did, we just happened to have them for a shorter period of time. It's sad, but it's life! So you go to this ball, Holly, and you embrace the fact that you had someone whom you loved and who loved you back."

Tears trickled down Holly's face as she realized he was right. She needed to remember Gerry and be happy about the love they shared and the love she still continued to feel; but not to cry about them, not to yearn for the many more years with him that would never come. She thought of the line he had written in his last letter to her, "Remember our wonderful memories, but please don't be afraid to make some more." She needed to put the ghost of Gerry that haunted her to rest but to keep his memory alive.

There was still life for her after his death.

Forty-five

"I'M SO SORRY, DENISE," HOLLY apologized to her friend. They were sitting in the staff room of Denise's workplace surrounded by boxes of hangers, rails of clothes, bags and accessories, which were untidily strewn around the room. There was a musty smell in the air from the dust that had landed on the rails and rails of clothes that had been sitting out for so long. A security camera attached to the wall stared at them and recorded their conversation.

Holly watched Denise's face for a reaction and saw her friend purse her lips and nod her head wildly, as if to let Holly know it was OK.

"No, it's not OK." Holly sat forward in her chair, trying to have a serious discussion. "I didn't mean to lose my temper on the phone. Just because I'm feeling extrasensitive these days, it doesn't give me the right to take it out on you."

Denise looked brave enough to finally speak. "No, you were right, Holly . . ."

Holly shook her head and tried to disagree but Denise kept on talking, "I've been so excited about this wedding that I didn't stop to think about how you might be feeling." Her eyes rested on her friend, whose face looked pale against her dark jacket. Holly was doing so well it was easy for them all to forget that she still had ghosts to be rid of.

"But you're right to be excited," Holly insisted.

"And you're right to be upset," Denise said firmly. "I didn't think, I just didn't think." She held her hands to her cheeks as she shook her head. "Don't go to the ball if you don't feel comfortable. We will all understand." She reached out to hold her friend's hands.

Holly felt confused. Chris had succeeded in convincing her to go to the ball, but now her best friend was saying it was OK not to go. She had a headache, and headaches scared her. She hugged Denise good-bye in the shop, promising to call her later to give her a decision about the ball.

She headed back to the office feeling even more unsure than before. Maybe Denise was right, it was only a stupid ball and she didn't have to go if she didn't want to. However, it was a stupid ball that was hugely representative of Holly and Gerry's time together. It was a night they had both enjoyed, a night they would share with their friends and an opportunity to dance to their favorite songs. If she went without him she would be destroying that tradition, replacing happy memories with an entirely different one. She didn't want to do that. She wanted to hang on to every single shred of memory of the two of them together. It was scaring her that she was forgetting his face. When she dreamed about him he was always somebody else; a person she made up in her mind with a different face and a different voice.

Now and again she rang his mobile phone just to hear his voice on his answering machine, she had even been paying the mobile company every month just to keep his account open. His smell had faded from the house; his clothes long gone under his own orders. He was fading from her mind, and she clung to every little bit of him that she could. She deliberately thought about him every night right before she went to sleep just so that she would dream about him. She even bought his favorite aftershave and splashed it around the house so she wouldn't feel so alone. Sometimes she would be out and a familiar smell or song would transport her back to another time and place. A happier time.

She would catch a glimpse of him walking down the street or driving by in a car and she would chase that person for miles only to discover it wasn't him; just a look-alike. She couldn't seem to let go. She couldn't let go because she didn't want to let go, and she didn't want to let go because he was all she had. But she didn't really have him, so she felt lost and confused.

Just before reaching the office Holly poked her head into Hogan's. She was feeling much more at ease with Daniel. Since that dinner where she had felt so uncomfortable in his company, she had realized that she was being ridiculous. She understood now why she had felt that way. Before, the only close friendship she had ever had with a man was with Gerry, and that was a romantic relationship. The idea of becoming so close to Daniel seemed strange and unusual. Holly had since convinced herself that there didn't need to be a romantic link for her to share a friendship with an unattached man. Even if he was good-looking.

And the ease she felt had become a feeling of companionship. She had felt that from the moment she'd met him. They could talk for hours discussing her feelings, her life, his feelings, his life, and she knew that they had a common enemy: loneliness. She knew that he was suffering from a different kind of grief and they were helping each other through the difficult days, when they needed a caring ear or someone to make them laugh. And there were many of those days.

"Well?" he said, walking around from behind the bar. "Will Cinderella go to the ball?"

Holly smiled and scrunched up her nose, about to tell him that she wouldn't be going, when she stopped herself. "Are you going?"

He smiled and scrunched up his nose and she laughed. "Well, it's going to be another case of Couples 'R' Us. I don't think I could cope with another night of Sam and Samantha or Robert and Roberta." He pulled out a high stool for her at the bar and she sat down.

Holly giggled, "Well, we could just be terribly rude and ignore them all."

"Then what would be the point in going?" Daniel sat beside her and rested his leather boot on the footrest of her chair. "You don't expect me to talk to you all night, do you? We've talked the ears off each other by now; maybe I'm bored of you."

"Fine then!" Holly pretended to be insulted. "I was planning on ignoring you anyway."

"Phew!" Daniel wiped his brow and pretended to look relieved. "I'm definitely going then."

Holly became serious. "I think I really need to be there."

Daniel stopped laughing. "Well then, we shall go."

Holly smiled at him. "I think it would be good for you too, Daniel," she said softly.

His foot dropped from her chair and he turned his head away

from her to pretend to survey the lounge. "Holly, I'm fine," he said unconvincingly.

Holly hopped off her chair, held him by the cheeks and kissed him roughly on the forehead. "Daniel Connelly, stop trying to be all macho and strong. It doesn't wash with me."

They hugged each other good-bye and Holly marched back to her office, determined not to change her mind again. She banged loudly up the stairs and marched straight by Alice, who was still staring dreamily at her article. "John Paul!" Holly yelled. "I need a dress, quick!"

Forty-six

Holly was running late as she rushed around her bedroom trying to get dressed for the ball. She had spent the past two hours applying her makeup, crying and smudging it and then reapplying it. She rolled the mascara brush over her eyelashes for the fourth time, praying the tear reservoir had run dry for the night. An unlikely prospect, but a girl could always hope.

"Cinderella, your prince has arrived!" Sharon yelled upstairs to Holly.

Holly's heart raced, she needed more time. She needed to sit down and rethink the idea of going to the ball all over again, as she had completely forgotten her reasons for going. Now she was faced with only the negatives.

Reasons not to go: She didn't want to go at all, she would spend all night crying, she would be stuck at a table full of so-called friends who hadn't talked to her since Gerry had died, she felt like shit, she looked like shit and Gerry wouldn't be there.

Reasons to go: She had an overwhelming feeling that she needed to go.

She breathed slowly, trying to prevent a whole new batch of tears from appearing.

"Holly, be strong, you can do this," she whispered to her reflection in the mirror. "You need to do this, it will help you, it will make you stronger." She repeated this over and over again until a creak at the door made her jump.

"Sorry," Sharon apologized, appearing from around the door. "Oh Holly, you look fabulous!" she said excitedly.

"I look like shit," Holly grumbled.

"Oh, stop saying that," Sharon said angrily. "I look like a blimp and do you hear me complaining? Accept the fact that you're a babe!" She smiled at her in the mirror, "You'll be fine."

"I just want to stay home tonight, Sharon. I have to open Gerry's last message." Holly couldn't believe the time had come to open the last one. After tomorrow there would be no more kind words from Gerry, and she still felt that she needed them. In all her excitement back in April, she couldn't wait for the months to pass so that she could rip the envelopes open and read that perfect handwriting, but she had wished the months away all too quickly and now it was the end. She wanted to stay in that night and savor their last special moment.

"I know," Sharon said, understanding. "But that can wait for a few hours, can't it?"

Holly was just about to say no when John shouted up the stairs. "Come on, girls! The taxi's waiting! We have to collect Tom and Denise!"

Before Holly followed Sharon downstairs she slid open the drawer of her dressing table and took out the November letter from Gerry she had opened weeks ago. She needed his words of encouragement to help her out now. She ran her fingers over the ink and pictured him writing it. She pictured the face he made when he wrote that she always used to tease him about. It was a face of pure concentration; his tongue even licked his lips as he wrote. She loved that face. She missed that face. She slid the card from the envelope. She needed strength from this letter, and she knew she would find it. Every day, she read:

> *Cinderella must go to the ball this month. And she will look glamorous and beautiful and have the time of her life just like always . . . But no white dresses this year . . .*
> *PS, I love you . . .*

Holly took a deep breath and followed Sharon downstairs.

"Wow," Daniel said, his mouth dropping open. "You look fabulous, Holly."

"I look like shit," Holly grumbled, and Sharon shot her a look. "But thanks," she quickly added. John Paul had helped her choose a simple black halter-neck dress, with a split to the thigh up the middle. No white dresses this year.

They all piled into the seven-seater taxi, and as they approached each set of traffic lights Holly prayed that they would turn red. No such luck. For once the traffic on the streets of Dublin cleared, and after picking up Tom and Denise, they made it to the hotel in record time. Despite her prayers, a mud slide didn't cascade down the Dublin Mountains and no volcano erupted. Hell refused to freeze over too.

They stepped up to the table just inside the door of the function room and Holly looked to the ground as she felt all eyes in their direction from the women eager to see how the newcomers were dressed. When they were satisfied that they were still the most beautiful people there, they turned away and continued their conversations. The woman sitting behind the desk smiled as they approached her. "Hello Sharon, hello John, hi Denise . . . oh gosh!" Her face might actually have gone whiter under her streaky fake-tanned face, but Holly couldn't be sure. "Oh hello, Holly, it's so good of you to come considering . . ." She trailed off and quickly flicked through the guest list to tick off their names.

"Let's go to the bar," Denise said, linking her arm in Holly's and dragging her away from the woman.

As they walked across the room to the bar a woman Holly hadn't spoken to for months approached her. "Holly, I was sorry to hear about Gerry. He was a lovely man."

"Thank you." Holly smiled and was dragged away again by Denise. They finally reached the bar.

"Hi there, Holly," a familiar voice behind her said.

"Oh hello, Paul," she said, turning to face the large businessman who sponsored the charity. He was tall and overweight with a bright red face, probably due to the stress of running one of Ireland's most successful businesses. That and the fact that he drank too much. He looked like he was choking underneath the tightness of his bow tie and he pulled at it, looking uncomfortable. The buttons on his tuxedo looked like they were about to pop any moment. Holly didn't know him very well; he was just one of the people she knew from meeting at the ball every year.

"You're looking as lovely as always." He gave her a kiss on the cheek. "Can I get you a drink?" he asked, holding his hand up to attract the barman's attention.

"Oh no, thanks," she smiled.

"Ah let me," he said, taking his bulging wallet out of his pocket. "What'll you have?"

Holly gave in, "A white wine then, please, if you insist." She smiled.

"I might as well get a drink for that miserable husband of yours," he laughed. "What's he having?" he asked, searching the room for him.

"Oh, he's not here, Paul," Holly said, feeling uncomfortable.

"Ah why not? The dryshite. What's he up to?" Paul asked loudly.

"Em, he passed away early in the year, Paul," Holly said gently, hoping not to embarrass him.

"Oh," Paul reddened even more and he cleared his throat nervously. He stared down at the bar. "I'm very sorry to hear that," he stuttered and looked away. He pulled at his bow tie again.

"Thank you," Holly said, counting the seconds in her head till he made an excuse to leave the conversation. He left after three seconds, saying he had to bring his wife her drink. Holly was left standing at the bar alone, as Denise had made her way back to the group with their drinks. She picked up her glass of wine and headed over.

"Hi, Holly."

She turned to see who had called her name.

"Oh, hello, Jennifer." She was faced with another woman she knew only from attending the ball. She was dressed in an over-the-top ball gown, dripping in expensive jewelry, and she held a glass of champagne between the thumb and forefinger of her gloved hand. Her blond hair was almost white, and her skin was dark and leathery as a result of too much sun.

"How are you? You look fab, the dress is fab!" She sipped on her champagne and looked Holly up and down.

"I'm fine, thank you, you?"

"I'm just fab, thanks. Gerry not with you tonight?" she looked around the room for him.

"No, he passed away in February," she repeated gently.

"Oh gosh, I'm so sorry to hear that." She placed her glass of champagne down on the table next to them and her hands flew to her face, her forehead creasing with worry. "I had no idea. How are you keeping, you poor love?" she reached out and placed her hand on Holly's arm.

"I'm fine, thank you," Holly repeated, smiling to keep the atmosphere light.

"Oh, you poor thing." Jennifer's voice was hushed and she looked at her pityingly. "You must be devastated."

"Well yes, it is hard, but I'm dealing with it. Trying to be positive, you know?"

"Gosh, I don't know how you can be, that's awful news." Her eyes continued to bore into Holly. She seemed to look at her differently now. Holly nodded along and wished this woman would stop telling her what she already knew.

"And was he ill?" she probed.

"Yes, he had a brain tumor," she explained.

"Oh dear, that's *awful*. And he was so *young*." Every word she emphasized became a high-pitched screech.

"Yes he was . . . but we had a happy life together, Jennifer." She once again tried to keep the atmosphere positive, a concept she didn't think this woman was aware of.

"Yes you did, but what a shame it wasn't a longer life. That's devastating for you. Absolutely *awful* and so unfair. You must feel miserable. And how on earth did you come here tonight? With all these couples around?" She looked around at all the couples as though there were suddenly a bad smell in the air.

"Well, you just have to learn to move on," Holly smiled.

"Of course you do. But it must be so difficult. Oh, how *awful*." She held her gloved hands up to her face, looking appalled.

Holly smiled and spoke through gritted teeth, "Yes, it's difficult, but like I said you just have to stay positive and move on. Anyway, speaking of moving on, I better go and join my friends," she said politely and dashed off.

"You all right?" Daniel asked as she joined her friends.

"Yes I'm fine, thank you," she repeated for the tenth time that night. She glanced over at Jennifer, who was in a huddle with her female friends talking and staring over at Holly and Daniel.

"I have arrived!" a loud voice announced at the door. Holly turned around to see Jamie, the party animal, standing at the door with his arms held high in the air. "I have once again dressed in my penguin suit and I am ready to partaaay!" He did a little dance before joining the group, attracting stares from around the room. Just what he wanted. He made his way around their circle greeting the men with a handshake and the women with a kiss on the cheek, sometimes "hilariously" switching the gesture. He paused when he got to Holly and he glanced back and forth from Holly to Daniel a couple of times. He shook Daniel's hand stiffly, pecked Holly on the cheek quickly as though she were diseased, and rushed off. Holly tried to swallow the lump in her throat angrily. That had been very rude.

His wife, Helen, smiled timidly over at Holly from across the other side of their circle but didn't come over. Holly wasn't surprised. It had obviously been too difficult for them to drive ten minutes down the road to visit Holly after Gerry died, so she would hardly expect Helen to take ten steps toward her to say hello. She ignored them and turned to talk to her real friends, the people who had supported her for the past year.

Holly was laughing at one of Sharon's stories when she felt a light tapping on her shoulder. She turned around mid-laughter to face a very sad-looking Helen.

"Hi, Helen," she said happily.

"How *are* you?" Helen said quietly, touching Holly gently on the arm.

"Oh I'm fine," Holly nodded. "You should listen to this story, it's very funny." She smiled and continued to listen to Sharon.

Helen left her hand on Holly's arm and eventually tapped her again after a few minutes. "I mean, how are you since Gerry . . ."

Holly gave up listening to Sharon.

"Since Gerry died, do you mean?" Holly understood that people sometimes felt awkward about these situations. Holly often did too, but she felt that if someone had brought the subject up themselves they could at least be adult enough to carry the conversation through properly.

Helen appeared to wince at Holly's question. "Well yes, but I didn't want to say . . ."

"It's OK, Helen; I've accepted that that's what happened."

"Have you?"

"Of course I have," Holly frowned.

"It's just that I haven't seen you for a very long time so I was beginning to get worried . . ."

Holly laughed. "Helen, I still live around the corner from you in the same house as before, my home phone number is still the same, as is my mobile number. If you were ever that worried about me I was never that difficult for you to find."

"Oh yes, but I didn't want to intrude . . ." She trailed off as if that were her explanation for not seeing Holly since the funeral.

"Friends don't intrude, Helen," Holly said politely, but she hoped she had gotten her message across.

Helen's cheeks blushed slightly and Holly turned away to answer Sharon.

"Keep me a seat beside you, will you? I just need to run to the ladies again," Sharon asked, doing a little dance on the spot.

"Again?" Denise blurted out. "You were just there five minutes ago!"

"Yes, well, this tends to happen when you have a seven-month-old baby pushing down on your bladder," she explained before waddling off to the toilet.

"It's not actually seven months old, though, is it?" Denise said, scrunching her face up. "Technically it's minus two months, because otherwise that would mean that the baby would be nine months old when he was born and then they would be celebrating his first birthday after only three months. And usually babies are walking by the time they're one."

Holly frowned at her. "Denise, why do you torment yourself with thoughts like that?"

Denise frowned and turned to Tom, "I'm right though, aren't I, Tom?"

"Yes love," he smiled sweetly at her.

"Chicken," Holly teased Tom.

The bell was rung, signaling that it was time to take their places in the dining area and the crowds began to swarm in. Holly took her seat and placed her new handbag down on the chair beside her to reserve it for Sharon. Helen wandered over and pulled out the chair to sit down.

"Sorry Helen, but Sharon asked me to save this seat for her," Holly explained politely.

Helen waved her hand dismissively. "Oh, Sharon won't mind," she said, plonking herself down on the chair and squashing Holly's new handbag. Sharon made her way over to the table and stuck out her bottom lip in disappointment. Holly apologized and motioned over to Helen as her excuse. Sharon rolled her eyes and stuck her fingers in her mouth and pretended to gag. Holly giggled.

"Well, you're in high spirits," Jamie announced to Holly, sounding very unimpressed.

"Is there any reason why I shouldn't be?" Holly replied tartly.

Jamie answered with some smart retort that a few people laughed at because he was "so funny," and Holly ignored him. She didn't find him funny anymore, though she and Gerry had always been among those people who hung on his every word. Now he was just being stupid.

"Are you OK?" Daniel asked quietly from beside her.

"Yes I'm fine, thank you," she replied, taking a sip of wine.

"Oh, you don't have to give me that bullshit answer, Holly. It's me," he laughed.

Holly smiled and groaned. "People are being very nice and all by offering me their sympathies," she lowered her voice to a whisper so Helen couldn't hear, "but I feel like I'm back at his funeral again. Having to pretend to be all strong and superwoman-like even though all some of them want is for me to be devastated because it's so *awful*." She mimicked Jennifer and rolled her eyes. "And then there are the people who don't know about Gerry and this is *so* not the place to have to tell them." Daniel listened to her patiently.

He nodded when she finally stopped talking. "I understand what you're saying. When Laura and I broke up I felt that for months everywhere I went I was telling people that we had broken up. But the good thing is that eventually word goes around so you can stop having those awkward conversations with people all the time."

"Any word on Laura by the way?" Holly asked. She enjoyed having bitching sessions about Laura even though she had never met her. She loved to hear stories about her from Daniel and then the two of them would spend the night talking about how much they hated her. It passed the time, and right now Holly really needed something to avoid having to talk to Helen.

Daniel's eyes lit up. "Yes, actually I do have a bit of gossip about her," he laughed.

"Oooh good, I love a bit of gossip," Holly said, rubbing her hands together with delight.

"Well, a friend of mine named Charlie who works as a barman in Laura's dad's hotel told me that her boyfriend tried to come on to some other woman who was a guest in the hotel and Laura caught him, so they split up." He laughed evilly and had a twinkle in his eye. He was delighted to hear of her heartbreak.

Holly froze because that story sounded rather familiar. "Eh . . . Daniel, what hotel does her father own?"

"Oh, the Galway Inn. It's a real kip of a place but it's in a nice area, across the road from the beach."

"Oh." Holly didn't know what to say and her eyes widened.

"I know," Daniel laughed. "It's brilliant, isn't it? I can tell you, if I ever met the woman who split them up I would buy her the most expensive bottle of champagne I could find."

Holly smiled weakly, "Would you now . . ." He better start saving his money then . . . Holly stared at Daniel's face curiously, interested to know why on earth Daniel had once been interested in Laura. Holly would have bet all her money against those two ever being together; she didn't seem his type, whatever his "type" was. Daniel was so easygoing and friendly and Laura was . . . well, Laura was a bitch. Holly couldn't think of any other word to describe her.

"Em, Daniel?" Holly nervously tucked her hair behind her ears, preparing herself to question him on his choice of women.

He smiled at her, eyes still twinkling from the news of his ex-girlfriend and ex–best friend's breakup. "Yes, Holly."

"Well, I was just wondering. Laura seems to sound like a bit of a . . . em . . . a . . . bitch, to be honest." She bit her lip and studied his face to see if she had insulted him. His face was blank as he stared at the candlesticks in the center of the table and listened. "Well," she continued, feeling as though she had to tiptoe carefully around this subject, knowing how badly Laura had broken Daniel's heart. "Well, my question is really, what ever did you see in her? How could you two *ever* have been in love? You're both so different, well, at least you *sound* like you're so different." She backpedaled fast, remembering she wasn't supposed to have ever met Laura. Daniel was silent for a moment and Holly feared she had stepped into the wrong territory.

He dragged his eyes away from the flame dancing around on the candlestick to face Holly. His lips broke into a sad smile. "Laura isn't really a bitch, Holly. Well, for leaving me for my best friend she is . . . but as a person, when we were together, she was never a bitch. Dramatic, yes. A bitch, no." He smiled and turned his body around to face Holly properly. "You see, I loved the drama of our relationship. I found it exciting; she *enthralled* me." His face became animated as he explained their relationship and his speech quickened with the excitement of the memory of his lost love. "I loved waking up in the morning and wondering what kind of mood she would be in that day, I loved our fights, I loved the passion of them and I loved how we would make love after them." His eyes danced. "She would make a song and dance about most things, but I suppose that's what I found different and attractive about her. I used to always tell myself that as long as she kept making a song and dance about our own relationship, then I knew she cared. If she hadn't, then it wouldn't have been worth it really. I loved the drama," he repeated, believing himself even more this time. "Our temperaments contrasted, but we made a good team; you know what they say about opposites attracting . . ." He looked into the face of his new friend and saw her concern. "She didn't treat me badly, Holly, she wasn't a bitch in that way . . ." He smiled more to himself. "She was just . . ."

"Dramatic," Holly finished for him, finally understanding. He nodded.

Holly watched his face as he got lost in another memory. She supposed it was possible for anybody to love anybody. That was the great thing about love; it came in all different shapes, sizes and temperaments.

"You miss her," Holly said gently, putting her hand on his arm.

Daniel snapped out of his daydream and stared deeply into Holly's eyes. A shiver went down her spine and she felt the hairs on her arms stand up. He snorted loudly and twisted back around in his chair, "Wrong again, Holly Kennedy." He nodded his head and frowned, as though she had said the most bizarre thing ever. "Completely and *utterly* wrong." He picked up his knife and fork and began to eat his salmon starter. Holly gulped back some cool water and turned her attention to the plate that was being set before her.

. . .

After dinner and a few bottles of wine Helen stumbled over to Holly, who had escaped over to Sharon and Denise's side of the table. She gave her a big hug and tearily apologized for not keeping in touch.

"That's OK, Helen. Sharon, Denise and John have been very supportive friends, so I wasn't alone."

"Oh, but I feel so awful," Helen slurred.

"Don't," Holly said, anxious to continue her enjoyable conversation with the girls.

But Helen insisted on talking about the good old times when Gerry was alive and when everything was rosy. She talked about all the times that she and Gerry had shared together, which were memories that Holly wasn't particularly interested in. Eventually Holly had enough of Helen's tearful whinging and realized that all her friends were up having fun on the dance floor.

"Helen, please stop," Holly finally interrupted. "I don't know why you feel you have to discuss this with me tonight when I am trying to enjoy myself, but you obviously feel guilty for not keeping in touch with me. To be honest, I think that if I hadn't come to this ball tonight I still wouldn't have heard from you for another ten months and more. And that's not the kind of friend I need in my life. So please stop crying on my shoulder and let me enjoy myself."

Holly felt that she had phrased it reasonably, but Helen looked like she had been slapped in the face. A small dose of what Holly had felt for the past year. Daniel appeared out of nowhere, took Holly by the hand and led her to the dance floor to join all her friends. As soon as they reached the dance floor the song ended and Eric Clapton's "Wonderful Tonight" began. The dance floor began to empty out bar a few couples and Holly was left facing Daniel. She gulped. She hadn't planned on this. She had only ever danced with Gerry to this song.

Daniel placed his hand lightly on her waist and gently took her hand and they began to circle around. Holly was stiff. Dancing with another man felt wrong. A tingle went down her spine and she shuddered. Daniel must have thought she was cold and he pulled her closer to keep her warm. She was led around the floor in a trance until the song ended and she made the excuse of having to go to the toilet. She locked herself in the cubicle and leaned against the door taking deep breaths. She had been doing so well up until now. Even with everyone asking her about Gerry she had remained calm. But the dance had shaken her. Perhaps it was time to go home while the going was good. She was about to unlock the door when she heard a voice outside say her name. She froze and listened to the women chatting outside.

"Did you see Holly Kennedy dancing with that man tonight?" a voice asked. The unmistakable whine of Jennifer.

"I know!" another voice spoke with a tone of disgust. "And her husband not yet cold in his grave!"

"Ah leave her alone," another woman said lightheartedly, "they could just be friends."

Thank you, Holly thought.

"But I doubt it," she continued and the women giggled.

"Did you see the way they were wrapped around each other? I don't dance with any of my friends like that," Jennifer said.

"That's disgraceful," another woman said. "Imagine flaunting your new man in a place you used to come to with your husband in front of all his friends. It's disgusting." The women tutted and a toilet flushed in the cubicle beside Holly. She stood frozen in her position, shocked by what she was hearing and embarrassed they were saying it where others could hear.

The toilet door opened beside her and the women were silenced. "Would you bickering old bitches ever go and get yourselves lives?" Sharon's voice yelled. "It is absolutely no business of yours what *my best friend* does or does not do! Jennifer, if your life was so bloody perfect then what are you doing sneaking around with Pauline's husband?"

Holly heard someone gasp. It was probably Pauline.

Holly covered her mouth to stop herself from laughing.

"Right, so keep your noses in your own business and piss off the lot of you!" Sharon yelled.

When Holly felt she had heard everyone leave she unlocked the door and stepped outside. Sharon looked up at her from the sink in shock.

"Thanks, Sharon."

"Oh Holly, I'm sorry you had to hear that," she said, giving her friend a hug.

"It doesn't matter, I couldn't give a crap what they think," Holly said bravely. "But I can't believe Jenny is having an affair with Pauline's husband!" Holly said, shocked.

Sharon shrugged, "She's not, but it'll give them something to bitch about for the next few months."

The girls giggled.

"I think I'll go home now, though," Holly said, glancing at her watch and thinking about the final message from Gerry. Her heart sank.

"Good idea," Sharon agreed. "I didn't realize how shite this ball was when you're sober."

Holly smiled.

"Anyway, you were great tonight, Holly. You came, you con-
quered, now go home and open Gerry's message. Ring me and let
me know what it says." She hugged her friend again.

"It's the last one," Holly said sadly.

"I know, so enjoy it," Sharon smiled. "But memories last a lifetime, remember that."

Holly made her way back to the table to say good-bye to
everyone and Daniel stood up to leave with her. "You're not leaving
me here on my own," he laughed. "We can share a cab."

Holly was slightly irritated when Daniel hopped out of the
taxi and followed her to her house, as she was looking forward to
opening the envelope from Gerry. It was a quarter to twelve,
which gave her fifteen minutes. She hoped he would drink his
tea and be gone by then. She even called another taxi to arrive at
her house in half an hour, just to let him know he couldn't stay
too long.

"Ah, so this is the famous envelope," Daniel said, picking the
tiny envelope up from the table.

Holly's eyes widened; she felt protective over that envelope,
and she wasn't happy with him touching it, removing Gerry's trace
from it.

"December," he said, reading the outside and running his fingers along the lettering. Holly wanted to tell him to put it down
but didn't want to sound psychotic. Eventually he placed it back on
the table and she breathed a sigh of relief and continued to fill the
kettle with water.

"How many more envelopes are left?" Daniel asked, taking his
overcoat off and walking over to join her at the kitchen counter.

"That's the last one." Holly's voice was husky and she cleared
her throat.

"So what are you going to do after that?"

"What do you mean?" she asked, feeling confused.

"Well, as far as I can see, that list is like your bible, your ten commandments. What the list says goes, as far as your life is concerned. So what will you do when there aren't any more?"

Holly looked up at his face to see if he was being smart, but his blue eyes twinkled back at her.

"I'll just live my life," she replied, turning her back and flicking the switch on the kettle.

"Will you be able to do that?" he walked closer to her and she could smell his aftershave. It was a real Daniel smell.

"I suppose so," she replied, confused and uncomfortable by his questions.

"Because you will have to make your own decisions then," he said softly.

"I know that," she said defensively, avoiding eye contact with him.

"And do you think you'll be able to do that?"

Holly rubbed her face tiredly. "Daniel, what's this about?"

He swallowed hard and adjusted his stance before her, trying to make himself comfortable. "I'm asking you this because I'm going to say something to you now, and you are going to have to make your own decision." He looked her straight in the eye and her heart beat wildly. "There will be no list, no guidelines; you will just have to follow your own heart."

Holly backed away from him a little. A feeling of dread pulled at her heart and she hoped he wasn't going to say what she thought he was about to say.

"Em . . . Daniel . . . I d-don't think that this is . . . the right time to . . . um . . . we shouldn't talk about . . ."

"This is a perfect time," he said seriously. "You already know what I'm going to say to you, Holly, and I *know* you already know how I feel about you."

Holly's mouth dropped open and she glanced at the clock.

It was twelve o'clock.

Forty-seven

G ERRY TOUCHED HOLLY'S NOSE AND smiled to himself as she wrinkled up her nose in her sleep. He loved watching her while she was sleeping; she looked like a princess, so beautiful and peaceful.

He tickled her nose again and smiled as her eyes slowly opened. "Good morning, sleepyhead."

She smiled at him. "Good morning, beautiful." She cuddled closer to him and rested her head on his chest. "How are you feeling today?"

"Like I could run the London marathon," he joked.

"Now that's what I call a quick recovery," she smiled, lifting her head and kissing him on the lips. "What do you want for breakfast?"

"You," he said, biting her nose.

Holly giggled. "I'm not on the menu today unfortunately. How about a fry?"

"No," he frowned. "That's too heavy for me," and his heart melted as he saw Holly's face fall. He tried to perk himself up. "But I would love a big, huge bowl of vanilla ice cream!"

"Ice cream!" she laughed. "For breakfast?"

"Yes," he grinned, "I always wanted that for breakfast when I was a kid but my darling mother wouldn't allow me to have it. But now I don't care anymore." He smiled bravely.

"Then ice cream you shall have," Holly said happily, hopping out of bed. "Do you mind if I wear this?" she asked, putting his dressing gown on.

"My dear, you can wear it all you like." Gerry smiled, watching her modeling the oversized robe up and down the bedroom for him.

"Mmm, it smells of you," she said, sniffing it. "I'm never going to take it off. OK, I'll be back in a minute," and he heard her racing down the stairs and clattering around in the kitchen.

Lately he had noticed her racing around every time she left his side, it was as though she were afraid to leave him for too long on his own, and he knew what that meant. Bad news for him. He had finished his radiation therapy, which they had prayed would target the residual tumor. It had failed, and now all he could do was lie around all day, as he felt too weak to get up most of the time. It just seemed so pointless to him because it wasn't even as if he were waiting to recover. His heart beat wildly at the thought. He was afraid; afraid of where he was going, afraid of what was happening to him and afraid for Holly. She was the only person who knew exactly what to say to him to calm him down and ease his pain. She was so strong; she was his rock and he couldn't imagine his life without her. But he needn't worry about that scenario, because it was she who would be without him. He felt angry, sad, jealous and scared for her. He wanted to stay with her and carry out every wish and promise they had ever made to each other, and he was fighting for that right. But he knew he was fighting a losing battle. After two operations the tumor had returned, and it was growing rapidly inside him. He wanted to reach into his head and tear out the disease that was destroying his life, but that was just another thing he had no control over.

He and Holly had become even closer than before over the past few months, which was something he knew was a bad idea for Holly's sake, but he couldn't bear to distance himself from her. He was enjoying the chats they carried on till the early hours of the morning, and they found themselves giggling just like when they were teenagers. But that was only on their good days.

They had their bad days, too.

He wouldn't think about that now, his therapist kept telling him to "give his body a positive environment—socially, emotionally, nutritionally and spiritually."

And his new little project was doing just that. It was keeping him busy and making him feel like he could do something other than lie on a bed all day. His mind was kept occupied as he mapped out his plan to remain with Holly even when he was gone. He was also fulfilling a promise he had made to her years ago. At least there was one he could follow through on for her. Shame it had to be this particular promise.

He heard Holly thudding up the stairs and he smiled; his plan was working.

"Babe, there's no more ice cream left," she said sadly. "Is there anything else you would prefer?"

"Nope," he shook his head. "Just the ice cream, please."

"Oh, but now I have to go to the shop to get it," she complained.

"Don't worry, hun, I'll be fine for a few minutes," he assured her.

She looked at him uncertainly. "I really would rather stay, there's no one else here."

"Don't be silly," he smiled, and he lifted his mobile off the bedside table and placed it on his chest. "If there's a problem, which there won't be, I'll call you."

"OK." Holly bit her lip. "I'll only be five minutes down the road. Are you sure you'll be OK?"

"Positive," he smiled.

"OK then." She slowly took off his robe and threw on a tracksuit and he could see she still wasn't happy about the arrangement.

"Holly, I'll be fine," he said firmly.

"OK." She gave him a long kiss and he heard her race down the stairs, rush out to the car and speed off down the road.

As soon as Gerry knew he was safe, he pulled back the covers and slowly climbed out of bed. He sat on the edge of the mattress for a while, waiting for the dizziness to pass, then he slowly made his way to the wardrobe. He took out an old shoe box from the top shelf that contained junk he had collected over the past few years and that also contained the nine full envelopes. He took out the tenth empty envelope and neatly wrote "December" on the front. Today was the first of December, and he moved himself forward one year from now, knowing he wouldn't be around. He imagined Holly to be a karaoke genius, relaxed from her holiday in Spain, bruise-free as a result of the bedside lamp and hopefully happy in a new job that she loved.

He imagined her on this very day in one year's time possibly sitting on the bed right where he was now and reading the final installment to the list, and he thought long and hard about what to write. Tears filled his eyes as he placed the full stop beside the sentence; he kissed the page, wrapped it in the envelope and hid it back in the shoe box. He would post the envelopes to Holly's parents' house in Portmarnock, where he knew the package would be in safe hands until she was prepared to open it. He wiped the tears from his eyes and slowly made his way back to bed, where his phone was ringing on the mattress.

"Hello?" he said, trying to control his voice, and he smiled when he heard the sweetest voice on the other end. "I love you too, Holly . . ."

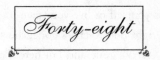

Forty-eight

"No Daniel, this isn't right," Holly said, upset, and pulled her hand away from his grip.

"But why isn't it right?" he pleaded with her with his twinkling blue eyes.

"It's too soon," she said, rubbing her face tiredly all of a sudden, feeling so confused. Things for her just seemed to get worse and worse.

"Too soon because that's what people have been telling you, or too soon because that's what your heart's telling you?"

"Oh Daniel, I don't know!" she said, pacing the kitchen floor. "I'm so confused. *Please* stop asking me so many questions!"

Her heart beat wildly and her head spun, even her body was telling her this wasn't a good situation to be in. It was panicking for her, allowing her to see that danger was ahead. This felt wrong, it all felt so wrong. "I can't, Daniel, I'm married! I love Gerry!" she said in a panic.

"Gerry?" he asked, his eyes widening as he went over to the kitchen table and grabbed the envelope roughly. "This is Gerry! This is what I'm competing with! It's a piece of paper, Holly. It's a *list*. A list you have allowed to run your life for the past year without having to think for yourself or live your own life. Now you have to think for yourself, right now. Gerry's gone," he said gently, walking back over to her. "Gerry's gone and I'm here. I'm not saying that I could ever take his place, but at least give us a chance to be together."

She took the envelope from his hand and hugged it close to her heart as tears rolled down her cheeks. "Gerry's not gone," she sobbed. "He's here, every time I open these, he's here."

There was a silence as Daniel watched her crying. She looked so lost and helpless, he just wanted to hold her. "It's a piece of paper," he said, softly stepping closer to her again.

"Gerry is *not* a piece of paper," she said angrily through her tears. "He was a living, breathing human being that I loved. Gerry is the man who consumed my life for fifteen years. He is a million billion happy memories. He is *not* a piece of paper," she repeated.

"So what am I?" Daniel asked quietly.

Holly prayed that he wouldn't cry, she didn't think she could bear it if he cried.

"You," she took a deep breath, "are a kind, caring and incredibly thoughtful friend who I respect and appreciate—"

"But I'm not Gerry," he interrupted her.

"I *don't want* you to be Gerry," she insisted. "I want you to be Daniel."

"How do you feel about me?" His voice shook slightly.

"I just told you how I feel about you," she sniffed.

"No, how do you *feel* about me?"

She stared at the ground. "I feel strongly about you, Daniel, but I need time . . ." she paused, ". . . lots and lots of time."

"Then I will wait." He smiled sadly and wrapped his strong arms around her weak body.

The doorbell rang and Holly silently breathed a sigh of relief. "That's your taxi." Her voice shook.

"I'll call you tomorrow, Holly," he said softly, kissing her on the top of her head, and he made his way to the front door. Holly continued to stand in the middle of the kitchen going over and over the scene that had just occurred. She stood there for some time tightly gripping the crumpled envelope close to her heart.

Still in shock she eventually made her way slowly up the stairs to bed. She slipped out of her dress and wrapped herself in Gerry's warm, oversized robe. His smell had disappeared. She slowly climbed into bed like a child and tucked herself under the covers and flicked on the bedside lamp. She stared at the envelope for a long time thinking about what Daniel had said.

The list *had* become some sort of a bible to her. She obeyed the rules, lived by the rules and never broke any of the rules. When Gerry said jump, she jumped. But the list had helped her. It had helped her get out of bed in the morning and start a new life at a time when all she wanted to do was curl into a ball and die. Gerry had helped her and she didn't regret one thing she had done in the past year. She didn't regret her new job or her new friends or any new thought or feeling she had developed all by herself without Gerry's opinion. But this was the final installment to the list. This was her tenth commandment, as Daniel had phrased it. There would be no more. He was right; she would have to start making decisions for herself, live a life that she felt happy about without holding back and wondering whether or not Gerry would agree with it. Well, she could always wonder, but she needn't let it stop her.

When he was alive she had lived through him, and now he was dead and she was still living through him. She could see that now. It made her feel safe, but now she was out on her own and she needed to be brave.

She took the phone off the hook and switched the power off her mobile. She didn't want to be disturbed. She needed to savor this special and final moment without interruptions. She needed to say good-bye to Gerry's contact with her. She was alone now and she needed to think for herself.

She slowly tore open the envelope, carefully trying not to rip the paper as she slid the card out.

> *Don't be afraid to fall in love again. Open your heart and follow where it leads you . . . and remember, shoot for the moon . . .*
>
> *PS, I will always love you . . .*

"Oh Gerry," she sobbed, reading the card, and her shoulders shook as her body heaved from the pain of her tears.

She got very little sleep that night and the times she did nod off, her dreams were obscure images of Daniel's and Gerry's faces and bodies being mingled together. She awoke in a sweat at 6 a.m. and decided to get up and go for a walk to clear the jumbled thoughts from her head. Her heart felt heavy as she walked along the path of her local park. She had bundled herself up well to protect herself from the stinging cold that whipped at her ears and numbed her face. Yet her head felt hot. Hot from the tears, hot from her headache, hot from her brain working overtime.

The trees were bare and looked like skeletons lining the pathway. Leaves danced around in circles around her feet like wicked little elves threatening to trip her up. The park was deserted; people had once again gone into hibernation, too cowardly to brave the winter elements. Holly wasn't brave nor was she enjoying her stroll. It felt like punishment to be out in the icy cold weather.

How on earth had she found herself in this situation? Just as soon as she was getting around to picking up the pieces of her shattered life, she dropped them all again and sent them scattering. She thought she had found a friend, someone she could confide in. She wasn't looking to become entangled in some ridiculous love triangle. And it was ridiculous because the third person wasn't even around. He wasn't even a possible candidate for the job. Of course she thought of Daniel a lot, but she also thought about Sharon and Denise, and surely she wasn't in love with them? What she felt for Daniel wasn't the love she felt for Gerry, it was an entirely different feeling. So perhaps she wasn't in love with Daniel. And anyway if she were, wouldn't she be the first person to realize it, instead of being given a few days to "think about it"? But then why was she even thinking about it? If she didn't love him, then she should come right out and say it . . . but she was thinking about it . . . It was a simple yes or no question, wasn't it? How odd life was.

And why was Gerry urging her to find a new love? What had he been *thinking* when he wrote that message? Had he already let go of her before he died? Had it been *so* easy for him to just give her up and resign himself to the fact that she would meet someone else? Questions, questions, questions. And she would never know the answers.

After hours of tormenting herself with further interrogations and the freezing cold nipping at her skin, she headed back in the direction of her house. As she walked down her estate, the sound of laughter caused her to lift her gaze from the ground. Her neighbors were decorating the tree in their garden with tiny Christmas lights.

"Hi, Holly," her neighbor giggled, stepping out from behind the tree with bulbs wrapped around her wrists.

"I'm decorating Jessica," her partner laughed, wrapping the tangled cords around her legs. "I think she'll make a beautiful garden gnome."

Holly smiled sadly as she watched them laughing together. "Christmas already," Holly thought aloud.

"I know," Jessica stopped laughing long enough to answer. "Hasn't the year just flown?"

"Too fast," Holly said quietly. "It went far too fast."

Holly crossed the road and continued on her way to her house. A scream caused Holly to swirl around and see Jessica lose her balance and collapse onto the grass wrapped in a pile of lights. Their laughs echoed down the street and Holly stepped into her house.

"OK, Gerry," Holly announced as she stepped into the house. "I've been for a walk and I've thought deeply about what you said and I have come to the conclusion that you had lost your mind when you wrote that message. If you really really mean it, then give me some sort of sign, and if not I'll completely understand that it was all a big mistake and that you have changed your mind," she said matter-of-factly into the air. She looked around the living room waiting to see if anything happened. Nothing did.

"OK then," she said happily. "You made a mistake, I understand. I will just disregard that final message." She looked around the room again and wandered over toward the window. "OK, Gerry, this is your last chance . . ."

The lights on the tree across the road flew on and Jessica and Tony danced around the garden giggling. Suddenly the lights flickered and went out again. They stopped dancing and their faces fell.

Holly rolled her eyes. "I'll take that as an I don't know."

She sat down at the kitchen table and sipped on a hot mug of tea to thaw out her frozen face. Friend tells you he loves you and dead husband tells you to fall in love again, so you make a cup of tea.

She had three weeks left at work until she could take her Christmas holidays, which meant that if she had to, she would only have to avoid Daniel for fifteen working days. That seemed possible. She hoped that by the time of Denise's wedding at the end of December she would have made a decision about what to do. But first she had to get through her first Christmas alone, and she was dreading it.

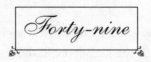

Forty-nine

"O K, WHERE DO YOU WANT me to put it?" Richard panted, dragging the Christmas tree in her living room. A trail of pine needles led all the way out the living room door, down the hall, out the front door and into her car. Holly sighed, she would have to vacuum the house again today to get rid of the mess and she stared at the tree with disgust. They smelled so fresh, but damn, were they messy.

"Holly!" Richard repeated, and she jumped from her thoughts to face him.

She giggled, "You look like a talking tree, Richard." All she could see were his little brown shoes sticking out from underneath the tree resembling a skinny little brown stump.

"Holly," he grunted, losing his balance slightly under the weight.

"Oh sorry," she said quickly, suddenly realizing that he was about to fall over. "Over by the window."

She bit her lip and winced as he sent everything crashing around him while he made his way over to the window.

"There now," he said, wiping his hands and stepping back to take a look at his work.

Holly frowned. "It looks a little bit bare, don't you think?"

"Well, you will have to decorate it of course."

"Well, I know that, Richard, but I was referring to the fact that it only has about five branches left. It's got bald patches," she moaned.

"I told you to buy a tree earlier, Holly, not leave it until Christmas Eve. Anyway, that was the best of a bad lot; I sold the best ones weeks ago."

"I suppose," Holly frowned. She really didn't want to get a Christmas tree at all this year. She wasn't even in the mood to celebrate and it wasn't as if she had any children in the house to please by putting up decorations. Richard had insisted, though, and Holly felt that she had to help him out with his new Christmas tree–selling venture, in addition to his flourishing landscaping business. But the tree was awful and no amount of tinsel could hide that; looking at it made her wish she had just bought one weeks ago. At least then maybe it would have looked like a real tree instead of a pole with a few pine needles hanging off.

She couldn't believe it was Christmas Eve already. She had spent the past few weeks working overtime trying to get the January issue of the magazine ready before they all took their Christmas break. They had eventually finished up the day before, and when Alice had suggested they all go for Christmas drinks at Hogan's she had politely declined. She still hadn't spoken to

Daniel; she had ignored all of his calls, had avoided Hogan's like the plague and had ordered Alice to tell him she was in a meeting if he ever called the office. He called the office nearly every day.

She didn't intend to be rude, but she needed more time to think things through. OK, so it wasn't as if he had just proposed to her, but it almost felt like she was thinking over a big decision like that. Richard's stare snapped her back to reality.

"Sorry, what?"

"I said would you like me to help you decorate it?"

Holly's heart fell. That was her and Gerry's job, nobody else's. Every year without fail they would put the Christmas CD on, open a bottle of wine and decorate the tree . . .

"Eh . . . no, it's OK, Richard, I'll do it. I'm sure you've better things to be doing now."

"Well, actually I would quite like to do it," he said eagerly. "Usually myself, Meredith and the children do it together, but I missed out on that this year . . ." He trailed off.

"Oh." Holly hadn't even thought about Richard's Christmas as being difficult too, she was too selfishly caught up in her own worries.

"OK then, why not?" she smiled.

Richard beamed and he looked like such a child.

"Oh, but the only thing is I'm not too sure where the decorations are. Gerry always used to store them away in the attic somewhere . . ."

"No problem," he smiled encouragingly. "That used to be my job too. I'll find them." He bounded up the stairs to the attic.

Holly opened a bottle of red wine and pressed play on the CD player; Bing Crosby's "White Christmas" played softly in the background. Richard returned with a black sack slung over his shoulder and a dusty Santa hat on. "Ho-ho-ho!"

Holly giggled and handed him his glass of wine.

"No no," he waved his hand, "I'm driving."

"You can have one glass at least, Richard," she said, feeling disappointed.

"No no," he repeated, "I don't drink and drive."

Holly threw her eyes up to heaven and knocked back his glass of wine before beginning her own. By the time Richard left she had finished the bottle and was opening another. She noticed the red light flashing on the answering machine. Hoping it wasn't from who she thought it was, she hit the play button.

"Hi Sharon, it's Daniel Connelly here. Sorry to bother you, but I had your phone number from when you called the club months ago about entering Holly into the karaoke. Em . . . well, I was really just hoping you could pass on a message for me. Denise has been so busy with the wedding arrangements that I knew I couldn't rely on her to remember . . ." He laughed slightly and cleared his throat. "Anyway, I was wondering if you could just tell Holly that I'm going down to my family in Galway for Christmas. I'm heading down there tomorrow. I haven't been able to get through to her on her mobile, I know she's on holidays from work now and I don't have her home number . . . so if you . . ."

He got cut off and Holly waited for the next message to be played.

"Eh, sorry Sharon, it's me again. Eh . . . Daniel, that is. I just got cut off there. Yeah, so anyway, if you could just tell Holly that I'll be in Galway for the next few days and that I'll have my mobile with me if she wants to reach me. I know she has some things to think about so . . ." He paused. "Anyway, I better go before I get cut off again. I'll see you all at the wedding next week. OK thanks . . . bye."

The second message was from Denise telling her that Daniel

was looking for her, the third message was from her brother Declan also telling her that Daniel was looking for her and the fourth message was from an old school friend who Holly hadn't seen in years, telling her that she'd bumped into a friend of hers called Daniel in a pub the previous night, which reminded her of Holly, oh yeah, and Daniel was looking for Holly and he wanted her to call him back. The fifth message was from Daniel again.

"Hi Holly, it's Daniel here. Your brother Declan gave me your number. I can't believe we've been friends so long and you never gave me your home number, yet I've a sneaking suspicion I've had it all along without realizing . . ." There was a silence as he exhaled. "Anyway, I really need to talk to you, Holly. I think it should be in person, and it should be before we see each other at the wedding. Please Holly, please take my calls. I don't know how else to get to you." Silence, another deep breath and exhalation. "OK, well, that's all. Bye."

Holly pressed play again, lost in thought.

She sat in the living room staring at the tree and listening to Christmas songs. She cried. Cried for her Gerry and for her baldy Christmas tree.

Fifty

"Happy Christmas, love!" Frank opened the door to a shivering Holly standing on the doorstep.

"Happy Christmas, Dad," she smiled, and gave him a big bear hug. She inhaled as she walked around the house. The beautiful smell of pine mixed with wine and Christmas dinner cooking in the kitchen filled her nostrils, and she was hit with a pang of loneliness. Christmas reminded her of Gerry. Gerry was Christmas. It was their special time together when they would hide from the stresses of work and just relax and entertain their friends and family and enjoy their time alone. She missed him so much it gave her a sick feeling in the pit of her stomach.

She had visited the graveyard that morning to wish him a happy Christmas. It was the first time she had been there since the funeral, and it had been an upsetting morning. No parcel under the tree for her, no breakfast in bed, no noise, no nothing. Gerry had wanted to be cremated, which meant that she had to stand in front of a wall that had his name engraved on it. And she really did feel like she was talking to a wall. However, she had told him about her year and what her plans were for the day, she had told him Sharon and John were expecting a baby boy and they were planning on calling him Gerry. She told him that she was to be his godmother; that she was to be maid of honor at Denise's wedding. She explained what Tom was like because Gerry had never met him, and she talked about her new job. She didn't mention Daniel. She had felt peculiar standing there talking to herself. She wanted to get some deep spiritual feeling that he was there with her and listening to her voice, but she really just felt like she was talking to a drab gray wall.

Her situation was no extraordinary sight on Christmas day. The graveyard had been packed with visitors, families bringing their aged mothers and fathers to visit their departed spouses, young women like Holly wandering alone, young men . . . She had watched as a young mother broke down over a gravestone while her two startled children watched on not knowing what to do. The youngest child could only have been three years old. The woman had quickly dried her eyes to protect her children. Holly was thankful that she could afford to be selfish and only have to worry about herself. How on earth that woman could find the strength to carry on through the day with two toddlers to worry about jumped into Holly's head regularly that day.

All in all, it hadn't been a good day.

"Oh, happy Christmas, dear!" Elizabeth announced, walking out of the kitchen with her arms held open to embrace her child. Holly started to cry. She felt like the young child at the graveyard.

She still needed her mummy, too. Elizabeth's face was flushed from the heat of the kitchen and the warmth of her body warmed Holly's heart.

"I'm sorry." She wiped her face. "I didn't want to do that."

"Hush," Elizabeth said soothingly, hugging her even tighter. She didn't need to say anything more; just being there was enough.

Holly had called around to visit her mother the previous week in a panic about what to do about the Daniel situation. Elizabeth, not usually the baking kind of mother, was in the middle of making the Christmas cake for the following week. Her face was powdered with patches of flour, the sleeves of her sweater were rolled up to her elbows, bits of flour gathered in her hair. The kitchen counter was covered in stray raisins, sultanas and cherries. Flour, pastry, baking trays and tin foil cluttered the surfaces. The kitchen was decorated in colorful glittery decorations and that wonderful festive smell filled the air.

The moment Elizabeth laid eyes on her daughter, Holly knew that she could sense there was something wrong. They sat at the kitchen table, which was overflowing with red and green Christmas serviettes with picture prints of Santa, reindeers and Christmas trees. There were boxes and boxes of Christmas crackers for the family to get competitive over, chocolate biscuits, beer and wine, the whole lot . . . Holly's parents had stocked up well for the Kennedy family.

"What's on your mind, love?" Holly's mother asked, pushing a plate of chocolate biscuits toward her.

Holly's stomach rumbled but she couldn't handle any food. Once again she had lost her appetite. She took a deep breath and explained to her mother what had happened between her and

Daniel and the decision she was faced with. Her mother listened patiently.

"So how do you feel about him?" Elizabeth asked, studying her daughter's face. Holly shrugged helplessly, "I like him, Mum, I really do but . . ." She shrugged again and trailed off.

"Is it because you don't feel ready just yet for another relationship?" her mother asked gently.

Holly rubbed her forehead roughly. "Oh, I don't know, Mum, I don't feel like I know anything anymore." She thought for a while. "Daniel is a brilliant friend. He is always there for me, he always makes me laugh; he makes me feel good about myself . . ." She picked up a biscuit and began to pick away at the crumbs. "But I don't know if I'll *ever* feel ready for another relationship, Mum. Maybe I will, maybe I won't; maybe this is as ready as I'll ever feel. He's not Gerry, but I'm not expecting him to be. What I feel now is a different kind of feeling; but a nice one, too." She paused to think about that feeling. "I don't know if I'll ever love the same way again. I find it hard to believe that will happen, but it's a nice thought to have that maybe someday I could." She smiled sadly at her mother.

"Well, you don't know if you can if you don't try," Elizabeth said encouragingly. "It's important not to rush into things, Holly. I know you know that, but all I want is for you to be happy. You deserve it. Whether being happy is with Daniel, the man on the moon or without anybody, I just want you happy."

"Thanks, Mum." Holly smiled weakly and rested her head on her mother's soft shoulder. "I just don't know which of those things will do that for me."

As comforting as her mother was to her that day, Holly was no closer to making her decision. First she had to get through Christmas day without Gerry.

The rest of Holly's family, minus Ciara who was still in Australia, joined them in the living room and one by one they greeted her with warm hugs and kisses. They gathered around the tree and exchanged gifts and Holly allowed the tears to flow all throughout. She hadn't the energy to hide them; she hadn't the energy to care. But the tears were a strange mixture of happiness and sadness. A peculiar sensation of feeling alone yet loved.

Holly sneaked away from the family so she could have a moment to herself; her head was a jumble of thoughts that needed to be sorted and filed. She found herself in her old bedroom staring out the window into the dark blustery day. The sea was fierce and threatening and Holly shuddered at its power.

"So this is where you were hiding."

Holly turned to see Jack watching her from the bedroom door. She smiled weakly and turned around to face the sea again, uninterested in her brother and his recent lack of support. She listened to the waves and watched the black water swallow the sleet that had begun to fall. She heard Jack sigh loudly and felt his arm around her shoulder.

"Sorry," he said softly.

Holly raised her eyebrows, unimpressed, and continued to stare ahead.

He nodded to himself slowly. "You're right to treat me like this, Holly, I've been acting like a complete idiot lately. And I'm so sorry."

Holly turned to face him and her eyes glistened. "You let me down, Jack."

He closed his eyes slowly as though the very thought of that pained him. "I know. I just didn't handle the whole situation well, Holly. I found it so hard to deal with Gerry . . . you know . . ."

"Dying," Holly finished for him.

"Yeah." He clenched and unclenched his jaw and looked like he had finally accepted it.

"It wasn't exactly easy for me, you know, Jack." A silence fell between them. "But you helped me pack away all his things. You went through his belongings with me and made the whole thing so much easier," Holly said, feeling confused. "You were there with me for that, why did you just suddenly disappear?"

"God, that was so tough to do," he shook his head sadly. "You were so strong, Holly . . . you *are* strong," he corrected himself. "Getting rid of his things just tore me up, being in the house and him not being there just . . . *got* to me. And then I noticed you were getting closer to Richard, so I just figured it would be OK for me to take a step back because you had him . . ." He shrugged his shoulders and blushed at the ridiculousness of finally explaining his feelings.

"You fool, Jack," Holly said, thumping him playfully in the stomach. "As if Richard could ever take your place."

He smiled. "Oh, I don't know, you two seem very pally-pally these days."

Holly became serious again. "Richard has been very supportive over the past year, and believe me people haven't failed to surprise me at all during this whole experience," she added, getting in a dig. "Give him a chance, Jack."

He stared out to the sea and nodded slowly, digesting this.

Holly wrapped her arms around him and felt the familiar comforting hug of her brother. Hugging Holly even tighter, Jack said, "I'm here for you now. I'm going to stop being so selfish and take care of my little sister."

"Hey, your little sister is doing just fine on her own, thank you very much," she said sadly as she watched the sea crash violently against the rocks, its spray kissing the moon.

. . .

They sat down for their meal and Holly's mouth watered at the spread of food before her.

"I got an e-mail from Ciara today," Declan announced.

Everyone oohed and aahed.

"She sent this picture of herself." He passed around the photograph he had printed off.

Holly smiled at the sight of her sister lying on the beach eating barbecued Christmas dinner with Mathew. Her hair was blond and her skin was tanned and they both looked so happy. She stared at it for a while feeling proud that her sister had found her place. After traveling around the world searching and searching, she reckoned Ciara had finally found contentment. Holly hoped that would happen to her eventually. She passed the photo on to Jack and he smiled and studied it.

"They're saying it might snow today," Holly announced, taking a second helping of dinner. The top button on her trousers had already been opened, but it was Christmas, after all; the time of giving and eh . . . eating . . .

"No, it won't snow," Richard said, sucking on a bone. "It's too cold for that."

Holly frowned. "Richard, how could it be too cold to snow?"

He licked his fingers and wiped them on the napkin that was tucked into his shirt and Holly tried not to laugh as she noticed he was wearing a black woolly jumper with a big picture of a Christmas tree emblazoned across the front. "It needs to get milder before it can snow," he explained.

Holly giggled. "Richard, it's about minus a million in the Antarctic and it snows there. That's hardly mild."

Abbey giggled.

"That's the way it works," he said matter-of-factly.

"Whatever you say." Holly rolled her eyes.

"He's right, actually," Jack added after a while and everyone stopped chewing to stare at him. That was not a phrase they often heard. Jack went on to explain how snow worked and Richard helped him out on the scientific parts. They both smiled at each other and seemed satisfied they were Mr. Know-it-alls. Abbey raised her eyebrows at Holly and they shared their secret look of shock.

"You want some vegetables with your gravy, Dad?" Declan asked, seriously offering him a bowl of broccoli.

Everyone looked at Frank's plate and laughed. Once again it was a sea of gravy.

"Ha-ha," Frank said, taking the bowl from his son. "Anyway we live too close to the sea to get any," he added.

"To get what? Gravy?" Holly teased and they all laughed again.

"Snow, silly," he said, grabbing her nose like he used to when she was a child.

"Well, I bet you all a million quid that it snows today," Declan said, eagerly glancing around at his brothers and sisters.

"Oh well, you better start saving, Declan, because if your brainiac brothers say it ain't so, it ain't so!" Holly joked.

"You better pay up then, boys." Declan rubbed his hands together greedily, nodding toward the window.

"Oh my God!" Holly exclaimed, excitedly jumping out of her chair. "It's snowing!"

"So much for that theory then," Jack said to Richard, and they both laughed as they watched the white flakes sparkling down from the sky.

Everyone deserted the dinner table and threw on their coats

to run outside like excited children. But then again, that's exactly what they were. Holly glanced down into the gardens lining the street and spotted the families of every household standing outside staring up into the sky.

Elizabeth wrapped her arms around her daughter's shoulders and squeezed her tight. "Well, it looks like Denise will have a white Christmas for her white wedding," she smiled.

Holly's heart beat wildly at the thought of Denise's wedding. In just a few days she would have to confront Daniel. As though her mother had been reading her mind she asked Holly gently and quietly so no one else would hear, "Have you thought about what to say to Daniel yet?"

Holly glanced up at the snowflakes glistening down from the black star-filled sky in the moonlight. The moment felt so magical; right there and then she made her final decision.

"Yes I have." She smiled and took a deep breath.

"Good." Elizabeth kissed her on the cheek, "And remember, God leads you to it and takes you through it."

Holly smiled at the phrase. "He better, because I'm going to need him a lot over the next while."

"Sharon, don't carry that case, it's too heavy!" John yelled at his wife, and Sharon dropped the bag angrily.

"John, I am not an invalid. I am *pregnant!*" she shouted back at him.

"I know that, but the doctor said not to lift heavy things!" he said firmly, walking around to her side of the car and grabbing the bag.

"Well screw the doctor, he's never been bloody pregnant," Sharon yelled, watching John storm off.

Holly banged down the boot of the car loudly. She had had

enough of John and Sharon's tantrums; she had been stuck listening to them bicker all the way down to Wicklow in the car. Now all she wanted to do was to go to the hotel and relax in the peace and quiet. She was growing quite afraid of Sharon as well, her voice level had raised three octaves in the past two hours and she looked like she was going to explode. Actually, by the size of her pregnancy bump Holly was afraid she really would explode, and she didn't want to be around for that happening.

Holly grabbed her bag and glanced up at the hotel. It was more like a castle. It was the place Tom and Denise had chosen as the venue for their New Year's Eve wedding, and they couldn't have picked a more beautiful place. The building was covered in dark green ivy climbing up its aging walls and a huge water fountain adorned the front courtyard. Acres and acres of beautifully kept lush green gardens crept out around all sides of the hotel; Denise didn't get her white Christmas wedding after all, the snow had melted minutes after it had arrived. Still, it had been a beautiful moment for Holly to share with her family on Christmas day, and it had succeeded in lifting her spirits for a short time. Now all she wanted to do was find her room and pamper herself. She wasn't even sure if her bridesmaid's dress would still fit her after she had piled on the pounds over Christmas. It was a fear that she wasn't willing to share with Denise, as she would probably have a heart attack. Perhaps some minor alterations wouldn't be too difficult . . . She also regretted telling Sharon she was worried about the fit as Sharon had screamed that she couldn't even fit into the clothes she had worn the day before, never mind a dress she was fitted for months ago.

Holly dragged her bag behind her over the cobblestones and was suddenly jerked forward and sent flying as someone tripped over her luggage.

"Sorry," she heard a singsong voice say and she looked back angrily to see who had almost caused her to break her neck. She watched the tall blonde as her hips went boom-boom heading toward the hotel. Holly frowned, that walk was familiar. She knew she knew it from somewhere but . . . uh-oh!

Laura.

Oh no, she thought, panicking, Tom and Denise had invited Laura after all! She had to find Daniel quickly so that she could warn him. He would be disgusted to find out she had received an invite. And then if the moment was right she would finish off that chat with him. If he still wanted to hear from her; after all, it had been almost a month since she had last spoken to him. She crossed her fingers tightly behind her back and rushed toward the reception area.

She was greeted with mayhem.

The reception area was crowded with angry people and luggage. Denise's voice was instantly recognizable above all the noise.

"Look, I don't *care* if you've made a mistake! *Fix it!* I booked fifty rooms *months* ago for my wedding guests! Did you hear me? *My wedding!* Now I am not sending ten of them to some crappy B&B down the road. Sort it out!"

A very startled-looking receptionist gulped and nodded wildly and tried to explain the situation.

Denise held her hand up in his face. "I don't want to hear any more excuses! Just get ten more rooms for my guests!"

Holly spotted Tom looking perplexed, and she headed over to him.

"Tom!" she beat her way through the crowd.

"Hi Holly," he said, looking very distracted.

"What room is Daniel in?" she asked quickly.

"Daniel?" he asked, looking confused.

"Yes, Daniel! The best man . . . I mean, *your* best man," she corrected herself.

"Oh, I don't know, Holly," he said, turning away to grab a member of the hotel staff.

Holly jumped to face him, blocking his view of the staff member. "Tom, I really need to know!" she panicked.

"Look, Holly, I really don't know; ask Denise," he mumbled, and he ran off down the corridor chasing the hotel staff member.

Holly looked at Denise and gulped. Denise looked possessed, and she had no intention of asking her in that mood. She queued in line behind all the other guests and twenty minutes later and a few sneaky moves to skip the queue, she reached the top.

"Hi, I was wondering if you could tell me what room Daniel Connelly is in, please," she asked quickly.

The receptionist shook his head. "I'm sorry, we can't give out guests' room numbers."

Holly rolled her eyes. "Look, I'm a friend of his," she explained and smiled sweetly.

The man smiled politely and shook his head again. "I'm sorry, but it's against hotel policy to—"

"Listen!" she yelled and even Denise shut up screaming from beside her. "It's very important that you tell me!"

The man gulped and shook his head slowly, apparently too afraid to open his mouth. Finally he said, "I'm sorry but—"

"Aaaaaggghhh!" Holly screamed with frustration, interrupting him again.

"Holly," Denise said, gently placing her hand on Holly's arm, "what's wrong?"

"I need to know what room Daniel is staying in!" she yelled, and Denise looked startled.

"It's room three forty-two," she stuttered.

"Thank you!" Holly yelled angrily, not knowing why she was still screaming, and she stormed off in the direction of the elevators.

Holly rushed down the corridor dragging her bag behind her and checking the door numbers. When she reached his room she knocked furiously on the door, and as she heard footsteps approaching the door she realized she hadn't even thought about what she was going to say. She took a deep breath as the door was pulled open.

She stopped breathing.

It was Laura.

"Honey, who is it?" she heard Daniel's voice call. Holly saw him walk out of the bathroom with a tiny towel wrapped around his naked body.

"You!" Laura screeched.

Fifty-one

H OLLY STOOD OUTSIDE DANIEL'S BEDROOM door and
glanced from Laura to Daniel and back to Laura again. She
gathered from their seminakedness that Daniel had already known
Laura was coming to the wedding. She also assumed that he
hadn't informed Denise or Tom either, as they hadn't been able to
warn Holly. But even if they had known, they wouldn't have considered it important to tell her. Holly hadn't shared what Daniel
had told her before Christmas with any of her friends. As Holly
stared into the hotel room, she realized this meant that she had
absolutely no reason to be standing where she was right then.

Daniel hung on to his tiny towel tightly, glued to the spot, his
face a picture of shock. Laura's face was stormy. Holly's mouth had
dropped open. Nobody spoke for a while. Holly could almost hear
everybody's brains ticking. Then eventually someone spoke and

Holly wished it hadn't been that particular person. "What are *you* doing here?" Laura hissed.

Holly's mouth opened and closed like a goldfish's. Daniel's forehead wrinkled in confusion as he stared from one girl to the other. "Do you two . . ." He stopped asking the question as if the idea were totally ridiculous, but then thought about it and decided to ask anyway, "Do you two know each other?"

Holly gulped.

"Ha!" Laura's face twisted in contempt. "She is *no* friend of mine! I caught this little bitch kissing my boyfriend!" Laura yelled and then stopped herself as she realized what she had said.

"Your *boyfriend?*" Daniel yelled, crossing the room to join them at the door.

"Sorry . . . ex-boyfriend," Laura mumbled, staring at the floor.

A small smile crept across Holly's face, glad that Laura had dumped herself in it.

"Yeah, Stevie, wasn't it? A good friend of Daniel's, if I remember correctly."

Daniel's face reddened as he looked at them both, seeming completely lost. Laura stared back at Daniel, angrily wondering how this woman knew her boyfriend . . . her current boyfriend, that was.

"Daniel's a good friend of mine," Holly explained, crossing her arms over her chest.

"So have you come to steal him from me too?" Laura said bitterly.

"Oh please, like you're one to talk," she fired at Laura and her face reddened.

"You kissed Stevie?" Daniel said, slowly getting the gist of the story. He looked angry.

"No, I did *not* kiss Stevie." Holly rolled her eyes.

"You did too!" Laura yelled childishly.

"Oh, would you ever shut up?" She looked at Laura and laughed. "What does it matter to you anyway? I take it you're back with Daniel, so it looks like everything worked out for you in the end!" Holly then turned to Daniel.

"No, Daniel," Holly continued. "I did not kiss Stevie. We were down in Galway for Denise's hen weekend and Stevie was drunk and tried to kiss me," she explained calmly.

"Oh, you're such a liar," Laura said bitterly, "I saw what happened."

"And so did Charlie." Holly ignored Laura and continued to face Daniel. "So ask him if you don't believe me, but if you don't believe me I really don't care either," she added. "Anyway, I came to have that chat with you but you're obviously busy." She glanced down at the skimpy towel wrapped around his waist. "So I'll see you both later at the wedding." And with that she turned on her heel and marched off down the corridor dragging her suitcase behind her. She glanced back at Daniel, who was still staring at her from his door, and she turned her head and turned the corner. She froze when she realized she had reached a dead end. The elevators were the other way. She kept on walking to the end of the corridor so she wouldn't look completely stupid for walking past their door again. She waited at the end of the corridor for a while until she heard the door close. She tiptoed back up the hall, rounded the corner and sneaked past his bedroom door and rushed down to the elevator.

She pressed the button and breathed a sigh of relief, closing her tired eyes. She didn't even feel angry with Daniel, in fact, in a really childish way, she was glad he had done something to stop them from having their little chat. So she had been dumped and not the other way around, as she was expecting. But Daniel couldn't have been that much in love with her, she reasoned, if he was able to get over her and go back to Laura so quickly. Ah well, at least she didn't hurt his feelings . . . but she did think he was a complete fool for taking Laura back . . .

"Are you getting in or what?"

Holly's eyes flew open; she hadn't even heard the elevator doors open. "Leo!" she smiled, stepping in and hugging him. "I didn't know you were coming down!"

"I'm doing hair for the queen bee today," he laughed, referring to Denise.

"Is she that bad?" Holly winced.

"Oh, she was just in a tizzy because Tom saw her on the day of her wedding. She thinks it'll be bad luck."

"Well, it will only be bad luck if she thinks it's bad luck," Holly smiled.

"I haven't seen you for ages," Leo said, glancing at Holly's hair and making it *very* obvious.

"Oh I know," Holly moaned, covering her roots with her hand. "I've been so busy at work this month I just haven't had time."

Leo raised his eyebrows and looked amused. "Never did I think I would ever hear you say those words about work. You're a changed woman."

Holly smiled and was thoughtful. "Yes. Yes, I really think I am."

"Come on, then," Leo said, stepping out onto his floor. "The wedding isn't for another few hours; I'll tie your hair up so we can cover those awful roots."

"Oh, are you sure you don't mind?" Holly bit her lip, feeling guilty.

"No, I don't mind at all." Leo waved his hand dismissively. "We can't have you ruining Denise's wedding photos with that head on you, can we?"

Holly smiled and dragged her suitcase out of the elevator after him. That was more like it, for a minute there he was just being too nice.

Denise looked at Holly excitedly at the head table of the hotel's function room as someone rapped a spoon against their glass and the speeches began. Holly fumbled nervously with her hands in her lap going over and over her speech in her head and not even listening to what the other speakers were saying.

She should have written it down because now she was so nervous, she couldn't remember the start of it. Her heart beat wildly as Daniel sat down and everyone applauded. She was next and there was to be no running into the toilets this time. Sharon grabbed her trembling hand and assured her she would be fine. Holly smiled back at her shakily, not feeling at all fine. Denise's father announced that Holly was going to speak and the room turned to face her. All she could see was a sea of faces as everyone stared up at her. She stood up slowly from her chair and glanced over at Daniel for encouragement. He winked at her. She smiled back at him and her heartbeat slowed down. Her friends were all there. She glanced down the room and spotted John sitting at a table with his and Gerry's friends. John gave her the thumbs-up and Holly's speech went out the window as a new one formed in her head. She cleared her throat.

"Please forgive me if I get a little emotional while I speak but I am just so happy for Denise today. She is my best friend . . . ," she paused and glanced down at Sharon beside her, ". . . well, one of them."

The room laughed.

"And I am so proud of her today and delighted that she has found love with a wonderful man like Tom."

Holly smiled as she saw tears fill Denise's eyes. The woman who never cried.

"Finding someone you love and who loves you back is a wonderful, wonderful feeling. But finding a true soul mate is an even *better* feeling. A soul mate is someone who understands you like no other, loves you like no other, will be there for you *forever*, no matter what. They say that nothing lasts forever, but I am a firm believer in the fact that for some, love lives on even after we're gone. I know a thing or two about having someone like that, and I know that Denise has found a soul mate in Tom. Denise, I'm glad to tell you that a bond like that will never die." A lump formed in Holly's throat and she took a moment to compose herself before continuing. "I am both honored and petrified that Denise asked me to speak today."

Everyone laughed.

"But I am delighted to have been asked to share this beautiful day with Denise and Tom, and here's to them having many more beautiful days like this together."

Everyone cheered and reached for their glasses.

"However!" Holly raised her voice over the crowd and held her hand up to silence them. The noise died down and once again all eyes were on her.

"However, some guests here today will be aware of the list that a marvelous man thought up." Holly smiled at John's table; Sharon and Denise cheered. "And one of those rules was to *never, ever* wear a 'spensive white dress."

Holly giggled as John's table went wild and Denise broke down into hysterics remembering the fateful night when the new rule was added to the list.

"So on behalf of Gerry," Holly said, "I will forgive you for breaking that rule only because you look so amazing, and I will ask you all to join me in a toast to Tom and Denise and her very, very 'spensive white dress, and I should know, because I was dragged around every bridal shop in Ireland!"

The guests in the room all held up their glasses and repeated, "To Tom and Denise and her very, very 'spensive white dress!"

Holly took her seat and Sharon hugged her with tears in her eyes. "That was perfect, Holly."

Holly's face beamed as John's table held their glasses up to her and cheered. And then the party began.

Tears formed in Holly's eyes as she watched Tom and Denise dancing together for the first time as husband and wife, and she remembered that feeling. That feeling of excitement, of hope, of pure happiness and pride, a feeling of not knowing what the future held but being so ready to face it all. And that thought made her happy; she wouldn't cry about it, she would embrace it. She had enjoyed every second of her life with Gerry, but now it was time to move on. Move on to the next chapter of her life, bringing wonderful memories with her and experiences that would teach her and help mold her future. Sure it would be difficult; she had learned that nothing was ever easy. But it didn't feel as difficult as it had a few months ago, and she assumed that in another few months it would be even less difficult.

She had been given a wonderful gift: life. Sometimes it was cruelly taken away too soon, but it was what you did with it that counted, not how long it lasted.

"Could I have this dance?" A hand appeared before her and she looked up to see Daniel smiling down on her.

"Sure." She smiled and took his hand.

"May I say that you're looking very beautiful tonight?"

"You may," Holly smiled. She was happy with how she looked, Denise had chosen a beautiful lilac-colored dress for her with a corset top that hid her Christmas belly, and there was a large slit up the side. Leo had done a beautiful job with her hair, pinning it up and allowing some curls to tumble down onto her shoulders. She felt beautiful. She felt like Princess Holly, and she giggled to herself at the thought.

"That was a lovely speech you made," he smiled. "I realize that what I said to you was selfish of me. You said you weren't ready and I didn't listen," he apologized.

"That's OK, Daniel; I don't think I'll be ready for a long, long time. But thank you for getting over me so fast." She raised her eyebrows and nodded over at Laura, who was sitting moodily on her own at the table.

Daniel bit his lip. "I know it must seem crazy fast to you, but when you didn't return any of my calls, even I got the hint you weren't ready for a relationship. And when I went home for the holidays and met up with Laura, that old flame just sparked again. You were right, I never got over her. Believe me, if I hadn't known with all my heart that you weren't in love with me, I never would have brought her to the wedding."

Holly smiled at Daniel. "Sorry for avoiding you all month. I was having a bit of 'me' time. But I still think you're a fool." She shook her head as she watched Laura scowl back at her.

Daniel sighed, "I know she and I have a lot to discuss over the next while and we're really going to take things slowly, but like you said, for some people love just lives on."

Holly threw her eyes up to heaven. "Oh, don't start quoting

me on that one," she laughed. "Ah well, as long as you're happy, I suppose. Although I don't see how you ever will be." She sighed dramatically and Daniel laughed.

"I am happy, Holly, I guess I just can't live without the drama." He glanced over at Laura, and his eyes softened. "I need someone who is passionate about me, and for better or for worse, Laura is passionate. What about you? Are you happy?" He studied Holly's face.

Holly thought about it. "Tonight I'm happy. I will worry about tomorrow when tomorrow comes. But I'm getting there . . ."

Holly gathered in a huddle with Sharon, John, Denise and Tom and awaited the countdown.

"Five . . . four . . . three . . . two . . . one! HAPPY NEW YEAR!" Everyone cheered and balloons of all colors of the rainbow fell from the ceiling of the function room and bounced around on the heads of the crowd.

Holly hugged her friends happily with tears in her eyes.

"Happy New Year." Sharon squeezed her tightly and kissed her on the cheek.

Holly placed her hand over Sharon's bump and held Denise's hand tightly. "Happy *New* Year for all of us!"

Epilogue

HOLLY FLICKED THROUGH the newspapers to see which one contained a photo of Denise and Tom on their wedding day. It wasn't every day that Ireland's top radio DJ and a girl from "Girls and the City" got married. That's what Denise liked to think anyway.

"Hey!" the grumpy newsagent yelled at her. "This is not a library, you either buy it or put it down."

Holly sighed and began to gather every newspaper from the newsstand once again. She had to take two trips to the counter due to the weight of the papers and the man didn't even think to help her. Not that she would have wanted his help anyway. Once again a queue had formed behind the till. Holly smiled to herself and took her time. It was his own fault, if he would just let her flick through the papers she wouldn't have to hold him up. She made her way to the top of the queue with the last of the papers and began to add bars of chocolate and packets of sweets to the pile.

"Oh, and can I have a bag too, please." She batted her eyelashes and smiled sweetly.

The old man stared down at her over the rim of his glasses as though she were a naughty schoolgirl. "Mark!" he yelled angrily.

The spotty teenager appeared from the shopping aisles once again with a pricing gun in his hand.

"Open the other till, son," he was ordered, and Mark dragged his body over to the till.

Half the queue behind Holly moved over to the other side.

"Thank you." Holly smiled and made her way toward the door. Just as she was about to pull the door open it was pushed from the other side, causing her purchases to once again spill out all over the floor.

"I'm so sorry," the man said, bending down to help her.

"Oh, it's OK," Holly replied politely, not wanting to turn around to see the smug look on the old man's face that was burning into her back.

"Ah, it's you! The chocoholic!" the voice said, and Holly looked up startled.

It was the friendly customer with the odd green eyes who had helped her before.

Holly giggled, "We meet again."

"Holly, isn't it?" he asked, handing her the king-size chocolate bars.

"That's right, Rob, isn't it?" she replied.

"You've a good memory," he laughed.

"As do you," she grinned. She piled everything back into her bag, lost in thought, and got back onto her feet.

"Well, I'm sure I'll bump into you again soon." Rob smiled and made his way over to the queue.

Holly stared after him still in a daze. Finally she walked over to him. "Rob, is there any chance you would like to go for that coffee today? If you can't, that's fine . . ." She bit her lip.

He smiled and glanced down nervously at the ring on her finger.

"Oh, don't worry about that," she held her hand out. "It only represents a lifetime of happy memories these days."

He nodded his head understandingly. "Well, in that case I would love to."

They crossed the road and headed over to the Greasy Spoon. "By the way, I'm sorry for running off on you the last time," he apologized, looking into her eyes.

"Oh, don't worry; I usually escape out the toilet window after the first drink," Holly teased.

He laughed.

Holly smiled to herself as she sat at the table waiting for him to bring back the drinks. He seemed nice. She relaxed back in her chair and gazed out of the window to the cold January day that caused the trees to dance wildly in the wind. She thought about what she had learned, who she once was and who she had now become. She was a woman who had been given advice from a man she loved, who had taken it and tried her hardest to help heal herself. She now had a job that she loved and felt confidence within herself to reach for what she wanted.

She was a woman who made mistakes, who sometimes cried on a Monday morning or at night alone in bed. She was a woman who often became bored with her life and found it hard to get up for work in the morning. She was a woman who more often than not had a bad hair day, who looked in the mirror and wondered why she couldn't just drag herself to the gym more often, she was a woman who had sometimes hated her job and questioned what reason she had to live on this planet. She was a woman who sometimes just got things wrong.

On the other hand, she was a woman with a million happy memories, who knew what it was like to experience true love and who was ready to experience more life, more love and make new memories. Whether it happened in ten months or ten years, Holly would obey Gerry's final message. Whatever lay ahead, she knew she would open her heart and follow where it led her.

In the meantime, she would just live.

Acknowledgments

Thank you, Mom, Dad, Georgina, Nicky, all my family and friends.

Thank you, Marianne Gunn O'Connor.

Thank you to my Hyperion editor, Peternelle van Arsdale.

READERS' GUIDE

The following questions are intended to provide individual readers and book groups with a starting place for reflection or discussion. We hope they will suggest a variety of perspectives from which you might approach *PS, I Love You*.

Discussion Questions

1. Who is narrating *PS, I Love You*? Where is the story located? What effect, if any, does location have on the story. Why?

2. At what point does the book hook you? What makes you keep reading? What is your favorite part?

3. Keeping in mind that Ahern was twenty-one when she wrote *PS, I Love You*, discuss her strengths as a storyteller. How effective is she at describing Holly's experiences? If you have lost a loved one, or know someone who has, discuss how much you relate to Holly's mourning process.

4. Look at the first two paragraphs of Chapter One. What is going on? What information does Cecelia Ahern provide at this early stage to set up the story that follows?

5. Thinking about the book's early dialogue, like Holly's wedding preparation in Chapter Two, explore Ahern's word choices. What do they convey about the story? Read aloud the long paragraph on page 10. What does Ahern reveal about the characters?

6. Briefly describe Holly's family and friends. Which characters do you like most? Why?

7. How does the idea of "a list" come about? What is so compelling about a list left by a loved one who has died? How does the list help Holly? Talk about which item was the most difficult for her, and why. If you know anyone who has been left such a list, share how it affected them.

8. Consider the last two paragraphs of Chapter Four, beginning with "Her stomach did a little dance. . . " Discuss your response. What is the author sharing with the reader? How successful is she? Why?

9. Looking at Gerry's letter to Holly in the package with the envelopes/list, discuss what you feel while reading it. Why does Holly feel both sad and relieved?

10. Overall, which item or items on the list move you the most? Why?

11. Think about Holly's reaction to Gerry's karaoke instruction. How does the experience help her? What happens to her when she learns her name had been placed on the list for karaoke months earlier?

12. Even though Gerry is dead, how does he come alive in the book? At what point in the book do we learn the most about Gerry? Describe him both physically and mentally.

13. In Chapter Five, what does Holly mean when she says she knew that she needed Gerry more than he needed her (when he was sick)? Why does she say that the list is the

best thing that could have happened right now, three
months after Gerry's death?

14. Look at Chapter Ten and discuss Richard's interaction
with Holly. Share your opinions of him—both at the
beginning of the book and at the end. What do you think
of Richard?

15. Discuss who experiences a transformation in *PS, I Love
You*. Why is it important that we see the characters moving on? Who is Holly at the book's start, and at the book's
end?

16. What is some of the evidence that shows Holly moving
on? Why does Holly cool toward Jack? How do Sharon's
pregnancy and Denise's marriage help Holly?

17. How does Ahern set up Holly's relationship with Daniel?
Did you think Holly was going to hook up with Daniel?
Why? Discuss what happens in Daniel's love life, and why
he makes the choice he does.

18. Consider Declan's film about girls, *Girls and the City*. Does
it remind you of anything else? What do you think of it?
Why does it strike a chord with its audience?

19. Who did you think the secret gardener was? Are you surprised that it is Richard? The garden is one of many
metaphors Ahern uses in *PS, I Love You*. What are some
others? How do these metaphors enrich the story? How do
they amplify Holly's journey?

20. What effect does the vacation to Spain have on Holly? How does the magazine job change her?

21. When the film of the book is made, what actors might make the story come alive for you?

22. Share how *PS, I Love You* has affected you? Has it had any impact on your close relationships? How?

If you enjoyed PS, I LOVE YOU,
be sure to catch Cecelia Ahern's new book,

THERE'S NO PLACE
LIKE HERE

An excerpt follows.

Jenny-May Butler, the little girl who lived across the road from me, went missing when I was a child.

The Gardaí launched an investigation, which led to their lengthy public search for her. For months every night the story was on the news, every day it was on the front pages of the papers, everywhere it was discussed in every conversation. The entire country pitched in to help; it was the biggest search for a missing person I, at ten years of age, had ever seen, and it seemed to affect everyone.

Jenny-May Butler was a blond-haired blue-eyed beauty who smiled and beamed from the TV screen into the living rooms of every home around the country, causing eyes to fill with tears and parents to hug their children that extra bit tighter before they sent them off to bed. She was in everyone's dreams and everyone's prayers.

She too was ten years old and in my class at school. I used to stare at the pretty photograph of her on the news every day and listen to them speak about her as though she was an angel. From the way they described her, you never would have known that she threw stones at Fiona Brady during yard time when the teacher wasn't looking, or that she called me a frizzy-haired cow in front of Stephen Spencer just so he would fancy her instead of me. No, for those few months she had become the perfect being, and I didn't think it fair to ruin that. After a while even I forgot about all the bad things she'd done because she wasn't just Jenny-May anymore: she was Jenny-May Butler, the sweet missing girl from the nice family who cried on the nine o'clock news every night.

She was never found, not her body, not a trace; it was as though she had disappeared into thin air. No suspicious characters had been seen lurking around, no CCTV was available to show her last movements. There were no witnesses, no suspects; the Gardaí questioned everyone possible. The street became suspicious, its inhabitants calling friendly hellos to one another on the way to their cars in the early morning but all the time wondering, second-guessing, and visualizing surprisingly distorted thoughts they couldn't help about their neighbors. Washing cars, painting picket fences, weeding the flowerbeds, and mowing lawns on Saturday mornings while surreptitiously looking around the neighborhood brought shameful thoughts. People were shocked at themselves, angry that this incident had perverted their minds.

Pointed fingers behind closed doors couldn't give the Gardaí any leads; they had absolutely nothing to go on but a pretty picture.

I always wondered where Jenny-May went, where she had disappeared to, how on earth anyone could just vanish into thin air without a trace, without someone knowing something.

At night I would look out my bedroom window and stare at her house. The porch light was always on, acting as a beacon to guide Jenny-May home. Mrs. Butler couldn't sleep anymore and I could see her perpetually perched on the edge of her couch, as though she was on her marks waiting for the pistol to be fired. She would sit in her living room, looking out the window, waiting for someone to call by with news. Sometimes I would wave at her and she'd wave back sadly. Most of the time she couldn't see past her tears.

Like Mrs. Butler, I wasn't happy with not having any answers. I liked Jenny-May Butler a lot more when she was gone than when she was here and that also interested me. I missed her, the idea of her, and wondered if she was somewhere nearby, throwing stones at someone else and laughing loudly, but that we just couldn't find her or hear her. I took to searching thoroughly for everything I'd mislaid after that. When my favorite pair of socks went missing I turned the house upside down while my worried parents looked on, not knowing what to do but eventually settling on helping me.

It disturbed me that frequently my missing possessions were nowhere to be found and on the odd time that I did find them, it disturbed me that in the case of the socks I could only ever find one. Then I'd picture Jenny-May Butler somewhere, throwing stones, laughing and wearing my favorite socks.

I never wanted anything new; from the age of ten, I was convinced that you couldn't replace what was lost. I insisted on things having to be found.

I think I wondered about all those odd pairs of socks as much as Mrs. Butler worried about her daughter. I too stayed awake at night running through all the unanswerable questions. Each time my lids grew heavy and neared closing, another question would be flung from the depths of my mind, forcing my lids to open again. Much-needed sleep was kept at bay and each morning I was tireder yet none the wiser.

Perhaps this is why it happened to me. Perhaps because I had spent so many years turning my own life upside down and looking for everything, I had forgotten to look for myself. Somewhere along the line I had forgotten to figure out who and where I was.

Twenty-four years after Jenny-May Butler disappeared, I went missing too.

This is my story.

~ 2 ~

M y life has been made up of a great many ironies, my going missing only added to an already very long list.

First, I'm six foot one. Ever since I was a child I've been towering over just about everyone. I could never get lost in a shopping center like other kids, I could never hide properly when playing games, I was never asked to dance at discos, I was the only teenager who wasn't aching to buy her first pair of high heels. Jenny-May Butler's favorite name for me well, certainly one of her top ten was 'Daddy-long-legs,' which she liked to call me in front of large crowds of her friends and admirers. Believe me, I've heard them all. I was the kind of person you could see coming from a mile away. I was the awkward dancer on the dance floor, the girl at the cinema who nobody wanted to sit behind, the one in the shop that rooted for the extra-long-legged trousers, the girl in the back line of every photograph. You see, I stick out like a sore thumb. Everyone who passes me, registers me and remembers me. But despite all that, I went missing. Never mind the odd socks, never mind Jenny-May Butler; how a throbbing sore thumb on a hand so bland couldn't be seen was the ultimate icing on the cake. The mystery that beat all mysteries was my own.

The second irony is that my job was to search for missing persons. For years I worked as a garda. With a desire to work solely on missing persons but without working in an actual division assigned to these, I had to rest solely upon the 'luck' of coming across these cases. You see, the Jenny-May Butler situation really sparked off something inside me. I wanted answers, I wanted solutions, and I wanted to find them all myself. I suppose my searching became an obsession. I looked around the outside world for so many clues, I don't think that I once thought about what was going on inside my own head.

In the Guards sometimes we found missing people in a state I won't ever forget for the rest of this life and far into the next, and then there were people who just didn't want to be found. Often we uncovered only a trace, too often not even that. Those were the moments that drove me to keep looking far beyond my call of duty. I would investigate cases long after they were closed, stay in touch with families long after I should. I realized I couldn't go on to the next case without solving the previous, with the result that there was too much paperwork and too little action. And so knowing that my heart lay only in finding the missing, I left the Gardaí and I searched in my own time.

You wouldn't believe how many people out there wanted to search as much as I did. The families always wondered what my reason was. They had a reason, a link, a love for the missing, whereas my fees were barely enough for me to get by on, so if it wasn't monetary, what was my motivation? Peace of mind, I suppose. A way to help me close my eyes and sleep at night.

How can someone like me, with my physical attributes and my mental attitude, go missing?

I've just realized that I haven't even told you my name. It's Sandy Shortt. It's OK, you can laugh. I know you want to. I would too if it wasn't so bloody heartbreaking. My parents called me Sandy because I was born with a head of sandy-colored hair. Pity they didn't foresee that my hair would turn as black as coal. They didn't know either that those cute podgy little legs would soon stop kicking and start growing at such a fast rate, for so long. So Sandy Shortt is my name. That is who I am supposed to be, how I am identified and recorded for all time, but I am neither of those things. The contradiction often makes people laugh during introductions. Pardon me if I fail to crack a smile. You see, there's nothing funny about being missing and I realized there's nothing very different about being missing: every day I do the same as I did when I was working. I search. Only this time I search for a way back to be found.

I have learned one thing worth mentioning. There is one huge difference in my life from before, one vital piece of evidence. For once in my life I want to go home.

What bad timing to realize such a thing. The biggest irony of all.

I was born and reared in County Leitrim in Ireland, the smallest county in the country with a population of about 25,000. Once the county town, Leitrim has the remains of a castle and some other ancient buildings, but it has lost its former importance and dwindled to a village. The landscape ranges from bushy brown hills to majestic mountains with yawning valleys and countless picturesque lakes. Leitrim is landlocked, bounded to the west by Sligo and Roscommon, to the south by Roscommon and Longford, to the east by Cavan and Fermanagh, and to the north by Donegal. When there, I feel it brings on a sudden feeling of claustrophobia and an overwhelming desire for solid ground.

There's a saying about Leitrim, and that is that the best thing to come out of Leitrim is the road to Dublin. I finished school when I was seventeen, applied for the Guards, and I eventually got myself on that road to Dublin. Since then I have rarely traveled back. Once every two months I used visit my parents in the three-bedroom terraced house in a small cul-de-sac of twelve houses where I grew up. The usual intention was to stay for the weekend but most of the time I only lasted a day, using an emergency at work as the excuse to grab my unpacked bag by the door and drive, drive, drive very fast on the best thing to come out of Leitrim.

I didn't have a bad relationship with my parents. They were always so supportive, even ready to dive in front of bullets, into fires, and off mountains if it meant my happiness. The truth is they made me uneasy. In their eyes I could see who they saw and I didn't like it. I saw my reflection in their expressions more than in any mirror. Some people have the power to do that, to look at you and their faces let you know exactly how you're behaving. I suppose it was because they loved me, but I couldn't spend too much time with people who loved me, because of those eyes, because of that reflection.

Ever since I was ten they had tiptoed around me, watched me warily. They had pretend conversations and false laughs that echoed around the house. They would try to distract me, create an ease and normality in the atmosphere, but I knew that they were doing it and why and it only made me aware that something was wrong.

They were so supportive, they loved me so much and each time the house was about to be turned upside down for yet another grueling search, they never gave in without a pleasant fight. Milk and cookies at the kitchen table, the radio on in the background and the washing machine going, all to break the uncomfortable silence that would inevitably ensue.

Mum would give me that smile, that smile that didn't reach her eyes, the smile that made her back teeth clench and grind when she thought I wasn't looking. With forced easiness in her voice and that forced face of happiness, she would cock her head to one side, try not to let me know she was studying me intently, and say, 'Why do you want to search the house again, honey?' She always called me honey, like she knew as much as I did that I was no more Sandy Shortt than Jenny-May Butler an angel.

No matter how much action and noise had been created in the kitchen to avoid the uncomfortable silence, it didn't seem to work. The silence drowned it all out.

My answer. 'Because I can't find it, Mum.'

'What pair are they?'

The easy smile, the pretense that this was a casual conversation and not a desperate attempt at interrogation to find out how my mind worked.

'My blue ones with the white stripes,' I answered on one particular occasion. I insisted on bright-colored socks, bright and identifiable so that they could be easily found.

'Well, maybe you didn't put both of them in the linen basket, honey. Maybe the one you're looking for is somewhere in your room.' A smile, trying not to fidget, swallow hard.

I shook my head. 'I put them both in the basket, I saw you put them both in the machine and only one came back out. It's not in the machine and it's not in the basket.'

The plan to have the washing machine switched on as a distraction backfired and was then the focus of attention. My mum tried not to struggle with losing that placid smile as she glanced at the overturned basket on the kitchen floor, all her folded clothes scattered and rolled in messy piles. For one second she let the façade drop. I could have missed it with a blink but I didn't. I saw the look on her face when she glanced down. It was fear. Not for the missing sock, but for me. She quickly plastered the smile on again, shrugging like it was all no big deal.

'Perhaps it blew away in the wind; I had the patio door open.'

I shook my head.

'Or it could have fallen out of the basket when I carried it over from there to there.'

I shook my head again.

She swallowed and her smile tightened. 'Maybe it's caught up in the sheets. Those sheets are so big; you'd never see a little sock hidden in there.'

'I already checked.'

She took a cookie from the center of the table and bit down hard, anything to take the smile off her aching face. She chewed for a while, pretending not to be thinking, pretending to listen to the radio and humming a song she didn't even know. All to fool me into thinking there was nothing to be worried about.

'Honey,' she said with a smile, 'sometimes things just get lost.'

'Where do they go when they're lost?'

'They don't go anywhere.' She smiled. 'They are always in the place we dropped them or left them behind. We're just not looking in the right area when we can't find them.'

'But I've looked in all the places, Mum. I always do.'

I had; I always did. I turned everything upside down; there was no place in the small house that ever went untouched.

'A sock can't just get up and walk away without a foot in it.' Mum false-laughed.

You see, just like how Mum gave up right there, that's the point when most people stop wondering, when most people stop caring. You can't find something, you know it's somewhere, and even though you've looked everywhere there's still no sign. So you put it down to your own madness, blame yourself for losing it, and eventually forget about it. I couldn't do that.

I remember my dad returning from work that evening to a house that had been literally turned upside down.

'Lose something, honey?'

'My blue sock with the white stripes,' came my muffled reply from under the couch.

'Just the one again?'

I nodded.

'Left foot or right foot?'

'Left.'

'OK, I'll look upstairs.' He hung his coat on the rack by the door, placed his umbrella in the stand, gave his flustered wife a tender kiss on the cheek and an encouraging rub on the back, and then made his way upstairs. For two hours he stayed in my parents' room, looking, but I couldn't hear him moving around. One peep through the keyhole revealed a man lying on his back on the bed with a face cloth over his eyes.

On my visits in later years they would ask the same easy-going questions that were never intended to be intrusive, but to someone who was already armored up to her eyeballs, they felt as such.

'Any interesting cases at work?'

'What's going on in Dublin?'

'How's the apartment?'

'Any boyfriends?'

There were never any boyfriends; I didn't want another pair of eyes as telling as my parents' haunting me day in and day out. I'd had lovers and fighters, boyfriends, men-friends, and one-night-only friends. I'd tried enough to know that anything long-term wasn't going to work. I couldn't be intimate; I couldn't care enough, give enough, or want enough. I had no desire for what these men offered, they had no understanding of what I wanted, so tight smiles all round while I told my parents that work was fine, Dublin was busy, the apartment was great and no, no boyfriends.

Every single time I left the house, even the times when I cut my visits short, Dad would announce proudly that I was the best thing to come out of Leitrim.

The fault never lay with Leitrim, nor did it with my parents. They were so supportive, and I only realize it now. I'm finding that with every passing day, that realization is so much more frustrating than never finding anything.

W hen Jenny-May Butler went missing, her final insult was to take a part of me with her. I think we've established that after her disappearance there was a part of me that was missing. The older I got, the taller I got, the more that hole within me stretched until it was gaping throughout my adult life, like a wide-eyed jaw-dropping fish on ice. But how did I physically go missing? How did I get to where I am now? First question and most importantly, where am I now?

I'm here, and that's all I know.

I look around and search for familiarity. I wander constantly and search for the road that leads out of here, but there isn't one.

Where is here? I wish I knew. It's cluttered with personal possessions: car keys, house keys, mobile phones, handbags, coats, suitcases adorned with airport baggage tickets, odd shoes, business files, photographs, can openers, scissors, earrings scattered among the piles of missing items that glisten occasionally in the light. And there are socks, lots of odd socks. Everywhere I walk, I trip over the things that people are probably still tearing their hair out to find.

There are animals too. Lots of cats and dogs with bewildered little faces and withering whiskers, no longer identical to their photos on small-town telephone poles. No offers of rewards can bring them back.

How can I describe this place? It's an in-between place. It's like a grand hallway that leads you nowhere, it's like a banquet dinner of leftovers, a sports team made up of the people never picked, a mother without her child, it's a body without its heart. It's almost there but not quite. It's filled to the brim with personal items yet it's empty because the people who own them aren't here to love them.

How did I get here? I was one of those disappearing joggers. How pathetic. I used to watch those B-movie thrillers and groan every time the credits opened at the early morning crime scene of a murdered jogger. I thought it foolish that women went running down quiet alleyways during the dark hours of the night, or during the quiet hours of the early morning, especially when a known serial killer was on the prowl. But that's what happened to me. I was a predictable, pathetic, tragically naive early morning jogger, in a gray sweatsuit and blaring headphones, running alongside a canal in the very early hours of the morning. I wasn't abducted, though; I just wandered onto the wrong path.

I was running along a canal, my feet pounding angrily against the ground as they always did, causing vibrations to jolt through my body. I remember feeling beads of sweat trickling down my forehead, the center of my chest and down my back. The cool breeze combined to cause a light shiver to embrace my body. Every single time I remember that morning, I have to fight the urge to call out to myself and warn me not to make the same mistake. Sometimes in that memory, on more blissful days, I stay on the same path, but hindsight is a wonderful thing. How often we wish we'd stayed on the same path.

It was five forty-five on a bright summer's morning, silent apart from the theme tune to *Rocky* spurring me on. Although I couldn't hear myself, I knew my breathing was heavy. I always pushed myself. Whenever I felt I needed to stop, I made myself run faster. I don't know if it was a daily punishment or the part of me that was keen to investigate, to go new places, to force my body to achieve things it had never achieved before.

Through the darkness of the green and black ditch beside me, I spotted a water-violet up ahead, submerged. I remember my dad telling me as a little girl, lanky, with black hair and embarrassed by my contradictory name, that the water-violet was misnamed too because it wasn't violet at all. It was lilac-pink with a yellow throat but even still, wasn't it beautiful and did that make me want to laugh? Of course not, I'd shaken my head. I watched it from far away as it got closer and closer, telling it in my mind, I know how you feel. As I ran I felt my watch slide off my wrist and fall against the trees on the left. I'd broken the clasp of the watch the very first moment I'd wrapped it around my wrist, and since then it occasionally unlatched itself and fell to the floor. I stopped running and turned back, spotting it lying on the damp estuary bank. I leaned my back against the rugged dark brown bark of an alder and, while taking a breather, noticed a small track veering off to the left. It wasn't welcoming, it wasn't developed as a rambler's path, but my investigative side took over; my inquiring mind told me to see where it led.

It led me here.

I ran so far and so fast that by the time the play list had ended on my iPod I looked around and didn't recognize the landscape. I was surrounded by a thick mist and was so high up in what seemed like a pine-tree-covered mountain. The trees stood erect, and needles to attention, immediately on the defensive like a hedgehog under threat. I slowly lifted the earphones from my ears, my panting echoing around the majestic mountains, and I knew immediately that I was no longer in the small town of Glin. I wasn't even in Ireland.

I was just here. That was a day ago and I'm still here.

I'm in the business of searching, and I know how it works. I'm a woman who packs her own bags and doesn't tell anyone where she's going for a straight week in my life. I disappear regularly, I lose contact regularly, no one checks up on me, and I like it that way. I like to come and go as I please. I travel a lot to the destinations of where the missing were last seen, I check out the area, ask around. The only problem was, I had just arrived in this town that morning, driven straight to Shannon Estuary, and gone for a jog. I'd spoken to no one, hadn't yet checked into a B&B, nor walked down a busy street. I know what they'll be saying, I know I won't even be a case. I'll just be another person who's walked away from my life without wanting to be found; it happens all the time, and this time last week they probably would have been right.

I'll eventually belong to the category of disappearance where there is no apparent danger to either the missing person or the public: for example, persons aged eighteen and over, who have decided to start a new life. I'm thirty-four, and in the eyes of others, have wanted out for a long, long time now.

This all means one thing: that right now nobody out there is even looking for me.

How long will that last? What happens when they find the battered, red 1991 Ford Fiesta along the estuary with a packed bag in the trunk, a missing persons file on the dashboard, a cup of, by then, cold not-yet-sipped coffee and a mobile phone, probably with missed calls, on the car seat?

What then?

Wait a minute.

The coffee. I've just remembered the coffee.

On my journey from Dublin, I stopped at a closed garage to get a coffee from the outside dispenser and he saw me; the man filling his tires with air saw me.

It was out in the middle of nowhere, in the midst of the countryside at five fifteen in the morning, when the birds were singing and the cows mooing so loudly I could barely hear myself think. The smell of manure was thick but sweetened with the scent of honeysuckles waving in the light morning breeze.

This stranger and I were both so far from everything but yet right in the middle of something. The mere fact that we were both so completely disconnected from life was enough for our eyes to meet and feel connected.

He was tall but not as tall as me; they never are. Five eleven, with a round face, red cheeks, strawberry-blond hair, and bright blue eyes I felt I'd seen before, which looked tired at the early hour. He was dressed in a pair of worn-looking blue denims, his blue-and-white checked cotton shirt crumpled from his drive, his hair disheveled, his jaw unshaven, his gut expanding as his years moved on. I guessed he was in his mid- to late thirties, although he looked older, with stress lines along his brow and laughter lines... no, I could tell from the sadness emanating from him that they weren't from laughter. A few gray hairs had crept into the side of his temples, fresh on his young head, every strand the result of a harsh lesson learned. Despite the extra weight he

looked strong, muscular. He was someone who did a lot of physical work, my assumption backed up by the heavy work boots he
wore. His hands were large, weather-beaten but strong. I could
see the veins on his forearms protruding as he moved, his sleeves
rolled up messily to below his elbows as he lifted the air pump
from its stand. But he wasn't going to work, not dressed like that,
not in that shirt. For him this was his good wear.

I studied him as I made my way back to my car.

'Excuse me, you dropped something,' he called out.

I stopped in my tracks and looked behind me. There on the
tarmac sat my watch, the silver glistening under the sun. Bloody
watch, I mumbled, checking to see that it wasn't damaged.

'Thank you,' I said with a smile, sliding it back onto my wrist.

'No problem. Lovely day isn't it?'

A familiar voice to match the familiar eyes. I studied him for
a while before answering. Some guy I'd met in a bar previously, a
drunken fling, an old lover, a past colleague, client, neighbor or
school friend? I went through the regular checklist in my mind.
There was no further recognition on either side. If he wasn't a
previous fling, I was thinking I'd like to make him one.

'Gorgeous.' I returned the smile.

His eyebrows rose in surprise first and then fell again, his face
settling in obvious pleasure as he understood the compliment.
But as much as I would have loved to stay and perhaps arrange a
date for sometime in the future, I had a meeting with Jack Ruttle,
the nice man I had promised to help, the man I was driving from
Dublin to Limerick to see.

Oh, please, handsome man from the garage that day, please
remember me, wonder about me, look for me, find me.

Yes, I know; another irony. Me, wanting a man to call? My parents would be so proud.

Jack Ruttle trailed slowly behind a HGV along the N69, the coast road which led from North Kerry to where he lived in Foynes, a small town in County Limerick a half-hour's drive from Limerick city. It was five a.m. as he travelled the only route to Shannon Foynes Port, Limerick's only seaport. Staring at the speedometer, he telepathically urged the truck to go faster while he gripped the steering wheel so tightly his knuckles turned white. Ignoring the advice of the dentist he had seen just the previous day in Tralee, he began to grind his back teeth. The constant grinding was wearing down his teeth and weakening his gums, causing his mouth to throb and ache. His cheeks were red and swollen, and matched his tired eyes. He'd left the friend's couch he was sleeping on in Tralee to drive home through the night. Sleep wasn't coming easily to him these days.

'Are you under any stress?' the dentist had asked him while studying the inside of Jack's mouth.

An open-mouthed Jack had swallowed a curse and fought the urge to clamp his teeth down on the white surgical finger in his mouth. Stressed wasn't even the word.

His brother Donal had disappeared on his twenty-fourth birthday after a night out with friends in Limerick city. After a late-night snack of burger and chips in a fast-food restaurant, he had separated himself from his friends and staggered off alone. The chipper was too packed for any particular person to be noticed; his four friends were too drunk and too distracted by their attempts to bring a female home for the night to care.

CCTV showed him taking ?30 out of an ATM on O'Connell Street at 3:08 a.m. on a Friday night, and later he was caught on camera stumbling in the direction of Arthur's Quay. After that, his trail was lost. It was almost like his feet had left the earth and he'd floated up toward the sky. Jack prepared himself for the fact that, in a way, maybe he had. His death was a concept he knew he could eventually accept if only there was a shred of evidence to support it.

It was the not-knowing that tortured him. It was the worry that kept him awake and the fear that drove him from his bed at night to the toilet to be physically ill. But it was the inconclusive search of the Gardaí that fueled his continuous search. He had combined his trip to the dentist in Tralee with a visit to one of Donal's friends who had been with him the night he went missing. Like the other crowd that were there that night, he was a person Jack felt like punching and hugging all at the same time. He wanted to shout at him, yet console him for his loss of a friend. He never wanted to see him again, yet he didn't want to leave his side in case he remembered something, something he'd previously forgotten that would suddenly be the clue they were all looking for.

He stayed awake at nights looking through maps, re-reading reports, double-checking times and statements while, beside him, Gloria's chest rose and fell with her silent breathing, her sweet breath sometimes blowing the corners of his papers as her sleeping world crept in on his.

Gloria, his girlfriend of eight years always slept. She had slept soundly through the entire year of Jack's horrid nightmare, and, still she dreamed. Still she had hopes for tomorrow.

She had fallen into a deep sleep after hours spent at the garda station, the first day they worried about not hearing from Donal after four days of silence. She slept after the Gardaí had spent the day searching the river for his body. She slept after the day they'd spent hours attaching photos of Donal to shop windows, supermarket notice boards and lamp-posts. She slept the night they thought they had found his body down an alley in the town and slept the next night when they discovered it wasn't him. She slept the night the Gardaí said there was nothing more they could do after months of searching. She slept the night of his mother's funeral, after seeing the coffin of a grief-stricken mother being lowered into the dirt, to join her husband at long last after twenty years in this life without him.

It frustrated Jack, but he knew it wasn't a lack of caring that caused Gloria's lids to close. He knew this because she held his hand when they sat through the questions at the garda station that first time. She stood beside him as the wind and rain lashed at their faces, by the river, watching the divers appear on the surface of the gray, murky water with faces more gloomy than when they had disappeared to the world below. She had helped him stick posters of Donal to windows and poles. She had held him tightly when he cried the day the Gardaí stopped looking and she stood in the front row of the church and waited for him while he helped carry his mother's coffin to the altar.

She cared all right, but one year on, she still slept at night during the longest hours of his life. The hours when Jack cared most about everything but the hours when deep in her sleep, Gloria didn't and couldn't care at all. Every night he felt the distance grow between her sleeping world and his.

He didn't tell her about coming across the woman, Sandy Shortt, from the missing person's agency in the Golden Pages. He didn't tell her he had called her. He didn't tell her about the late-night phone calls all last week and the new sense of hope this woman's determination and belief had filled his head and heart with.

And he didn't tell her that they had arranged to meet on this very day in the next town because . . . well, because she was sleeping.

Jack finally managed to overtake the long vehicles, and as he neared home he found himself alone on the now-quiet country road in his twelve-year-old rusting Nissan. The interior of his car was silent. Over the past year he found he was intolerant of unwanted noise; the sound of a TV or a radio in the background was merely a distraction to his pursuit of answers. Inside his mind was manic: shouting, screaming, replays of previous conversations, imaginings of future ones all leaped around his head like a bluebottle trapped in a jam jar.

Outside the car the engine roared, the metal rattled, the wheels bounced and fell over every pothole and bump in the surface. His mind was noisy in the silent car; his car clattered in the quiet countryside. It was five fifteen on a sunny Sunday morning in July and he needed to stop for air, for his lungs and for the front deflated wheel.

He pulled over at the deserted petrol station that would be closed until later in the morning and parked beside the air pump. He allowed the birdsong to fill his head temporarily and push out his thoughts while he rolled up his sleeves and stretched his limbs from the long journey. The bluebottle momentarily settled.

Beside him a car pulled up and parked. The population of the area was so small he could spot an alien car a mile away . . . and the Dublin license plate gave it away too. Out of the tiny battered car, two long legs dressed in gray sweatpants appeared, followed by a long body. Jack stopped himself from gawking, but from the corner of his eye he watched the curly-black-haired woman taking long strides to the coffee dispenser by the door of the shuttered garage. He was surprised that someone of her height could even fit into the small car. He noticed something fall from her hand and heard the sound of metal sound against the ground.

'Excuse me, you dropped something,' he called out.

She looked behind her in confusion and walked back to where the metal was glistening on the ground.

'Thank you,' she said with a smile, sliding what looked like a bracelet or a watch onto her wrist.

'No problem. Lovely day, isn't it?' Jack felt the pain in his swollen cheeks worsen as they lifted in a smile.

Her green eyes sparkled like emeralds against her snow-white skin and glinted as they caught the sunlight streaming through the tall trees. Her jet-black curls twirled around her face playfully, revealing parts of her features, hiding others. She looked him up and down, taking him in as though analyzing every inch of him. Finally she raised an eyebrow. 'Gorgeous,' she replied, and returned the smile. She, her jet-black curly hair, the Styrofoam cup of coffee, legs and all, disappeared into the tiny car like a butterfly into a Venus flytrap.

Jack watched the Ford Fiesta drive into the distance, wanting her to have stayed, and once again he noted how things between him and Gloria, or perhaps just his feelings for her, were changing. But he hadn't time to think about that now. Instead he returned to his car and leafed through his files in preparation for his meeting later that morning with Sandy Shortt.

Jack wasn't religious; he hadn't been to church for more than twenty years. In the last twelve months he had prayed three times. Once for Donal not to be found when they were searching the river for his body, the second time for the body in the alley not to be him, and the third time for his mother to survive her second stroke in six years. Two out of three prayers had been answered.

He prayed again today for the fourth time. He prayed for Sandy Shortt to take him from the place he was in and to be the one to bring him the answers he needed.